Praise for Barbara Elsborg's *Cowboys Down*

"When I think of an author who can wring every single emotion out of me, only one name stands out in my mind: Barbara Elsborg. She's the Queen of Angst, hands down supreme ruler of the realm."

~ *Long and Short Reviews*

"…this book is worth investing the reading time if you like M/M, hunky cowboys, flamboyant agents and cute doggie friends."

~ *Guilty Pleasures Book Reviews*

"When you put all the pieces of *Cowboys Down* together with bantering conversation, fear, danger and some unexpected twists and turns, you come up with an entertaining read I thoroughly enjoyed. I think you will too."

~ *Romance Junkies Reviews*

Look for these titles by *Barbara Elsborg*

Now Available:

Cowboys Down
Worlds Apart

Cowboys Down

Barbara Elsborg

Samhain Publishing, Ltd.
11821 Mason Montgomery Road, 4B
Cincinnati, OH 45249
www.samhainpublishing.com

Cowboys Down
Copyright © 2013 by Barbara Elsborg
Print ISBN: 978-1-60928-883-9
Digital ISBN: 978-1-60928-753-5

Editing by Sue Ellen Gower
Cover by Scott Carpenter

This book is a work of fiction. The names, characters, places, and incidents are products of the writer's imagination or have been used fictitiously and are not to be construed as real. Any resemblance to persons, living or dead, actual events, locale or organizations is entirely coincidental.

All Rights Are Reserved. No part of this book may be used or reproduced in any manner whatsoever without written permission, except in the case of brief quotations embodied in critical articles and reviews.

First Samhain Publishing, Ltd. electronic publication: February 2012
First Samhain Publishing, Ltd. print publication: January 2013

Chapter One

Jasper turned and glared at the couple behind him, but more particularly at the agent of Satan sitting between them whose hooves were pummeling his seat. "Could you please control your child?"

"Sit still, sweetie," the mother said.

Jasper slumped back and sighed. On his third flight since he'd set off from London, the landing in Jackson Hole, Wyoming couldn't come soon enough. The boy kicked again and a tic fluttered across Jasper's cheek. Before he exploded with fury and ended up snapped into handcuffs, he unclipped his seat belt and stepped into the aisle. He envied the trio of women sitting near the exit a few rows in front of him. Envy turned to borderline hatred when he looked at the length of their legs and considered his own six-three frame.

The line for the bathroom gave him an excuse to linger and stretch his muscles. Jasper's head buzzed, filled with the competing sounds of people chattering, a woman in the exit row coughing and jet engines roaring. He'd come all this way for peace and quiet, but he hadn't anticipated the tortuous journey to find it. The thought of the return trek filled him with dread.

When the tone of the coughing changed, Jasper turned. His eyes widened as he registered the pallor of the hacking woman. She leaned forward, gripping the armrests, fighting for breath, and the pair on either side weren't doing a damn thing except gaping at her. Jasper didn't hesitate. He strode forward, unclipped the woman's seat belt and hauled her to her feet. Pulling her back against his chest, he wrapped his arms around her and squeezed tight under her ribs. She'd stopped struggling to breathe, and her body hung limp in his embrace. Another jolt from his clenched fists but nothing happened. *Jesus, don't let me have got this wrong.* Was he trying to perform the Heimlich maneuver on some poor sod with asthma like him or maybe she'd had a heart attack? Hesitation might have been the right option in this scenario.

One more thrust and—*thank Christ*—something purple flew from her mouth and landed on the carpet. The suck of uninterrupted air by the woman was matched by Jasper's deep sigh of relief. He relaxed his grip, his hands resting just below her breasts. *Put her down, idiot.* Jasper lowered her onto her seat, patted her on the hand and fled back to his seat.

He became aware of people clapping and suspected the tips of his ears had gone red. Fortunately his dark hair covered them. Not possible at school where short hair was compulsory and he'd been known for years as Rudolph the Red-Eared Reindeer. With a name like Jasper Randolph, he was doomed.

The flight attendants were all over the woman now. *Too bloody late.* Jasper settled in his seat and closed his eyes as he heard a hoarse voice berate the crew, threatening to sue. Why did someone have to be blamed for accidents? How could that have been anyone's fault? Except what if he hadn't managed to dislodge the object? Would he have been arrested if she'd died? Actually he *should* have ignored her. In this litigious society, walking away was the safer option, just not the ethical one.

An insistent hand tapped his shoulder and Jasper reluctantly opened his eyes.

"Thank you," a dark-eyed attendant said and smiled.

Jasper nodded. He was uncomfortable with praise, always had been, probably because he didn't get much of it when he was a child.

"Are you a doctor?" the guy asked.

"No." Jasper closed his eyes again before the risk of conversation increased to the point he'd have to be rude. The steward was obviously gay and Jasper wasn't keen on men who seemed so feminine, though maybe that was part of his problem. He was looking for the proverbial needle in a haystack—a gay guy who acted more like a straight man. *But I'm not looking.*

The fasten seat belt sign came on as the plane began its descent. With a bit of luck, he wouldn't have to open his eyes until the aircraft landed. And though he was looking forward to arriving, he was no longer excited about what would follow. Yet another mistake to talk himself into something that had seemed like a good idea at the time and had now topped the list of the worst ideas ever.

The vacation he worked hard for all year would not be his usual solo tramp around Italy or Greece exploring ruins, but a stay on the Neilson Ranch where Jasper hoped to learn how to relax, to get dirty without worrying, to be sociable without blushing and to ride a horse without throwing up.

Except Jasper wasn't sure any of that was possible. He was an uptight, upper-class stockbroker, product of a private education and a top-flight university—for a while at least, whose mother was desperate for him to settle down, get married and provide her with a houseful of grandchildren. Well, when she was having one of her better days. And having grandchildren was something else that wasn't going to happen. Not in the way she wanted anyway.

Jasper's hope of scuttling off the plane without any fuss died the moment the seat belt sign pinged. Two of the women from the exit row rushed back and were all over him like an unpleasant rash.

"Oh my God. I could have died," the woman croaked. "Thank you so much for saving me. I'm Melissa." The woman with her elbowed her in the side. "This is Janie."

"Delighted to meet you," Jasper lied.

"Oh, you're English. Say something else. I love your accent." Melissa all but fluttered her eyelashes at him.

"Kind of you to say so," Jasper said through gritted teeth.

It was only the cabin crew urging people to leave the aircraft that saved him from becoming their *bestest* best friend. Jasper lingered, making a big deal of gathering together his book and—well, his book. He waited until everyone else had disembarked before he grabbed the Tumi briefcase from the overhead locker, shoved his book inside and moved toward the front of the small plane.

The captain stopped him.

"Mr. Randolph, thanks for your prompt action today. The airline will be writing to you, but I'd like to offer you this bottle of champagne with our compliments."

"There's really no need," Jasper mumbled.

The bottle was pressed into his hands, and Jasper couldn't escape fast enough.

He jammed the champagne into his bag, and once he was inside the terminal, made for the nearest washroom. Jasper splashed cold water over his face and, leaning with his hands on the basin, stared into the mirror. Considering the length of time he'd been traveling, he didn't look too bad. He took a comb from his pocket and pulled it through his hair, and then dragged his fingers over his stubbled cheeks. Maybe he should retrieve his razor and— *Stop it*, he told himself. Who was there to care how he looked? He straightened his tie, tucked in his shirt and went to find his suitcase.

His fellow passengers were crowded around the carousel and Jasper hung back, but Melissa spotted him, waved and headed in his direction. *Shit*.

"We wondered where you'd gone. Thanks again for saving me."

"It was nothing," Jasper mumbled.

"A yogurt-covered cranberry went down the wrong way. They shouldn't sell snacks that can kill you. I'm going to write to the airline."

Jasper thought about pointing out any food inhaled rather than ingested had the potential to kill, but didn't bother.

"My voice is really croaky. Think I ought to see a doctor?" she asked.

"I'm sure you'll be fine."

Janie came up and smiled at him. She and Melissa wore denim jackets covered with sparkly...bits, tight jeans and heavily patterned, silver-tipped cowboy boots. They looked like twin dolls.

"Are you here on business?" Janie asked.

"Holiday."

"You mean vacation," Melissa said. "Us too. We're going to spend the week on a ranch."

Oh fuck. He couldn't be *that* unlucky.

"Where are you staying?" Janie asked.

Jasper hoped for a miracle. "The Neilson Ranch."

Both women squealed and heads turned in their direction. "Omigod," came from two sets of lips. Simultaneously. Then they high-fived and squealed again. Jasper cringed.

Oh my God, indeed. Thanks a lot, pal. Though God had never done anything for Jasper when he'd really needed help. Why would he start now?

"Would you be an absolute angel and help with our bags?" Melissa asked.

What choice did he have? He was still a gentleman, though by the end of this holiday...er...vacation, he hoped not to be.

Jasper piled a large flatbed cart with their luggage—small, medium and large bags and cases in bright pink and purple.

"I hope we brought enough," Melissa said, and only when Jasper caught a glimpse of her worried face did he realize she wasn't joking. He hated to think how much they'd paid in excess baggage.

"Ooh, over there." Melissa pointed toward a guy holding a sign.

The fifty-year-old looked like he'd stepped straight out of an old Western, with a deeply wrinkled, weather-beaten face, denims sliding off his hips and a blue flannel shirt stretched over his belly. He was as tall as Jasper but much broader. As Jasper pushed the cart over, another guy joined the first. He tipped up the rim of his Stetson with his thumb then took the hat off and ran his fingers through hair the color of corn. Jasper stifled his groan. Melissa and Janie didn't bother.

"Oh my Lord," Janie whispered. "That cowboy is—"

"Mine," Melissa snapped a moment before Janie's, "Mine."

The new guy looked around Jasper's age. He was maybe an inch taller than Jasper with sun-streaked shaggy blond hair and sparkling blue eyes. His gray shirt was rolled above his elbows, and Jasper took in tanned muscular forearms before he let his gaze drop to a flat belly, faded jeans, narrow hips and the generous bulge on the left side of the zipper. Jasper averted his gaze and tightened his mouth. This holiday was not about finding a guy, it was about finding himself.

Though if he did the latter quickly, maybe he could move on to the former.

Calum stood next to Pete, the ranch foreman, watching the new arrivals and trying to pick out which were theirs. Pete half-heartedly rocked a badly written sign saying *Neilson Ranch* that he'd hastily cobbled together after he forgot the one Calum's sister had worked on for hours. Angie had decorated the sign with foam flowers and little horses she'd cut out of magazines. It had been fancier than the ones she usually made. Calum frowned. Maybe Pete had deliberately forgotten it.

They had nine guests arriving today to spend the week experiencing life on a working ranch. Calum thought his granddaddy would have rolled like a cement mixer in his grave if he'd seen what his son and grandson had sunk to in order keep the ranch going. But times had changed and there was more money to be made in entertaining rich folks than the cattle business. Though with fifteen rooms to fill, this week wasn't going to make them as much as usual.

The idea that these people thought they were getting a taste of cowboy life made Calum chuckle. They didn't sleep in a bunkhouse, share a bathroom or eat beans out of a can. He hated beans. Each guest had their own room with bathroom attached, high quality meals, a pool to relax in and a massage if they wanted one. It was nothing like ranch life.

"Here they come," said Pete. "Smile."

Calum sighed and put a broad smile on his face.

The newlyweds weren't hard to spot. They were glued at the hip, love in their eyes as they chattered to each other. The other married couple would be the pair walking apart, the young, slim wife scowling, the older, gray-haired husband tight-lipped and pulling both suitcases. They'd bicker for the entire time and she'd flirt with everyone except her husband. Calum wondered which of them had suggested this vacation.

"Howdy, folks," Pete said, and in a lower voice added, "Oh Christ, I hope these aren't ours."

As Calum introduced himself to the guests, out the corner of his eye he saw two women in matching denim jackets sparkling with rhinestones, walking in front of a cart piled with luggage. In their early twenties, one blonde, one brunette, they were made up to the gills with red polish on their fingers, designer sunglasses perched on their heads, and designer smiles on their faces. They looked like dolls.

Calum couldn't see the guy pushing the piled-up luggage until the cart stopped. When he appeared, the breath caught in Calum's throat and his fingers tightened around the brim of his hat. *Oh shit.* Tall, dark, slim, large brown eyes. *Fuck, fuck, fuck.* Calum's heart stuttered and stalled. The dude looked like he'd walked off an ad for Abercrombie and Fitch. Maybe he wasn't the English guy—then Calum noticed the tie around his neck. Yep, he was.

"Matt Dunn and Paul Kenyon," said a voice at his ear.

Calum turned to look at the last two guests. The smirk on their faces made Calum suspect he'd been caught ogling Mr. Smooth. These two Americans were big guys in their thirties. Calum mentally picked out their horses.

"Calum Neilson. Welcome to Jackson Hole."

The guests started to talk to each other, but the English guy stood apart, staring in another direction as if he wished he were someplace else. He looked as though he was off to a business conference, not a riding vacation. Tailored pants, dress shirt and that fucking dark blue tie. Except there was something about the way he dressed that turned Calum on big time. He gulped.

"What the hell are we going to do with all this luggage?" Pete scratched his head.

"We didn't bring anything we didn't need," said the blonde woman.

Calum tore his gaze from dangerous temptation and concentrated on the pair of chattering women in front of him. "You're Janie and Melissa. Janie's the blonde, right?"

The blonde beamed at Calum. "How did you guess?"

Lucky guess. "Intuition," Calum said. He'd once fucked a blonde Janie. "Pleased to meet you. And you, Melissa."

Melissa held his hand too long. Calum pulled away.

"I'm so looking forward to this," Melissa said, staring straight at him.

In the periphery of his vision, Calum noticed the English guy heading in their direction.

"Jasper Randolph." He held out his hand. "How do you do?"

"Hi." Calum barely let their hands collide before he pulled away. Even then, his stomach knotted into a tight ball. He saw the guy blink in confusion at the curt welcome. *Shit, I'm a dickhead.*

"Welcome to Jackson Hole," Calum said in a loud voice before he remembered he'd already said that. "Transport's in the parking lot if you'd like to follow us."

Pete spoke with the newlyweds as they walked out into the sunshine. Calum put his hat back on, tugged down on the brim and stalked off, yelling at his brainless dick. Not only did the guy's looks tick every box, his accent just about made Calum come in his pants. But he wasn't going to do this. It wasn't what he wanted.

Yeah, well, if he kept telling himself that maybe one day he'd believe it. Still, he shouldn't do anything to rock the boat with his dad. He'd spent too long getting the damn thing to float more or less level. No way was he getting involved with Jasper Randolph. *No, no, no.*

Yes, yes, yes, said his cock.

It quickly became clear there was no way the luggage would fit as well as the passengers. Just as well Calum had brought the SUV to Jackson to pick up supplies. He could take some of the bags.

"You sure you ladies brought enough?" Pete stacked two suitcases on the front seat of his vehicle and then lifted another from Calum's hand. "Looks like you're planning on moving in." He nodded toward the Englishman standing with a pristine navy blue suitcase and leather bag. "Calum, you're going to have to take him with you."

It flittered through Calum's head to object, but if he made a fuss, it would look rude. He was damn sure Pete had done this deliberately. Calum could have taken the excess luggage and let Jasper ride with the other guests, but that would mean unpacking and Jasper would think he had some problem transporting him. He did.

Jasper turned in his direction and gave him a tentative smile and Calum's dick grinned back. *Oh fuck.*

"Over here," Calum muttered to Trouble with a capital T and strode down the line of parked vehicles to a battered SUV.

"Porsche in for a service?" Jasper asked.

Calum stumbled to a halt. Was that a joke? "Watch out for—" Too late.

As Jasper opened the passenger door, Bessie leapt off the floorboards and her paws hit his chest. The dog knocked the guy backward, sending him staggering into the vehicle parked alongside. As he tried to get his balance, Bessie barked and jumped up at him.

"Down, Bessie," Calum snapped. "She won't hurt you." He picked up Jasper's case and slung it on top of the boxes in the back of the SUV, then slotted the expensive-looking leather carryon into a gap between bags of feed.

When he looked back, Bessie had her teeth in the bottom of Jasper's pants, growling as she tugged at the material.

Calum frowned. This wasn't like her. "Bessie, cut it out."

Jasper twisted free and jumped into the car. The dog followed and stuffed herself into the foot well, glaring up at Jasper. As Calum climbed in the other side, there was a loud doggie rumble followed by a human yelp. "Ouch."

"Did she bite you?" *Oh God.* "Bessie, what the hell's the matter with you?"

The dog sat up, rested its chin on the seat between Jasper's legs and bared her teeth. Jasper stayed absolutely motionless.

"Tell me you've fed her today," Jasper said.

"Christ." Calum got out and walked round to Jasper's door. "Out," he snapped.

Jasper pulled himself up.

"Not you. Bessie, get out."

The dog jumped down and Calum opened a rear door and put her between two boxes. He climbed back in the front and sighed. "I'm sorry. She's never been this aggressive before. I don't know what's gotten into her."

"It's okay. Don't worry about it." Jasper lifted the leg of his pants and looked at his ankle.

Fuck it. Is that blood? "She's broken the skin? Oh shit. Do you want to go to the doc?"

The guy laughed. "It's just a scratch. Only..."

"What?"

"I'm assuming she doesn't have rabies."

Calum shuddered. "I hope not. I've had her since she was a pup."

"Australian cattle dog."

Calum gave a surprised laugh. "Yeah, she is. And she's usually docile with most people—maybe she sensed you're afraid of dogs."

"I'm not scared of dogs," Jasper snapped and then sighed. "She was being protective. It's fine."

He closed his eyes and rested his head against the window. Almost before Calum had pulled out of the airport, soft snores were coming from his passenger.

What the fuck had made Bessie nip him? Calum gave a little smile because he was kind of jealous. Biting this uptight dude sounded like fun. Then he frowned. He wasn't supposed to be thinking that way. In any case, what would a polished guy like Jasper see in a rough cowboy like him? Calum didn't own a pair of pants that weren't jeans. His natural odor was horse sweat and...dirt, not the fragrant kind. He didn't manage to keep a shirt clean longer than an hour and his body was scarred and battered.

Calum glanced at Jasper again. He could have come straight from the office. A tie, for Christ's sake? But that shadow of stubble on his chin and cheeks, those soft-looking lips, the dark hair, the thick black eyelashes that were longer than any he'd ever seen, and those fucking huge brown eyes—this guy had Calum swallowing hard.

Jasper's hands lay across his crotch. His fingers were long and slender. Clean, neat nails. Large unblemished hands. Office worker's hands. He'd wreck them if he didn't wear gloves. Even holding the reins would give him calluses. Seemed a shame. Calum sighed. That wasn't what he was really thinking. He was imagining those hands stroking him, soft fingers trailing down his spine, sweeping over his hips to wrap around his cock, long fingers sliding into his asshole. *Christ, now I've got a boner.* Good thing the guy was asleep.

Jasper hoped he was managing a realistic impression of a guy asleep. He kept his hands relaxed on top of his cock, willing it to stay flaccid. Mind over matter, but it was a struggle. As often as he might tell himself the purpose of this holiday was to unwind into a guy who could enjoy life, the thought that he might meet a cowboy he could unwind into, one he could get down and dirty with, had been there as well.

That bloody dog knew what he was thinking. Australian cattle dogs weren't an aggressive breed, but very protective of their owners. They nipped at the heels of cattle to herd them. So in nipping at Jasper, Bessie was establishing both her ownership of Calum and the pecking order in any potential relationship.

The message was clear. *Hands off. He's mine.*

Yeah, well Jasper didn't even know whether Calum was gay, straight or bi. Not that it mattered. He'd do what he always did, fall in lust with someone who was either unobtainable or uninterested, and jack off while he thought about them.

Jasper jolted awake when the SUV came to a stop. What had started as pretence had turned into him sleeping for—he checked his watch—over an hour. *Fuck, I hope I didn't snore for real. Or dribble.* He stretched his legs and blinked.

"Reckon you needed that," Calum said.

Jasper yawned. "I've been traveling for over twenty-four hours." His ears still rang with fatigue.

"It's a long way to come. Hope you enjoy your stay. Just join the others up at the ranch for the welcome."

Calum climbed out, opened the back door for Bessie to jump out and walked off.

Well fuck you too. Jasper tore his gaze from Calum's tight backside and exited the vehicle. On that side of the SUV, a line of mountains stretched as far as he could see, snow dusting the peaks, the rocks below running though a kaleidoscope of colors down to smoky green foothills and a river. The sky was the most intense blue Jasper had ever seen, rather like Calum's ocean eyes. No washed-out English gray overhead, but miles of bright sky and not a cloud in sight. He took a deep breath and sighed. Mountain air would do him good. Lusting after a guy he couldn't—shouldn't—have would do him no good at all.

Jasper turned in a circle. Mountains rose on either side, with the ranch nestling in a long undulating valley between. The main building was a sprawling wooden structure with a wraparound porch that looked like an overgrown alpine chalet, and Jasper felt a pang of disappointment it wasn't some beaten-up shack with creaking shutters and a hitching post. Then he smiled at the thought of his reaction if it had been. He already knew this place had a gym, a pool and a hot tub. He intended to use all three. Jasper took another deep breath. Maybe he wouldn't even need his inhaler. The air smelt fresh and clean with the tangy scent of pine and sage.

When he heard snuffling around his feet, Jasper looked down to see Bessie tentatively wagging her tail.

"So you're sorry now?" He bent and extended his hand. "I know he's yours, but a guy can look, can't he?"

The dog allowed him to tickle her behind the ears and a moment later lay on her back so he could stroke her belly. Jasper smiled. Animals were easy in comparison to humans.

"Hey! Got time to join us?"

Suspecting that had been aimed at him, Jasper turned to see the rest of the guests milling at the bottom of the steps leading up to the ranch. A tall, gray-haired guy in his mid-fifties stood at the top. He frowned as he beckoned to Jasper. *Great, I'm in trouble already.*

Jasper reached for his luggage and tagged on at the back of the group, Bessie at his heels, wagging her tail hard enough to raise bruises. Jasper wished he knew what she was thinking. What had happened on the way to the ranch? Had Calum told her that he fancied—*for fuck's sake.*

"Welcome to the Neilson Ranch," said the guy on the steps. "My name's Erik Neilson. You already met my son Calum and my ranch manager Pete at the airport. But these two beauties by my side are the heart of this operation. My wife Vera and our lovely daughter Angie."

One step below Erik, a pretty girl in her early twenties with long blonde hair thrust her arm in the air and waved. A woman with a kind smile stood at her side. There was something not right about the girl, though Jasper wasn't sure what.

"In a moment you'll be shown to your rooms. Only a few rules. First, no wandering off the ranch on your own without telling someone. Easy to get lost around here and there are wild animals always on the lookout for an easy meal. Including bears and mountain lions. Second, remember this is a working ranch so the needs of our cattle and horses come first, but if there's something particular you want to do, tell me. If I can make it happen, I will. This is your vacation and we aim to please. We want you to forget your troubles and enjoy yourself."

Jasper found his gaze wandering toward Calum, and when the guy quickly looked away, he wondered if Calum had been looking at him. Could he be gay? That was the problem with not fancying guys who were obviously that way inclined. It was much harder to trust his gaydar. Jasper tuned back in.

Erik's gaze seemed directed at him and Jasper shuffled in discomfort. *Shit, did I miss anything important?* Or had Erik seen him staring at his son?

"When you've settled, we have drinks and snacks ready in the lounge. Dinner is at seven. One final thing. Our horses don't spook at gunfire, but they sure don't like to hear cell phones playing some crazy tune. If your phone rings while you're out on a ride, expect to eat some dust. These are working stock horses and not particular about their manners. If you persist in talking on your cell phone while you're riding, you might find one of the wranglers will shoot it out of your hand. Better hope you don't have it pressed against your ear at the time." He flashed a toothy smile.

Everyone laughed, but when Erik's gaze locked on him again, Jasper had the feeling he wasn't joking.

Note to self: Don't take phone when I go riding.

Chapter Two

Calum walked into the dining room to see Angie and Vera serving drinks to guests who chatted and milled about in front of the roaring fire. It took a lot of heat to warm a room with a cathedral ceiling. The room was impressive but their family lounge was much more cozy—well, when his father wasn't being an ass. Temperatures were already falling under clear skies. This time of year the days were warm but the nights cold. Snow wasn't impossible. Calum scanned the room for Jasper and didn't see him. Disappointment tussled with relief and neither won. In any case, Calum wasn't sure he could have made polite conversation. What did he have in common with an uptight English guy? He didn't even know if Jasper was gay.

"He's not here," Calum's father said at his ear.

"Who?" Calum hadn't been able to help jumping. He swore sometimes his father could read his mind, but Calum put as much indifference into his voice as he could. "What are you talking about?"

"You know damn well who I'm talking about. You maneuvered your way into bringing him here in the SUV when you could have transported luggage instead. I saw the way you watched him outside. I saw him looking at you."

Oh fuck. Calum made sure his face showed nothing, though he knew it was a waste of time. His father didn't trust him. Pointless explaining that Pete had loaded the luggage and that Pete had told him to take Jasper in the SUV. As far as his father was concerned, Pete was a fucking god who could do no wrong, which was why he was ranch foreman and not Calum.

"Keep away from the English guy," his father muttered.

Calum bit his lip before he snapped something he'd regret. It hurt that his father assumed he wanted to leap on every good-looking guy who came to the ranch. Would he have reacted the same if Calum was straight?

"Chat with those pretty girls and be nice," his father said.

Probably not.

Calum did as he was told. Gradually the long table in the dining area began to fill. Pete and the other wranglers sat down, and Ring, Pete's son, took the seat between Melissa and Janie. That guy only had to open his mouth to annoy Calum. Often he didn't even have to do that. Just looking at Ring put Calum in a bad mood. The slimy, sneaky, sarcastic son of a bitch took every opportunity to make trouble for him.

Vera and Angie joined them at the table. His father insisted the family and ranch hands dine with the guests. He insisted they smile about it too, and Calum tried to look happy. The kitchen help began to bring out platters of steaming roast beef, and Calum wondered what was keeping Jasper. Any moment his father would notice he was still missing and get annoyed. Staying under the radar was the best response to Erik Neilson. Not turning up for a meal or turning up late would just plain piss him off.

"Anyone seen the English guy?" asked Calum's father in a loud voice.

Here we go. His father looked straight at him. Calum tried to stare him down, but felt his gaze drift away. *Fuck it, and I haven't even done anything wrong.*

"I hope the damn fool's not gone wandering off," Pete muttered.

Calum's stomach lurched. Might Jasper have done that, even after the warning? Had he been listening? It was all too easy for arrogant city slickers to underestimate the danger of the Wyoming wilderness, particularly when they were in search of a photo. They'd had more guests injured because they weren't looking at what they were doing than through any other means.

But it was dark. Couldn't take photos in the dark.

His father sighed and turned to Vera. "Which room's he in?"

"Seven."

Angie stood. "Want me to check on him?"

"Let Calum go," Vera said.

Calum didn't miss the look his father shot Vera. There was an awkward pause before his father said, "Fine."

Calum pushed back his chair and made his way to the guest wing. As far as his father was concerned, Calum trod a line of respectability so thin it was almost invisible, which was probably why Calum kept slipping off it. He didn't like being treated as if he were the biggest disappointment of his father's life. He worked hard without complaining. He'd stayed there on the ranch when he could have left. What more did the man want?

Yeah, well, Calum knew the answer to that, but it was one thing he couldn't do even if he wanted to, and he didn't. He ran his fingers through his hair and then rapped at Jasper's door. When there was no answer, he knocked harder.

"Jasper? You in there?"

Nothing. *Christ.* Now what was he supposed to do? What if the English guy had wandered off and gotten lost as night fell? Or fallen and injured himself? Been bitten by an annoyed snake? Mauled by a bear?

Calum tried the door and it clicked open. The light from the hallway shone on Jasper who lay on his back, fast asleep, still in the clothes he'd arrived in, tie included, though it was loosened. Calum's breath caught in his throat. Something about watching guys sleeping that calmed him. No matter what they were really like, you could make them what you wanted them to be while they slept. Calum smiled, closed the door and returned to the dining room.

"He's sleeping," he told his father and sat. "Long journey, I guess."

His father tsked.

"Angie, when you're done eating, put a note under his door telling him we've left him a snack in the fridge," Vera said. "Then make sure you remember to leave him one."

"Okay. I'll make him my favorite sandwich."

"Not peanut butter and chocolate spread, sweetheart," Vera said. "Beef would be good or there's some chicken."

Angie was twenty years old and a mite slow, but she had the sweetest nature. She'd come to the ranch, age eight, when her mother had married Calum's father, and had been Calum's shadow ever since. It hurt that his father seemed to love her more than he'd ever loved his son, but Calum couldn't begrudge Angie that affection. *Shouldn't.*

"So folks," his father said, addressing the table. "Looks like our English guy's tuckered out already and he hasn't even been on a horse yet."

There was a burst of laughter and Calum prickled with annoyance. Jasper had been travelling for over a day and Jackson Hole was seven hours behind London time, which meant it was two in the morning as far as the guy's body clock was concerned.

"How about we stand up and introduce ourselves," his father said. "You already know who I am, but I'll start us off. Erik Nielson. Owner of the Neilson Ranch. This spread belonged to my father and my grandfather before him and one day it will be Calum and Angie's."

And why did that feel like a noose around his neck? Calum had known since he was a small boy that this was his life, all mapped out for him, but as much as the place was in his blood, he wanted staying here to be his decision, not his father's. There was a world out there he'd never seen and he resented the fact that his father didn't care.

The wranglers stood up one after the other, mumbled their names and sat down again. The first of the guests to speak was the newly married guy. He had one of those faces that always seemed to be smiling. "I'm Brad Olsen and this is my wife, Nita. We're from LA. We've been married for seven weeks, one day and," he checked his watch, "three hours. I'm a lawyer and Nita's a realtor, so if you need a house in California, talk to us."

The husband of the other couple stood. "Sam West and my wife, Judy. From Tucson. I run a greenhouse business. Judy doesn't work." He sat down.

"We have three kids," Judy hissed. "That's work."

"You make it work," he snapped back.

Oh God. Calum hoped he didn't have to take this pair out tomorrow.

"How about the two beauties at the end of the table?" his father asked.

"I'm Melissa Saxon. This is my best friend Janie Dunmore. We're from LA too. We don't have jobs yet, but we do have wealthy daddies." She giggled.

The wranglers were going to love them. Spoiled rich girls with more money than sense. The grin on Ring's face widened.

"I paint," Janie said.

Calum perked up. She might want to spend an afternoon painting. He could take her to the place he liked to draw.

Melissa snorted. "Squares and circles. You haven't sold anything yet."

Calum swallowed his sigh. More bickering.

"Better not get any ideas about not working, Angie," his father said. "If you don't do your chores, you don't get paid."

Angie's pretence of pouting made Calum's heart ache.

"I'm Matt Taylor from New York. I own an air-conditioning company. Married, two kids."

"Paul Kenyon. I run a modeling agency in New York. Divorced, no kids."

Calum chuckled to himself as Melissa and Janie straightened up and smiled in Paul's direction with perfect white teeth. The grin had fallen off Ring's face. He wasn't going to be much competition for a guy who ran a modeling agency.

"Our absent guest's name is Jasper Randolph," said Calum's father. "He's from London, England. You'll have to ask him what he does for a living when he's not lazing around in bed."

"He saved my life on the plane."

In the silence that followed Melissa's announcement, Calum's jaw dropped along with several others.

"She was choking," Janie said. "Coughing and coughing. She couldn't breathe. It was so frightening."

Melissa glared at her. "My story." She milked the moment as everyone looked at her. "I couldn't get air into my lungs. Jasper did the Hind...lick maneuver and out popped the yogurt-coated cranberry and I breathed again."

"Good for him." Calum's father struggled to keep a straight face. The guys from New York and a couple of the wranglers didn't even try.

"Have any of you ridden before?" Vera asked in a loud voice and glared at the sniggering ranch hands.

Apparently, they all had, though Calum knew they'd have to go through an assessment tomorrow. No way would the horses be put at risk through hotshot riding. A know-it-all attitude would get guests a week on an old horse for beginners. Calum wondered what sort of a rider the Englishman was.

What sort of ride he'd be?

Shit.

Jasper looked at the clock on the bedside table and groaned. If he didn't get this jet lag sorted out fast, he'd miss all the evening meals. Once he'd reached his room, he'd shaved, decided to close his eyes for a few minutes before he checked his emails, and now it was almost three in the morning. He rolled off the bed, looked at his creased clothes and managed a grin. He couldn't remember the last time he'd fallen asleep still dressed. *I'm off to a good start in loosening up.*

He spotted a piece of paper by the door and padded over. A snack had been left in the fridge. His stomach rumbled. He needed a shower and to check his messages, but that could be delayed until he'd had something to eat. *Wow, I am lightening up.*

According to the agenda, breakfast was at eight. It was a long while to wait when the last decent meal he'd had was dinner the night before he set off. Jasper put on his shoes, slipped out of the room, wandered along dimly lit corridors and eventually stumbled across the kitchen. He found a plate of sandwiches in the fridge along with water and soda. He took the water.

Jasper pushed open the front door, intending to sit on one of the rockers, but sucked in a breath at the chilly air. Maybe he'd stay inside.

"The one on the left creaks," a voice said, and Jasper almost dropped everything.

Calum sat in a rocker on the other side of the door, wearing his Stetson, booted feet with spurs attached propped up on the rail of the porch. Jasper's cock tried to unfurl. *Oh dear God, is this going to happen every time I look at this guy?* Nevertheless, he banished thoughts of going back indoors. If his teeth started to chatter, he'd stuff the sandwich in his mouth.

"The one next to you okay?" Jasper asked, relieved those few words came out without a squeak.

"Yep."

Jasper settled on it and put the water on the deck. "I missed dinner." Well, that was an impressive conversation opener.

"Yep," Calum said.

Jasper's shoulders sagged. So neither of them was good at conversation. Didn't mean they wouldn't be good at— *Don't go there.* The guy was probably married with kids. Goose bumps prickled Jasper's skin and he took a bite of the sandwich as he gazed over the dark shadows of the mountains and up into the sky, clotted with stars. The night looked blacker, the stars more plentiful and brighter than at home. Ambient light in central London made star gazing virtually impossible. Yet it was still hard to find what you were looking for in this indigo sky smothered with opportunity.

Jasper shivered. He should have worn a sweater.

Oh crap. Had Calum noticed he hadn't even changed his clothes? His tie still hung around his neck. He ought to have washed. *Fuck it.* Calum could probably smell him. That thought lead to another. Jasper wanted to press his face into the cowboy's neck and inhale him.

Probably earn a fist in the face.

Might be worth it.

I could just do it. Find out right now if I'm going to spend the week longing for the impossible.

On the other hand, Jasper knew life would be discovered on other planets before he worked up enough courage to make the first move.

Though it was him who cracked first on the conversation front. "What are you doing out here?"

"Protecting the guests from bears."

He had Jasper for a moment. "Pretty kind of you to sacrifice yourself on our behalf," he said.

"Yeah, well, they *would* have eaten me first, but now I reckon they'll go for you and those sandwiches."

Jasper smiled. "I miss anything at dinner, apart from food?"

"Your heroics on the plane."

Jasper stopped smiling. "Ah."

Calum chuckled. "Apparently, you performed the Hind Lick maneuver. The ranch hands are jealous as hell."

Jasper burst out laughing.

"Wish I'd been there to see it." Calum rose to his feet and stretched. "I better get back to bed. I have to be up at dawn." There was a short pause. "You need help to find your way back to your room?"

"I'm fine, thanks."

After Calum disappeared into the ranch, his spurs jingling, Jasper let out a quiet groan. What had that question meant?

I'll show you back to your room and say good night?

I'll show you back to your room, shove you inside and fuck your brains out?

Jasper had an overactive and over-optimistic imagination directly linked to his cock. Now he had to sit there, and if necessary freeze to death, until his cock gave up and returned to respectability.

It wasn't just the cowboy's looks, it was the way he spoke, the way he moved, the way he smelled. *I want him.*

Calum closed the door of his room, leaned back against it and exhaled noisily. It wasn't just Jasper's looks, it was the way he spoke, the way he moved, the way he smelled. *I want him.*

This was going to be a long, frustrating week.

He threw his hat onto the chair and shucked off his clothes as he made his way to the bed. He hadn't got his jeans all the way down before he wrapped his hand around his erect cock and began to pump. Kicking his way out of his clothes, Calum knelt by the side of his bed and yanked open his bedside cabinet. He pulled out a sandwich bag, squirted lube inside, then squished up the plastic to spread the gel around. Calum slid his cock into the bag and pushed it between the mattress and the box spring base. To think he'd complained when Vera had ordered him a new bed and he'd lost the one with wooden slats. Calum shuddered with pleasure at the pressure on his cock, the slick feel of the lube, and then leaned over the bed, grabbed the quilt in his fists and thrust his hips back and forth.

Calum had a hundred-and-one ways to make himself come without the aid of a partner or a hand. He wondered if there was anything he hadn't tried, wouldn't try. With his cock trapped in wet, tight heaven, this felt pretty good, not his favorite, but maybe as near to actual fucking as he could get. Then a jolt of awareness hit him that he was fucking his bed and his hips faltered.

He closed his eyes and tried to think of the last guy he'd fucked, but the face of the Texan faded and it was the uptight Englishman who filled his head. That thin blue tie. Calum wanted to wrap it around Jasper's wrists, his mouth, his cock—*oh fuck, fuck.* His breathing speeded up and he shunted his hips faster, pressing his chest down on the bed. His balls ached as if they'd been pumped up like an overfilled water balloon. His cock grew hotter by the second and his nerves hummed with tension.

Ah Christ, this is fast.

As if he'd been grabbed by a grizzly bear, orgasm seized him and shook him hard. Calum convulsed and slammed his face into the bed to muffle his cry as his come spurted out in long, hard blasts into…Jasper's ass. *Nice thought.*

Jasper struggled with the lock on his door until he realized that it didn't work and he'd obviously not locked it when he'd left. He'd tell someone in the morning, but then would that look as if he thought someone was going to steal from him? He didn't want to further piss off Calum's father. Jasper flipped open the button on his pants and eased down his zipper with a faint moan. *My bloody cock hurts.* How the hell was he going to manage to spend a week near Calum Neilson with a dick that was going to stand up and wave a flag if the guy came into sight? How could he even ride with an erection? He'd have to wank off before he left his room and even then, that wouldn't work. Jasper was usually proud of his recovery time, but now he saw it as an inconvenience.

He stripped and folded his clothes. Not that he could wear them again until they were laundered. He hung up the rest of his things in the closet and ignored his boner. By the time he'd neatly placed his underwear and socks in the chest of drawers, his cock was even harder and leaking pre-come. Too much thinking about the cowboy. Jasper sighed. *Shower and wank.*

His room was at the end of the hallway, so he hoped he wouldn't disturb anyone by showering at this early hour. He hated to think what he smelled like. He sniffed under his arms and winced. Jasper checked for shampoo and soap and turned on the water. His hand was working his cock even before he'd stepped under the flow. He drew his fist down to his swollen balls before slowly dragging his hand up again. Jasper felt obliged to hurry, still concerned about the sound carrying, though imagining Calum in the shower with him meant speed wasn't a problem. What the fuck had the cowboy being doing awake at this time of the morning?

Would he be there tomorrow?

While one hand pumped at the base of his cock, Jasper rubbed the crest with his thumb, teasing the foreskin over the tip before pushing it down to let his palm wrap around the head. More shampoo on his hands and he worked his cock faster, squeezing hard. Orgasm built inside him like a brewing storm. Dark clouds rolled in, his vision wavered and his balls tingled as if low-wattage electricity hummed through his veins. Jasper turned to face the tiles, wrapped both hands around his shaft and shunted his hips faster and faster as he jerked his hands in a matching rhythm.

Fire raced down his spine and long ribbons of come spurted into...Calum's ass. *Nice thought.*

Jasper managed a couple more hours sleep before breakfast, but he'd set his alarm to give him time to check his emails. He'd meant to look at them when he came back to his room but been distracted by his cock. Nothing urgent in his inbox—yet—though he still had to reply to fifteen messages. One of his important clients hadn't reacted well to the news that Jasper was taking a week's holiday. Despite reassurances that a colleague would be available to deal with any problems, the client would probably still email him every day. And because Jasper was a conscientious idiot, he'd respond.

There was no sign of Calum in the dining room, and Jasper wanted to hit himself upside the head for looking. He introduced himself to the other guests while they collected food from a buffet but picked a place to sit on his own toward the end of the long communal table. The moment he sat, he realized it was the wrong thing to do, but if he got up and moved, he'd look even more stupid. While everyone else tucked into huge amounts of food, Jasper had two slices of toast, an apple and coffee. He'd never seen plates piled so high with such a mixture—fruit, bacon, sausage, pancakes and maple syrup running into scrambled eggs. Everyone ate as if this were their last meal.

Janie and Melissa came to sit either side of him and Jasper sighed into his coffee.

"That all you're eating?" Janie pressed her leg against his.

"Not very hungry," Jasper lied. He was far more concerned about throwing up when the time came to sit on a horse.

"We missed you at dinner last night," Melissa said. "What if I'd choked again?"

He glanced at her expecting to see a smile, but she was serious. Oh God. When Jasper felt the push of her leg as well, he locked his knees together.

"Do you know Prince William and Kate?" Melissa asked.

"No."

"Have you met Queen Elizabeth?" asked Janie.

"Yes." She'd given his father an award and Jasper had been with him.

"Wow," Melissa said. "I had my life saved by a friend of the Queen of England."

Jasper opened his mouth to correct her and then thought—why bother? When she turned to tell the couple next to her, he wished he had. By the time it had spread around the table, he'd probably be a minor royal. He picked up his toast and put it down again. There was no way he could eat anything. Why wasn't he in Greece looking forward to exploring an ancient amphitheater?

"Morning, folks," Erik said as he walked into the room. "A beautiful day for riding. And if by lunchtime, your aching muscles tell you they've had enough, we have fishing or a scenic Jeep trip arranged for this afternoon."

I can lie in the sun and do nothing all day. I don't have to ride.

"It's up to the wranglers to pick you out a pony. Don't argue or you'll find you get the most ornery animal we have and he'll drive you crazy by the end of the day because he won't go one damn place you ask him, and he won't move a fraction faster than he wants to."

Sounded like a dream horse to Jasper. His hand slipped over the roll of sugar-free mints in his pocket. The way to any horse's heart. Though knowing his luck, he'd probably get a mutant horse that hated mints. He slipped the apple into his other pocket.

"Now I can see some of you are already dressed in suitable clothes." Erik smiled at the two couples standing near him who were in tatty jeans, long-sleeve shirts and vests. "Don't forget your hats."

Erik wandered down the table to Melissa and Janie, who got up to pose. "You look real pretty, ladies, but you'll ruin those outfits."

"That's okay. We bought lots with us." Melissa gave him a broad smile.

Jasper had been trying to think what the two of them reminded him of and he suddenly got it. The cowgirl in the animated movie about toys he'd watched while babysitting his neighbors' kids. White shirts trimmed with yellow, jeans with cow-print chaps and red cowboy hats dangling down their backs.

Erik looked at their boots.

"Seven pairs of boots too," Janie said.

Christ. No wonder they had so much luggage.

"Something wrong with the food?" Erik snapped.

That was aimed at him. Jasper flinched. "No, I—"

"Boss," Pete called from the door. "Can I have a word?"

As Erik walked away, Jasper sighed. He was dressed okay, wasn't he? No tie, a crisp, cream cotton shirt and blue chinos tucked into his old riding boots. And he wasn't going to care if he got dirty.

Well, not too much.

He'd packed a stain remover just in case.

One look at the wranglers leaning on the corral fence and the line of horses at their side and a day by the pool seemed even more attractive. *I look like an idiot.* Jasper hadn't mastered the art of dressing down. He'd very nearly put on his tie, but it was his boots that looked stupid. Knee high, tight and black, they were show-jumper's boots. He held the riding helmet behind his back. He'd assumed they'd all need hard hats for insurance purposes and he had one of his own, so why not bring it?

Because no one else was going to be wearing one.

He saw a couple of sly nudges and mutters pass between the wranglers when they saw his boots, but actually, in the grand scale of things, he didn't care. Jasper was far more concerned about not freaking out when it was time to mount the horse. His heart thumped like an overloud bass on a car music system and his mouth had lost all moisture. Good thing Calum wasn't around to laugh at him too.

Oh shit, of course he is.

Calum walked over with his father and Pete. Christ, he was wearing chaps. Well, Pete was too but Jasper wasn't looking at Pete. Something about the way the leather—

"Who's first?" Erik asked.

That won't be me. Jasper set his jaw. He had a list of excuses to avoid climbing over the fence. A need to retrieve something from his room, a stone in his boot, a coughing fit, an urge to take a leak, to get a drink, spontaneous combustion, alien abduction—oh, he could be very inventive.

Melissa climbed over the fence. "Yaaaay. Me first."

Jasper watched as Pete spoke quietly to Melissa and then signaled to a stocky wrangler who led a gray horse into the corral. Melissa looked like she'd been born in the saddle.

One by one, each guest showed what they could do and the line of horses grew smaller as they rode away. They all looked enthusiastic and competent. Great. When Jasper had filled in the details of his riding experience on the booking form, that he'd ridden for several years, he'd neglected to mention something rather important. His stomach roiled. The only good news was that as a guest met with Erik's approval, they left with a wrangler so in the end, only Pete, Calum and Erik remained to witness Jasper's humiliation.

Not sure my feet are going to move. I really need to piss. Oh Christ. Is that a spaceship?

"Your turn." Erik smirked at Jasper's knee-high black boots. "Show jumper?"

"No," Jasper muttered, though once upon a time he had been.

His fingers clenched around the helmet. He slammed it onto his head and clipped it in place before he could change his mind. Jasper averted his gaze so he didn't catch anyone's eye, particularly Calum's, but anxiety ballooned in his chest, making it hard to swallow the bile surging up his throat. He sensed he was fighting a losing battle to control his nerves. Even the thought of taking the apple bribe from his pocket made him feel sick.

"Climb over and show us what you can do," Erik said.

Oh God, shit, fuck, crap. As if he could read Jasper's mind, the horse gave him a look of disdain, flaring his nostrils.

Erik gave an impatient sigh. "When you're ready."

"One minute," Jasper mumbled, turned and threw up. *Oh fuck, fuck, fuck.*

"Shit," Pete muttered.

Jasper didn't think he had that much in his stomach but he'd been mistaken. Oh God. He dragged a tissue from his pocket and wiped his mouth. "I'm sorry. I'll clean it up if you'd point me in the—"

"Don't worry about it," Erik said.

"You okay?" Calum asked.

"Must have eaten something that disagreed with me." Jasper backed away. "Sorry."

He practically ran back to the ranch, tearing off his helmet as he went. Why the hell had he thought forcing himself to confront this was the way to go? There were plenty of other things to do in life, why throw himself over this particular cliff?

Note to self: Look more carefully before I leap. I might land in quicksand.

Chapter Three

Calum stared after Jasper's retreating back and sighed. A guy with issues was not what he needed to be hot for because he had enough of his own. *Fuck.*

"Looks like you're not going to be riding today, Pete," Erik said. "You can see to those damaged boards on the barn. Put Bonny back in the pasture and get Gunner to deal with that mess. Calum, go see if the guy needs a doctor. At least we know it's nothing he's eaten here. He didn't touch his breakfast."

"He had that sandwich Angie made," Calum said.

"How do you know?" his father snapped.

Calum thought quickly. "Because it's gone from the fridge. I assume he ate it."

"Oh Christ. Get after him."

Calum didn't rush. Jasper had to be embarrassed. He'd give him a chance to compose himself. He'd watched the English guy as one by one the guests went through their paces, proving they knew how to mount and hold the reins correctly, to cue the horse to walk, stop, turn and canter and most important—they didn't yank at the animal's mouth. With every passing minute, Jasper's face had steadily paled, taut lines bracketing his lips.

But Calum didn't think the dude was sick. More like scared.

When Calum knocked on the door of Jasper's room, it swung open. A suitcase sat on the bed, a few clothes lay inside together with an apple. Packing or not unpacked yet? Packing, Calum guessed. There was no sign of Jasper. Bathroom, maybe? Calum stayed where he was and banged harder on the door.

It took a couple of moments before Jasper appeared, dark shadows evident under those beautiful eyes, and it was all Calum could do not to pull him into his arms.

"Okay?" Calum leaned on the doorframe. "Deserting us already?" He nodded toward the bed.

"I started to pack and then realized I was being an idiot. Nothing new there." He backed up to the bed and sat next to his case, elbows on his knees, head in his hands.

"Calum, is he okay?"

Angie came running up the corridor, her long blonde hair tumbling down her back. She pushed past him and burst into the room before he could stop her.

"I just made you what I like," she blurted. "Not my favorite, but still good."

Jasper straightened and sent Calum a confused look.

"Angie made the sandwich," Calum said. "We're worried it made you throw up."

Jasper rose to his feet. "That sandwich was delicious. One of the best, if not *the* best I ever had. That's not why I was sick."

Angie's chin wobbled. "But Pete said it made you sick."

Damn Pete. Why did he have to do that?

"Can you keep a secret?" Jasper asked.

Angie nodded hard. She pulled him to the far side of the room and glared at Calum. He rolled his eyes and put his hands over his ears as Jasper bent to whisper to Angie. Calum didn't hear what he said.

"There's no need to be scared of horses," she said in a loud voice.

Jasper's face flushed with a tinge of red and Calum groaned.

"I'll let you ride Misty," Angie said. "She's good as gold. She's never thrown me. Well, only once and that was my fault."

Calum opened his mouth, but Jasper shook his head and smiled at Angie. *Oh God, this guy is going to break my fucking heart.*

"That's really kind of you, Angie. I think I might lie by the pool instead today. I'd love another sandwich for lunch." He sat back on the bed.

"Go tell Mom you make the best sandwiches," Calum said. Angie raced off and Calum flashed Jasper a look of apology. "She likes the idea of a secret, but she can't keep one. She's..." Oh God, he didn't want to say.

"Sweet," Jasper said. "And special."

Calum's jaw twitched. "Yeah, she is." He realized he'd taken a step nearer Jasper and backed up. "Why did you choose this kind of vacation if you don't like horses?"

"I *do* like horses. It's not horses I have a problem with, it's getting on their backs that's the issue." His fingers fidgeted on the bed. "I used to ride a lot, but I...haven't for some time."

Why did you stop? "Sure you want to lie by the pool? Can I convince you to try again? Everyone's gone now. We can take it as slow and easy as you like." Oh God, slow and easy sounded good, but listening to his dick, Calum suspected fast and hard would be more likely.

"*You'll* take me out?" Jasper asked.

Calum nodded. He hadn't missed the interest in Jasper's voice and his cock nodded an I-told-you-so.

"My stomach's empty now. You should be safe." Jasper gave a wry grin.

"Wait here. I'll be back in a sec." Calum turned at the door. "Unpack. You don't look like a quitter to me."

On his way to his room, Calum bumped into his father who grabbed his arm to bring him to a halt. "Angie says the pansy's scared."

Oh shit. If his father didn't keep his mouth shut, everyone on the ranch would find out and Jasper would be a laughing stock.

"What the fuck's he doing here?" his father asked.

"He's not scared of horses."

"Well he did a damned good impression of it. At least we know it wasn't the food. I don't want someone else threatening to sue us."

"That didn't come to anything."

They'd had a guest who'd almost taken them to court a few months ago. Some crap about bedbugs. Pest control had found no evidence of any problem, but word spread based on internet comments. Calum had jumped on every post he saw and eventually squashed the rumor, though there was no way of knowing if they'd have had that level of cancellations without the issue. It damn well annoyed him his father had refunded the bedbug guy's money. The lying bastard had probably made up the whole thing.

His father glared at him. "We had four cancel that should have been here this week."

"Coincidence," Calum said, though he wasn't sure it was.

He knew his father was worried. Even when they weren't running at capacity, the wranglers and other help still had to be paid and horses had to be fed. They weren't the only dude ranch in Wyoming. They couldn't afford to make mistakes.

"Go and help Pete replace that boarding on the barn," his father said.

"I'm going to take the English guy out. He wants to ride."

His father scowled. "Think that's a good idea?"

Calum stiffened. "Don't you trust me?"

They stared at each other and Calum thought if the wrong thing was said, he'd walk off this ranch and never speak to his father again. But then he'd thought that a lot of times and he'd never left. Calum backed down from confrontation just like he always did.

"Sorry," he muttered.

His father nodded. "I'll tell Gunner to saddle Zander."

Calum carried on to his room, his heart hammering. Just him and Jasper? At least he'd know by the end of the ride if the guy was only going to figure in his dreams. But if Zander wasn't in the right mood, they'd be lucky to make it to the bottom of the first pasture by lunchtime. He snatched up boots and gloves, turned to leave and then went back to grab a couple of foil packets from his bottom drawer. Fuck what his father thought. Calum was listening to his dick. It was more fun.

When he got back to Jasper's room, the suitcase had gone.

"These should fit." Calum handed him the boots. "We look about the same size."

"I don't want spurs. I don't need them."

Calum sucked in his cheeks. "The horses are used to them."

"But I'm not. I don't want to risk injuring a horse if I…"

If you panic. Shit. "Here, I'll take them off."

Calum removed the metal and passed the boots back.

Jasper slipped them on and stood to press his heels down into the boots. "Thank you."

"You should wear these too." Calum handed him the gloves. "You don't want to end up with hands like mine."

"Nothing wrong with yours," Jasper murmured.

Calum's breath caught. "Come on, then. Let's see if Zander likes you. Leave the helmet, you won't be going above walking pace."

Jasper was silent all the way to the corral. Calum couldn't help but notice he trudged the worn path like he was walking to his execution. The sunglasses were back in place. Hard to tell what he was thinking. Calum wondered what had happened. Had to be some sort of accident. Hence the helmet. *Shit, I should have let him wear it.*

The docile brown horse they used for beginners was tethered to the rail of the corral. No one else was around.

"You don't have to do this if you don't want to," Calum said.

Jasper remained tight-lipped.

"You could try again later."

Calum could almost see the battle going on in Jasper's head. He wanted and didn't want at the same time.

"Why don't you just say howdy to him?" Calum climbed over into the enclosure.

He was a little surprised when Jasper followed.

"Good boy, Zander." Calum patted the horse at the base of its neck.

Jasper tipped his sunglasses onto his head and held out his hand, palm flat and let the horse sniff. "You look older than me," he said and laughed quietly, though the smile didn't make it all the way to his eyes.

"He's been around for as long as I can remember."

As Jasper stroked the horse's shoulder, Calum moved away. The petting turned into a firm scratch and Zander dropped his head so Jasper would keep doing it. Calum's gaze was glued to Jasper's hand and his mind returned to an earlier train of thought. What would it feel like being stroked by Jasper? Soft fingers sliding into his pants, wrapping— *Oh fuck.* There was a distinct lack of room in his jeans and Calum swallowed his groan. *I'm jealous of a horse?*

"Those long brown eyelashes don't have me fooled." Jasper ran his hand along Zander's flank. "We both know if I do something you don't like, I'm going to be eating dirt."

Zander bobbed his head.

Jasper turned to Calum, and sighed. "Did he just agree?"

Calum chuckled. The chances of Zander mustering enough energy to throw anyone off were zero. He'd pretty much put up with anything except overuse of spurs. He was a good boy, unlike Calum. "Keep stroking him. Let him get used to the sound of your voice and your scent." He moved up behind Jasper, his heart jumping.

"Good lad," Jasper whispered and scratched between the horse's ears.

Zander swung his head round hard and knocked Jasper into Calum. Calum couldn't help himself. As he caught hold of Jasper, he breathed in. Soap, coconut shampoo, musk. *Fuck it.* Calum jerked away.

"Sorry," Jasper said.

"Oh yeah, and don't mess with his ears."

Funny how he hadn't thought to mention that. Jasper turned and gave Calum a look that said he knew exactly why he hadn't mentioned it. Calum's cock continued to grow. He couldn't tear his gaze from Jasper as he petted Zander. *Want him, want him, want him.* Except someone like Jasper could probably have any guy at all. *And it won't be a guy like me.*

"So, Zander, are you going to play nice?" Jasper whispered as he stroked the horse's neck. "Not going to bolt for a fence the moment I sit on your back and try to launch me into the next paddock?"

The horse whickered.

"Sorry my hands are clammy, only I'm kind of nervous."

"Someone you know have an accident?" The question escaped before Calum could stop it.

"My brother."

Jasper continued to scratch Zander, his face turned away from Calum. He didn't say anything else, but Calum couldn't leave it there.

"Bad?" he asked.

Jasper turned to look at him. "Ben died."

Why didn't I leave it? Me and my big fucking mouth. "Oh Christ. I'm sorry." *Shut the fuck up.* "How long ago?" *Quiet! Now!*

"Five years."

Calum took a deep breath. "I figure you're allowed to be nervous. You want me to go grab that helmet?"

"No. I'm guessing I've got the horse you use for beginners. He's not going to buck or kick or move faster than a snail, are you, sunshine? It's just that the other half of my brain is telling me he's been waiting for an idiot like me so he can show his hidden demon side."

Jasper took a roll of mints from his pocket and Zander almost knocked them out of his hand in his desperation to snaffle one. The white mint on Jasper's palm disappeared and Zander whinnied.

"You're welcome," Jasper said.

Calum laughed. "You just made a friend for life."

Jasper stared straight at Calum and offered him the roll. The grin on Jasper's face didn't last long, but it was deadly. Calum took a mint and smiled. Jasper popped one in his own mouth. After he put the mints back, Zander tried to get his head in Jasper's pocket.

"No more until you've let me get on your back," Jasper said. "I've done enough sweet-talking. You'll be wanting flowers and chocolates next."

Zander's ears twitched, but Jasper stepped away from the horse not toward him. The set of his jaw told Calum that for all his chatter, Jasper was on the point of walking away.

"Zander won't throw you," Calum said.

"Right." Jasper took a deep breath.

"What happened to your brother?"

"He came off his horse and…hit a car. Ended up paralyzed from the neck down. Ben was only fifteen years old. He spent the next nine years unable to even breathe on his own before he died." Jasper's voice had dropped to a whisper. "I don't want that to happen to me."

"Oh fuck."

"Oh fuck sums it up."

Calum struggled for something to say. "How about I promise to shoot you if it does?" *Oh crap, not that you idiot.*

But Jasper released a strangled laugh and then looked straight at him with those big chocolate eyes. "Would you? If I asked?"

Calum's answer came straight from his heart. "Doesn't seem right to let humans suffer when we're prepared to put animals out of their misery."

"Not as simple as that though, is it?"

And that told Calum a lot. "Did your brother ask you to kill him?"

"All the time." Jasper untied the reins and slipped on the gloves. He put his left foot in the stirrup, grabbed the pommel, swung up onto the horse and then pulled down his sunglasses.

Drop the subject now. Calum sighed. "You made that look pretty easy."

"I've got my eyes closed. Am I sitting the right way round?"

Calum laughed. "You're fine."

"I'm fucking scared shitless."

"Need me to fix your stirrups?"

"I can do it." Jasper reached down and then gave Calum a puzzled look. "Where's the strap?"

Calum smiled. "Maybe you'd better let me get that. Kick your foot out of the stirrup."

Jasper moved his leg forward and Calum lifted the fender and adjusted the stirrup leathers in the buckle. Jasper murmured quietly to Zander as Calum fixed the other side.

"Walk him round a spell when you're ready."

Jasper made a clicking sound, squeezed with his legs, kicked once with his heels and Zander moved out into the corral. Calum saw a confidence in Jasper that hadn't been there a moment ago, though he was holding a rein in each hand.

"Western horses neck rein," Calum said. "I suspect you're used to horses responding more to direct pressure on their mouths than reins on the side of the neck."

"I use a combination of the two."

"Try holding the reins in one hand, palm up with one rein between the thumb and forefinger and one between the forefinger and middle finger." Calum watched as Jasper changed his hold. "That's it."

When he saw Jasper got it, Calum relaxed and leaned on the rail. He tried to imagine being unable to do anything for himself, if he couldn't scratch an itch, fuck or jack off, and what he'd do if someone begged him to flip a switch and end a life. Hell, whichever way he looked at it. Had Jasper cracked in the end and done what his brother had asked? Killed him?

"I'll get Blue. You okay in here on your own?" Calum asked.

"Fine."

I'm doing it. Jasper's pulse raced, excitement overwhelming his fear. After making such a fool of himself earlier, there was no way he'd have given up and retired to the pool when Calum stood watching him. If the animal had been foaming at the mouth and pawing the air with his hooves, Jasper would have still tried to ride. To think he'd spent all this time worrying about getting on a horse, when all he needed for that extra push was a good-looking guy's gaze fixed on him.

Jasper patted Zander on the neck. "Good boy. Are we going to have some fun? That doesn't include you throwing me and then standing there whickering. You treat me well and I'll return the favor. Okay?"

The horse whinnied and Jasper laughed. "I'll take that as a yes."

Calum returned on a lively looking black quarter horse, followed by Bessie, and leaned down to open the corral gate to let Jasper out.

"Is she rounding us up?" Jasper asked, nodding at the dog.

"She'll follow to the bottom of the first pasture. She's too old now to run along with me." Calum reined Blue back so the two horses walked side by side, but from his snorting and blowing, Blue was clearly anxious to race off. "You okay?"

"Yes. I think I'd built this up in my mind to be something akin to taking a parachute jump. The fear of it worse than doing it—once I'd been pushed out of the plane, that is. Though now I've seen you've brought a rifle, I'm wondering if there's something else for me to worry about."

"Nope, it's just in case we meet a bear. When we've had one reported in the area, we don't take chances."

Jasper smiled. "Nothing to worry about at all then."

"Not for me. Blue's way faster than Zander."

Calum grinned and Jasper wished he'd worn looser pants.

They travelled for quite awhile in comfortable silence before Calum spoke.

"What do you do for a living?"

"Stockbroker."

Calum chuckled. "Me too. Part of my job's breaking stock. Any good at it?"

"You don't survive in the business for long if you're not. Same for you I'd imagine. Have you always worked on the ranch?"

"I went away to college, though not far. Wyoming's in my blood, I guess."

Jasper looked around. Powder-blue skies stretched as far as he could see, punctuated by craggy peaks, some of them capped with snow. "You're very fortunate to have this on your doorstep. A sky blue enough to swim in, snow-capped mountain peaks, rolling plains. It's hard to think of anything more beautiful." *Don't think about Calum naked.*

"Yeah, it's great until you want to go to the movies or need your laptop repaired or you want to dance where no one's going to laugh at you."

Jasper raised his eyebrows. "You like to dance?"

"No, because I get laughed at. What about you?"

"I don't get laughed at because I don't dance." *But I might with the right person.*

Calum smiled. "Want to encourage Zander to pick up the pace?"

"I thought you said we wouldn't be going above a walk."

"I lied. Going to show me you can persuade him without spurs?" He tugged his hat farther down on his head, kicked Blue and cantered away.

Jasper dug his heels into Zander's flanks, clicked his teeth, flicked the reins and the horse set off after Blue. At a slow trot.

"That won't do," Jasper muttered. "Come on, boy. Don't show me up."

He kicked harder at Zander's flanks and urged the horse into a canter. As the ground began to run away beneath him, Jasper wanted to whoop.

Oh Christ. He'd forgotten the fun, the exhilaration of being carried at speed on a horse's back, the sound of hooves pounding, the sensation of all that muscular power between his legs. Calum glanced over his shoulder to check he was following and then yelled something that was carried away on the wind. Blue was much faster, but Zander tried to catch up. After a few minutes, Jasper reined him back. The last thing he needed was a horse to collapse under him because he'd pushed too hard.

By the time he reached Calum, the cowboy was grinning ear to ear.

He wheeled Blue alongside. "Like riding a bike."

"I thought you said Zander was old and slow."

"Maybe he needed someone with the right touch to bring him to life."

Jasper was glad his sunglasses hid his eyes. It would be easy to read too much into that.

"Blue and Zander are pals. Zander will follow him anywhere. Even when he shouldn't."

What was he supposed to read into *that*?

Nothing, idiot.

They walked the horses for a while and spectacular views kept opening up of sagebrush plains, grassy meadows and rocky gorges—all framed by snow-capped mountains. Compared to London, this was another planet. No traffic, no police sirens polluting the air, just the sounds of a rushing river and snuffling horses. Large birds circled overhead, wings spread as they soared on warm currents.

"Wow, eagles," Jasper said.

Calum looked up and laughed. "Buzzards. Probably looking for something that's died."

Jasper snorted. "Wreck the moment, why don't you? It's beautiful anyway."

"Yep, everywhere you look."

Jasper caught a glimpse of Calum staring at him and his heart lurched.

"What can you see out of your window?" Calum asked.

"At work? The concrete and glass of an office block. An occasional bird flies past. Usually a pigeon. At home, well I have a small house with enough space to park my car at the front and at the back there's a tiny flagstone yard with a small table and chairs. It's all closed in, claustrophobic. Everything here is so big."

"Yep, it sure is."

Jasper's mind got sidetracked and his cock pressed against his zipper. He sighed and tipped his face to the sky. Even surrounded by mountain ranges, the sky looked huge, endless.

"You live on your own?" Calum asked.

Jasper's heart skipped a beat. "Yes."

"No wife, fiancée, girlfriend, boyfriend, dog, cat?"

"No." Jasper tried to think of some witty come back. An imaginary friend? Maybe not. A minute went by, his mind remained blank and the moment had passed.

"I've never lived on my own," Calum said. "I'm used to having lots of people around."

"It can get lonely when there's just one of you," Jasper said.

"It can get lonely when there's a crowd." Calum kicked Blue on. "Some of the cattle are over the next ridge. We'll go take a look at them. We don't bring them back down to the lower grazing until mid-September."

Jasper urged Zander on. "I saw on the website you let guests help with that."

Calum snorted. "Help, yeah, if they can ride. They don't realize it's all day in the saddle and not just one day either and they're expected to look after their horse when they get back, not pass the reins and responsibility to someone else."

Jasper heard a mechanical buzz and Calum pulled a phone from his pocket.

"Yep," Calum said.

"Whereabouts are you?" asked a crackly voice.

"Dutton Ridge. Why?"

"Fence down at the southeast corner. I'll find someone nearer."

Calum put the phone away.

"I thought your father said anyone using a cell phone would be shot."

"Yeah well, we can't police the sounds guests' phones are going to make. It's easier to ban them, but the wranglers all carry phones or walkie-talkies in case of an emergency."

As they reached the top of the ridge, Jasper looked down to see brown and black longhorn cattle meandering through the trees. He suddenly felt like a cowboy and smiled.

"Hey, there's Bonnie and Clyde and little Jimmy," Calum said.

Jasper gave him an incredulous glance. "You give names to your herd?"

"Just the ones we eat." Calum only held his face straight for a moment. He laughed and Jasper chuckled.

"We'll head for that rocky outcrop and rest the horses for a while. Follow me." Calum kicked Blue on.

Jasper let Zander have his head to pick his way down the rough slope and ducked tree branches that threatened to knock him off. When Calum slipped from his mount, Jasper did the same and pulled Zander to where Calum was tethering Blue. Calum tied Zander next to him. He took two bottles of water from his saddlebag and tossed one to Jasper.

Calum hung his hat on the pommel and chugged half the bottle straight down. He upended the rest over his head and as the water poured down his hair and over his face onto his shirt, Jasper's cock turned hard as stone. *Oh Christ.* Had Calum done that knowing how fucking sexy it looked? Or because he was hot?

"That's better," Calum said with sigh. "Course, it won't last long in this heat. You need to wear a hat."

Jasper stood with his back toward Calum, pretending to look at the view. His fingers fumbled with the screw top of the bottle and then he tipped the water into his mouth. He'd never upended a bottle over his head and fought an urge to copy Calum. The idea of pouring cool water over his face was appealing. When Jasper turned, he made sure he held the bottle so it disguised the bulge in his pants. Calum sat on a rock in front of him, his wet hair dripping down his tanned cheeks and Jasper suspected the attempt to hide his rather obvious reaction was doomed to failure.

The water glistened like diamonds in Calum's hair. As the drips fell off his chin and trickled down his neck, Jasper wanted to leap on him and lick up every one. Calum leaned back on his hands and closed his eyes. He tipped his head so the sun fell on his face, and Jasper sighed at the knowledge that his cock wasn't going to give up anytime soon. He still wasn't completely certain Calum was gay, but Jasper was edging that way.

Calum had rolled up the sleeves of his shirt to reveal strong forearms, the fine light blond hair shining in the sun. His long, denim-and-leather-clad legs were stretched out in front of him, crossed at the ankle, spurs glinting. The bulge at Calum's groin grew as Jasper stared. *Guess that answers one question.*

Note to self: Put my tongue away.

Chapter Four

Excitement bubbled inside Jasper. He sat on the rock beside Calum but faced the other way. His heart pounded, his voice trapped in his throat as he stared through the trees toward the river. Much safer than looking at the guy next to him...or that swelling at his crotch. But almost immediately Jasper began to convince himself he was mistaken. Could be any number of reasons for Calum having an erection.

"I suppose you've got what you came here for," Calum said. "You're riding again. Didn't seem like such a big deal."

Jasper snorted and his chest loosened. He turned to face Calum. "You missed me throwing up then? Anyway, that wasn't the only reason I came."

I want to get down with a cowboy. Oh shit. Is that really why I'm here?

"Why else did you come all this way?"

"To learn how to get dirty and not mind."

Calum chuckled. "I'm an expert in that."

Oh fuck. Take a deep breath and be sensible.

"I also thought it was about time I learnt how to...unwind. I work in a hectic, constantly changing environment where I have to make important decisions quickly. There's no chance to relax. I spend most of my day on the phone pitching stock ideas to potential or existing clients and then issuing sell or buy orders involving vast sums of money. High octane, high adrenaline stuff and I have to maintain tight control, keep everything balanced or it would come crashing down around my ears to not only ruin me but my clients."

"The keeping control and balanced part's not so different from riding a horse."

Jasper laughed. "True, but here there's no urgency to this, no requirement to take a particular route, to make a certain point at a particular time."

"Not so sure about that. We need to be back for lunch or Vera won't be happy. And if I pick the wrong path, we could end up lost."

Jasper's heart had calmed, his cock soft again. Conversation was safe. Just because they'd both had erections didn't mean—*oh fuck, yes it does*—but it didn't mean they had to do something about it.

"You say you wanted to relax yet you picked a vacation you knew would be stressful," Calum said.

"I assumed once I'd conquered my fear of riding, I'd enjoy it."

"And get dirty."

Something in the way Calum said that made Jasper swallow hard.

"So riding's important for you to get back under control?"

Jasper supposed it was. Another box to tick in his life.

"You have to be in control of everything?" Calum asked in a quiet voice.

"Not everything." Jasper's cock uncurled like a sprouting plant.

"Because I'm a sort of controlling guy too."

Shit, shit, shit.

Calum brushed a smear of dust from the knee of Jasper's pants. The slightest touch and Jasper's breathing hitched. Every muscle tensed.

"You resisted wiping that off," Calum said with a mouth-watering grin.

Maybe I was hoping you'd do it for me. Jasper averted his gaze and stared at a tree. Of course the words stayed in his head. Ultra-decisive in his professional life, he was a different person in his private. The chances of Jasper making a move were zero.

Calum lifted Jasper's sunglasses off his face and set them aside. *Oh fuck.* Now Jasper had to look at him.

"The getting dirty thing could be because you grew up too fast." Calum stared straight at him. "No time to be a kid. Probably had something to do with what happened to your brother. You stayed under the radar by being a good boy."

Clever guy. Except how could Jasper begrudge the time his parents had spent with Ben and not with him? Jasper had to behave, stay in his room, keep out of trouble, not make a nuisance of himself. How could he have fun and laugh when his brother was able to do little more than blink? How could he be happy when everyone in the house was steeped in misery, when every conversation was about Ben and never about him?

"The control thing," Calum said, "I understand that. When I'm breaking in a horse, I can't let my concentration slip for a second. I have to show the animal I'm in charge, and that I understand what he needs. But work is work and pleasure's pleasure."

Calum's hand lay flat on the rock between them. Jasper's hand mirrored it, their fingers inches apart. A small gap the size of the Grand Canyon. Jasper imagined his hand sliding over to touch Calum's fingers.

So easy.

So damn difficult.

Jasper's heart thumped so hard it hurt.

"You know the first thing I noticed about you?" Calum asked and swung round so he was sitting the same way as Jasper.

"You thought I had pink luggage?"

He laughed. "No, the purple."

Jasper couldn't dislodge the lump in his throat.

"Your huge brown eyes," Calum whispered.

Oh God. Jasper's cock made a determined attempt to get through his zipper and his grip tightened around the water bottle held at his groin as if he could push the thing back down.

"I have a thing for sparkling blue eyes," Jasper blurted. Like a pool he wanted to dive into and then never climb out.

"Is that right?"

"And tanned skin that looks as though it's always warm." *Shit.* Where did that come from?

"Not in the winter. I get so cold I feel like my skin's freezing." Calum's voice was hoarse. "I like soft hands."

Oh God, he's flirting with me. And I'm flirting back.

"For me, there's something about a rough touch," Jasper choked out.

Calum barked out a laugh.

Jasper sighed. "I wasn't sure about you."

"Nor me about you."

But I am now.

Jasper swallowed to bring moisture to his mouth. "Which makes you just about perfect."

"Hell, I'm a long way from perfect."

Not me for, you're not.

"So," Calum said. "We going to ignore this?"

Jasper tightened his mouth. Calum wanted to slam the lid back on the box already?

"Or do something about it?" Calum asked. "Only I've just ridden seven miles with a cock so stiff it hurts." He gave a wry grin.

"Me too."

"I know we *should* ignore it," Calum said. "The wranglers aren't allowed to fuck the guests. It causes complications and that rule applies to me too even though I'm the boss's son. Especially to me since I'm supposed to be setting an example. My father will just about kill me if he finds out, but you're distracting me beyond reason. I came so hard after I left you last night, I thought my heart would stop."

The effect on Jasper's cock was as effective as if Calum had stroked it. Jasper glanced down to check it hadn't burst his zipper and wasn't out scenting the air.

"I sort of understand how Eve felt when she was tempted with that apple." Calum grinned. "So bad, so good."

How many before me? Does it matter?

Jasper stared at their hands, fingers inching closer and closer until the tips touched. The jolt that went through him could have been a lightning strike for the impact it had. Jasper burned head to toe. His throat dried so fast he couldn't speak. His cock strained against his zipper and made the water bottle jump. Then their fingers linked, and their hands clasped and tightened.

"Oh fuck," Calum whispered.

It was as if they'd been welded together, and while their entwined hands didn't shift, to Jasper's astonishment, his other hand let go of the bottle and rose to slide up Calum's forearm. It was Jasper's hand that crept to the damp hair at the nape of Calum's neck, Jasper's hand that tugged Calum nearer. Their faces were so close they breathed each other's air. Calum brought his free hand to the back of Jasper's neck, and when Jasper slid his fingers into Calum's hair to press into his scalp, Calum did the same to him.

Their other hands unlinked as if by mutual consent, and as Calum lifted his fingers to Jasper's face and stroked his chin with his thumb, Jasper's palm settled over Calum's chest. Then their lips were together and Jasper wasn't sure who'd moved first, nor did he care. Their kiss was wet and open, tongues tangling as the sound of their ragged groans filled the air. Calum's tongue teased his while his fingers twisted harder in Jasper's hair, urging him closer.

The first deep thrust of Calum's tongue surprised him.

Calum pulled away, muttered, "Oh God, you taste good," and then he kissed him again.

Jasper curled his tongue under Calum's, exploring his mouth, but a gentle kiss grew rougher by the second. Deeper and harder lunges as they dueled, each fighting for control and then they were on their feet, bodies plastered together, hands on backs, on butts, on necks as they staggered around and writhed and humped and fucked each other's mouths until they couldn't breathe.

They came up for air like kids in a swimming pool competing over who could stay under longest. They gasped and laughed, wanting to do it all over again. Jasper's senses were consumed by need. Damp mouth, hot tongue, strong hands—if his cock could have moaned, it would have.

Calum's breathing rasped in his ear. "Oh fuck, fuck."

Jasper panted into Calum's neck. "Oh fuck, fuck."

Then they went at it again, kissing, groping, grinding their hips together until it almost hurt. Calum's fingers tugged at Jasper's shirt until it came out of his pants. A warm hand slid onto his lower back and tingles raced up Jasper's spine. Roughened fingertips wormed their way into the back of his chinos, and pressure spiraled from Jasper's balls to set fire to his belly. Calum groaned into Jasper's mouth as he squeezed one of his butt cheeks, his thumb sliding into the crease. He rocked his cock against Jasper's and they bucked and rutted as if there were no clothes between them.

Vaguely, somewhere in Jasper's head, buried under a mountain of greedy lust, he knew they ought to slow down, take their time, at least make sure no one but the horses watched, but it was as though he'd stepped onto a speeding train with no way off until the destination was reached. And if Jasper was going to come in his pants, he was determined not to be the only one. He pushed his hand between their excited hips and while his cock rubbed one side of Calum's dick, his hand pressed against the other.

Calum gasped into his mouth. "We can't go back with wet patches on our jeans, and if you keep doing that with your hand, that's exactly what's going to happen."

"Don't want to stop," Jasper panted.

He found the head of Calum's cock and rubbed his finger over the denim.

"Jesus," Calum gasped and grabbed Jasper's hand.

"I want to suck you off," Jasper blurted.

Calum jerked away and backed up a few steps, but the look in his eyes told Jasper he wasn't running far. Jasper's pulse kicked up a notch. Calum ran his tongue over his lower lip and then reached for his belt. But before he touched it, he straightened and looked around.

"Fuck it," he snapped. "Someone's coming."

Jasper groaned.

By the time three horses came into view, Calum had remounted Blue. He adjusted his hat on the pommel to ensure it obscured his crotch, but his cock knew when it was beaten. His balls, on the other hand, made their displeasure very clear. They ached like hell. There was some comfort in knowing he wasn't the only one.

"Howdy, dudes," Melissa shouted. "What are you guys up to?"

Jasper had retrieved his bottle of water and sat on the rock with his left leg bent. Calum slapped a smile on his face.

"Call of nature." Calum nodded to Ring, who nodded back.

"Ooh, what have you seen?" Janie asked. "Anything interesting? We spotted antelope and mule deer."

Calum stifled his laugh at Janie's misunderstanding and belatedly remembered he'd been supposed to point out the local flora and fauna to Jasper.

"We've seen prairie dogs too," Melissa said. "They were so cute."

Ring gave a pointed snort.

"And what do we find to add to our list when we come around that rock but a couple of good-looking guys." Melissa wolf-whistled.

"We were hoping for elk," Janie said.

Jasper's laugh rang out.

"Or a bear," Melissa said. "Ring said there might be one in these rocks."

"Yeah?" Calum glanced at the wrangler who smirked.

"Did you use to be a rodeo star too?" Janie asked.

"No." Calum walked Blue over to Ring's horse. "You mean that one time you tried bull-riding and broke your arm?"

The wrangler scowled. "You ever sat on a bull's back?"

"No, I have more sense."

"I doubt that." Ring glanced toward Jasper with a sneer on his face and Calum felt a ball of fury writhe in his gut.

My fucking father. The reason for the earlier call now clear, Calum slapped his Stetson back on his head.

"Since we're here," Ring said, "Jasper can join us for the rest of the ride. Go and help my father work on the barn."

Calum imagined himself planting his fist in Ring's smug face, and then thought of Jasper's reaction, and the report back to his father by the women of an unprovoked attack. Before he did or said something that couldn't be undone, he wheeled Blue away and headed up the slope.

By the time Calum was in sight of the ranch, he'd calmed down. He felt bad he'd ridden off without saying anything to Jasper. It was possible his father hadn't sent Ring after him. It was too easy to see conspiracy where there was none, especially if you had something to feel guilty about, though the fact that Calum even *felt* guilty infuriated him.

After a blazing row with his father three years ago, Calum's sexuality had never been openly mentioned again. Instead, Calum put up with all the snide comments, veiled threats and looks of disgust because he'd do anything to avoid an all-out confrontation and risk what happened during that vicious argument. His father had had a heart attack, ended up in the hospital and Calum spent three days thinking if he died, it would be his fault.

When he reached Bessie patiently waiting by the Neilson Ranch sign, Calum slid off Blue's back and stroked his dog.

"Hi, girl. You been sitting here or did you sense me coming?" Or *not* coming, as it happened.

Calum walked Blue the rest of the way to cool him down, Bessie padding along beside. It was just as well he and Jasper had been interrupted. His father had made it clear that if he discovered Calum had messed around with a male guest again, he'd write him out of his will and it wouldn't be Calum taking the reins on retirement—whatever came first.

Sometimes, Calum didn't care.

But most times, the thought of losing the ranch made his heart ache fit to break.

When he led Blue through the large wooden doors into the stables, Gunner was in there cleaning tack.

"Want me to see to him?" Gunner asked.

"Thanks." Calum handed over the reins to the elderly, white-haired ranch hand and patted Blue on the neck.

Gunner had worked for his grandfather as well. The man was well past the age when he should have retired, but Calum suspected his father would let Gunner keep going as long as he wanted.

"Thought you took someone out with you on Zander," Gunner said. "Lose them?"

"He's coming back with Ring. Seems the rodeo star needed help handling the rhinestone cowgirls."

Gunner laughed.

As Calum headed to the ranch house, he saw his father coming the other way looking unsurprised to see him. *Bastard.* Harsh words bubbled in Calum's throat but he held them back.

"I need you to go to Jackson," his father said. "Vera has a list of stuff and there's a bunch of documents I want picked up from Hardy's."

And you couldn't have asked me to do this yesterday when I went to the airport?

"Okay," Calum said, and added, "Did you get that fence sorted?" Because he couldn't help but think the whole thing had been made up just to find out where he was.

"Yep, Dave went."

"Any cattle get loose?"

"I called Marty and asked him to check."

Marty ran the adjoining ranch, but he and Calum's father didn't get on. Calum wasn't sure if he'd ever known why. He *did* know that no man alive could hold grudges as long as his father. The guy had made it a work of art. Which led Calum to suspect his father lied about phoning Marty as well.

As Calum carried on walking, his father called, "Ask your sister if she wants to tag along."

Calum clenched his jaw. It was almost as though his father could guess what he was thinking—which had been to wait until Jasper returned and then the two of them could go to Jackson together.

"Hardy's waiting on you, Calum. You need to set off straightaway. Take the SUV."

"Okay, Boss." *And fuck you too.*

Calum ran up the steps and found Vera in the private lounge.

"Dad says you need something from Jackson."

She handed him a strip of paper. "Thanks, Calum. It wasn't urgent, but—"

"Does Angie want to come?"

"I doubt it. She's desperate to finish her necklace."

"Okay. I'll go on my own." He turned to his dog. "Bessie, stay." Calum snagged the keys to the SUV from the rack and headed out. Maybe a drive would help him sort out his head.

The inane chatter of Melissa and Janie ruined Jasper's ride back to the ranch. He tried riding ahead, but it wasn't easy to make a horse lead when he didn't want to. Zander didn't have an alpha bone in his body. That bastard Ring managed to wedge Jasper between the two girls by riding his horse with its nose up Zander's backside. Jasper ignored all the wrangler's comments about Zander being gay. Ring obviously missed the point that his horse was the one interested in Zander. Ring was such a bloody wanker.

Maybe Calum was too. His sudden disappearance had been disappointing. He'd ridden off without a word, and considering what Jasper had been about to do, he couldn't help but feel hurt. Though maybe it was for the best. They hadn't talked much, but enough for Jasper to understand Erik Neilson wasn't happy about his son's sexuality. Jasper didn't want to make trouble for Calum.

Within minutes, the girls had given him a splitting headache. Jasper refused to believe it was the sun. It appeared neither female had an unspoken thought.

"I can't wait to do the overnight trip," Melissa said.

"It sounds so romantic, sleeping under the stars." Janie sighed.

"Cooking our own food," Melissa added. "It's going to be fun."

"It's cold at night," Ring said behind them.

"We could snuggle up." Melissa grinned at Jasper. "Share body heat."

"What happens when the sun goes down?" Janie turned to Ring.

"We build a fire, cook, eat, drink. I play the guitar, some like to sing and tell stories. Then we go to bed. It could even snow."

"That would be so great," Melissa said.

Jasper thought Ring was going to choke laughing.

"Cooking on a campfire, roasting marshmallows." Melissa sighed. "Do you have those in England? Marshmallows I mean, not campfires. They're sort of round and mainly white and pink but at Easter and Christmas and Halloween, you can get them in different shapes and colors."

She went on and on, and finally Jasper had more than he could stand. "Do you know what marshmallows are made of?"

"Sugar," Janie said.

"And gelatin," Jasper said. "Know what gelatin is?"

"No." Melissa shook her head.

"It's a thickening agent made from animal bones and skin."

After a few exclamations of disgust, they were quiet for a blissful two seconds before it started all over again.

"It never gets really cold in LA. Does it get cold in the UK?" Melissa asked.

"At times," Jasper said. *Oh God, will she ever shut up?*

"Not like here," Ring said. "You have to be a real man to cope with our winters. The wind's so strong, sometimes the snow doesn't even reach the ground."

Jasper bristled. "No pretend men live in Wyoming then? Only real men?"

The girls laughed and Jasper's spine prickled. No doubt Ring's laser eyes were boring into his back.

"That's rich, considering you probably spend your days sitting on your backside in air-conditioned comfort," Ring snapped.

"We're a bit short of open ranges in London."

Jasper kicked Zander on and after some hard, persuasive work with his thigh muscles, he managed to get him ahead of the other horses. Jasper pulled away on a diagonal and then mentally pleaded with Zander to pick up the pace. He wouldn't.

"Where are you going?" Ring called.

"I'll call if I need you for anything." Jasper clicked Zander on and to his relief, this time the horse cooperated.

According to the literature guests were not required to ride with the wrangler. They only needed to stay within shouting distance in case they needed help. Jasper wouldn't lose sight of Ring, but he damn well didn't need to ride with him.

It wasn't long before the three of them were well ahead and Jasper turned back to tag along behind. When the ranch was in sight, he slipped off Zander's back and walked him the rest of the way. Ring and the girls didn't bother. That was fine with Jasper. He couldn't stand another minute of their company. He just hoped he wasn't supposed to ride with them tomorrow.

By the time he led Zander into the stable, his shirt was sticking to his back. Ring was in there taking the saddle off the horse Janie had been riding while a white-haired guy removed the tack from Melissa's. There was no sign of the girls. Guests might not *have* to look after their horses, but he disagreed. How could you bond with the animals if you didn't take care of them? Jasper had already loosened Zander's cinch. Now he went through the rest of the procedure—removing the bridle, putting on the halter, taking off the saddle. Years since he'd done this, but it was second nature.

He talked quietly to the horse as he worked and then walked him over to a bucket holding a damp sponge so he could wipe him down. Aware of Ring's gaze, Jasper treated Zander like a prince. He cleaned the horse's mouth and even brushed his hair flat.

"Like handling all that male flesh?" Ring whispered. "Does it make you hard?"

Bastard. Jasper ignored him, but how did the guy even know he was gay? Though ignoring him rather than reacting with indignation had probably told Ring what he wanted to know. Jasper checked Zander's hooves to make sure he hadn't picked up any rocks and then ran his hand over his flank. Zander nuzzled insistently against the pocket with the mints and Jasper smiled. "Not yet."

"In a stall or outside?" Jasper asked.

"Inside," Ring told him.

The stalls were all named so he walked him down the center until he found Zander's, between Blue and Misty. Both horses were in their stalls. So Calum was back.

"Halter off?" Jasper asked.

"Yep. Hang it on the hook." It was the older guy who spoke this time.

Jasper shut the door on Zander and offered him a mint.

"Did a good job there," the guy said as he came up behind him. "Makes a change not to have to take over."

"Thanks. I'm Jasper." Jasper offered his hand and the man shook it with a smile.

"The guy who threw up. I'm Gunner."

Oh Christ. "Am I going to always be known as the guy who threw up?"

Zander snorted. *Traitor.*

Gunner laughed. "Until you earn yourself a new name."

Note to self: "Guy who fucked the owner's son" had a nice ring to it.

Chapter Five

While the guests ate lunch and exchanged stories about their morning ride, Jasper sat and listened, thinking how he'd freak them out if he told them what he and Calum had been up to. *Nearly been up to.* Except he had an unhappy suspicion that the chances of finding himself with his arms around the cowboy didn't look good. No sign of Calum at lunch, though Jasper tried not to read anything into that.

He considered going fishing that afternoon with Matt and Paul until Melissa and Janie decided to go. The thought of it set off Jasper's headache again. The two couples wanted to do the Jeep tour. Jasper wouldn't be joining them either. Nor did he want to go for a ride in case he ended up with Ring. When he'd booked this, he hadn't thought he'd be the only single. He'd imagined several people riding together every day. Jasper slunk back to his room and changed into his swimming trunks. With a bit of luck, he'd have the pool to himself.

Jasper sighed with relief when he saw he'd been right. Almost. Calum's dog appeared from nowhere, her tail wagging.

"Hi, Bessie." Jasper rubbed her head and the dog arched her shoulders so he'd scratch behind her ear. "We friends now?"

She rolled onto her back and presented her belly. Jasper laughed. He snagged a blue towel from a neat pile on a table and laid it on a lounger. Bessie moved to lie in the shade beneath. Jasper gave her a final stroke and then slid into the cool water, dropping beneath the surface to wet his head. He enjoyed swimming, liked imagining life was different as he did a slow crawl for lap after lap. Jasper didn't often get the chance to swim in the open air under warm blue skies.

As he swam, he thought about Calum. What was he supposed to do when he saw him? Pretend the kiss, the touching, the offer to suck his cock had never happened? Treat him with civil cordiality? Spend the rest of the week riding as the third wheel with Ring and the sparkly twins? Jasper thought he'd rather not ride, except being on Zander had reminded him of what he'd been missing. *And it is my fucking holiday.*

If there were fewer guests than usual, maybe he could ask Erik to send him out with Gunner.

Swimming relaxed his body but not his mind. Jasper couldn't stop thinking about Calum, wanting Calum. It had been a long time since Jasper had been with anyone, which was probably the reason for his current slobbering. If it hadn't been for the fact that Calum seemed just as keen until his sudden departure, Jasper would be worried he'd lost his touch. There *had* been something between them. So why hadn't Calum appeared at lunch.

Jasper hoisted himself out of the pool to find Bessie still lying under his sun lounger and Angie sitting on the one next to it threading beads on a strand of thread. She was a really pretty girl, but Jasper could see there was something not quite right in her expression, as though the world she saw was not the same as the one seen by everyone else. She wore a pink T-shirt and denim cut-offs, and looked longingly from Jasper to the pool.

"I'm not allowed in the water without supervision," she said.

Jasper dropped onto his lounger and brushed the water from his face. "Can you swim?"

"Yep, I can swim real good. Calum taught me."

He glanced around before he asked his next question. "Is Calum on the ranch?"

"He had to go to Jackson to do stuff for Mom and Dad." A cascade of small blue beads fell onto the pool deck and Angie groaned. "Ah darn it."

Jasper bent to help her pick them up. "What are you making?"

"A necklace."

He could see that the beads would drop off the end again if she didn't enlarge the knot in the thread. "Can I do something to help?"

"Sure."

He made the knot bigger and handed the beads to Angie for her to rethread. She chewed her lip as she concentrated, and although Jasper had thought she'd chat, she didn't. Tempted as he was to ask questions about Calum, he resisted.

Angie attached fastenings to the necklace and hung it around her neck.

"That looks lovely," he said and she beamed.

"I'm going to make you something now."

Oh God. "Oh good. Thank you."

Jasper lay back on the lounger, turned his face to the late-afternoon sun and closed his eyes.

The next thing he knew cold water hit his face and he jerked upright. Bessie emerged growling from under his lounger as Jasper coughed, blinking drops from his eyes. *What the fuck?*

"No," Jasper snapped at the dog as she darted toward Matt and his ice bucket.

Melissa shrieked with laughter and jumped in the pool to join Janie and Paul. Matt put the bucket down and dived in before Jasper could follow up on the reconsidered inclination to let Bessie bite him. He stood and picked up his sodden towel. A bracelet made of blue beads had been tied around his wrist. He must have been in a really deep sleep not to notice Angie doing that.

"You're mean," Angie shouted and Jasper jerked around. She stood at the edge of the pool with her hands on her hips and glared at Matt. "You shouldn't do things like that."

"Don't you like being splashed?" Matt took in a mouthful of water and spat it at her. It fell well short.

"You're a big bully," Angie said.

Jasper stepped up to her. "Where should I put my wet towel, Angie?"

She opened her mouth as if she was going to shout again and then sagged. "I'll show you."

Jasper followed her. "Thank you for my bracelet. It's very beautiful. No one's ever given me anything like this before."

She smiled at him. "It's a glow-in-the-dark friendship bracelet. I like you."

"And I like you too."

"Will you sit next to me at dinner?"

"If you like." *Especially if Calum's nearby.*

"You can never take the bracelet off otherwise we won't be friends anymore."

Christ. "Okay." It wouldn't kill him to wear it for a week.

Calum arrived back just before dinner. He fed Bessie, checked on the horses, cleaned himself up and found everyone drinking and chattering in the lounge. No sign of Jasper. Was he asleep or avoiding him? Calum sighed.

"Will you go knock on his door?" Vera asked him.

Crap, had it been *that* obvious he'd been looking? "Whose?"

He supposed he deserved the look Vera gave him.

"Okay, okay. I've put your supplies in the kitchen," Calum said. "Dad's papers are in his study. I won't be eating. I met a friend from college in Jackson and we're going for a drink."

Vera stared straight at him and Calum had the uncomfortable feeling she knew what he was planning. But she'd tell his father the lie and it would come better from her than him. Calum hurried into the guest wing and headed for Jasper's room. He hoped Jasper wasn't pissed off with the way he'd left this morning. *Of course he is, you prick.* Calum swallowed hard and rapped on his door. Harder when he didn't answer.

When Jasper appeared, the jolt of lust hit Calum like a cattle prod. The English guy wore jeans and a creased white linen shirt, a thin blue tie loose at his neck and no shoes on his feet. He still looked like a model, an unattainable dream.

"Oh God, I fell asleep *again*?" Jasper dragged his fingers through his hair. "Have I missed the meal?"

"Want to go out to eat instead?" Calum blurted. "There's a bar in Landon that does good burgers."

"Okay."

The fast response smacked Calum right in the groin. He smiled and was rewarded with one from Jasper.

"I'll tell Vera you're not hungry, that you want to sleep and would like Angie to leave another sandwich. I need them to think you're still here."

He watched the Adam's apple shift in Jasper's throat before the guy nodded. Calum didn't want to have to sneak around, but there was no choice.

"I'll show you the back way out. Wait in the silver truck and I'll be there in a couple of minutes."

"Should I duck down out of sight?" Jasper's voice was cool.

Shit, have I pissed him off? "Would you mind?"

Jasper slipped on a pair of shoes and tucked his wallet in his pocket. "Do I need a jacket?"

"We only have to walk across a parking lot. You'll be fine."

Jasper went to the bed and arranged a couple of pillows under the cover. "Years since I've done that."

Relief flooded Calum at the sight of Jasper's grin. He led the way downstairs, through the basement gym and out the emergency exit. Bessie bounded over.

"Stay, girl," Calum said and turned to Jasper. "Truck's unlocked."

Once he was sure no one but Bessie saw Jasper get into his truck, Calum raced back to the dining room. His father glared. Roast chicken had already been served. Calum headed for Vera and bent his head to her ear.

"He's skipping dinner. Jet lag."

"Where's Jasper?" Angie asked in a loud voice. "He said he'd sit by me."

"He's tired, sweetheart," Vera said.

Angie's shoulders slumped.

"You can leave him another sandwich," Calum told her.

"Okay." Angie looked so disappointed, he felt guilty.

Vera caught his arm as he turned to leave. "Careful," she whispered.

"Now where would be the fun in that?" he whispered back.

Vera rolled her eyes.

There was no sign of Jasper in the passenger window of the truck, but when Calum pulled open the driver's door, he saw him curled on the backseat and his cock twitched.

"Let me drive off the ranch and then you can sit up front."

As soon as they cleared the gate, he pulled up at the side of the road and Jasper came to sit next to him.

"Sorry and thanks," Calum said. He almost added "please" in there too, just in case.

"The subterfuge is because of your father?" Jasper asked.

"He won't accept that I'm gay. I feel bad about asking you to keep this quiet, but—"

"It's okay. I don't want to make trouble for you. Well, not in that way." Jasper grinned.

Calum gulped. "How about your folks?"

"My father's dead. My mother's in denial. She wants grandkids."

"Ah. Well, it's not impossible."

"No, not impossible," Jasper said.

They were both quiet for a moment and Calum wondered if Jasper was thinking the same as him, that he'd like kids one day and a home to share with a guy he loved. Maybe Angie could live with him and help look after the children. Which reminded him.

"Angie thought you were going to sit with her at dinner."

Jasper groaned. "She asked and I said I would. I'll apologize tomorrow."

"Talking of apologizing, sorry I rode off this morning without saying anything. I'm fairly certain my father called to find out where I was and then sent Ring to make sure I was showing you the appropriate flora and fauna."

Jasper laughed.

"I'm not Ring's favorite person. Hell, I'm not anyone's favorite person." Calum sighed. "So are you riding again tomorrow?"

"Not if I have to go out with the dazzling duo. Unless I can take duct tape."

Calum chuckled.

"Is this a gay bar we're going to?" Jasper asked.

"Christ no. There are no gay bars in Wyoming. Well, none that I know of."

"Really?"

"If you're different out here, you keep your head down and your mouth shut because people don't want to know. I went to a high school where no one spoke about being gay—well, not in a positive way." Calum didn't imagine it to be like that in England.

Jasper frowned. "That must make life difficult."

"Sometimes. Especially if you can't keep your cock under control. So I could be in trouble tonight."

Jasper's face creased in laughter, and Calum wanted to find a place to park, and then drag him into the backseat by his tie and kiss him.

"Did you have a problem at school because you were gay?" Jasper asked.

"Not at school. I wasn't gay when I was at school."

"What?"

Calum sighed. "Well yeah, I was but I wasn't. I dated girls." He glanced across at Jasper but he didn't look surprised.

"Do you still date women?" Jasper asked.

"No." Calum pulled into the parking lot of the bar. "I don't date anyone."

When he got out of the vehicle, Jasper came round and sidled up to him. "So no kissing, no fondling and no touching while we're in here?"

"Not unless you want us to get beaten up." *That tie might do it, all on its own.*

Jasper straightened. "Are you serious?"

Calum nodded.

"Have you ever been—?"

"I'm hoping for plenty of kissing, fondling and touching later." Calum prayed Jasper accepted the deflection.

"I'll think about it." Jasper stalked toward the bar.

Calum chewed his lip. He wasn't sure if Jasper was upset he had to go back in the closet for the night. Maybe it hadn't been a good idea to bring him to a place where they couldn't be themselves. But then Jasper turned and beckoned him, mischief in his eyes, and Calum felt a weight lift from his chest.

He noticed the beaded bracelet dangling around Jasper's wrist as he reached for the door. "Angie's work?"

"I'm forbidden to take it off. It glows in the dark. She snuck it on while I dozed by the pool."

Calum laughed. "Asleep again?"

"I was thinking I might not get much rest later."

The look in Jasper's eyes was unmistakably carnal. Maybe coming here was a mistake. Calum should have just found somewhere they could fuck this out of their systems. He sucked in his cheeks and followed the guy in. Jasper was here for a week and that was it. This could be nothing more than a fling and Calum had to be satisfied with that.

They sat at the bar. Jasper ordered a beer, Calum asked for orange and tonic water. No way would he risk getting caught

DUI. He had enough problems in his life. He hadn't been in this bar for years, but that didn't mean he'd remain unrecognized. The Neilson Ranch wasn't the biggest spread, but everyone in the county knew his father. No matter how far Calum drove, how obscure a place he picked, it only took one person to report he'd been in here and add the detail that he'd been sitting too close to a guy.

"Can I get you boys anything to eat?" the barmaid asked.

"Burger and chips...fries, please," Jasper said and Calum mentally groaned.

No one would mistake Jasper's accent. One detail Calum hadn't thought of. It was too late now. Fuck it, Calum didn't care. He wasn't going to spend the rest of his life doing what his father wanted without having some fun as compensation.

"Where you from?" the barmaid asked Jasper, looking at his tie.

"London."

"You as well?" she looked at Calum.

"Local. I'll have the same as him."

The drinks arrived and Calum looked on in envy as Jasper tipped the bottle to his lips, not sure whether he'd rather drink the beer or be the bottle.

"Want a mouthful?" Jasper asked.

Their fingers brushed as Calum took the beer, deliberate on both their parts. He stared at Jasper as he drank and Jasper stared back at him. Calum's cock began to harden as he thought about Jasper's lips on the bottle, on his mouth, on his dick. *Fuck it.*

He handed the beer back and shuffled farther under the bar counter. "Thanks."

"Oh Christ," Jasper whispered. "Why did you let me watch you do that?"

Calum smothered a laugh.

"What do you usually do for entertainment in the evening?" Jasper asked.

"Whatever the guests want."

A smile quirked Jasper's lips. "I should think so too. And when there are no guests?"

Jack off. "Watch TV." *Jack off.* "Listen to music." *Jack off.* "Mess around on the internet." *And jack off.* "And work with clay." Christ, how had that slipped out?

"Clay as in mud, not Clay as in long, lean and male?"

Calum glanced around to make sure no one was listening. "Modeling animals mostly," he mumbled. "Sometimes figures—cowboys." *Maybe an English guy next.*

Jasper's brown eyes opened wider. "Like Remington?"

Calum snorted. "Yeah, just like Remington. That's why I help run a dude ranch and still live with my folks. Nothing of mine has made it into bronze."

"Will you show me what you've made?"

He shifted in discomfort. "Okay, though most of my models are too fragile to keep. I tried baking a few, but it didn't work too well. It's expensive to get them cast. The nearest foundry's a couple of days' drive."

Now he'd told Jasper he'd looked into it. *Shit.* Out of sight under the overlap of the bar, Jasper's knee rocked against his.

"I wish I could do something like that," Jasper said quietly. "Use my hands and be creative. To squeeze and twist and bring a lump of something soft and pliable to life and make it go hard."

"Shut the fuck up," Calum hissed but he couldn't help laughing.

"That's what you have to do when you throw a pot, isn't it? You get your hands nice and wet. You draw up the clay taller and taller. Then you put your thumbs in the center and press down before you drag the thing up again. And you keep doing it over and over."

Jasper stared straight at Calum as he spoke. "Sadly all my erections eventually collapse, but they do it with a bang." He winked.

"Oh God." Calum's jaw twitched. "You're not fit to take out in public."

"How did a cowboy end up playing with clay?"

"You'll laugh."

Jasper chuckled.

"Told you," Calum said.

"You have to tell me now."

"I fell, got plastered in mud and picked it off my clothes. I molded the bits into a ball and made a figure."

"How old were you? Twenty-five?"

Calum quietly growled. "'Bout eight."

"Do you draw as well?" Jasper asked.

"Yeah, some."

"I'm not in the slightest bit artistic. I can't even manage a respectable doodle. They all turn out looking like—well, not decent."

Calum snorted. How come it felt so easy to talk to this guy?

Jasper took a swig of his beer. "My other problem with clay was that I didn't like—don't like—to get dirty. I blame my mother. She was obsessive about me and Ben being smart and clean at all times, mostly in case the vicar called. Ben was the rebel. I was the neat freak. Even now, I wouldn't dare turn up to see her not wearing a suit and tie."

"I like your tie."

Jasper smiled. "I wear it out of habit."

Calum kept his voice down. "I've been thinking of what bit of you I'd like to wrap it around."

When Jasper shuffled farther under the bar, Calum barked out a laugh.

Jasper groaned. "God, don't. I need food to distract me. I'm so hungry I've been thinking of chewing off my arm." He bent his head closer to Calum. "Or chewing on something of yours."

Calum sniggered. "You do realize that if we keep this up, neither of us is going to be able to move until they switch off the lights?"

The food arrived and Calum ordered more drinks. Jasper began to eat the burger with a knife and fork and Calum gaped at him.

"What?" Jasper asked.

"Nothing." Calum picked up his bun and sank his teeth into it. The filling oozed out and a slice of tomato dropped onto the plate.

"Hah." Jasper raised his eyebrows. "That could have fallen on your shirt."

"Men do *not* eat burgers with cutlery."

"Those who want to stay clean do. Anyway, I'm British. Everyone already thinks I'm weird."

And fucking gorgeous. Calum had known it was hopeless from that moment at the airport when Jasper had held out his hand. Nothing was going to stop them tonight. A reckless part of Calum didn't even care if his father found out. What the hell would he do? Shoot him? The threat to write Calum out of his will or sell the ranch from under him would hurt his father as much as Calum. No way would his dad follow through on the threat.

Then the sensible part of his brain took over. If his father had a fatal heart attack because of something Calum had done, how could he live with himself? Whether he liked it or not, whether he thought it was right or not, in the long run, Calum had little choice. In a way, it was just as well Jasper would be gone at the end of the week.

"You play any sport?" Calum asked.

"No."

"Watch it?"

"No."

"What do you do in your spare time?"

Jasper shrugged. "I don't have any. When I get back from the office, I'm too exhausted to do anything other than slump in front of the TV with something to eat and I usually fall asleep. Particularly if I've found something vaguely creative to do with my right hand." He grinned and Calum had to swallow the lump in his throat. "I work Saturday too. Sunday I clean and grocery shop."

Calum pushed his empty plate aside. "Doesn't sound like much of a life."

"It isn't."

"Do you like your job?"

"I hate it."

Calum was shocked at the vehemence in Jasper's response. "Then why do it?"

"Good question. Want a game of pool?"

"Sure." Calum accepted they both had things they didn't want to talk about.

Jasper pushed away Calum's wallet and put money on the bar. Calum thought about protesting, but it would draw attention and he'd get it next time. *Oh God, let there be a next time.*

There were three pool tables, two of them in use. Jasper racked up the balls and then as he deliberately chalked his cue, he stared at Calum and flicked his tongue over his lip. Calum couldn't help laughing. Jasper stood out in the room among all the jean-clad guys with their old shirts and worn hats and beer bellies. He looked like a fucking prince. Yet that thought made Calum sag. What could Jasper see in a guy like him with calloused hands and little brain? But when Jasper turned and smiled straight at him, it was as if the whole room lit up.

"Want to break?" Jasper asked.

A few minutes later, Calum realized he should have said no. Jasper was about to sink every ball. Calum's gaze hovered between the emptying pool table and Jasper's trim butt. His butt usually won, which was why Calum had tugged his shirt out the front of his pants. Shit, he'd be too distracted to make a decent shot anyway. Might just as well enjoy the view. Calum had a thing for slim-hipped guys. He imagined his fingers rubbing the soft skin below Jasper's hipbones, trailing his hands—

"Best out of three?" Jasper asked.

It was a miracle Calum won the next game. After one terrible shot by Jasper that flew off their table and almost landed on someone else's—thanks to a nudge against his butt by Calum with the pool cue—Calum concentrated on what he was doing and not on Jasper. Though it did cross Calum's mind after a couple more duff shots by Wonder Boy that Jasper might have let him win. A thought confirmed when he saw the smirk on Jasper's face.

Jasper moved to his side. "What does the winner get?"

Calum leaned against the wall and said in a quiet voice. "Well, since you're gonna win, why not tell me what you want?"

"Guess."

Shit. Calum didn't want to guess. He had no idea whether Jasper was a top or a bottom. Usually it was fairly easy to tell, but Jasper was both strong and weak at the same time. *Same as me.* Except Calum hadn't been fucked for a long time, and after it had happened, he'd sworn never to let it happen again. He stepped forward and racked the balls.

Note to self: Do I want to win or lose?

Chapter Six

Turned out it was irrelevant whether Calum wanted to win or lose. One mistake by Calum and Jasper was unstoppable. He called out ball after ball and sank every one despite the number of beers he'd consumed. After he sank the last, Jasper flashed a triumphant grin and held out his hand. Calum laughed and shook it. But the laugh faded as Jasper's fingers wrapped tighter around his. Calum pulled free and slotted his cue back in the stand.

"Coming?" he barked hoarsely at Jasper and then walked out of the bar.

His cock was so hard the damn thing throbbed. He slammed the truck door as he settled in the driver's seat and then turned to watch Jasper saunter across the parking lot. Calum yanked the other half of his shirt out of his pants so it disguised the bulge in his jeans. Jasper sat beside him and fastened his seat belt.

Calum hadn't pulled out of the lot before Jasper reached to slide his hand under Calum's shirt. He stroked his cock through his jeans, and Calum sucked in a breath. "Oh fuck." His body crackled as if he'd been touched by a naked flame.

"Want me to stop?"

Yes. No. Yes. No. That dialogue could go on for some time. Calum managed a gurgled grunt. Jasper could take it anyway he liked.

"Is there some place we could go?" Jasper asked. "A motel? A deserted beach."

"We're not near the sea."

"It was a joke. If there a motel around here?"

He massaged Calum's balls until a squeak escaped. A large bed, a comfortable mattress, sheets... It was too big a risk. Calum lied, "Not around here."

"No motels?" Jasper sounded incredulous.

"They're not big enough to slip in and out of without people noticing." Another lie, but Calum couldn't chance it.

"You won't have that problem with me," Jasper said then hiccupped, and Calum let out a choked laugh.

Oh God, can I let him fuck me? What if I freak out?

Jasper kept rubbing his cock as Calum pulled onto the main road leading home. Every speck of blood had rushed south. It was impossible to think, difficult enough to drive.

"Any more turns?" Jasper asked.

"Not for a while."

"Good. Don't get us killed."

Jasper flipped open the button of Calum's jeans and eased down the zipper.

"Oh Christ, if I crash, it's gonna be your fault." Calum gripped the steering wheel so hard he suspected he'd leave marks in it. It had to be the alcohol making Jasper this forward but Calum wasn't complaining. Well, not really.

The relief at the reduced pressure on his cock lasted a split second before fingers slid inside his shorts. Jasper rubbed his thumb over the head of Calum's erection and like throwing a match into a pool of gas, heat flashed through Calum's body and he went up in flames. He let out a strangled groan and his grip on the wheel slipped. The truck swerved, a horn blared and Calum yanked the vehicle straight.

"Jesus. Sorry, sorry." Calum blinked hard. He ought to tell Jasper to stop, but he didn't want to. He kept his gaze fixed on the road, though he wondered how much he was taking in. Good thing he knew this route like the back of his hand, except he didn't recognize the white knuckles gripping the wheel.

Calum's cock was out now, in front of his shirt, scenting the air like some ravenous, slavering wolf.

"Oh Christ," Jasper whispered. "I shouldn't have done that. It's like unwrapping a bar of chocolate and then not eating it."

He bent his head and Calum gasped. "Don't you fucking dare."

"I dare." But Jasper straightened up and laughed.

"It's not fucking funny."

At that, Jasper laughed harder. Calum quivered when he felt a finger and thumb roll over the crest of his cock and move away. He glanced across and caught Jasper's tongue snaking out to lick his fingers. Another brush against his dick and this time Jasper's hand touched Calum's mouth.

"Taste," Jasper whispered.

Calum licked and his foot pressed harder on the gas. *Oh fuck, fuck, fuck.* Nothing coming behind them, nothing in front, ditch at the side. Nowhere to fucking stop.

Jasper looped the seatbelt out of the way and then maneuvered until his head was between Calum's chest and the wheel. *Stop.* Calum yelled the word in his head, but it didn't come out of his mouth. One soft flutter over the tip of his cock with a hot tongue and Calum almost lost control of the vehicle and himself. *Oh God, if I come first, he'll want to fuck me.* Trouble was Calum didn't think that was a big enough incentive to stop his balls from exploding. A couple of miles before they were out in the countryside and where there'd be a place to pull off—could he last that long? When Jasper's lips settled around the sensitive head of his cock and sucked hard, Calum started to shake.

"Please," he pleaded.

Jasper lifted his head. "Please what? Stop or keep going?"

The feel of his exhalations hitting Calum's spit-slick cock made the breath catch in his throat. "I need to find a place to pull off the road before I get us killed. Or worse, we're injured and they find us doing this."

Jasper sat up again and Calum breathed a sigh of relief. He wanted Jasper to keep going, but there was no way he could drive with the guy's mouth around his dick. The first likely track Calum saw, he pulled off the pavement and they bounced between trees down the dirt road. Calum shoved the truck into park, switched off the engine, killed the lights and sat with his chest heaving. Jasper had his hand inside his own pants, stroking himself.

Calum groaned. "Take your shirt off and get in the back. Leave the...leave the tie on."

Jasper undid the top couple of buttons and peeled it over his head. Even in the dim light Calum could see the hills and planes of his body, sculpted muscles, hard abs and tight, dark nipples topping gently rounded pecs and that fucking tie hanging between. A dusting of hair led south—a treasure trail to unbuttoned pants and a partially lowered zipper.

"You work out?" Calum asked.

"Most days before work."

Calum pulled down the center seat between them and Jasper scooted into the back.

"Your shirt too," Jasper said.

Calum was already struggling with the buttons. He dragged his shirt over his head and scrambled after Jasper into the rear of the vehicle. They were all arms and legs until Calum forced Jasper to settle on his back while he knelt astride his hips. Calum groaned when Jasper wrapped his fingers around his cock, but he couldn't tear his hands away from Jasper's body, his calloused fingers intent on exploring every inch of skin. They panted into each other's faces, gazes locked. The scent of Jasper filled Calum's head—a mixture of soap and musk and beer. The guy had hair as dark as a starless night and eyes he could hide in. He'd never felt this level of attraction to any guy before.

"I have to undo the rest of the zipper before my cock does it for me," Jasper said with a grunt.

He groaned as he pulled it down, his eyelids fluttering. Calum couldn't stop touching him, his hands mapping Jasper's upper body, fingers trailing along ribs, the curve of his shoulders, down rounded triceps, over rock-hard biceps and back to graze the taut muscles of his stomach in a constant loop of flowing movement. As he reached for the waistband of Jasper's shorts, Jasper grabbed him and turned them both so Calum lay on his back with Jasper hovering over him, his tie tickling Calum's chest.

Oh God, why did I let him pin me?

"There's not enough room," Calum panted.

"Write and tell Chevrolet. Make back seats bigger to facilitate English guys giving blowjobs to American guys."

Calum laughed and gave in. He wasn't sure he could last long enough to get inside Jasper. They could bring each other off and then he'd have to make sure he was the one on top. Calum stroked Jasper's silky hair. "We could get out of the car."

"Too cold and I don't want a moose sticking its nose up my backside or a rattlesnake biting my butt or—"

"Okay, I get it. We're fine where we are." Calum tugged on Jasper's tie to bring his head down.

Jasper's mouth hovered over Calum's. "More than fine."

Calum tightened his grasp on Jasper's tie and pulled him down the last inch. The whispered groan issuing from Jasper's lips ripped through Calum like a whirlwind. Excitement raced along his veins and the moment those soft lips touched his, he was lost in a tornado of lust. Calum ate at his mouth and he could feel Jasper's arms trembling where they rested against his body. He traced around Jasper's tongue with his, tugged at it with his teeth and then sucked hard. Jasper moaned into his mouth and his fingers threaded Calum's hair.

Their cocks had their own way of kissing, slick heads sliding together, smearing pre-come one to the other. Hips rocked in a languid salsa, and Calum slipped a hand between their bodies to bring their dicks tight together. *Oh fuck, he's big.* A jolt of fear raised goose bumps on the back of his neck and he forced it into reverse.

Calum rubbed the head of Jasper's cock and Jasper jerked away and reared up. "If you keep doing that, I've had it. Move back a bit to give me room."

Calum lifted his butt to shift backward and Jasper seized the chance to pull Calum's pants farther down his thighs. Calum leaned his shoulders against the door, bent one knee against the back seat and dropped his other leg into the space at the rear of the driver's seat. Jasper leaned over and slowly licked a line from Calum's throat down the center of his chest. His tie, trailing over Calum's skin, added another level to the sensation.

"Shit, shit." Calum's breathing grew more ragged.

He stroked Jasper's hair as his head sank lower and lower. *Suck me, suck me, suck me.* Calum angled his hips so his cock brushed Jasper's lips and then moaned when a wet tongue swirled around the tip.

Up and down, round and round and over the crest, Jasper's tongue touched every part of his dick, laving him like he was a stick of candy. Muscles tightened in Calum's body as he tried to hold back from coming. His toes curled, his calves tensed and his butt cheeks went rigid as Jasper wrapped his hot, wet mouth tighter around him and sucked until his cheeks hollowed. Oh Christ. Calum's thumbs dug into Jasper's head, his fingers shaking as Jasper drew on him with his mouth.

"Oh God, that feels good," Calum muttered. "Jesus, Jesus."

Jasper sucked along the line of his shaft and nipped at the base with his teeth. *I'm going to come. Fuck.* As Calum reached a trembling hand to wrap around the root of his cock, Jasper got there first. As his grip hardened and the need to come receded, Calum let out a long sigh, one that turned into a whimper when Jasper mouthed his balls. *Now, I'm going to come.* But as though Jasper read his mind, he pressed down hard in exactly the right way, in exactly the right place and the pressure in Calum's head faded to a dull ache.

Lips pulled and tugged at the tight sac protecting his balls. Jasper's nose and cheeks rubbed Calum's cock while his mouth worked magic lower down, and the tension crept back into Calum's body, seeping up his spine, tightening every muscle until he was arching away from the door, hips bucking, urging Jasper to take more.

While Jasper maintained his hold at the base of Calum's cock, and his mouth played with his balls, the fingers of his other hand teased the tender strip of flesh between Calum's sac and his hole. Breathing became an issue. He'd forgotten how. When Jasper began to take more of his cock into his mouth, the steady rhythm pushed Calum into a different level of heaven. The warm, wet suction made his hips jerk, but Jasper pushed him down. No confusion as to who was in control but that was fine. Calum's turn would come. He felt a sharp prickle at the back of his head. His first warning. On five he'd lose it.

Jasper dipped his tongue into the slit and Calum shot straight to four and three quarters.

"F-fuck," Calum gasped.

He wanted to watch Jasper's dark eyes staring up at him, but Calum's eyes fluttered closed as his hips rose and Jasper swallowed him. Calum's cock brushed the back of Jasper's throat and his balls detonated. Lightning blazed down his spine and he shot spurt after spurt of thick fluid into Jasper's mouth, each jet accompanied by a guttural groan, until Calum collapsed back onto the seat. His shoulder was wedged against something hard, his ankle was twisted, but he didn't give a fuck.

Calum dragged energy from somewhere to open his eyes and looked up at Jasper staring down at him, a smile quirking his lips. Calum wiped a fleck of come from Jasper's lower lip with his finger and brought it to his own mouth.

"That was some dessert," Jasper said.

"I feel deprived."

Jasper swallowed, his eyes dark with need. "That could be quickly remedied—and I mean quickly. I'm not talking minutes."

Calum chuckled. "You make me laugh."

"Is that good?"

"I thought I'd forgotten how. Want to swap places?"

"Might be easier said than done."

It was, but in a tussle of arms and legs, amid a lot of laughing and groaning, Calum eventually pinned Jasper on his back and tugged down his pants and shorts to expose his cock. Long and thick, the head wet with pre-come, a dark purple vein tracing its length, the damn thing looked so beautiful, Calum's lungs locked.

"One lick would do it," Jasper said with a gasp. "Damn it, if you keep staring at it, that'll work too. Twenty seconds tops."

"Trying to spoil my fun?" Calum wrapped his hand around Jasper's cock and loosely stroked it, savoring the velvet-soft texture of the skin against the steel-hard muscle beneath.

"Shit," Jasper grunted. "No more than ten."

Calum squeezed the shaft, his thumb sliding off the shallow dip beneath the head. "Ten minutes?"

"If I didn't think it would tip me over the edge, I'd laugh at that pathetic joke."

Calum stroked and played with Jasper's cock, cupping his heavy balls and rolling them gently in his palm.

"Maybe five seconds," Jasper choked out.

One lick of the salty tip of Jasper's cock and Calum's head fogged. He knew Jasper was close, the strain evident on his face, a mixture of pleasure and pain. Calum sucked the tip into his mouth.

"God, God, God, God," Jasper panted.

Taking the swollen crest tighter between his lips, Calum slid his mouth up and down the top couple of inches. Jasper's hands clenched and unclenched against Calum's ribs. Calum teased the slit, bathing it in spit and pre-come and then screwed his mouth hard down Jasper's length.

Jasper's breathing grew so labored that for a moment Calum worried, and then a hand on top of his head urged him to continue while the other hand stroked his cheek.

"Shit, I never knew I could multi-task so well," Jasper blurted. "And I'm reciting the alphabet backward at the same time. Stuck at Y."

One deep swallow and Jasper's body went as stiff as his cock.

"Oh Christ, that...you...fuck...yesssss."

The thick shaft swelled and pulsed, and Jasper cried out as he emptied his load into Calum's eager mouth. Calum didn't move until he'd swallowed every drop of come. He licked Jasper clean and then he kissed his way up Jasper's body, lapping the salt from his skin until he nuzzled into the hollow of his throat above his tie. Calum lifted his head and looked straight into Jasper's face. Jasper grinned at him, still panting, his lower lip swollen from where he'd bitten it.

"You make my fucking heart jump," Calum whispered.

He laid his palm over Jasper's chest and felt his heart beating fast and furious under his hand. A flutter in the rhythm and Calum smiled. He slid his hands up Jasper's ribs until they wrapped around his neck to pull on the tie, his thumbs brushing Jasper's soft lips.

"I feel like a horny teenager, except I never did this in my car when I was a teen," Calum said. "Did you?"

"I didn't have a car."

"I want to fuck you, but I don't want to do it like this with no space to move, nothing special about it." Calum brushed Jasper's hair out of his eyes.

"Then take me back and show me your etchings—oops, I mean your models."

Calum swallowed hard. Take Jasper into his bed. Could he?

Calum drove the truck into its spot with the other vehicles at the back of the ranch and turned off the engine.

"You have to be absolutely silent when we walk down the corridor," he said. "Once we're in my bedroom, we should be okay as long as you don't scream." He gave Jasper a nervous smile. "One side of the room it's the end of the building, closet the other and beyond that a guest room. My father and Vera are at the far end of the corridor."

"Why do you call her Vera?"

Calum frowned. "When Dad brought her to meet me, she asked me to. Why?"

"I just wondered why you didn't call her Mum."

"I suppose I didn't want to at first, and by the time I could have, we'd both gotten used to me not doing it." Calum exited the vehicle and closed the door quietly.

As they walked back into the dark ranch, Calum thought about Jasper's question. Vera *was* his mother in every way that counted. She might love Angie best but she loved him too. *Christ, should I have been calling her Mom?*

His heart hammered as he led Jasper into the private side of the ranch. He had no excuse for bringing Jasper in here. If his father happened to walk out... Calum swallowed hard.

When he had the light on and the door closed behind them, he breathed a sigh of relief.

"Bloody hell," Jasper whispered.

Calum turned to look at him. Jasper's gaze flittered from one thing to the next. From Calum's shelf of clay models, to the drawings pinned to his walls, his cluttered desk strewn with paper and pencils, his shelves of books, DVDs, CDs and his untidy bed. Anxiety chewed at his gut. *What's he thinking?* Jasper walked over to the models and stared at them.

"I mean, Christ Almighty, they're fantastic." Jasper pointed to a reclining horse. "That cow is so realistic."

Calum laughed and slapped a hand over his mouth. He was thrilled by Jasper's response.

"I would really like to see them cast in bronze." Jasper trailed a finger down the back of another horse and then moved to the desk.

Jasper picked up his sketch pad and flicked through it. Calum was too slow to stop him.

"Who's this ugly mutt?" Jasper held up the pad next to his face and smiled at his image.

The best-looking guy I've ever seen.

"I'm so jealous that you can draw and carve...cows."

Calum sniggered.

"You're wasted here," Jasper whispered. "You could make a fortune in London. Any gallery would snap these up."

And just for a brief moment, Calum let himself imagine what his life might be like in a different world. And when he sensed Jasper was going to follow up on what he'd said, Calum pulled him into his arms and silenced him with a kiss. As Jasper wrapped his arms around him, Calum feathered his lips against Jasper's, his tongue snaking along the seam. Jasper melted against him.

"Christ, you make me so hot," Calum muttered into his mouth. "When did you realize you preferred guys?"

"The day my Latin teacher fucked me, and I liked it. He'd come to my house to give me lessons in the school holidays. My parents had gone out. After the renewed interest I showed in a dead language, and many private lessons later, my parents were disappointed I barely scraped a pass in my exam." Jasper smiled.

"How old were you?"

"Fourteen."

Calum raised his eyebrows.

Jasper pulled away and leaned against the wall. "I know. He could have gone to prison. He said he loved me and I believed him until the day I saw him touch my brother. I threatened to go straight to the headmaster and if he didn't get there first and resign, I'd confess everything. The idiot thought I was jealous, that a few kind words and a computer game would win me over."

"What happened?"

Jasper grinned. "He ran faster than me to the head's office. Just. I made him work for it."

"He left?"

"The new teacher was a woman with a moustache. I don't like moustaches."

Calum laughed.

Note to self: Shave every day.

Chapter Seven

Jasper had been serious about Calum making a fortune in London with his sculptures. He probably didn't need to come to London, but Jasper let the thought burst out without passing it through quality control. Images flittered through his head of setting up a studio for Calum in his house, Jasper supporting him until he'd established himself, the pair of them eating breakfast on the patio, fucking in his bed.

All this on the basis of a mutual blowjob in the back of a truck?

I've got it bad.

Not only that, Jasper had acted completely out of character. He was far more likely to overanalyze and do nothing than give in to his desires. Maybe a bit of his bravery came from the alcohol but not all. Calum made him feel brave.

He smiled, moved away from the wall toward Calum, and the cowboy took a step back. Jasper halted. Had he missed some signal here?

"I can't do this. I'm sorry," Calum muttered, his head down.

Jasper felt as though a metal bar had been slammed into his face. For a moment, he could neither move nor breathe. He swallowed hard, unlocked his lungs and managed to croak, "Did I do something wrong?"

"No, no. I...I need to wrap my head around some things. See you later, right?"

But I wanted to wrap my arms around you. No point torturing himself wondering why. Jasper nodded, turned and walked out.

He understood no.

Fuck it, I don't understand at all.

Jasper detoured via the kitchen and retrieved the sandwich from the fridge. He didn't want Angie to think he wasn't grateful, and rather than throw it away and risk her finding it, he took it back to his room.

What changed? What did I do?

He showered and soaped his flaccid cock. Even remembering the way Calum's mouth had felt on him didn't make Jasper hard. He was suffused with disappointment and confusion until he remembered Calum's fear of his father finding out he'd been with a guest. Was that it? The reason he'd not wanted to go further?

Jasper knew he'd get no sleep. He opened his laptop. He wished he could ignore work, but if he didn't keep his eye on what was happening in the markets, he'd be letting people down. Jasper didn't trust the guy covering for him. It had been a long while since Jasper had trusted anyone.

He ate Angie's sandwich as he worked.

Jasper poured a mug of coffee at the breakfast buffet. He scanned the room for Calum but wasn't surprised not to see him. Jasper had eventually decided it was fear of discovery that had come between them a few hours ago, though if that were the case, his cock reminded him, why had Calum taken him back to his room? Because he'd felt the same desperation as Jasper? It had worn off bloody quickly. Jasper exhaled. What he needed was for Calum to tell him what was wrong so he didn't go home fretting about what he'd done, hadn't done, could have done.

He glanced at the array of food, his stomach churned and Jasper turned away. He didn't feel well. He took a sip of his coffee before he looked for somewhere to sit. There was no sign of Angie, so no chance to apologize for not being there at dinner, or to thank her for the sandwich, though it had left a strange aftertaste. Jasper swallowed the moisture in his mouth and winced.

He took a seat across from Matt and Paul, away from the giggling cowgirls. Was it his imagination that he suddenly felt weak, his legs trembling?

"Only coffee?" Matt asked as he tucked into a plate of bacon and eggs.

"Not hungry," Jasper said. *Christ. I feel like I'm going to throw up.*

"Worried you'll puke again?" Erik walked up behind Jasper and slapped him on the back just as he picked up his drink. The coffee sloshed and a wash of hot liquid hit his hand. *Fuck.* Jasper put the mug down and grabbed a napkin to wipe his stinging flesh.

"No need to be nervous," Erik said in an overly loud voice. "Ring said you did okay yesterday on Zander. We'll put you on Spider today. She has a bit more spirit. Want to ride with these two?"

Framed as a question, but Erik wasn't asking. It flittered through Jasper's head to request Calum take him out. When they'd arrived, Erik had been at pains to tell them to ask for what they wanted.

I'd like to fuck your son.

On the other hand, Jasper didn't want to cause trouble. At least on a ride with Matt and Paul, he'd be spared the chattering chipmunks.

"Fine," Jasper said, glaring at the coffee stain on his shirt cuff. *Damn.*

"Vera's going to think you've got something against her cooking if you keep skipping dinner. You're missing out on our evening entertainment too. Found something better to do? Or maybe you don't like our company?"

Erik laughed but Jasper didn't miss the edge to the man's voice. *Shit.* Was this because he'd upset Angie or had he and Calum been seen last night? Maybe Erik was doing nothing more than fishing.

"I work fifteen-hour days, six days a week. I'm jet-lagged and I'm tired," Jasper said.

"Try rounding up cattle," Erik snapped. "Think about doing it in the pouring rain and freezing cold with the wind so strong it could knock you off your horse. Think about being knee-deep in mud while you drag cattle out of trouble. Amazing you find sitting behind a desk playing with your...pencil so exhausting." Erik walked away before Jasper could say anything, but the coldness in the guy's tone was unmistakable. *He knows something.*

"Someone got out of bed the wrong side this morning," Vera said with a forced laugh. "Ignore him. He's got a lot on his mind."

"It is tiring though sitting behind a desk," Paul said. "A different sort of weariness to the physical kind, but I'm exhausted by the end of a day in the office."

Jasper sipped his coffee, pleased he had an ally.

Matt raised his eyebrows. "You find enough energy to party most nights."

Paul grinned. "Perk of the job. Too many desperate models, not enough hours in the day."

"You can always toss a few more my way," Matt said.

"Sandy letting you off the leash again?" Paul asked.

"I'm here, aren't I?" Matt glanced at Melissa and Janie.

Jasper didn't think he'd misunderstood the conversation. The earlier camaraderie he'd felt with Paul evaporated.

Paul pushed a business card across the table to Jasper. "I'd like you on my books. You've got exactly the face one of my clients is looking for."

As though I'm going to throw up? Jasper left the card where it lay. As the men tucked into their towering plates of food, he felt more and more queasy. Was the presence of Calum the only reason he'd managed to get on the horse? Jasper didn't think he was worried about riding, but he did feel ill.

"I'll see you at the stables." Jasper jumped up.

Once he was out of the dining room, he rushed back into the guest wing and just managed to reach his bathroom before he vomited. Slumped over the toilet, Jasper retched and retched, his stomach seemingly intent on turning itself inside out.

When there was nothing left to throw up, Jasper cleaned his teeth, washed his face and stared at himself in the mirror. The color he'd acquired yesterday had disappeared. His eyes looked huge, the shadows beneath them darker. If it hadn't been for the fact that he didn't want Erik to think he was a coward, he'd forgo this morning's ride and stay by the pool. As it was, he grabbed his gloves and headed for the stable.

He was the last one there. He could see the other guests riding in the distance. Paul and Matt were already mounted and waiting. So was Ring. *Shit.* The wrangler pointedly looked at his watch. Jasper hadn't realized the wranglers would move between guests. He thought he might have preferred the chattering Calamity Janes to this sour-faced guy.

Gunner held the reins of a black mare. The horse's head was up, her nostrils flared. No quiet mount like Zander, Spider looked difficult. Jasper put his hand in his pocket and pulled out the tube of mints. When the horse showed no interest, his heart sank.

"This one's a picky lady," Gunner said. "You could bring her diamonds and she'd turn up her nose. Don't let her have her head until you're ready or she'll take charge of the whole ride."

Jasper stroked the horse's neck and grabbing the horn, put his foot into the stirrup and hoisted himself into the saddle. The moment his weight settled on Spider's back, the horse reared up on her hind legs. The reins flew out of Gunner's grasp and the old man shied away from the flailing hooves. *Oh Christ.* An image of Ben shot into Jasper's mind as he caught hold of the mane with one hand and made a grab for the trailing reins. Missed. Spider's hooves slammed down and then she tried to buck Jasper off.

Fuck, fuck, fuck. Jasper knew what to do but the horse was having none of it. Without even a loose grip on the reins, he had to yank on the mane to try and force up Spider's head. Jasper tightened his legs, neither foot was in a stirrup, and used the pressure of his thighs to urge the horse forward. If he could make her move in a tight circle, she wouldn't be able to buck. Ring yelled instructions, but Jasper sensed this was a horse in pain, not one who just didn't feel like being ridden. He was going to get thrown. Sooner rather than later. Better if Jasper chose when and how and not the horse.

He heard a familiar voice shout out his name. *Oh God.* If Calum tried to help, he'd get hurt. Jasper leaned forward, put his hand on the horn and swung his shoulders right at the same time as he shifted his right leg over the horse's hindquarters. Theoretically, he'd be able to get his balance before he dropped off, but pressure on the saddle seemed to make this horse jumpy. Jasper didn't hesitate. He pushed himself backward as Spider bucked. Jasper stayed airborne for a long second and then he hit the ground rolling.

Impact with the dusty earth knocked the sunglasses from his face and the air out of his lungs, but he knew he'd avoided serious injury. Jasper struggled to get up, more to prove to himself he could than to avoid Spider's dancing hooves. Jasper's sunglasses weren't so lucky. They lay in pieces in the dirt.

Gunner grabbed his arm and hauled him to one side. Jasper slumped down on his haunches, his breathing labored, his chest tight. *Please, not now.* He concentrated on taking deep, slow breaths. Calum snagged Spider's flying reins and talked to the horse, trying to calm her down.

"What the hell was that about?" Paul asked as his horse nervously pawed the ground.

None of the horses looked happy. Even Ring had trouble with his mount. Anxiety spread like flu among herd animals.

"You okay?" Gunner asked Jasper.

Jasper nodded. Nothing broken, but he was plenty bruised, particularly his pride.

"Gunner, come and hold Spider," Calum called.

Jasper could see the concern in Calum's eyes and forced himself to his feet. "You might as well go without me," Jasper said to Ring.

"Get back on the damn horse and show her who's boss," Ring snapped. "Damn pussy." The last two words were whispered though no one could have missed them.

Jasper sensed Calum moving and snapped, "No." He directed the word at Ring but it applied to Calum too. "I'm not riding Spider today."

"Got your eye on something else?" Ring muttered.

"Fuck off, you piece of shit," Jasper said quietly.

Ring stared at him and then spat at Jasper's feet. He wheeled his horse round and cantered off. Paul and Matt cast each other confused glances and then followed. Once Gunner took Spider's reins, Calum rushed over. Jasper wanted those strong arms around him, but knew he couldn't let Calum touch him. Bessie on the other hand, jumped up, licking his hand and Jasper kept the dog between them.

"I'm okay," Jasper said, trying to warn Calum that Gunner was watching. "There's nothing wrong with me, but there is with the horse."

Calum's hands clenched into fists at his sides. "Oh God. You could—"

"No need to reach for your gun." Jasper forced out the joke. He knew what Calum was thinking, because in that split second when he had to decide what to do, Jasper had thought of Ben, who'd landed on his head on a paved road. Dirt was a more forgiving surface on which to acquire bruises, but landing awkwardly could have snapped his neck just as easily.

"Spider's high strung," Calum said. "Who the hell said Jasper had to ride her?"

"Boss's orders." Gunner held the now docile animal.

"Out, Bessie," Calum snapped and the dog slipped under the rail of the corral.

Calum stroked Spider's neck. When he loosened the girth, the horse tried to skitter away. "Steady, girl. What is it?"

"Check the saddle." Jasper brushed dirt from his clothes, relieved his breathing had eased.

When Calum lifted the blanket from the horse's back, the reason for Spider's discomfort became plain. A smear of blood and a thorny twig in the wool.

"Shit." Calum turned to Gunner. "Who saddled her?"

"I did. I checked the blanket. Always do. Christ." Gunner put his hand to his jaw and rubbed the lower half of his face. "I'm sorry, Jasper. I must have missed it. That's never happened before. Let me saddle up another. Won't take but a minute."

"It's okay. I don't have anyone to ride with now."

"Calum can take you. You might catch up with Ring."

Jasper turned to look at Calum.

A slow smile spread across that beautiful face. "Sure. Did Ring say he was heading for Bonnet's Ridge?"

"No," Gunner said. "I thought I heard him mention—ah yep, I think he did. I'm sure he did. Course, I have been known to make mistakes."

Jasper tried not to limp as he followed Calum and Gunner back to the stable with Spider. Calum carried the saddle into the tack room.

"Look after Spider and I'll see to Blue," Calum said to Gunner. "Jasper can ride Star."

Calum lifted a gray Stetson from a peg and tossed it to Jasper. "It's mine. Wear it."

Jasper put it on and heard Calum give a quiet moan. A moment later, Calum had sidled up behind him. "You might have to leave that on, cowboy, and take everything else off."

Oh God, now we think alike? Jasper's cock purred despite the voice in his head reminding him of Calum's words last night.

"Star's good as gold." Gunner led a brown mare out into the sunshine. "Well, unless you try and ride her through a gap you could drive a semi-trailer through. She thinks she's fat."

"Polo?" Jasper offered one to Star who sniffed it. "Sugar-free," he added and the horse snaffled it off his palm.

Gunner snorted. He held the horse while Jasper climbed on and then handed him the reins. Once Jasper was safely seated and the horse showed no sign of not wanting him there, he relaxed. He ached so much he couldn't imagine moving at anything faster than walking pace, but then he looked at Calum's butt as he swung up onto Blue and thought there were a few things he might manage faster than that.

"Bessie, stay," Calum ordered and kicked Blue into a walk.

Jasper adjusted his Stetson so it shaded his eyes and set off after Calum.

"I take it we're not going to Bonnet's Ridge?" Jasper asked.

Calum looked back and smiled. Then his eyes focused behind Jasper and the smile fell off his face. Jasper turned and saw Angie running up.

"You told me you'd take me riding," she called to Calum.

"Not this morning," Calum said.

"But you promised."

"Go and help Vera make lunch. Maybe I can take you this afternoon."

Angie turned to Jasper. "And you said you'd sit with me at dinner."

"I'm sorry. I missed dinner. I ate your sandwich though. Thank you."

"Was it okay?"

Jasper couldn't detect any guile in her expression. "Lovely, thanks." He felt bad that he could even suspect her of trying to make him sick.

"We'll see you later," Calum said and kicked his mount on.

Jasper followed. When he glanced back, Angie still stood watching.

"Should we have brought her along?" Jasper asked.

"Nope."

"Are you going to be in trouble for taking me riding again?"

"Yep." Calum grinned. "But I have somewhere special to show you."

"I thought..."

"What?"

"You said you couldn't do this, what changed?"

Calum's smile fell off his face. "I didn't mean...it was there, the ranch, my room. I didn't want to fuck you thinking any minute someone was going to bang on the door." He licked his lips. "I *do* want you. A lot."

Jasper nodded. That was what he'd concluded and yet something still bugged him. Calum had known there was a risk of being heard before he'd taken him to his room. Was there something else?

They cantered and walked until they reached the foothills, and then Calum led the way up a rocky valley following the path of a stream. It was a good thing Star was watching where she was going because Jasper was too easily distracted by Calum. The way he pulled down his hat, his narrow waist, broad back, those muscular arms, the way he kicked Blue on—*everything he does turns me on.*

While they'd walked the horses side by side, they'd talked about all sorts of things—food, music, films, books. It was rare to find a guy who liked to read as much as he, let alone the same types of books. When they disagreed over the merits of an author, arguing with Calum had been entertaining. Yet in all they talked about, subjects close to the heart had been avoided. Past relationships, what they wanted out of life, how they felt.

You've known the guy a couple of days. And in a couple more days, Jasper would be leaving and he'd never see Calum again. Why did that choke him up? Jasper gave himself a hard mental slap. He was an idiot. They'd sucked each other off, and Jasper wanted them riding into the sunset forever. It was fine to be an incurable romantic in his dreams, but life wasn't like that. Life was mostly...shit.

"We'll leave the horses here in the shade." Calum slithered from Blue's back. He removed something from his saddle bag and stuck it in his back pocket. Then tossed water to Jasper and took one for himself.

They were at the edge of a small stand of slender trees, their smooth white bark pocked with black scars. Jasper looked up into the green leaves and smiled when he heard them rustle as if they were whispering to each other.

Calum tethered the horses. "Quaking aspens."

"Very pretty."

"Something special about them." Calum slid his arm over Jasper's back. He twisted his fingers in his hair and heat shot to Jasper's groin.

"The noise they make?" Jasper asked, thinking of the sounds he'd like to hear from Calum.

"Yes but not that. They can produce seeds, but that's generally not the way they reproduce. All these trees are genetically identical, growing from a shared root system. So really this is one individual entity rather than a group of individuals. The heaviest organism in the world is an aspen grove in Utah. Six thousand tons."

"Christ. That's impressive."

"They come from the same source, and so they're all the same sex. Male trees stand separately from females."

"How can you tell male from female?"

"Examine their catkins."

Jasper laughed.

"Course, there aren't any catkins on this time of year. You need to see them in the spring. Or come in the fall when the colonies change color together."

The leaves all trembled again, the shivering aspens asking Jasper to come back, or maybe warning him to stay away.

"I wonder why they developed like that," Jasper said.

"Protection against fire maybe, but it leaves them vulnerable. If one tree's sick, the whole group is in danger. Having said that, they're hard suckers to kill."

Calum groaned. "My phone. Fuck it." He took his arm from Jasper. "Yes?" he snapped into the cell.

"What the fuck do you think you're doing?"

Calum's bloody father. Jasper made to move away and Calum caught his arm.

"What I'm doing is taking a guest for a ride after Ring rode off without him."

"Why did Ring go without him?"

"Because Jasper couldn't ride Spider. That was your idea, I hear. Way to go, Boss. We have a guest who's overcoming an issue about riding and you put him on a horse like Spider. The reason she—"

Jasper shook his head and mouthed "No." He didn't want Gunner to get into trouble for the thorn under the saddle.

"We're trying to catch up with Ring now," Calum said.

"You let your sister down."

A muscle in Calum's cheek twitched. "I'll make it up to her." He cut off the call.

"Should we go back?" Jasper asked.

"Hell no. Come on."

They walked into the stand of trees, sunlight dappling ground covered in wild flowers, grasses and shrubs. Calum made for a grassy area, flung himself onto his back and looked up at Jasper.

"You have to lie flat to get the best effect," Calum said.

"Really?" Jasper smiled and checked the ground.

"What are you looking for?"

"Snakes, dirt, ants, blood-sucking roots that are going to spring up and drag me under the surface. Oh, and bears."

"I checked for all those. Come here."

Jasper tossed his hat and water next to Calum's, turned up his collar and carefully settled on the soft grass at his side. Calum's fingers wrapped around his, and Jasper's throat went dry.

"Look up," Calum whispered.

The color of the leaves shifted through shades of green as a gentle breeze rippled through the canopy. Sunlight winked through thousands of gaps. It was so peaceful, Jasper stopped worrying about what he was lying on and let the beauty of it sink in.

"What are you thinking?" Calum asked. "Still fretting about ants and dirt?"

I want you to fuck me. He swallowed hard. "I was wondering why the leaves move like this."

"Something to do with the part of the stalk that connects the leaves to the stem. They're flattened rather than cylindrical so they let the leaves flutter as they bend in the wind. And because they move so much, it allows the sun to shine on all the leaves...and on us."

Jasper turned to look at him and found Calum staring at him. "What did you study at college?"

Calum sighed. "Agriculture."

"You don't sound happy about it."

"My father pitched a fit when I said I'd like to study art. I went no farther than Laramie to please him, studied what he wanted and not what I wanted, and I've done a few other things besides just to keep him happy—I think I've had enough of doing what I don't want to do."

Calum shifted onto his side. A warm hand slipped around Jasper's throat and soft lips traced the length of his face from his hairline to his Adam's apple. The slight roughness of Calum's chin brushing against Jasper's temple sent waves of pleasure rippling to his groin. Calum's breathing hitched at the same time as Jasper's and they laughed.

"I feel like I've thrown myself off a cliff and I haven't hit the ground," Calum whispered.

"That was me, thanks to Spider."

Calum's eyes widened. "Shit, I'd forgotten you came off hard. Are you okay?"

Jasper nodded.

"That fucking thorn under the blanket. It's never happened before. Gunner's getting too old for this work, but my father won't make him leave. He's too fond of the guy. Though if he finds out about Spider, he might stop Gunner doing the saddling."

Calum sucked gently on Jasper's neck and then kissed his way back up to his forehead. At the same time, he pushed Jasper's legs apart with his knee, shifting over until he lay on top, steel-hard cocks pressing against each other.

For the briefest moment, Jasper caught sight of Calum's blue eyes staring into his, before Calum tilted his head and moved in for a kiss. They started slow and gentle but excitement pushed them into hot and greedy. Calum's tongue stabbed his mouth in an imitation of sex then Jasper did the same to him. Hands all over each other, groaning and laughing, they rolled around in the grass, each trying to pin the other down. Neither wanted to win. Neither wanted to lose.

They shed their clothes as they wrestled in a clumsy, tangled mess. Kisses shifted from soft to rough and back again. Hands stroked and then fingers tightened. Fists flew though punches were held. They laughed and groaned. Jasper wanted to kiss every scar on Calum's body, wanted Calum to kiss every inch of his. They pinned each other down, threw each other off and panted their way to painful arousal. This was play-fighting at its most arousing and Jasper's heart beat so loud it almost deafened him.

Finally, they lay buck naked on their backs, chests heaving, cocks bobbing, pre-come glistening. Jasper wanted to fuck, wanted to be fucked. *Who goes first?* Calum stretched out a hand and dragged his jeans closer. From his back pocket he pulled out a string of condoms, a small bottle of lube and a quarter.

"We're going to toss for it?" Jasper panted.

"You have a better idea?"

"Yeah, you go first."

Jasper saw a flash of relief on Calum's face and knew he'd made the right decision. Calum slipped a leg over Jasper's hip and straddled him.

"You'll be the one the bear grabs," Jasper said. "This way I get some warning."

Calum laughed.

Maybe that wasn't so funny. Jasper gulped.

Note to self: Keep a look out for bears and pissed-off dads.

Chapter Eight

Calum took a quick look round to check for bears or a pissed-off father storming out of the trees before he leaned down and licked the salty dip at the junction of Jasper's neck and shoulder. Jasper moaned. Had he guessed how much Calum needed to be on top? Was that why he'd foregone the coin toss or did he really not care who went first? Maybe he'd seen the coin and knew Calum was going to fix it.

He'll still want to fuck you at some point, warned his brain.

But Calum would deal with that when he came to it. For now, he was exactly where he wanted to be. He ran his teeth along the hard ridge of Jasper's collarbone, making the dude beneath him draw in his breath in a long hiss, which brought a smile to Calum's face. He laved the rounded contours of Jasper's pecs and teased the tight, dark nipples with his teeth. While Jasper panted and groaned beneath him, Calum's arousal kicked off like a bronco. Every sound Jasper made was echoed by one from him. He wanted to crawl under this guy's skin, get inside him, meld with him.

Jasper's hands were doing some exploring of their own, fingers of one hand trailing ribbons of fire down Calum's back while his others threaded Calum's hair then stroked his ears and neck. All the while, Calum continued his journey south. He trailed his tongue down the center of Jasper's chest and circled his navel over and over, chuckling as the skin there fluttered at his touch. He dipped his tongue inside, rhythmically pushing the wet tip into the shallow salty space, feeling his pulse climb as Jasper's cock brushed his nipple.

With half of his brain shouting, *Get inside him and fuck him hard and fast*, Calum struggled to listen to the sensible half telling him to go slow. He danced his thumbs over Jasper's firm abs, let his fingers slide into the creases of his groin and licked the head of his cock.

Jasper let out a ragged cry. "Oh shhh...it."

Calum pushed Jasper's knees up and spread his legs. Once he was sure Jasper would keep them there, he tucked down, ignoring the rough ground beneath him and sucked the tight sac holding Jasper's balls.

"Bloody hell." Jasper wrapped his hand around the base of his cock.

He wasn't the only one struggling for control. Calum's nuts were drawn up tight, threatening to blow. He shifted his attention from one ball to the other while above his nose, Jasper's fingers clenched tighter around his shaft.

"Oh fuck, fuuuuck." Jasper's legs trembled as his breathing grew noisier. "Enough, enough."

Calum released him and, using his palms to spread Jasper's cheeks, he trailed his tongue down the dark line separating the balls and on to the ultrasensitive strip of flesh beyond. He wanted to play there, show Jasper how good he could make this feel with the slightest of pressure changes, but inside his head, his need to come rose like magma trapped under a volcano. One swipe of his tongue over Jasper's pucker and Jasper drew up like a bow.

"Christ. Jesus. God. If I see a bear...I'm not telling you until I've come," Jasper blurted.

Calum laughed into his butt, blew on his puckered hole, and Jasper shuddered. Spreading his palms on the underside of Jasper's thighs to keep his body open, Calum buried his face between Jasper's butt cheeks. He fluttered his tongue over the taut entrance and sucked, licked and teased the ring of muscle until he felt Jasper begin to relax.

"Okay?" Calum lifted his head to ask.

"Don't interrupt. I'm just doing some complicated mental arithmetic. One plus one equals...ah damn."

Calum smiled, said, "Two," and slipped his tongue into Jasper's anus.

"Oh fu...ck. Two? Are you sure?" Jasper pulled at his hair.

No way was Calum stopping. He reached blindly for the lube and condoms and dragged them close as he kissed and licked and fucked Jasper with his tongue. Calum flipped off the top of the lube one-handed and spilt it onto his palm. He replaced his tongue with a finger and pulled up to look at Jasper's face as he pushed the digit in and out of his ass.

Jasper writhed beneath him.

Calum's cock was blood-red at the crest. It looked thicker than he'd ever seen it.

"Fuck me," Jasper whispered. "Please."

Calum fumbled with the condom but eventually got it on. *Way to look smooth.* More lube in his hand, though most went on the grass, and he rubbed it over his aching shaft. A loud moan from Jasper, and Calum glanced up to see Jasper's gaze fixed on his fingers. Taking a tight hold at the root, he lined the head of his dick against the entrance to Jasper's body and pressed until he felt the muscle barrier give way. Calum stared into Jasper's face as he pushed deeper, noting the reaction to everything he did, the way Jasper sucked in a breath, the flutter of his thick eyelashes, the wince, the sigh and finally the smile that curved his lips.

"Oh God that feels good." Jasper groaned. "You can use your cock instead of your finger now."

Calum snorted and, pulling Jasper's legs into the crook of his arms, he thrust hard to bury himself balls deep.

"Fuuuuck," Jasper gasped.

"Serves you right for joking at a critical point."

Jasper stared straight at him and laughed. "You were taking too long."

Now Calum's heart ached as badly as his balls. He'd never laughed and joked when he had sex. His partners, the few he'd had, only cared enough that he got them off after he'd fucked them and then they were gone. There was no cuddling, no sleeping together, no fun. It was just sex. Good sex, but nothing more.

This was.

Calum's heart ached. He stared down at Jasper and slowly withdrew his cock, dragging it through nerve-rich tissue while Jasper gazed up at him through hooded eyes. Rolling his hips, Calum thrust back into Jasper's anus. He kept his strokes slow and smooth, amazed he'd not come the moment he felt the clasp of Jasper's muscles, further amazed he'd not immediately driven himself to oblivion in some super-fast shunting motion.

Jasper pumped his cock in time with Calum's thrusts, and Calum's gaze dropped to Jasper's hand. The guy had managed to get hold of the lube and his cock glistened in the sunlight like some magic totem. Jasper's fingers squeezed the tip and then he twisted his fist as he dragged it down. Watching him bring himself off had Calum gulping. He began to move faster as pressure mounted in his head. The long, deep thrusts had Jasper gasping more loudly, his breathy cries ricocheting around Calum's head.

Calum slipped onto another plane as pleasure coursed through him, every muscle, every cell filled with ice and fire. Not even a bear could stop him now. He was pistoning into Jasper, the squelch of sweat-slick bodies, the sound of Jasper's ragged breathing, every grunt and groan propelling Calum to completion.

"Calum." Jasper closed his eyes as he groaned his name and Calum's balls drew up tight.

Jasper's hand jerked harder and faster at his cock and Calum's simmering orgasm approached the boil. He wanted Jasper to come first but wasn't sure how much longer he could hold on. He pushed harder at Jasper's legs, forcing his butt higher and then canted his hips to change the angle of entry.

"Jesus." Jasper sucked in a breath and opened his eyes.

A creamy jet spurted from Jasper's cock and landed close to his throat. Then as he splattered his stomach in ropes of come, Calum's cock jerked in the hold of Jasper's body. Orgasm boiled over to race through him, surging along veins, swelling at the back of his head before careening down his spine to ignite his balls. He exploded into Jasper with such force that it stole the air from his lungs. Over and over his cock jerked and released his load. Only as Jasper pulled him down for a kiss did Calum remember he needed to breathe.

When he regained enough awareness to register he had Jasper pinned awkwardly beneath him, Calum eased his semi-hard cock free and slumped at Jasper's side. When he felt fingers wrap around his and hold tight, the lump in Calum's throat threatened to choke him. *How am I going to let this guy go?*

How am I going to let this guy go? Jasper's heart hammered in his chest. This was turning out to be the best holiday he'd ever had and he didn't want it to end. He couldn't believe he was lying naked in a wood, come smeared all over his chest, next to a guy who could give him a hard-on by simply smiling.

Calum leaned up on one elbow and grinned. "I think we frightened away the bear." He put a finger in the come on Jasper's stomach and smeared it in circles. "Worried that you're messy?"

"No."

"Liar."

Jasper shrugged. "I was planning to wipe myself down on your shirt."

Calum laughed. "I can do better than that. Come on." He pulled off the condom, set it aside and then pushed himself to his feet.

"What about our clothes?"

"Leave them. They're not going anywhere."

As Jasper followed Calum through the trees, the sound of running water grew louder. They emerged from the stand of aspens at the foot of a rocky crag. Fifteen feet above their heads a waterfall poured into a plunge pool. Jasper pushed back his anxiety about wandering around naked and took in the view. Powder-blue skies stretching as far as the eye could see, shimmering aspens all around and this sparkling stream, falling to rush and ripple over rocks. Not to mention the lean, tanned male body that fulfilled all Jasper's fantasies, scars included.

Calum clambered down to the pool.

"It looks cold," Jasper said.

"It's not."

Before Jasper could shout a warning about depth or hidden rocks or piranhas, Calum took a flying leap and dive-bombed the water, sending spray arching into the air. For a moment, the sun shining on the water droplets created a rainbow and Jasper's eyes widened.

Calum surfaced and shook water from his gold-streaked hair. He swam to the opposite side of the pool and turned to look at Jasper. "Join me."

Jasper thought of the treasure at the end of a rainbow, looked at Calum's shining face and jumped.

He came up swearing, nipples hard as bullets, his cock and balls fleeing for warmer climes. "For fuck's sake. It's bloody freezing." Jasper swam across the pool to Calum's side and gaped as he reached him. "What the hell? The water's warm here. That's impossible." He frowned. "Unless you p—"

Calum splashed him. "No, I fucking didn't. I'll show you why one half's warm."

He pulled himself out onto a flat rock, giving Jasper a mouthwatering view of his butt and then clambered up several boulders before he disappeared. Jasper followed. When he reached the top, he found Calum sitting in another pool of water surrounded by rocks. Jasper slid in beside him and let out a deep sigh.

"Warm enough for you?" Calum asked.

"Hot spring?"

"Yep. It bubbles up here and flows into the plunge pool someplace below the surface."

Jasper leaned back against the warm rock and tilted his face to the sun. "It's perfect."

Calum's thumb brushed his lips. "You're perfect."

Eyes open again, warmed inside as well as out, Jasper smiled.

"We have about ten minutes before the bus tour arrives," Calum said.

"What?" Jasper reared up.

Calum chuckled and pulled him down. "I'm joking. Far as I'm aware, no one knows about this. There's hot springs all over Wyoming, but this one's off the beaten track."

Jasper settled deeper in the water. "What a great place to camp out—alfresco bathtub, stunning view, amazing company."

"Thanks." Calum tousled Jasper's hair.

"I meant me."

Calum snorted.

"Christ, this is too hot." Jasper hoisted himself out of the water onto a flat rock. He lay back and sighed as a warm breeze caressed his body. "A towel to lie on and this would be almost perfect."

Calum joined him on the rock, lying at a right angle with his head pressed against Jasper's ribs. "What else do you need?"

"An ice-cold beer."

"Yeah, that would be good."

Jasper took a deep breath. "Ben would have loved this. He talked about running away to be a cowboy when he was a kid. He had this old gun that fired caps and took it everywhere with him. His favorite game was shooting me. I perfected dying in many different ways. I thought about that a lot after his accident."

"You were close to Ben."

"I think that's why his asking me to pull the plug hurt so much. He kept saying if I really loved him, I should have been able to do it. And I thought, if he really loved me, he would never have asked."

Calum slipped his hand onto Jasper's leg and wrapped his fingers around his shin.

"The thing is," Jasper said, "What you think you can do and what you can actually do are two different things. Easy to *think* you could go through with it until the moment comes that you have to do it. I kept stringing Ben along, telling him I would, that I was waiting for the results of some test, or details of a new technology that could improve his life, or that I needed more time because I had to make sure no one knew what I'd done or I'd get arrested. Always some excuse and he knew I was too chicken-shit scared to do it. He never said it but I saw it in his eyes."

And Jasper hadn't wanted to look at Ben anymore because when he did, guilt swamped him.

"I don't think you were scared," Calum whispered. "If you'd really wanted to do it, the idea of the police getting involved wouldn't have stopped you."

Jasper exhaled. "Christ, am I that obvious?"

"He was your brother. Broken body, but he was still your brother."

"But I wanted him dead." Jasper laid his arm over his eyes. "Every night I prayed to a God I'd long since given up on that when I woke in the morning, Ben would be dead. And then I'd wake and walk along the corridor and hear the noise of the fucking machine that kept him alive, and it was like a knife in my heart reminding me of what I hadn't done."

"He was cared for in your home?"

"Once he was stable and the hospital said they could do nothing more. The house was adapted to cope with him. A room prepared downstairs. Another for his caregiver. Places to put all his stuff—the wheelchair, the hoists, the bath. Our home was converted into a hospital and I fucking hated him for it."

Jasper shuddered. He'd never told anyone that before.

"Sometimes I hate Angie," Calum whispered. "She's sweet and wouldn't hurt a fly, but she sucks up attention. From the moment my father told me he was marrying Vera, it was made clear Angie was my responsibility too. Times when I wanted to do things on my own, I had to take her with me or not do them. You lose your friends pretty quick when you have a girl tagging along, particularly one like Angie. Not that I had many friends."

Jasper pushed himself up and trailed his fingers through Calum's wet hair. "You think they love her more than you?"

"I *know* they do. Vera's her mom. I can understand it from her, but my dad..." Calum gave a short laugh. "I can't do a fucking thing right. He hates that I'm gay so he pretends I'm not. He gave Pete the job of foreman when he should have asked me. He made me get m—ah, fuck it." Calum sat up and looked at Jasper. "I've said more to you than I've ever said to anyone."

"I'm a good listener."

Calum ran a finger along Jasper's cheekbone. "Maybe it's because you live on the other side of the world."

Maybe it's because we have something here.

"You're mine for a week," Calum said.

Jasper's heart clenched. "I don't want to make life difficult for you. We should be careful. You have to live here after I've gone."

"I wish..." Calum sighed.

Jasper wished that too.

Back where they'd left their clothes, Jasper wrapped his arms around Calum and wrestled him to the ground. He didn't want this time together to end.

"Let me check my phone," Calum said and Jasper rolled off him.

What the fuck? One minute Calum couldn't keep his hands off him and now he needed to see whether he'd missed any calls? *Why?* Jasper's cock was hard, Calum's wasn't.

He doesn't want to be fucked.

Jasper didn't *know* that was what was wrong but he felt it. He grabbed his shorts and pulled them on as Calum retrieved his cell.

"Seven missed calls. Seven messages."

"Can I guess who from?" Jasper asked.

"No prizes."

Calum had offered a coin toss and Jasper refused because he'd had a gut feeling Calum wanted to go first, but maybe the gut feeling should have told him a little more. Maybe Calum didn't bottom. *Fuck. I'd like a look at that coin.* Jasper tugged on his chinos and zipped up. It wasn't the end of the world. Jasper liked one as much as the other. He was disappointed Calum didn't want—ah fuck, more than disappointed, but he'd get over it. Maybe. Jasper finished dressing and tugged on his hat. Calum had the phone on speaker, lying on the grass, and the angry voice of Erik rang out as he dressed.

"Where the fuck are you? Why aren't you answering your phone? Angie's gone missing. Call me."

Jasper's heart sank.

"Calum, get back here now."

Calum stared at his phone as if it were a snake.

"This is fucking urgent. Answer your phone."

The messages grew increasingly frantic. Jasper buried the condom under a tree as Calum paced with his phone off speaker.

"It's me. I must have been out of range. I didn't—no... I didn't... That's not fair... I don't care what... I had the phone with me... Jackson's Gully... Okay, I'll check on the way back."

Jasper registered that Calum had deliberately stopped him hearing what his father said and wondered why. Calum shoved the phone back in his pocket and untied the horses. Jasper climbed on Star.

"What's happened?" Jasper asked.

"Angie took Misty out while everyone was at lunch. They can't find her. And of course it's my fault because I was supposed to take her riding, not theirs because they didn't keep an eye on her."

Star followed Blue through the stand of trees.

"Any idea where she'd go?" Jasper called.

"They've checked all the obvious places."

"Does she have a phone?"

Calum looked over his shoulder. "Yeah, but she's not answering or we'd know where she was."

Jasper ignored the sarcasm. "Maybe she's not responding because she knows she'll get shouted at. Why don't *you* call her?"

Calum faced forward and pulled out his phone.

"Christ, Angie, what the... Where are you?... Call Dad." He sighed. "All right, I'll do it... Yes and I'll come. Stay put." Calum turned to Jasper again. "She's at Cookie Bend—it's on our way back."

"Better tell your father."

"Yeah." Calum grimaced. "Hi, Dad. I called her and she answered. She's fine... No, she wants me to get her... She asked me not to tell you where she was... That's not my fucking fault... Maybe an hour... Okay."

Calum turned in his saddle to face Jasper. "Maybe I have the chance to redeem myself here. I just don't need Angie thinking she can make a friend of a rattler."

Once they reached open ground, Calum kicked Blue into a canter and Jasper followed.

Calum sighed when they caught sight of Angie sitting on a rock. "Thank fuck," he mumbled.

As far as Jasper could tell, she looked fine. Calum slid off Blue when they reached his sister and she ran to Calum, a smile on her face and flung herself into his arms. Jasper stayed mounted and watched.

"Are you okay?" Calum smoothed down her hair.

"Yes."

"You do know you're going to be in trouble when we get back? What did I tell you about going off on your own?"

She pulled away and pouted. "You promised to take me riding." Then she glared at Jasper. *Uh-oh. My fault.*

"Let's go home," Calum said.

"I can't ride Misty. She's thrown a shoe."

"What? Again?"

"Same one."

Jasper slipped from Star's back and walked over to the gray mare. She stood still as he ran his hand down her neck.

"What have you been up to?" Jasper murmured. He could see a shoe missing from a front hoof, but something about the way she stood worried him.

"I've got a boot in my saddlebag," Calum said. "Does the hoof look damaged?"

"No." Jasper put three fingers on the inside of the widest point of the horse's fetlock, located the large vein and pressed it flat to find the artery.

"What are you doing?" Calum called.

"Just checking something." Jasper pressed hardest with the finger farthest from the heart, slightly less with the middle finger and even less with the last. In that way he amplified the pulse, and then felt what he'd hoped not to.

Calum turned to his sister. "See if you can find the shoe, Angie. We don't want nails sticking up for an animal to tread on." Once she'd walked away, Calum headed for Jasper carrying a hoof pick, a set of shoe pullers and a boot. "What is it?" he asked quietly.

"Throbbing pulse." Jasper checked the other leg. "Look how she's standing. It's hardly noticeable, but I think her back legs are slightly forward to take the weight off her front."

"Oh fuck. Laminitis?"

Jasper nodded. "You need to call the vet."

Angie came running up. "Found it." Her mouth turned down when she saw Calum's face. "What's the matter?"

"Misty might not be very well. I'm going to call the vet and ask him to come take a look. We need to walk back. You lead Blue, I'll lead Misty, okay? Head toward that pointed rock. Blue'll want to go first."

While Calum spoke to the vet, Jasper distracted Angie. "Sorry I wasn't there for dinner last night. I was really tired. There's a seven-hour time difference between here and where I live. That means when it's five o'clock in the afternoon in Jackson Hole, it's midnight in London."

"How can it be midnight when the sun's shining?"

"Well, it's..." Jasper gave up. "Did you make my sandwich?"

"All by myself."

"What did you put in it?"

She glared. "You ate it, didn't you? So you know."

So he did.

"Daddy was cross," Angie muttered. "He said you must have gone out with Calum and Calum was supposed to take me riding. You said you were my friend." Her lip wobbled.

Oh God. "Can't I be friends with both of you?"

"What's wrong with Misty?"

Jasper would take that as a no, then. Well, he'd won over Bessie, he'd just have try harder with Angie, though he wouldn't be rubbing her belly. He glanced back at Calum, but he was still on the phone.

"I suspect she has something the matter with her hooves. Sometimes when a horse keeps throwing a shoe from the same foot, it's a sign it needs to be looked at."

"She seems okay. I think you're wrong," Angie said.

"What do you feed her?"

"She has what the others have."

"Do you give her treats?" Jasper asked.

"Sometimes." Angie's head dropped.

"What sort of treats?"

"Apples and carrots."

"I bet she loves those," Jasper said.

Angie looked up again. "Sometimes I give her the special grain she likes and after Gunner cuts the lawn at the front of the ranch, I collect a bucket of grass for her."

"Grass?" Calum asked as he came up alongside.

"That's all I give her," Angie said. "Only after Gunner's cut the lawn."

Christ. Over-consumption of carbohydrate-rich lawn grass clippings was the most common cause of laminitis. Jasper hated to see horses suffering from it.

"It's not good for her, sweetheart," Calum said. "Don't give her any more."

"But everyone has to have treats." Angie's lip wobbled. "Grass is nice. Horses like grass."

"You can't feed lawn grass to—"

Jasper cut off Calum's snap. "You know you're not supposed to eat too many sweets?"

"Candy," Calum corrected.

"It's bad for my teeth," Angie said.

"That's right and too much grass and the wrong grain is bad for a horse's hooves," Jasper said. "But it might not be that. The vet needs to look at Misty and do some tests."

Angie gulped. "Is she going to be okay?"

"I'm sure she'll be fine," Jasper said and Calum frowned at him.

It looked very early stages to Jasper. Laminitis couldn't be cured but catch it in time and it could be treated.

"Don't give her false hope," Calum whispered. "She can't be protected from everything. And how come you knew what to look for?"

"Seen it before." Jasper didn't want to tell *that* story.

"Is Daddy going to yell at me?" Angie asked.

"He's going to hug you and tell you he's glad you're safe," Calum said. "He'll yell at me."

"You shouldn't do things to upset him," Angie said. "He doesn't want you to be friends with Jasper. He said Jasper's a bad f-fluence. What's that?"

"A measurement of the quantity of x-radiation in a beam," Jasper said.

Calum gaped at him.

"Diagnostic radiology." Jasper grinned. "I suppose a *bad* fluence would be if you miscalculated."

"Can I ride Blue?" Angie asked.

Calum nodded. "I'll give you a leg up."

Jasper sighed. He'd nearly said too much.

Note to self: Stop being such a clever dick.

Chapter Nine

Jasper watched a cloud of dust following a white SUV as it headed along the road parallel to where they walked with the horses.

"The vet," Calum said as they crossed the last stretch of pasture.

What a place to live and work. Jasper thought of his small, airless office and the chair from which he rarely lifted his butt and felt a pang of regret for what might have been.

There'd been no change in Misty's gait as they'd walked back, which was a good sign. Better if she hadn't had to walk at all, but then if she hadn't been able to walk, she'd need to be put down.

As they arrived at the stable, Bessie bounded to meet them, Erik strode out, scowling, and Angie started to cry.

"This is your fault," Erik snapped at Calum.

Jasper's spine prickled. He glanced at Calum and saw his jaw twitch. How the fuck was it Calum's fault? Jasper opened his mouth and then closed it again. Not his place to speak out, but he wished Calum would defend himself.

"Daddddy," Angie wailed.

Erik wrapped his arms around her. "Hush, angel." Over his daughter's shoulder, he glared at Jasper and then at Calum. "You know better than to promise her something and then go back on it." He patted Angie's back. "Let me have a look at Misty."

Angie released him, and Erik ran his hand down Misty's leg to inspect the hoof. "It looks okay. Any horse will walk differently with a shoe missing. If the vet's come out here for nothing, I'll take his fee out of your wages."

Jasper's fingers tightened around Star's reins. He expected Calum to say something, but his mouth remained a thin line.

"Want me to take Blue and Star?" Jasper asked.

"Thanks," Calum muttered.

Jasper led the horses away and Bessie followed. Erik Neilson was a jerk. Jasper felt sorry for Calum having to live and work with a father like him. Jasper missed his father. Well, missed the father he'd had before Ben's accident. He'd been fun, someone who'd played cricket in the rain, helped them fly kites and taught them how to fish.

As Jasper reached the stable door, Pete walked out and pointedly ignored him. *Oh great, someone else who hates me.*

Gunner emerged from a stall. "Good ride?"

"Yes." A very good ride.

"Want me to see to Blue?"

"Please."

Jasper's tension seeped away as he brushed Star down. There was a lot of comfort in giving pleasure to someone else, and Jasper knew Calum had enjoyed fucking him. Would he get the chance to return the favor? A surge of lust ran up Jasper's throat and emerged as a faint groan. Star nuzzled his shoulder as he worked, snorting into Jasper's neck as he chatted to her. He knew all too well the dangers of getting attached to animals—the danger in getting attached to anyone.

Bessie sat and watched, almost as though she was checking he was doing it right. The thought of a wagging tail and happy circling mutt to greet him when he came home made him sigh with longing. But it wasn't fair to keep an animal cooped up for hours. Even if he employed a dog walker, Jasper still didn't spend enough time at home.

I hate my job.
So do something about it.
It's too late.
Money isn't everything.

Easy to say when you have plenty.

Jasper had run this conversation through his head so many times he was sick of it.

He heard a commotion at the barn door and turned to see Misty being led in by Erik. Angie and Pete were with him and a tall, bearded guy in his forties who Jasper assumed was the vet. There was no sign of Calum.

"What's the verdict?" Gunner asked.

"Looks like laminitis," Erik said.

Jasper felt no pleasure in being right.

"Ah darn it." Gunner took off his hat and scratched his head.

"It's my fault Misty's ill because I fed her grass." Angie hiccupped and rubbed her eyes.

"Who told you that?" Erik asked.

"Him." She pointed at Jasper.

Every head turned his way. *Shit.* "I also said it might not be that. It's not a good idea to give horses grass mown from a lawn, but it can also be caused by too much rich feed, an infection or a hormonal imbalance."

"What makes you an expert?" Erik snapped.

As Jasper verged on snapping back, Gunner asked, "Is that what you've been doing with those buckets of grass?" He turned from Angie to Erik. "She said she'd been feeding her cow."

"I did feed Charlotte," Angie said. "I just shared the grass with Misty." Tears trickled down her cheeks.

"Mown grass is too rich for horses, but it's not necessarily the cause of Misty's problem." The vet glanced at Jasper. "I'll do some tests that should give us answers. But it was a good catch. Early enough for me to do something about it."

"Calum has a good eye," Erik said.

Jasper chewed his lip. *Erik would rather give his son credit than me?* Given the pair's relationship, that said a lot. Jasper didn't mind Calum getting praise for spotting the laminitis, particularly if it got his father off his back, but he suspected it would take a lot more than that. Jasper shut Star in her stall, gave her a mint and the horse whinnied with pleasure. He wondered if Erik liked mints.

Jasper was on his twentieth lap of the pool when a sudden splash startled him and he stopped swimming. He lifted his head and blinked water from his eyes to see Angie doing doggie-paddle in the shallow end. Reassured she could swim, albeit untidily, Jasper continued to the far end, did a tumble turn and swam back. It was another length before he realized Angie was in deep water and flailing. A shiver of unease flashed down his spine and he swam over to her.

"Are you—?"

"I can do it," she shouted and went under.

Fuck. Jasper hauled her up, but she wrapped her arms around his neck and pulled him under. Water poured into his mouth and Jasper kicked to the surface, dragging Angie with him. They were both coughing and spluttering. A couple of yards and he'd be able to stand, but Angie was in full panic, her arms wrapped tight around his neck while she kicked at his legs. A knee in his balls sent them both under again.

Jasper struggled to the surface, torn between dragging himself free of her grip and pinning her arms. He couldn't let her drown, but what should have been easy, just to shift them both a few feet to safety, took all his strength.

"Angie, hold still," he gasped.

She managed to land punches and kicks while still clinging to him and screaming and crying.

"Don't kick," he snapped. "I can keep us afloat...if you hold still."

She took no notice.

Jasper dragged her to the side. As he tried to lift her onto the edge of the pool, her bikini top came undone at her neck, exposing her breasts. *Shit.* As she continued to struggle, he sat her on the side and tried to help her cover up. *Oh God, I can't breathe.*

"I hate you," Angie screamed. "It's your fault Misty's sick. Your fault Calum didn't take me riding. Leave me alone."

"Fine." Jasper backed off, his chest heaving.

"What the fuck do you think you're doing?" snapped a deep voice.

Jasper spun around in the water. At the end of the pool, Angie's father shot him an icy glare. *Oh God.*

"Get inside, young lady," Erik barked. "You know you're not allowed in the water without supervision."

"He said I could go in."

What? Jasper didn't have the breath to speak.

"Inside now," her father shouted.

Angie wrapped herself in a towel and scuttled away. With no small amount of difficulty Jasper hauled himself out of the pool and pushed himself upright as Erik stormed to his side.

"She was—" His chest heaved.

"Shut. The. Fuck. Up." Erik's neck swelled and he flushed red as a cockerel's comb, his fists clenched tight in front of his belly.

"Look," Jasper panted. "I wasn't—"

"I don't want to hear one damn word, you fucking viper. Keep your hands off my daughter and off my son. The sooner you leave this ranch the better."

He stalked away and Jasper stared after him, open-mouthed and gasping. *Well, I'll let her fucking drown next time, shall I?*

No strength in his legs to keep him upright, Jasper lay on the towel and burned with humiliation. His heart hammered, his breathing still labored. There was no point hoping Angie would explain. Stuff got twisted in her head. Because he was the one who'd noticed Misty's problem, she blamed him. She probably thought he *had* been feeling her up. *Christ.* Though he wasn't sure how she rationalized he'd said she could go in the pool. Didn't matter. When Erik told Calum he'd found Jasper holding Angie with her top off, what the hell was he going to say? Jasper had hoped to remember this day as one of the most perfect he'd ever spent and it was sliding downhill faster than a luge.

When he could breathe normally again, he'd find Calum and at least put this straight. Maybe he ought to leave the ranch. Hire a car in Jackson Hole. They'd bring one out to him if he paid extra. Jasper had never seen Yellowstone National Park. Then he thought about Calum, what they'd done that afternoon, how he wanted to do it again, and he didn't want to run away. And how stupid was that? A few more days and he'd be leaving anyway.

Much as Jasper wanted Calum—and there was no point denying he did—this was going nowhere. The more involved with each other they became, the worse it would be when they split. Jasper spotted Vera heading toward him and scrambled to his feet. *Oh fuck.* He could guess what was coming. Angry mother, more yelling. Shouldn't take him long to pack. If she'd call him a cab, he could leave within the hour, though not without speaking to Calum.

"I didn't do anything," Jasper said quickly. "I was trying to help her and your husband misinterpreted the situation. It looked bad, but it was totally innocent, I swear."

"I'm sure it was." Vera's smile told him she meant it.

Relief rushed through Jasper like a cool breeze and he exhaled.

"I know that you don't—well, really don't worry. I believe you. Did you tell her she could go into the pool?" she asked.

"No, I don't know why she said that."

"I assume she panicked."

"She got out of her depth, and when I swam to her, she grabbed me. We both went under."

Vera wrapped her arms around herself. "Oh God. Thank you for helping her. I'd told her to wait for me. She can swim, but if she swallows water, she forgets to keep moving her arms and legs. She said you pulled her up and sat her on the side and that her top came undone. I realized Erik had got hold of the wrong end of the stick. Not for the first time."

"So he's okay with me?"

Her shoulders fell. "Not exactly."

Jasper should have known that was expecting too much.

"He knows Calum's interested in you and it's stirred up things Erik wants kept buried."

"I should leave. I don't want to cause trouble. Is there a cab company that would take me to Jackson?"

Vera put her hand on his arm. "Don't go. Maybe it would help if things were stirred up. Erik's too bull-headed and Calum goes out of his way to avoid confrontation. It's time he stood up to his father. I just don't want to see either of them get hurt."

What about me? What if I get hurt?

She turned away and then turned back. "I hope you manage dinner tonight. If not, Angie will leave you another sandwich."

He threw himself back on the lounger. Didn't seem fair the best day of his life could end up being one of the worst.

Calum slouched sulkily in the back seat of the Jeep, his hat tipped over his eyes. Gunner rode shotgun, Pete was driving, and Calum wondered if he was aiming for every damn pothole. *Bastard.* Calum had been on his way to find Jasper when he'd been shanghaied into this pointless trip. According to his father, there had been reports of a mountain lion close to where the guests were due to camp tomorrow night. The three of them had been sent to check for tracks.

Well, two of them had. No doubt Pete had been told to get Calum away from Jasper, but Calum had no idea why Gunner had wanted to come as well. Pete hadn't looked happy about it.

"Your father says we can eat on the way back," Pete said.

What a fucking surprise and that probably accounted for Gunner tagging along. The guy probably wanted to go to the steakhouse in Dawson.

"How about that steakhouse in Dawson?" Gunner asked.

Bingo. "Fine," Calum muttered.

He wouldn't be surprised if Pete manufactured some problem with the vehicle that kept them overnight. An ache gripped Calum's chest. What was wrong with liking guys better than women? It wasn't as if he were doing it on purpose. He couldn't help the way he felt. He wasn't hurting anyone or offending public decency by holding hands or kissing in public. Calum ground his teeth. Why the fuck couldn't his father let him be happy?

Pete pulled up abruptly and Calum lurched against his seat belt. He lifted his hat to see they were in the clearing below the site where they usually pitched camp. Course, they told the guests who had to ride here, they were miles out in the middle of nowhere. Not quite. His father wouldn't risk a guest's safety by not having a viable road close by.

"Where'd you learn to drive?" Gunner mumbled. "My bones are rattling."

Pete turned to Calum. "Know what you're looking for?"

Yeah, a tall dark Englishman with eyes that melt my heart. "Tracks wider than they are long. Heel pad with four lobes and no claw marks." Calum exited the Jeep and slammed the door. Hard.

"How long?" Pete asked.

Calum's jaw twitched. "About three inches." *Same as your dick.*

Pete let Toby out the back and the large hound bounded to the nearest tree to take a leak. Gunner followed to copy Pete's dog, and Calum swallowed his smile as he turned away. Calum hadn't brought Bessie. Damn thing would get herself killed if she tried to protect him.

Gunner and Pete picked up rifles.

"Where's mine?" Calum asked. "I thought you said you'd put it in?"

Pete rolled his eyes. "No. I told you to."

The fucking liar.

"Not much use anyway," Gunner said. "If it attacks, you won't see it coming."

Calum still wished he had a weapon.

"Calum, you head east and circle round," Pete ordered. "Gunner, go due north. We'll meet up at the camp."

"Shouldn't we stick together?"Gunner asked. "If Calum doesn't have—"

"We'll cover more ground my way." Pete strode off.

They had maybe an hour before sunset. Plenty of time to find nothing, particularly the more noise they made. Chances were a lion would see or hear them and leave. Gunner was right. A rifle was next to useless, but Calum would have still felt better holding one. He should have put it in the Jeep himself. Christ, he knew Pete hated his guts. Why would the bastard do him any favors?

Calum stamped across the ground. The chances were small of there being a big cat around here, let alone one getting ready to attack. He was convinced this trip was a waste of time. So when he saw what he thought was a paw print, for a brief moment Calum wondered if his father had sent someone out here to make it.

He bent to take a closer look, saw another print and then another before they disappeared in front of a rock where the cat must have jumped. Shit. A prickle of unease skittered up his spine. Calum took out his phone and called Pete.

"I found a set of prints. Less than hundred yards from where we parked."

"Fresh?"

Not that Calum was an expert but—yeah, they did look fresh. "Think so."

"Wait there. I'll call Gunner. Keep your eyes peeled."

No kidding. But before Calum could turn, he heard a hiss behind him and it wasn't a snake. He faced the noise. He couldn't see anything, but that didn't mean the cat wasn't there. Calum's heart surged up to block his throat and his spine prickled as if he'd backed into a sharp bush. The desire to flee grew alongside his need to piss. The knowledge that running was the wrong thing to do plus the fact that his knees shook were the only things that kept Calum standing where he was.

He risked a quick dip to grab a couple of rocks and then straightened, raised his arms and yelled, "Scat, pussy. Get out of here."

Calum kept looking round, trying to catch sight of it. Mountain lions usually backed down from confrontation. They liked to approach from above and behind but once their cover was blown, they'd lost their advantage. At least that's what he'd read. Calum kept yelling and made himself look as big as possible as he reversed in the direction of the Jeep. *Shit, I hope the cat hasn't circled around behind.* Wrong time to think about that scene in Jurassic Park.

Toby's barking grew louder. Maybe that was enough to scare the thing into fleeing. Then there was a blur of movement at the periphery of his vision and Calum saw the cat standing no more than ten feet away, its tawny color blending with the rock. *Oh fuck. Don't run.* How far could they jump? Maybe it was just as well he couldn't remember. He yelled louder, threw the rocks, missed with both, *crap*, and the cat flashed him a contemptuous look. *Don't run.* Calum rushed forward, arms out, fists clenched and screamed, "You want to fight, you fucker? If you think I'm going down, you bastard, you've another think coming."

Instead of running, the cat jumped. *Oh shit.* Calum didn't have time to be frightened, he thrust out his fist and connected with its jaw as a paw swiped at his shoulder. He felt as if he'd thumped a truck and then been run over by it. As Calum tumbled to the ground, the lion on top, he just had time to consider that maybe he wouldn't survive this encounter before a shot rang out. He could swear the bullet parted his hair. *Jesus.* The mountain lion bounded away and Toby jumped over Calum to dash after it.

"Toby, get back here!" Pete shouted and then turned to Calum. "You okay?"

"What the hell were you aiming at?" Gunner gasped from the other side of the clearing.

Calum levered himself upright and stood.

"Are you okay?" Gunner asked. "Jesus, Calum. You thumped it."

"I'm fine. Don't fuss." Except his knees were still shaking and the contents of his stomach were trying to emulate Houdini. He glowered at Pete. "You nearly shot me."

"But I didn't."

"There's no need to look so fucking disappointed," Calum snapped.

Pete stepped right into his face. "Don't be such a dickwad."

"Cut it out." Gunner nodded toward Calum's shoulder.

Calum tugged at his shirt to find the material ripped and wet. He felt pain then when he hadn't before, but the claw marks were little more than deep scratches.

"Up to date on tetanus?" Gunner asked.

"Yeah."

"Let's get back to the Jeep," Gunner said. "I'll clean that up."

Calum fell into step beside him, wondering if the cat was watching.

"I'll bring a couple wranglers out here tomorrow morning and look for it," Pete said. "Means a change of venue for the campsite."

"Reckon Black Ridge will do?" Gunner asked.

It lay on the other side of the Neilson spread.

"Yep." Pete strode on ahead, Toby at his heels.

"You did well there," Gunner said. "Remembered not to run or curl up in a ball."

"I was too scared."

"Like hell you were. You did exactly the right thing. Pete did the wrong thing in splitting us up, particularly when you had no rifle. We should have walked the circle together. Thin line between everything being okay and you ending up as cat food."

Oh Christ.

"Feel that bullet whizz past your head?" Gunner whispered.

"Yep."

Gunner caught his arm. "Watch your step with Pete." He kept his voice low.

Back at the Jeep, Calum stripped off his shirt and winced. There were three long scratches on the front of his shoulder. He was really lucky they weren't deep. He must have shoved the cat back when he'd thumped it, only a fraction, but enough to reduce the impact of the claws.

Gunner held Calum's bunched-up shirt under the wounds and poured water over them. Calum gritted his teeth.

By the time Gunner had cleaned him up and slapped a dressing on, Calum ached from head to foot. At least they could go back to the ranch now. They wouldn't let him in a restaurant without a shirt.

"There's a shirt in the back you can wear," Pete said.

Shit.

"I'm not missing out on ribs because you got sideswiped by a lion." Pete grinned.

"We might even get a free meal out of it," Gunner said.

Jasper missed the evening meal again, but this time by design. He just couldn't face everyone, particularly if the word had spread that he was a sexual predator. Vera might be on his side, but Erik wanted to think the worst and Jasper had yet to hear from Calum. While he waited and hoped, he answered emails, sent instructions to a colleague regarding a couple of clients, read a boring report about the markets and eventually Googled laminitis and found an article on a treatment using stem cells. He wasn't supposed to be interested in stuff like that anymore, but Jasper couldn't turn off the tap.

Pulled out of his room by hunger, he bypassed the lounge and headed for the kitchen. Relieved to find it empty, he opened the fridge and hesitated when he saw the sandwich and bottle of water. Made for him, no doubt, but after the last sandwich he wasn't sure if he wanted to risk eating it.

"What are you doing?"

Jasper turned to find Ring scowling at him.

"Getting a sandwich." Jasper grabbed it and the water and closed the fridge door.

"Think people were going to call you names at dinner?" the wrangler snarled.

"What? Like hero?"

"More like pedo."

"Fuckwit," Jasper muttered.

Ring clenched his fists and Jasper smiled. "Go on. Hit me. I dare you. I'll slap you with a lawsuit."

Jasper hoped he sounded braver than he felt.

"You won't be smiling soon," Ring sneered.

He walked off and Jasper went back to his room to slump on the bed. Why wouldn't he be smiling soon? Had that been just a throwaway line or did it mean something?

Jasper's stomach rumbled. He unwrapped the sandwich and as he was about to bite into it, realized what he was doing and opened it up to look inside. Beef, lettuce, pickle, tomato and mayonnaise. It looked okay and smelt fine, but Jasper only ate half.

Ten minutes later, he was vomiting into the toilet. *Oh Christ.* Angie was deliberately trying to make him ill. Or force him to leave. Jasper let out a choked groan. Though it didn't have to be Angie. *Fucking Ring?*

He crawled across the bathroom floor and sat leaning against the wall clutching his stomach. This was shaping up to be the craziest day ever. And it wasn't over yet. Once his heart slowed and his breathing eased, Jasper pushed himself up. He cleaned his teeth and drank water from the tap. The seal on the bottle appeared intact but he wasn't going to risk it. He dropped the rest of the sandwich in the waste bin and lay on his bed.

Was it crazy to think someone was trying to poison him? More likely to be an accident, some contaminated food. The mayonnaise? Should he tell Vera? Maybe Angie didn't realize she was using something that had gone off. Perversely, if others had been sick too, Jasper would feel better. One half of his head told him to say nothing, the other half persuaded him Vera ought to know.

Jasper smartened himself up before he left his room. He found everyone sitting in the lounge. All the furniture was large and looked comfortable, a mismatch of sofas and chairs with lots of cushions. They'd gathered to watch an elderly guy and a young woman, both dressed in Native American clothing, make arrows and thread beads.

There was no sign of Calum. Angie sat at a table sorting different colored feathers with Vera close by. Jasper waited for an opportunity to catch Vera on her own and then wasn't sure how to start the conversation.

"I wondered…um…the sandwich left in the fridge." A sudden thought struck him. "It was for me?"

"Yes."

"Did Angie make it?"

Vera frowned. "Yes. Why?"

Jasper lowered his voice. "I just ate half of it and it made me sick. It's happened before."

He could almost see Vera prickle.

"Something you're allergic to?" she asked.

"Not that I'm aware of. I wondered…"

"What?" she snapped.

Jasper changed his mind. Vera had been on his side and he was about to lose her as an ally. "Doesn't matter. Probably me. Jet lag." *Christ, if I blame anything else on jet lag, I'll never fly again.*

Vera gave him a steely glare. "If you have a problem with the sandwiches my daughter made, I suggest you make more effort to dine with everyone else."

"Of course, you're right. I'm sorry."

He looked up at the sudden lull in the buzz of conversation. Calum strolled in with Pete and Gunner. Jasper heard the sigh escape from his mouth and clamped his lips together. One glance from Calum and Jasper's ears burned. He forced himself to look away before his cock began to behave badly.

Jasper managed no more than a couple of seconds staring at the wall before Calum drew his gaze again. When he looked at the cowboy, somehow everything that held Jasper balanced tipped and slid beyond reach. His life in London was ordered and safe. Calum made him do reckless things like take off his clothes and fuck in a wood then jump in a waterfall. And he loved that. *Oh fuck.* Jasper wanted to walk across the room, pull him into his arms and kiss him. Only that was the last thing Calum needed. The cowboy had told him people here kept their differences to themselves.

I'm different and I'm not ashamed of it. Except Jasper didn't know who he was anymore. Working a job he hated, with a mother he could hardly bear to visit, lonely, hoping for something to happen, and now it had, he couldn't keep it.

"A lion?" Janie squeaked.

What? Jasper tuned back in.

Erik rushed over to his son, Vera on his heels. Erik actually looked concerned, as though he wanted to give Calum a hug. Maybe there was hope for the two of them, especially if Jasper left.

While Jasper listened to the story, he felt his heart pounding all over his body. Calum caught his eye and shot him a little smile. *The idiot is smiling?* Jasper wanted to kill him. Kiss him and then kill him. *Oh Christ.*

"Which is why we tell you not to go off on your own," Erik said and looked round pointedly at the guests. "This is dangerous country." His gaze lingered on Jasper. Of course Erik would be delighted if he became cat food.

"What should we do if we come face-to-face with a mountain lion?" Melissa asked.

"Just what Calum did," Gunner said. "Make a lot of noise."

She wouldn't find that a problem.

"I can do that," Melissa said with a laugh.

"Running is the worst thing to do," Gunner said. "Calum not only stayed where he was, he fought back. He smacked that f— 'Scuse me...the lion in the jaw."

Jasper thought his heart had stopped. Bloody hell. The lion would have eaten Jasper before he'd thought of doing that.

"I can't believe you did that." Vera stared wide-eyed at Calum.

"You're not supposed to play dead?" asked Matt.

"Lions aren't like bears," Erik said. "Play dead and they'll eat you. But the chances of getting attacked are small. Cats would rather run away. Best thing to do is make yourself look as big as you can and make as much noise as you can. Wave your arms in the air and yell. That way you won't look like prey."

"Just an idiot," Calum muttered.

Everyone laughed. Jasper didn't. Calum could have died. He felt like there'd been a sea change inside him, a movement from lust to something much deeper. The thought that the guy standing feet from him, the guy he yearned to pull into his arms and hug, could have been killed, shocked Jasper to the core. When Ben had his accident, it had been a lesson in how short life could be, how everything could change forever in an instant, how you had to seize the moment—and yet Jasper still hadn't.

Had he learned nothing?

Note to self: Be a bigger man. Don't run away from what you want.

Chapter Ten

While everyone crowded around Calum, Jasper hung back. He saw pride in Erik's eyes and hoped Calum could too. Jasper thought of his own father and a bubble of pain burst in his chest. Nothing could be put right there, but Calum still had a chance.

"It was a crap idea anyway," came a whisper from nearby. "Mine was better."

Jasper froze.

"Leaving the meat worked, but how was I to know Gunner would tag along?" That sounded like Pete.

Jasper moved nearer to the voices, which were coming from the side of the fireplace, and knocked into a coffee table making it scrape across the floor. Pete and Ring emerged.

"Cocksucker," Pete muttered and pushed past Jasper.

"If a mountain lion had come anywhere near you, you'd have pissed your pants." Ring picked up a glass of soda from the table. "You fucking fag."

Jasper gasped as the liquid hit his groin.

"Oops. You just did." Ring sniggered.

Jasper shivered as cold soda soaked through his chinos. "What the hell are you playing at?"

Ring laughed and moved away with Pete. Jasper was about to go after them and then noticed Erik ruffle Calum's hair. No one had seen what Ring had done. This wasn't the time to cause a scene, not when Calum was the man of the moment. Jasper grabbed a newspaper from a coffee table to hold over his groin and left.

As he approached his room, Jasper tensed. He hadn't left his door ajar. *That bloody lock. Or is someone in there?* His spirits sank even lower. This vacation was becoming more stressful than his job. Hoping to catch the intruder in the act, he pushed the door fully open and stalked in. Bessie lay on the floor, shaking and drooling.

"Bessie?"

She showed no reaction to Jasper's voice. He tried to get her to stand and it was clear she couldn't. Jasper checked her gums and then groaned as his gaze caught the upturned waste bin. "Oh fuck it."

The dog had eaten the other half of the sandwich. Jasper scooped her into his arms and ran back to the lounge. He burst in and shouted, "First-aid kit."

"Kitchen." Vera turned and ran.

Jasper bolted after her, Calum at his heels.

"What the hell's the matter?" Calum asked.

"Bessie's been poisoned."

Calum gasped. "What?"

Jasper laid her on the kitchen floor and Calum dropped to his knees at her side.

"Hey, Bess, what you been up to?" Calum stroked her head. He looked up at Jasper. "Poisoned? What's she eaten?"

"I don't know exactly." Jasper took the red first-aid box from Vera and opened it on the floor. He was relieved to see a bottle of three-percent hydrogen peroxide. "Spoon," he snapped.

Calum caught his arm. "If it's something caustic, we shouldn't be making her vomit."

"It isn't caustic." Jasper poured out a spoonful of the chemical. "Hold her mouth open."

"You said you didn't know what it was. How can you be sure it isn't dangerous to make her vomit?" Calum asked.

"Because I ate it too. Now hold open her mouth."

Calum gaped at him, but grasped Bessie's jaw and Jasper spooned in the liquid.

"What happened to your pants?" Calum asked.

"Ring threw a drink at me." And now Jasper wondered if it had been done to make him go back to his room to find Bessie. Did Ring want him blamed for her death? *Oh fuck.*

"Should we call the vet?" Vera asked.

"If the first dose doesn't work, we can try another, but by the time a vet gets here..." Jasper quieted.

Calum held Bessie's paw and stroked her head. "Come on, girl."

The dog convulsed and then made the noise Jasper had been hoping for and she threw up. By the time she'd emptied her stomach, she was just about standing on her own and trying to wag her tail. Vera bent to clean up the mess and her gaze locked with Jasper's.

"I'm sorry," she whispered.

It was obvious what the dog had thrown up.

"She ate the other half of my sandwich," Jasper said to Calum in a quiet voice.

Calum gaped. "What?"

"Anyone could have tampered with it," Jasper said. "It wasn't necessarily—"

"Will you let me deal with it?" Vera chewed her lip.

Jasper nodded.

She shot him a look of gratitude. "Thank you."

"Is someone going to explain what's going on?" Calum asked.

"I'll look after Bessie. Go and talk to each other." Vera gave Calum a push. "If I need you, I'll call."

"The stables," Calum muttered. "I'll be there in five."

Jasper turned to Vera. "Might I have a piece of fruit?"

"I could make you a sandwich." Then she winced.

"An apple would be fine," Jasper said.

Calum tossed him one.

Jasper returned to his room and stripped off his wet pants and shorts. He wondered if there was some way to do laundry.

He was running out of clean clothes. He reached for a pair of boxers then smiled and left them where they were. Even as he pulled on a pair of chinos, his cock was swelling.

When he stepped outside, Jasper shivered, but he couldn't be bothered to go back and get a sweater. He hoped Calum planned to warm him up. It was a clear night, starry curtains hanging over the mountains, the Milky Way sprawling like a splatter of paint across the heavens. Wrapped up in something warm, Jasper could have lay on his back and looked at them for hours, particularly if Calum was by his side. He took a bite of apple and trudged over to the barn.

He slid the large door across the track far enough for him to slip inside and was hit at once by the scent of horses, hay and leather. Jasper had been a little surprised he'd not had a problem yet with his breathing. Maybe it was only London traffic fumes that choked him.

There were a couple of dim fluorescent lights on in the building. Jasper walked down the line of stalls past the shuffling horses. Star whinnied a greeting and Jasper stroked her neck. He gave pieces of apple to Star and Xander and gave the rest to Spider. It disappeared in a flash.

"We friends again?"

Spider nudged his shoulder.

"No more apples, sorry."

The horse snorted. Jasper turned at the sound of the barn door opening and sighed when he saw Calum. They needed to talk but Jasper needed more to be held. He walked back and Calum unlocked the tack room. He flicked on the light as Jasper stepped inside, and then reached behind him to close the door and lock it. Calum took out the key and put it in his pocket.

"Are you okay?" Jasper asked.

"I am now." Calum stepped forward and kissed his neck—slow, soft presses with soft lips that made Jasper's cock jump in his pants like a Mexican bean as it tried to grow against the stricture of the material.

"This first, talk later." Calum kissed his way to Jasper's mouth and back-walked him to the wall where reins and bridles hung. They jingled as Jasper hit them. "You taste like apple."

Jasper slid his hands around Calum's waist, fingers tugging at his shirt until he could touch bare flesh. As he spread his hands over the warm skin of Calum's lower back, pressing his fingers into the dips either side of his spine, Jasper let out a deep sigh. An ache bloomed in his chest. This might only be lust, but it still hurt to want someone so much.

Calum's tongue slithered along Jasper's teeth, paused to curl around his canine and then plunged deep. Jasper let him have his fill and when Calum pulled back to breathe, Jasper took over, his tongue sliding into a moist, warm mouth as he threaded his fingers in Calum's hair. Their hips rolled and rubbed together, Calum pressing him to the wall with the full length of his body.

Jasper sucked Calum's tongue between his teeth and sucked a groan out of him too. They both trembled as the kiss deepened until they were eating at each other more greedily. Jasper blazed with heat as if he'd been lying in the sun. His hips danced a duet with his tongue and the hard thickness of Calum's cock seemed intensified by the one less item of clothing between them.

"Shit," Calum gasped and pressed his forehead to Jasper's for a moment before he straightened and stared him in the face. "Want to fuck you."

Seemed obvious they weren't playing turns, but Jasper felt a pang of disappointment as his earlier thought appeared confirmed. Calum didn't want to bottom, but Jasper wasn't that easy.

"Beg me," Jasper whispered.

"What?"

"You heard."

Calum jerked away. "Fuck you. I'm not begging."

Jasper began to unbutton his shirt, all the time maintaining eye contact with Calum. Away from the heat of the cowboy's body, Jasper shivered in the chill air as he tossed his shirt onto the workbench. Calum's gaze was glued to Jasper's tight nipples.

"Beg me," Jasper repeated, hoping Calum would play.

"Make me."

Jasper smiled. He reached for a horse blanket from a shelf and threw it on the floor. Then he kicked off his shoes and stood on it. Calum's hand massaged his crotch as he watched. Jasper slid open the button on his pants and then eased down the zipper a little way, enough to make his point.

"You fucker," Calum growled. "No shorts?"

Jasper played with the tab of his zipper, twisting it in his fingers.

"Take your pants off," Calum snapped.

"Say please."

Calum laughed. He dropped to his knees and, grabbing Jasper around the hips, he pulled him against his face.

"Please," he mumbled into the part-open V of Jasper's pants.

Calum pulled the zipper the rest of the way down and then carefully extricated Jasper's cock and balls. Jasper looked down at his cock, tip glistening, rearing dark and hard against his belly—Calum's mouth inches away.

"Beg me to fuck you." Calum breathed on the wet crest of his cock.

Aggravation warred with the tingle in Jasper's balls, but he groaned, "No."

It was *his* game, not Calum's, but then Calum's warm, wet mouth closed around the tip of his shaft and Jasper's head fogged. He leaned back against the leather straps, the buckles and snaps digging into his skin, and the discomfort helped him focus. He wouldn't beg. But Calum tightened his mouth, made a vacuum with his lips as he sucked and Jasper was lost again.

Calum's tongue delved into the slit at the head of his cock, and Jasper heard a keening noise. He realized with a touch of embarrassment that the sound had come from him. A bloody whimper. Even worse, he did it again. He couldn't stop the noises coming out of him. Every time Calum sucked, Jasper gasped or groaned or moaned or did something in between.

When Calum lifted his mouth from Jasper's cock, looked up at him and licked his lips, Jasper sucked in a breath. *Oh God, I can't deny him anything.* Calum's tongue shot out to flick the head of his cock, glistening with spit and pre-come, and Jasper's toes curled on the blanket. Calum lifted Jasper's feet one after the other to take off his pants and then stood and tossed them onto his shirt. Jasper was hugely turned on by the fact that he stood there buck naked while Calum was still dressed.

"You have to choose now," Calum said.

"Choose what?"

"Whether you want me to suck you off or fuck you."

"Can't I have both?"

Calum shook his head. "Depends whether you want to…fuck me."

Jasper was relieved to have a wall to lean against, but he heard the hitch in Calum's voice and knew there was an issue.

"I have some rules," Calum said and leaned forward to puff hot air over Jasper's neck.

Jasper prepared his answers. Yes, he'd wear a condom. Yes, he'd be careful. They'd be swimming in lube. Yes, he'd beg. Damn it.

"If I fuck you," Calum said, "you can't come. You have to wait." His hot tongue flicked along the line of Jasper's chin.

"Define wait."

Calum laughed and nipped the lobe of Jasper's ear. Jasper shuddered. His chance of not coming with Calum's cock in his ass was low. His chance of getting inside Calum's ass before he came all over his butt was low. If he got inside, and moved at all, even one slide, odds he'd not come were zero.

"Don't take your clothes off," Jasper whispered. Maybe that'd help him last longer.

Calum's zipper sounded over-loud in the room. Strong hands gripped Jasper by the shoulders and turned him to face the wall.

"Oh Christ," Calum muttered. "You look...fucking fantastic."

Jasper pressed his palms flat on the wooden wall, a horse's bridle rubbing against his cheek, reins digging into his chest. How the hell was he not going to come? Even the sound of Calum's Western drawl excited him. Calum stepped closer so he leaned against Jasper's back. He nudged his cock into the crease of Jasper's butt and then bit his shoulder.

"I'm going to fuck you right through the wall," Calum growled.

Jasper made that pathetic noise again, wished he could blame it on a mouse, and then let his forehead rest against the hanging leather.

Lube-slick fingers took the place of Calum's cock, sliding down the crease of his butt, homing in on Jasper's puckered asshole and coating it with moisture.

"Fuck you right through the wall and into the horse's stall on the other side," Calum spat the words against Jasper's neck.

Jasper exhaled at the burn of the thick finger pushing inside him. Calum's arm slid around his waist and grabbed Jasper's cock.

"Oh God. You can't do that and expect me not to come." But Jasper wasn't sure he cared anymore. He'd forgotten the rules of the game—if there'd been any. All he could think about was the climax brewing in his body, a seismic shift waiting to happen. One perfect touch, two surfaces slipping against each other and he'd shatter. Calum pumped his cock in smooth, hard strokes in time with his finger spearing Jasper's anus.

"Not fair," Jasper blurted.

"Is that right? You should have made conditions. You can't come until I have."

"Take your hand off my cock."

"Too late now and you don't mean it anyway."

Jasper could feel his chance to fuck Calum slipping away.

"Beg me to stop," Calum whispered in his ear.

Jasper let out a strangled laugh. "Please." Calum could take that anyway he liked.

Calum pulled away and the coolness of the tack room washed over Jasper's sweaty back to raise goose bumps. He heard the sound of ripping, the snap of latex and then Calum was back. Well part of him, his thick shaft sliding along the cleft of Jasper's butt. Warm hands spread his cheeks, and when the rounded head nestled against his hole, Jasper tensed.

"Okay?" Calum's fingers stroked his hips as he rubbed his mouth over Jasper's shoulder.

"I can't speak *and* fuck. Oh and not come. I'd forgotten about that."

Calum pressed harder with his cock, and Jasper concentrated on relaxing into the intrusion, willing his muscles to allow Calum in. Fingers tightened on his hips as the pressure on his anus grew more firm. It seemed to Jasper as though his senses were heightened—the slightly rough feel of Calum's fingers, the hardness of his cock, the softness of his shirt and worn jeans, the way his breath stuttered against Jasper's neck. So much for thinking Calum staying dressed would help.

Jasper bore down, braced for the bite of pain when Calum's cock pushed through, knowing the pleasure that would follow. The ring of resistant muscle flexed and Calum kept pushing, stretching Jasper's passage until he was buried deep.

"Oh God," Calum gasped.

Jasper's toes were curled again while his fingers pressed hard at the boards of the wall. If Calum left his cock alone, he had a vague chance of not coming. Then Calum pulled back and made his first drive into him and Jasper knew he had no chance at all. He might as well just enjoy it. He flexed his hips back into Calum's thrust and spread his legs wider.

"This feels so good," Calum whispered. "Christ, you're so sexy."

His head dropped to Jasper's shoulder and he rested his face there as he moved faster, lunging into Jasper's ass. When Calum changed the angle of his thrusts and his cock brushed Jasper's prostate, Jasper let out a long exclamation—part cry, part moan.

"Yeah, yeah," Calum panted.

Jasper stopped thinking about *not* coming and threw his hips back harder against Calum, clenching his muscles around the thick cock. Jasper wanted to be fucked hard. He could feel his ass burning as Calum thrust deep, shoving him forward so his face scraped against the horses' leathers. Calum inhaled with every withdrawal, grunted with every lunge and rode Jasper faster and faster.

"Fuck, fuck, fuck," Calum gasped. "Close. Ah fuuuck."

The movements of Calum's cock grew choppier as he drove into Jasper in short, hard jabs that made Jasper's legs tremble. Electric shivers raced up and down his spine until his entire body was quaking. Calum bit down on Jasper's shoulder and he felt the guy's cock swell. When Jasper's balls tingled, he gritted his teeth. He'd lasted this long, he didn't want to lose it now.

"Yes, yes, yes, yes," Calum rammed up hard against him and tucked his arms under Jasper's to pull him upright.

Jasper felt the cock inside him pulse, and then Calum let out a long sigh and melted against him. Jasper tipped his head back and turned to find Calum's mouth. The kiss was long and slow. Calum's rough palms rubbed Jasper's nipples and then one hand slid down his stomach to his cock. Jasper knocked his fingers away.

"You know what happens when you shake a can of soda before you rip off the tab?" Jasper asked.

Calum pulled out of his ass. "You didn't come."

Jasper turned to face him. "Good God, didn't I? I hadn't noticed."

Calum burst out laughing. He wrapped the used condom in a tissue and then tucked himself back in his pants and zipped up. *Ah. So I don't get to fuck him.* Jasper reached up with one hand for the rail behind him and gripped tight.

"I'd like to paint you looking like that," Calum blurted.

"That'd be one to hang on the wall and frighten small children and dogs."

"No, your face, the expression on it."

"Pain?" Jasper smiled. "Frustration?"

Calum leaned against the workbench. "Need. Anticipation. Desire. L—lust."

"Are you going to put me out of my misery?"

"If you ask nicely."

"Bastard."

Calum raised his eyebrows.

"Fucking bastard," Jasper said.

"That's better." Calum dropped to his knees in front of Jasper and swallowed his cock.

Jasper stopped breathing and his knees turned to jelly. Caught in the grip of an orgasm so powerful it neared the point of pain, his balls exploded and come flooded up his cock and splashed into Calum's mouth. Jasper threaded his fingers in Calum's hair, as if that would keep him upright. Air rushed back into his lungs and he let out a choked groan.

Calum licked him clean, and then kissed his way to Jasper's mouth. "Now, we talk," he said.

Jasper dressed as he went over what had happened, trying to make sure he missed nothing including the conversation he'd overheard between Pete and Ring, and Erik's reaction to finding Angie half-naked in the pool.

"You think Angie poisoned the sandwich?" Calum asked, the disbelief clear in his voice.

"No. Maybe it was Ring. He knew I'd have to go back to my room after he threw the drink on my crotch. But how did he know I'd left half the sandwich? Why would he want to hurt Bessie?"

Jasper perched next to Calum on the workbench, their knees just touching.

"On the other hand, it could all be coincidence," Jasper said. "Some ingredient gone off that so far has only been used to make me something to eat. I noticed the lock on my door isn't working right. Bessie might have nudged it open and then found the sandwich in the wastebin. Pure chance."

"I don't think Angie would know *how* to poison anyone and she certainly wouldn't hurt Bessie."

"So what did Pete and Ring mean about their idea working if Gunner hadn't tagged along? And leaving meat? Had they deliberately drawn the lion to that place?"

"That's pretty fucked up if they did."

"Maybe it's all focused on persuading me to leave. Don't have a homicidal ex lurking anywhere?" Jasper smiled and then groaned. "Ah shit, I forgot to ask you about the mountain lion. Are you okay?"

"Yep, lucky it didn't swallow."

Jasper's burst of laughter was broken by the sound a key turning in the lock. Calum hopped to his feet as his father walked in. *Shit.* Jasper wrapped his fingers around the tissue-covered condom and slipped it into his back pocket as he pushed himself off the bench.

"What's going on?" Erik demanded.

"We've been talking," Calum snapped.

Erik's snort showed what he thought of that. Jasper thought about saying something and changed his mind. It wasn't his place. Nor his fight. Then Erik turned to glare at him. Maybe it *was* his fight.

"You think if you accuse my daughter of trying to poison you that it'll deflect attention from what you're really up to?"

Oh Christ. "I—"

"Angie wouldn't hurt a fly," Erik barked. "She wouldn't know how to poison a sandwich. You would—though you wouldn't need to. You can pretend it's made you sick then feed half of it to Calum's dog to prove it. What did you give Bessie to make her fit like that? Chocolate? Anyway, you make sure *you* save the dog and suddenly you're a hero. First on the plane then at the pool, now with the dog. Makes me wonder how Angie got into trouble in the water in the first place."

Jasper was too flabbergasted to speak. He glanced at Calum, but his lips were pressed in a tight line.

"You know what I think?" Erik looked Jasper up and down. "I think you're some sick fuck who gets off on the idea of being a hero." He strode across the tack room to stand right in front of Jasper. "Stay away from my son. Stay away from my daughter. Stay off my fucking radar. That was your final warning."

Jasper was desperate to hear Calum stand up for him, but he said nothing, and that hurt. When Jasper glanced at him, his face was blank as he stared at his boots. Was he wondering if his father was right? That Jasper had somehow engineered all this?

"You're wrong," Jasper said. "I haven't lied. But I'm not a hero. I'm just a guy who works long hours who wanted to come to terms with riding again and do it under wide blue skies. Except it turns out Wyoming's not so beautiful under the surface." He looked from Erik to Calum. "I've done nothing to be ashamed of. I've never intentionally hurt anyone, man or animal. If I hadn't returned to my room when I did, Bessie could have died. Maybe you'd better start thinking about who on this ranch would benefit from causing trouble."

"That's crap," Erik snapped. He turned to Calum. "Not hard to guess what you two have been up to in here. I can smell it. I can't believe you let this guy stick his cock up your ass."

"I didn't," Calum blurted.

Oh God, this is over.

"I hope you used protection," Erik snarled. "Christ knows where this dude's been."

Jasper's gut bubbled with fury, anxiety and deep sadness. "I feel sorry for you," he said, the message for both Calum and his father, though Jasper was addressing Erik. "You have so much and you're too blind to see it."

He walked out.

Note to self: Cancel thought about not running. It's time to leave.

Chapter Eleven

Calum started to follow Jasper but his father pulled him back.

"I want to speak to him." Calum jerked free of his grasp.

"Please, Son, think. You don't need this sort of complication. The guy's leaving in a couple of days. Sooner if I have my way."

Calum bristled.

His father sighed and lowered his voice. "He's not good for you. You were just getting better and—"

"Getting better?" Calum gaped. "I'm not fucking ill. I'm attracted to men not women. There's nothing you can do to change that, though Christ knows you've tried hard enough."

His father's jaw tensed but now Calum had started, he didn't want to stop. He'd just stood there and let Jasper be insulted while he felt everything bubble up inside him until the dam finally burst.

"Being gay doesn't make me any less of a man. Makes no difference to the way I do my job. If people choose to treat me differently, then that's their problem."

"The wranglers don't respect you."

"And whose fault is that?" Calum snapped. "If you don't show me respect, then why should they? You made Pete foreman when it should have been me, and Pete hates my guts. Ring's the same. I get the shittiest jobs and I never complain. I work harder and longer than any other wrangler and I never say a word. When I find something that makes me happy, can you blame me for wanting to make the most of it?"

Shut up, shut up. I'll make him explode.

Erik stepped into his face. "You weren't ready to be foreman. The wranglers wouldn't have listened to you."

The words readied to spill out. Calum couldn't stop them. "How do you know? You never gave them the chance. You made me look the lesser man because you chose Pete over your son. I know this ranch inside out. My mother gave birth to me here, but guess what? I hate the damn place as much as I love it because it's turned into a fucking prison."

Calum reached for the door and Erik thrust out his hand and stopped it from opening.

"You ungrateful little shit. Everything I've done, I've done for you." His father spat out the words.

"And Angie," Calum barked.

"Yes. She's as much my daughter as you are my son, and for all her problems, a lot less damn trouble."

"You have it all planned out, don't you? What are you and Vera going to do? Retire to Florida in a few years and leave Pete to run this place, with me doing whatever he says and Angie hanging on my heels?"

"Forget Pete. Angie's always going to need looking after."

"I know that, but I also know you don't encourage her to look after herself." Calum felt as though there were another person inside him who'd finally burst out of a cage. He knew he should shut up but he couldn't. "When she wanted to go and stay with that friend she made at school, you said no. When she was asked out by that boy who was a touch slow like her, you said no. She doesn't have any friends outside the ranch."

"I'm protecting her."

"You're controlling her, just like you do me."

"I'm doing what's best," Erik barked, his face reddening. "What the hell do you think a man like him wants with a guy like you whose major skill is throwing peanuts up in the air and catching them with your mouth?"

Calum bristled. "He likes me just as I am."

"Doesn't matter what the bastard likes. You can't go to London. He's not welcome here. There's no future in this. Give it up."

Calum yanked open the tack room door and stalked out. He knew his father was right about one thing. It ended between him and Jasper in a couple of days. But every time he touched Jasper, he wanted him more. Calum was making things more difficult by fucking him and he'd moved beyond lust into much more dangerous territory. The guy made him hard, made him laugh, made him come so violently, his heart ached. Right this moment, all Calum could think was how wonderful it would be to walk into Jasper's room and fuck him again.

Only at some point, Jasper would want to fuck him back, and Calum wasn't sure he could let that happen. He'd deflected the issue tonight, partly through the arrival of his father. Until Calum got his head round this...fear, he had to stay away from Jasper because if Jasper tried to fuck him and Calum freaked, it would definitely be over before Jasper even got back on that plane.

Jasper could no longer blame jet lag for his sleepless night. He'd lain half-awake and hungry for more than food. He'd been waiting for Calum's knock and it never came. He wanted to know why Calum hadn't defended him. Now it was morning and Jasper couldn't help but wonder if Calum believed his father about that hero crap. Hard to conceive Jasper had ever thought his life boring. He'd never had so much happen in so short a time.

One thing was certain—forget the overnight trip. Jasper didn't want to put his feet into a sleeping bag into which someone had stuffed a rattler. His inclination was to revert to plan B and go to Yellowstone in a rental car—with or without Calum.

He suspected he was reading too much into what was going on between them. They were bad for each other. *Oh Christ and yet so right.* But there was no point prolonging it. *This* was why

Jasper had never had a boyfriend who lasted more than a couple of weeks. If there was ever any of depth to the attraction, it was always one-sided. He'd not yet found that elusive balance. Maybe until now.

Fuck it, fuck it, fuck it. He dragged his fingers through his hair. Thinking too much was going to drive him crazy.

A stomach growling with hunger pulled him to breakfast. He stuck to food others were eating and sat by Matt and Paul who had large steaks on their plates. Jasper had never thought of eating steak for breakfast.

"Got your appetite back?" Paul nodded at Jasper's plate.

"Yes, though not enough to eat what you're having. It's not my sort of thing."

Matt smirked. "Yeah, well we all know what your sort of thing is."

Jasper bristled. *Oh great.*

"Different sort of meat," Paul said and laughed. "You'd fit right in with my male models."

Jasper wished he was wandering around Pompeii. It would be a damn sight more interesting than listening to these two. All he'd achieved this holiday was overcoming his fear of getting on a horse, only instead of breaking his neck, he'd broken his heart. It was less painful to stay alone, and when he got desperate, find someone just as desperate, have a quick fuck in a pub toilet and then walk separate ways.

When he'd finished eating, he went back to his room and started to pack. Then he unpacked. Jasper gave a heavy sigh. He knew better than to run away from trouble. It doubled in size and came after you with sharper teeth. On the other hand, why stay and be miserable? He sat on the bed and put his head in his hands. Hesitation, indecision—how come he could be decisive in his business life and yet wallow like a wounded whale in his private life?

Someone knocked at the door and Jasper sprang up. It wasn't Calum and his shoulders slumped.

"Can I talk to you?" Vera asked.

"Come in. Better leave the door open, I don't want any more trouble."

Jasper gestured to a chair, and after Vera sat, he perched on the bed.

"I spoke to Angie—carefully—and I'm as certain as I can be that she didn't put anything in your sandwich to make you sick. She worships Bessie, who seems no worse for her ordeal, by the way. If Angie thought it was her fault the dog had been ill, I'd be able to tell."

"Right." *So long as the dog's okay, I don't matter.*

"Erik thinks you're making it all up."

Of course he does. Jasper's heart felt like it was being squeezed by an iron fist. "Why would I do that?"

"Seeking attention? Trying to get Calum to feel sorry for you?"

For fuck's sake. "To what end?"

"To have sex with you." Vera looked down and blushed. It was catching. Jasper's ears burned under his hair.

He took a deep breath. "I spent a lot of money on this holiday—vacation. I've traveled halfway around the world. So far, I've thrown up twice after I've eaten a sandwich made by your daughter. I saved her from drowning and your husband thinks I was molesting her. Spider almost threw me after a thorn was left—probably deliberately—under the saddle. I've had a drink chucked at my pants by one of your wranglers and I've put up with snide comments from the same wrangler as well as some of the guests. As far as your husband's concerned, I'm the son of Satan. It's not been the vacation—damn it—the word's holiday—I hoped for, though meeting Calum has been one of the highlights. But I know when I'm not welcome and I'm leaving as soon as I can arrange a hire car." *And spoken to Calum.*

Vera sighed. "I need to explain about Erik. He's worried that being gay will get Calum killed."

"Killed?" Jasper gaped at her.

"While Calum was at the University of Wyoming in Laramie, another student was robbed, tortured and left tied to a fence in a remote area. He died of his injuries. He'd been beaten beyond recognition and it was done because the boy was gay."

Oh my God. "Did Calum know him?"

Vera nodded. "Erik thought he could make Calum not be gay and he put him through a lot of—well, he can't accept it. I don't know if he ever will, and now both he and Calum are miserable. You've put a smile on Calum's face for the first time in a long while, but come Friday, you'll be gone and Calum will still be here."

"So you think I should leave." It wasn't a question.

"I can't tell you what to do. Part of me thinks now that you should go, but by being here you've given Calum courage to stand up to Erik. Judging by Erik's temper when he came to bed last night, he and Calum argued. I actually think that's a good thing. Calum needs to speak out for what he wants. But it's also a bad thing. Erik's already had one heart attack. He's on medication and we try to keep stress to the minimum. Calum blames himself for his father's ill health and I've watched him bite his tongue ever since."

Shit. So that was why Calum hadn't spoken out last night.

Vera gave him a tight smile.

"I'd better leave."

"Please speak to Calum before you go. Erik's sent him to take equipment out to the campsite. He should be back soon."

With nothing better to do until the cab arrived to take him to Jackson, and since he'd been warned they were short of drivers and it would be a three-hour wait, and because he didn't want to skulk in his room like a coward, Jasper went to the lasso demonstration. He leaned against the corral fence, watching a wrangler twirl a rope in the enclosure.

"Amazing how a piece of rope has the ladies so entranced," Gunner said at his elbow.

"Not so sure it's his rope they're looking at."

Gunner laughed. "Dean used to work here full time but he travels around demonstrating his skill with a lasso. Ring won't get a look in now with the rich girls."

Melissa and Janie sat on the top rail, clapping for Dean, and when Jasper looked at Ring, he was scowling at *him* as if it were his fault. *Fuckwit.*

Jasper hadn't realized so much could be done with a lasso. Dean flicked and spun it high, twirled it low and then made it dance somewhere in between. He jumped over, through and around the spinning rope in a whirl of continuous elegant motion. Even though this was a guy skipping, which didn't sound good in theory, in practice, Jasper was mesmerized. Dean made it look simple, so of course it wouldn't be.

After showing off on foot, Dean repeated some of it on horseback. He even stood on his saddle as his horse cantered and still roped his target. His exuberance reminded Jasper of Ben who always threw himself wholeheartedly into every activity, mostly without thinking.

Pete let seven calves into the corral and called, "Janie, which calf do you want Dean to catch?"

"That cute one with the white patch on his head. He's so sweet."

Gunner rolled his eyes. A moment later, the calf was roped and Dean was off his horse pinning the animal down. Jasper felt a rope being pushed into his back. Gunner was handing out lariats to everyone.

"We'll show you what to do," Ring said. "Then those brave enough can climb into the corral and try to rope a steer."

Wranglers had drifted out to watch and Jasper guessed this was a chance to laugh at the guests. Gunner pulled Jasper to one side.

"Hold the loop lightly in your right hand and coil the rest in your left. Okay? Leave about five feet of rope between the two." Gunner stood back and waited while Jasper sorted himself out.

"Now relax your wrist and swing the rope over your head, right to left. Keep going until it feels right."

Jasper was determined to do this.

"Once you have it in a nice spin, you need to throw the loop forward quickly. As you bring your wrist down to the level of your shoulder, swing the loop toward the target. The trick is to keep it smooth and straight. The stronger you throw, the farther it goes. Then pull on the length in your left hand to tighten the loop. Got that? Try and catch me."

Jasper had enough problems getting the rope to swing around his head let alone throw it at a target, but he waited and waited until it felt right and then released it like a slingshot. The rope flew through the air and settled around Gunner's shoulders. Jasper was so shocked he stood there gaping.

"Your calf's wriggled free because you didn't tighten the loop," Gunner said and pulled the rope off his head. "But that was pretty good for a first attempt."

A fluke. But it wasn't. Jasper roped Gunner the next three times despite him moving farther and farther away—though Jasper had done something like this before, just with less panache.

"I'd run so you could see what it's like to rope a calf, but I'd probably give myself a heart attack," Gunner said.

Jasper guessed Gunner wanted him to laugh, but since Vera had told him about Erik, Jasper didn't find the idea of a heart attack very funny. He practiced throwing the lasso over the fence posts. A couple of the guests seemed to be pretty good at it. Melissa and Janie were useless.

"Okay," Ring said. "Climb in when you're ready. Choose your calf and go for it."

Instant chaos. The calves ran all over the place pursued by rope-swinging idiots while the wranglers roared with laughter. Melissa and Janie squealed as they ran from the animals not toward them. Jasper kept his eye on a little brown calf and followed it, swinging the rope around his head. When he let the lasso go, it flew straight and true but another got there a fraction before his, knocking his rope aside. Jasper followed the lasso back to Ring and didn't miss the smirk on his face.

A rope smacked Jasper hard across his cheek, then something hit him behind the knees and the next moment he was eating dirt in the middle of a mini-stampede. Jasper gasped in pain as a hoof stomped on his lower back and he inhaled a lungful of dust. As he pushed himself to his feet, rubbing his eyes, Jasper began to cough and knew he was in trouble. Apart from the throbbing in his back, he had a tight ache in his chest and his breathing was short and shallow. *Oh fuck.* A lot of good his inhaler did in his room.

Jasper wasn't the type to panic but he was breathing way too fast in an attempt to get more oxygen. He hadn't had a full-blown asthma attack in months, and he put his hands on his thighs as he tried to slow his breathing. A rope landed around his neck, yanked tight and fear surged. Jasper wrenched it off, laughter ringing in his ears as he staggered to the side of the corral.

As he climbed the fence, Gunner came over to him. "You okay?"

He nodded and headed back toward the ranch. Jasper heard catcalling behind him, but he blanked his mind and kept going. He didn't have the breath to explain what was wrong and he doubted they'd care. Dry dirt under his feet, but he might as well have been wading through mud. What was no distance at all looked fucking miles. Why hadn't he brought his inhaler with him?

He was almost at the house, wheezing like an old man, when he heard Calum call.

"What's happening? Been running?"

Jasper forced out the word. "In...haler."

"In your room?" Calum snapped.

The relief that Calum understood allowed Jasper's focus to slip and he stumbled to his knees. "Bag. Bed."

"Hang on." Calum raced up the steps.

Jasper sat and leaned back on his elbows, trying to force himself to breathe more deeply. Clammy sweat beaded his brow and he felt chilled despite the strong afternoon sun. Bessie nuzzled and whined at his side, but he didn't have the strength to reassure her. He kept his eyes on a car moving toward the ranch, a cloud of dust billowing in its wake. *My taxi?* Calum would be back with his inhaler before the vehicle arrived. *Ten more seconds. Count.*

Calum jumped down the steps and pressed the inhaler into his hand. "I've been shaking it. The cap's off."

Jasper breathed out, put the mouthpiece between his lips and as he pressed down on the canister, he inhaled. He was supposed to hold his breath for ten seconds but barely managed five.

"Okay?" Calum asked as he dropped down to sit beside him.

Jasper nodded. He needed another dose but he had to wait. Calum's hand pressed on his lower back where he'd been kicked and Jasper flinched. Calum dragged his hand away and Jasper would have groaned if he had the energy.

He shook the inhaler again.

Calum rose to his feet. "Oh fuck it."

Breathe out. Press. Breathe in. Count. He only got as far as five before he had to breathe but panic stalled as the medication took effect and enlarged his airways. The car skidded to a halt and a woman in a tight dress emerged from the driver's side. Not the cab. Bessie growled.

"Bessie, quiet," Calum snapped and then turned to the redhead. "What the fuck are you doing here?"

"That's not a nice way to greet your wife."

No dust this time clogging Jasper's lungs, but shards of glass. *Wife?* He should've stayed where he was until he had his lungs under control, but that one word kicked Jasper to his feet. He staggered up the steps into the ranch.

What the fuck had Calum been playing at?

As he pushed open the door, he heard Angie yell, "Suz! Suz!" Jasper glanced back before he stepped inside and watched the attractive woman wrap her arms around Angie. His gaze drifted to Calum who stood with his shoulders down, his lips a tight line, dog at his side. *Oh fuck it, and I still fancy the idiot.* While Jasper paused, he hoped Calum would at least look at him, but the cowboy bolted toward the barn.

Jasper passed Vera on the way back to his room.

"You okay?" she asked.

Jasper nodded. He didn't have the energy to speak. He concentrated on walking in a straight line and once he was in his room with the door closed, the inhaler fell from his fingers and Jasper dropped to his knees. He rolled onto his back and flung his arm over his eyes. *Christ. Talk about everything being right and wrong at the same time.*

This was his fault. Partly. Messing around with a guy he knew virtually nothing about. Calum had asked if he was attached but Jasper hadn't asked him the same. He'd assumed. So was Calum bi? Jasper sighed. *Idiot.* Of course he was. *Did it matter?* It did if he had a wife.

He wished he could put the tight feeling in his chest down to the asthma attack, but he knew part of it was bitter disappointment. Those moments when he and Calum had held each other, kissed—Jasper had felt more alive than he had for years.

And that was all he was going to get.

He could hide in his room and nurse his broken heart while he waited for the cab or put a brave face on and go for a swim. At least that would help his asthma. Jasper stripped. His shirt and pants were filthy and he wasn't bothered. His indifference almost made him smile. Jasper washed his face and hands, pulled on his swimming trunks and slunk to the pool. The cab wouldn't leave without him.

The gentle exercise eased his chest, forcing his body into a pattern of regular breathing and he felt tension slide from his muscles. He didn't overdo it. Once he'd calmed down, he climbed out, and lay on a lounger facing the sun. The nagging ache in his lower back hadn't diminished. Impossible to get kicked by a cow, no matter how small, and not feel it.

"You're not his usual type," said a woman.

Not hard to guess who this was.

Kicked twice by a cow. But maybe he was being unfair. He didn't know this woman. Calum must have seen something in her to marry her. But the way things were going, he fully expected Suz to be wielding a knife. Bloody imagination. Now he *had* to open his eyes. She stood looking down at him. No knife. Her hands rested on her hips and a scowl twisted her pretty face.

"You're blocking my light," Jasper said and closed his eyes again.

He knew she'd moved because he felt the heat of the sun back on his face.

"Don't you want to know what his type is?" she asked.

No. Yes. Jasper kept his mouth shut.

"Blonder than him, smaller than him, younger than him."

If he couldn't even lie in the sun in peace, he'd sit in his room until the car came from Jackson.

"Leave him alone," Calum snapped.

Bloody hell, this is like a TV soap. Take one sulky woman. Add a pissed-off husband. Stir.

"Suz, I want you to come and see my necklaces. Please," Angie said.

Throw in a bewildered sister.

Jasper opened his eyes. He was surprised Suz let Angie pull her away. She went up slightly in his estimation. He rolled over and turned away from Calum.

Result—a wounded idiot.

"Christ," Calum whispered.

Rough fingers touched Jasper's lower back and he bit his lip.

"That's quite a hoof mark." Calum gently rubbed Jasper's upper back with his thumb. "Was the calf okay?"

Jasper laughed. *Oh shit.* And his cock didn't have an ounce of sense. The good news was that facedown, Calum couldn't see the effect of his touch. The bad news, that Jasper couldn't get up anytime soon and stalk off in a righteous temper.

Calum took his fingers away and Jasper turned his head to look at him. Calum sat on the adjoining sun lounger, his Stetson tipped back on his head, his eyes narrowed in concern.

"You okay?" Calum asked.

Of course I'm not fucking okay. I have an asthma attack because some jerk deliberately trips me, I get kicked in the back by a cow and I find out you're married.

"Yes," Jasper said.

"I can explain," Calum whispered. "It's not what it looks like."

"You married her?"

"Yes."

"Then it is what it looks like." He turned the other way again.

Note to self: Don't get up until your cock has deflated.

Chapter Twelve

Calum sat on the lounger next to Jasper and stared down at his tanned back. He didn't blame Jasper for not wanting to listen, but he wasn't going to walk away without explaining.

"Suz went to the same high school as me. Her parents moved to Utah while I was at college, and a couple of years ago she came to work in the ranch kitchen. We got on okay, though there was never anything sexual between us." Calum licked dry lips. Would Jasper believe him? "But Suz wanted there to be." Her obsession with him had grown embarrassing.

"Did you?"

"No," Calum snapped. "Christ, no. Once I even found her in my bed, lying there naked, waiting for me. She flirted with all the wranglers, but she was fixated on me. Everyone liked her. She was fun and feisty, and when I kept turning her down, they all thought I was crazy. Particularly my father." Calum swallowed hard. "We ended up having a terrible row and I told him I was gay. Then he had a fucking heart attack." He blew out a long breath.

Jasper sat up and faced him, his dark eyes wide with concern.

"Guilt does stupid things to people. So does alcohol." Calum winced. "I got drunk, asked Suz to marry me. The next day, instead of apologizing, we drove six hundred miles to Las Vegas. A day later we were married, and during the ten-hour journey back, I had plenty of time to think about how I'd made the biggest mistake of my life. Only Suz was so excited, I also thought—maybe I can do it, maybe I can be what everyone wants. Maybe I'm wrong and they're all right."

Calum wondered now how he'd gone through with it, how he'd said "I do" at the crucial moment. He remembered thinking he was going to throw up and then the words were out and he couldn't take them back.

"Then what?" Jasper asked.

"Instead of making things better, I'd made them worse. My father was ecstatic, talking about building us a house, having grandkids and how he'd teach them to ride. Vera knew I'd done the wrong thing. She said it would end in tears and she was right. I couldn't...I couldn't be what Suz wanted. I had sex with her, but it wasn't good for either of us. I came back from a trip to Laramie to find she'd fucked one of the wranglers."

Calum gave a huff of cold laughter. "The irony was I'd been faithful and she hadn't. But she was unhappy and I didn't have a way to change that other than divorce. I gave her all my savings and she gave me back my freedom, along with the everlasting disapproval of my father and the outright hatred of Ring, who'd wanted Suz for himself. He wasn't even the guy Suz chose to fuck. That was Dean, lasso boy, though he doesn't realize I saw him coming out of our room."

"Oh God. How long were you married?"

"Six months."

"Idiot," Jasper whispered and slid his leg alongside Calum's.

The breath caught in Calum's throat and his "yep" came out choked.

"Why did she say she was your wife?"

"To irritate me. Christ, she doesn't even need to open her mouth to do that. She should have married Ring. The two of them have a lot in common."

Jasper smiled.

"So we divorced. Irreconcilable differences." Calum snorted. "Those two words covered a mountain of problems."

"What's she doing here?"

"My guess is my dad called her to stir up trouble between us."

Jasper's brow wrinkled. "We didn't have enough already?"

Fuck. Calum stared straight at him. "Don't leave."

"You didn't stand up for me in front of your father. I could have accepted that if you'd come to me afterward to explain, but you didn't. I think you'd decided last night we'd gone far enough. I'm happy to go with the flow, for the moment to dictate how things play, but I don't think you are. The blowjobs have been great, you fucking me was great, but I wanted more. I wanted you under me, moaning and writhing, while I fucked you." Jasper's mouth twitched in a nervous smile. "Why don't you want that too?"

"I...I need—"

"Calum, you need to come here," Vera shouted from near the house.

Calum jumped to his feet.

Jasper looked up at him with those big eyes. "Saved by the bell?"

Calum hesitated. Jasper's sad face made his stomach clench. *Tell him I'll talk to him later.* But he walked away without saying anything. *Coward, coward, coward.*

Vera waited by the door and beckoned him inside. "Suz is here."

"I know. I've been trying to find Dad. Did he call her?"

"No."

"I don't believe you," Calum snapped. "Christ. That's it. I've had enough of the controlling bastard."

He stalked off and Vera dashed after him. Calum halted outside his father's office as Vera jerked at his arm.

"Don't," she pleaded. "You're not going to get him to see sense, just make things worse. And there's something you need to know."

"I'm thirty years old. He can't tell me how to live my life. I tried to be what he wanted and look what happened."

Vera fixed him with her gaze. "Calum, this guy will be gone at the end of the week. You'll still be here."

He removed her hand from his arm. "Maybe I won't."

Vera paled. "You don't mean that."

"Don't I? I'm beginning to think this is a simpler choice than I'd imagined. Stay here and be miserable or leave and give myself a chance of happiness."*Oh God, could he?*

"You don't know this guy."

Calum sighed. "This isn't about Jasper. It's about me. It's about what I want. My life."

"There's something else you need to know. Suz—"

"I don't give a f—damn about Suz. She cheated on me, walked out of here with all my money and I hoped never to see her again."

His father came out of his office. "What's all the noise?"

"What's Suz doing here?" Calum demanded.

"Suz is here?"

The surprise on his father's face looked genuine and pulled Calum up short for a moment.

"Suz arrives and Jasper's leaving. How about that? Are you going to apologize to Jasper before he goes?" Calum asked.

"What the hell for? The guy's a wimp. I heard one of the calves kicked him and he ran off. Didn't want people to see him sniveling."

"He had a fucking asthma attack," Calum snapped. "I had to get his inhaler. For Christ's sake give the guy a break."

Vera put her hand on his father's arm. "Don't let the man leave like this. If any of it gets in the papers, that a guest's been bullied, what chance—"

"If he wants to go, I'm not going to stop him." His father went back into his office and slammed the door.

Calum yanked it open again. "He's not at fault here. You could at least apologize to him for what happened with Angie."

His father glared and slammed the door again.

Vera caught Calum's arm. "Leave him be."

Calum pulled away and leaned against the wall. "He has no respect for me at all." And deep down Calum wondered if he ever would. The pain of it choked him.

"He loves you."

Calum gave a humorless laugh. "He has a strange way of showing it. Is Suz another weapon in his arsenal? He still trying to make me not-gay?"

"He doesn't understand."

"He's living in the dark ages and I'm not staying in there with him."

Vera took a deep breath and put her hand on his chest. "There's something you need to know, something you need to see. Come with me."

Calum followed her to the private lounge and stopped in his tracks, his stomach sliding to his feet. Suz held the hand of a tow-haired boy with bright blue eyes. *Oh fuck, fuck, fuck.* The kid looked about two years old and Calum knew what Vera was thinking, but she was wrong. If Suz had told this kid he was his father, he'd fucking kill her.

Well, no he wouldn't but still... Calum stared straight at Suz. "Don't say one word in front of him. The two of us need to talk."

Jasper called the cab company in Jackson to see what the delay was and learned the driver had broken down. Another vehicle had set off. He didn't want to sit in his room, waiting, so he headed for the stables. The guests and most of the wranglers would have embarked on the overnight trip by now, which suited him just fine. As Jasper approached the barn, the sound of a horse whinnying in pain and fear set his teeth on edge.

Gunner and the vet were in the corral with a horse Jasper didn't recognize. The brown mare danced around while the vet tried to calm her down.

"Lucy, it's okay. No one's gonna hurt you," Gunner said.

"Good girl." The vet ran his hand down her flank and the horse shied away.

Jasper thought about Ben's horse. His brother wasn't the only one hurt in the accident. Jasper had looked on helplessly as the ambulance crew dealt with Ben, listening to Samson's screams. No one could do anything until the vet came and those long minutes after Ben had been whisked away, Jasper had sat with Samson's head on his lap, stroking the horse's neck, trying not to look at the blood, at the way the bones in his back legs protruded through his black coat.

He swallowed hard and leaned against the rail, watching as the vet tried to examine Lucy while Gunner struggled to keep the horse still. Even as Jasper was thinking of climbing in to give them a hand, the animal reared up, jerked the reins out of Gunner's grasp and knocked him to the ground before cantering with an awkward gait to the far end of the corral. When the mare got there, she almost fell but then turned and raced back. Gunner was right in the horse's path, pushing himself to his feet. Jasper vaulted over the top rail of the corral and ran toward the old man.

"Careful," the vet shouted. "I think she might have rabies."

Oh fuck. Jasper stood between Gunner and the advancing horse and held up his hand. *Christ, as if that's going to stop her.* "Stop," Jasper snapped. Then he said it again. Louder.

The mare staggered as she pulled up and Jasper grabbed the leading rein. "Hey, Lucy. It's okay. You're safe." Jasper spoke quietly to the horse and stroked her flank. He waved his right hand in front of Lucy's left eye and she tried to rear away. "Okay, okay, girl," Jasper whispered. He fumbled in his pocket for a mint and she snuffled it.

"Did you hear what I said?" the vet asked.

He and Gunner stood a little way away.

"I don't think it's rabies," Jasper said.

"Increased saliva, excitability, disorientation, running blindly?" the vet barked.

"She's supposed to have been vaccinated." Gunner brushed dust from his clothes.

Lucy yanked her head to try and pull away.

"Shh, you're fine," Jasper said to her. "Good girl." Except she wasn't fine. "Don't make any sudden movements on her left side. It's upsetting her."

"I'll take another look. You're the one who spotted the laminitis, aren't you?" the vet asked Jasper. "Are you a vet?"

"I didn't qualify," Jasper muttered. "I didn't do the final year."

"So what do you think it is?" the vet asked, his tone more reasonable.

"Any other symptoms?" Jasper asked.

"Suddenly spooking for no reason," Gunner said. "She's tried to climb out of her stall a couple of times. And just like she did now, she runs flat out from one end of the pasture to the other."

"She's usually calm and affectionate?" Jasper asked.

"Yep, she's a charmer." Gunner scratched his head. "I can't figure it out."

"It could be West Nile virus, equine herpes, EPM," the vet said.

"It might be neurological." Jasper had been thinking equine protozoa myeloencephalitis, EPM for short. "But it looks like she has a problem with the vision in her left eye."

"There's no sign of cancer," said the vet.

"I did a case study of a horse like this. The owner thought he was blind in one eye, tests showed he wasn't, but the vision came and went. So did the crazy behavior. The horse had a CT scan and there was a massive circulatory blockage in his brain. When he got excited, the blood supply was cut off to the front lobes. It caused intermittent blindness and erratic behavior, things like trying to climb out of his stall and racing around like a creature possessed."

"Brain tumor." The vet sighed.

"That's not good," Gunner muttered. "Explains why she's been getting worse."

The three of them stared at the now docile horse.

"I might be wrong," Jasper said. "It's just my unqualified opinion."

"I could do tests, but I think you're right. No point throwing money away. I'll go speak to Erik." The vet turned and then swiveled back. He held out his hand. "We were never introduced. I'm Frank Hess."

"Jasper Randolph."

"Why didn't you finish the course?"

"A change of heart about my future."

Frank frowned. "You threw away eight years of study?"

"Five in the UK. I studied for four but I needed a job that paid more."

Frank shrugged, disapproval clear on his face. He turned to Gunner. "Take Lucy to your back barn." Then he stalked off.

"You just disappointed him," Gunner said. "Money ain't everything."

"I know, but I had obligations and little choice. Are you okay with her now?"

"Yeah, she's good as gold again. Poor girl. Come on, Lucy."

Gunner walked the horse away and Jasper knew the likelihood was that she'd never see the sky again. Brain tumors in horses were basically inoperable. Medicine might help, but the cost made it likely Erik would have Lucy put to sleep today.

Christ. He'd come out here to cheer himself up and now he was even more depressed. Five years since he'd walked away from what he thought would be his future. His reasons were personal though he'd told the truth to the head of the school of veterinary medicine who'd tried to dissuade him, but Jasper had made up his mind.

He headed back to the ranch and saw Angie walking toward him holding the hand of a small blond boy, who looked no more than two. Jasper had no idea whether Angie was going to play nice or nasty, but relief hit him when she walked up with a broad smile on her face.

"I'm going to show Misty to Seth."

"Don't let him get too close," Jasper said and wondered if Seth's mother knew Angie had him.

"I know. Are you still wearing your bracelet?"

Jasper pulled back his cuff and showed her.

"I made that," she said to Seth. "Do you want one?"

The little boy shook his head.

The pair entered the barn and the thought that followed hit Jasper like a spear in the chest and he sagged. Calum's ex-wife had arrived a little while ago. What if this boy was hers and Calum's? *Christ.* Even more of a reason for Jasper to leave.

He went back to his room to wait for the cab.

"Where are we going?" Suz asked.

"Someplace private," Calum muttered.

Unfortunately, the only place that was really private was his room. He opened the door and gestured Suz inside.

"Still playing with mud?" She picked up one of his figures.

Calum took a deep breath. Her parting gift, apart from the quick divorce, was the smashing of his clay models. Not all of them, but enough to hurt.

"Seth is two years old. His birthday's March 28. Do the math."

"He's not mine," Calum said.

"He's the image of you."

Calum snorted. "Like I'm the father of every blond-haired, blue-eyed kid?"

Suz crossed her arms. "You are this one."

Calum's heart cartwheeled. "In the handful of times we had sex, I always used protection."

"Accidents happen."

"But they didn't. Even if it's true, why keep quiet about it until now?"

Her mouth curved in a smile. "Spite."

Calum sucked in a breath. That at least sounded like the truth.

Suz sat on his bed and leaned back on her elbows. "I wanted to punish you."

"For what? We both agreed the marriage was a mistake. I gave you every cent I'd saved. The agreement was that you went away and didn't come back."

"I need money to look after Seth."

Calum didn't believe this, neither that Seth was his son, nor that she'd wait until now to ask for money. He suspected his father had engineered Suz's visit as a way to break him from Jasper. Had he poisoned the sandwiches too? *Jesus Christ.*

"How much did he offer you?" Calum asked.

Suz wrinkled her brow. "I don't know what you're talking about."

"I know you slept with at least one of the wranglers. Why should I accept the kid is mine?"

"Because he is. And because if you don't, I'll go to the local paper and tell them why we broke up."

Calum wished he could shake some sense into her. "Won't that defeat the purpose? How thrilled will people be with you that you want a gay guy as your son's father?"

"You beat me."

Calum gaped at her. "I never touched you."

"Mud sticks." She glanced at his models. "You'd know."

"No one will believe I hit you." Oh Christ, he hoped not. "I want a paternity test."

"Costs five hundred dollars."

Calum glowered. "How much do you want to go away and not come back?"

She rose to her feet and walked over to stand in front of him. "Fifty thousand."

Calum laughed. The sum was nonsensical. "Five hundred seems like the better deal."

"Twenty-five thousand."

"I hope you didn't tell him I'm his father."

"Twenty thousand and I'll go now. If you haven't got it, your father has. I want the money by tomorrow noon or I'll start to tell everyone he's yours, you beat me and you're gay."

There was a bang on the door and his father called, "Calum!"

Calum reached for the handle, braced himself and pulled the door open.

"Bad news. Frank needs to put Lucy down." He smiled when he saw Suz. "Hey there. What brings you out here?"

Calum clenched his fists.

"Just passing," Suz said. "Thought I'd pop in and see how you're all doing. Sounds like it's a bad time. I remember riding Lucy."

"She's been a good horse. Calum and I need to go see to her. We'll catch up later." His father nodded to Calum.

"Out of my room." Calum hustled her out and locked the door.

"I'll come with you," Suz said. "Angie took my son to see the horses."

Calum held his breath.

"You have a son?" his father asked.

"Name's Seth. He's a real cutie."

"What's wrong with Lucy?" Calum asked, wondering if his father was jumping to conclusions yet knowing there was nothing he could do to head this off.

"Frank reckons a brain tumor."

"Ah damn," Calum muttered. That accounted for the erratic behavior. Maybe Suz had one too. Could they put her down—two for the price of one?

The three of them exited the building and headed for the stables. Suz struggled to keep up in her heels.

"Is Frank sure?" Calum asked.

"Sure enough to recommend she be euthanized."

Shit.

Gunner came out of the stable as they approached. "Frank's with Lucy in the back barn. He's waiting on you. I'll take Angie and the boy to the house."

"Take Suz with you," Calum's father said.

Angie and Seth walked out of the stable and Calum's father's face went through a variety of expressions—shock, joy, love. *Fuck.*

"Hello there, young man," his father said.

Angie pulled at her father's arm. "Daddy, this is Seth. He wants to ride Misty."

"Not now, sweetheart. I've got something to do. Go back to the house with Gunner." He stared at Seth, glanced at Calum, and Calum's stomach churned.

By the time Lucy had been injected with euthanasia solution, Calum felt even worse. It always hurt to see a horse put down, and Lucy had been a faithful, solid pony. He volunteered to dig a grave with the ranch's ancient backhoe and knew he'd slipped into avoidance mode. The only person he wanted to speak to was the one person who wouldn't want to speak to him.

Note to self: Make the hole big enough for myself as well.

Chapter Thirteen

Jasper lifted the champagne the airline had given him out of the bathroom sink. The ice he'd snagged from the kitchen had chilled the bottle to a drinkable level. He wasn't going to take the champagne with him. It seemed unlikely Calum would be joining him so he might as well drink it himself.

He filled a glass and toasted as he drank.

"To the weirdest holiday I've ever had."

"To the most fucked-up, fucking fan-fucking-tastic guy I've ever fucking met."

"To his happiness."

"To his son."

In a few hours, Jasper would be ensconced in a motel in Jackson Hole, planning his visit to Yellowstone. Tomorrow he'd watch Old Faithful spurt—alone. Try to spot bison—alone. Eat a meal—alone.

"To Yellowstone." *Fuck.*

Shouldn't be hard to finish the bottle. Jasper just wished it made him feel happier and not more depressed.

By the time Calum had filled in Lucy's grave, it was getting dark. He had no reason to linger but he checked the horses, checked the tack room, checked that all the gates were closed before he went back to the house.

He shouldn't have let things finish like that with Jasper. The guy was right. Calum hadn't stood up for him in front of his father. He had afterward, but so what? That wasn't the main issue. Jasper had figured out Calum didn't want to bottom. Except, it wasn't a matter of *want*, Calum couldn't. And he didn't want to tell Jasper why. He clenched his fists as memories surged and had to take a few deep breaths to calm himself.

As Calum passed the lounge on the way to his room, he heard Suz laughing. The sound drove splinters of ice into his heart. Maybe he should offer to remarry her. Assuming Seth was his. Why make a kid suffer for the mistakes of his parents? Only Calum wasn't sure he could live the rest of his life forcing himself to have sex he didn't care for. No, the better option was to share caring for Seth.

"Calum?" Vera called. "You finished?"

"Yep." He forced his feet to take him into the lounge. Angie was playing with Seth, building a tower of plastic boxes.

"Come and talk to your boy," Calum's father snapped.

Every nerve in Calum's body went tight as a bow string. "We don't know that he's mine."

"How can you say that?" Suz whispered.

"When I see the results of a paternity test, I'll do the right thing." Calum glared at her.

Vera rose to her feet with a resigned sigh. "Get cleaned up and I'll fix you something to eat."

"I've arranged for a company to send a representative out tomorrow," Suz said. "They courier the test to the lab. It takes about seventy-two hours. But I can't afford—"

"I'll pay," Erik said.

"You going to give her the twenty thousand she wants to go away?" Calum ground out.

"What are you talking about?" Suz asked.

Calum turned his back and left. His life was falling apart.

Vera caught up with him before he reached his room. She put her hand on his arm. "Are you okay?"

"What do you think?"

"Is he yours?"

Calum shuffled in embarrassment. "We used condoms. I don't remember any accidents and there weren't that many times. I didn't say—but..."

"What?"

"When she was here, I saw Dean coming out of our room. He didn't see me. When I went in, Suz was naked. Not hard to guess what they'd been doing."

Vera gasped. "Why didn't you tell us?"

Calum shrugged. "What was the point? It was over between me and her. It had never begun. I shouldn't have married her. The whole mess was my fault."

"Why's she come?" Vera frowned. "I don't understand. A paternity test will tell us the truth. She has to be certain Seth's yours."

"Or certain that she can make it so." Thoughts ticked over in Calum's mind. "Could she do that? Fix the results?"

Vera patted his arm. "Maybe you should go to a lab rather than let someone collect a sample from here."

Calum nodded.

"By the way," Vera said. "Jasper's still here, though your father thinks he's gone."

Calum gulped. *Oh Christ.* "He was leaving?"

Vera nodded. "There was a problem with the cab and they said they'd send another, but it hasn't arrived yet. Jasper said he didn't want anything to eat, but maybe if I make you both something?"

Thank fuck he hadn't gone. Though Calum couldn't figure out how he felt. Happy and excited he had a chance to put things right, nervous about how he'd be received and sad this could be goodbye? Calum pulled Vera into his arms. "Thank you."

"Wash up first," she said and held her nose.

"Yes, Mom."

When Calum saw the smile on her face, he knew he'd made a mistake all those years ago when he'd taken Vera at her word. He'd thought she told him to use her name because she didn't want him to think she was taking the place of his mother. She'd been more of a mother to him than he deserved.

Calum put down the tray of food and knocked on Jasper's door. When it opened, Jasper stood in front of him, in his shirt and tie, holding his suitcase, his leather satchel slung over his shoulder.

"Is the cab here?" he asked and swayed slightly.

"Not yet. Hadn't known you called one."

Jasper's shoulders fell and he went back into his room, dumping the briefcase on a chair and the suitcase next to it before he lay on the bed. Calum picked up the tray and closed the door behind him with his backside.

"I brought you something to eat."

"Not hungry."

Calum put the tray on the floor and sat on the bed next to Jasper's legs. Jasper had his arm flung over his eyes. Calum caught sight of the champagne bottle.

"Save any for me?" he asked.

"I toasted you," Jasper mumbled.

"He's not mine," Calum blurted.

Jasper lifted his arm from his eyes. "Sure about that?"

"Almost."

"Would you like him to be?"

Calum took a deep breath. "A bit of me would. Suz wants money. I'm sure that's what all this is about. Don't leave like this."

"Leave like what?"

Calum sighed. "Pissed with me."

"I'm not pissed with you, I'm pissed with myself." Jasper hiccupped. "For expecting too much. S'okay. I'll be gone soon and things will go back to normal. I enjoyed these few days—mostly." He reached for Calum's hand and laid his on top. "I'll miss you."

The lump in Calum's throat grew larger. "Is that right?"

"I shouldn't have said that to you." Jasper pushed himself up to a sitting position. "About you not wanting me to fuck you. We've known each other a few days. I know what it's like to want something and yet not want it at the same time. It isn't so different from what Ben wanted me to do. It had to be my decision not his. Just like this is your decision not mine." Jasper stared straight into Calum's eyes. "What I'm saying is that it's okay. What you want and don't want is fine with me. I understand."

Calum lifted his hand to Jasper's face and trailed his fingers down his cheek. "I want you." He gulped. "I know I can't have you, but I still want you."

There was a long pause before either of them spoke.

"Lock the door," Jasper whispered.

OhGodohGodohGod. Calum crossed the room and flipped the latch only for it to spring open again. His fingers shook. He tried again and this time it held. When he turned, Jasper had stood to kick off his shoes. He'd unfastened his shirt and tie, his hand now massaging his groin.

"Undo your fly," Calum croaked.

He watched as Jasper flipped the button on his chinos and then slowly eased down the zipper. His cock tented blue boxers, a wet spot at the head. Jasper slid one hand inside his briefs and ran the other over his chest, squeezing his pecs, pulling a nipple between his fingers, sliding his hand over his abs.

Calum was riveted by the flex and play of Jasper's muscles. He reached to trail his thumb along the line of Jasper's jaw, down his throat, into the depression between his rounded pecs, down the line of dark hair to join Jasper's hand inside his boxers. Calum pressed his lips against Jasper's while their hands played with the same hot, hard toy. Jasper moaned into Calum's mouth and the sound echoed through him, sending pulses of heat racing to his cock. Inside Jasper's briefs, their hands worked together, rubbing and stroking his erection. Calum let Jasper guide his hand, felt his fingers tighten as they reached his tip and then relax as Calum drew his hand down.

Their tongues surged in time with their hands, and Calum couldn't think straight, couldn't concentrate on anything but the way this felt, the way Jasper felt.

Then Jasper's hand was gone and he was undoing Calum's jeans, reaching for his cock, and Calum sighed into Jasper's mouth. Their hands moved together again, cocks pressed one alongside the other and Calum gritted his teeth against the pressure building in his balls. Desperate to stave off the inevitable, he pulled Jasper's fingers away and pushed the guy back to the bed and onto his back before licking his way down his chest, leaving a trail of hot, moist kisses in his wake. Jasper's fingers threaded his hair, pushing him down, but Calum set his own pace, laving a slow path over chiseled abs to the jut of Jasper's hipbone.

"Calum," Jasper whispered in a long drawn-out sigh.

He loved hearing his name come from Jasper's lips, loved the way he said it. Calum pressed his face into the warm, fragile skin between Jasper's cock and the angle of his hip and inhaled him—dark musk, soap, essence of Jasper. Calum refused to think this might be the last time. He brushed Jasper's fingers away from his cock so he could have it all to himself and tugged at the guy's chinos to get better access.

A moment later, they were almost ripping clothes off each other until they were left naked, panting on the bed. They sat face-to-face, balls to balls, Jasper's legs tucked under Calum's, hands on their own cocks. Jasper tucked his toes around Calum's back and Calum did the same to him. They kissed again, pressed tight against each other, cocks rubbing side by side between them. They writhed and bucked and rocked and every touch against his cock, against his balls, against Calum's skin felt as if he'd dived from cold water into hot to make his entire body tingle.

"Want to suck each other off at the same time?" Jasper bent his head and licked Calum's nipple. It crinkled and tightened, and Calum felt an ache grow in his balls.

"Sounds good."

"Like to see my party trick?" Jasper asked. "Not that I've ever done it at a party."

"That sounds good too."

They untangled themselves and Calum stared at Jasper's heavily veined cock, rising from a nest of dark curls. Christ, he was beautiful. Jasper lay on his back, head and shoulders on the pillow. He put his arms behind his knees and—*oh fuck*. Calum's jaw dropped as Jasper folded up and licked his own cock.

"How the hell can you do that?" Calum asked. "I'm jealous."

"Long cock, bendy spine and years of practice," Jasper gasped. "Just don't expect me to talk at the same time."

"Fuck that is so hot." Calum licked his lips as Jasper took the top inch of his cock in his mouth and sucked.

"Now all the rest of it," Calum said.

Jasper laughed and uncurled. "I'm too tall really. It's not comfortable. Not as good as—"

Calum planted his mouth on Jasper's, tasted salty-sweet pre-come and moaned. They swiveled round and lay on their sides so their faces were in each other's groins. As Calum took the head of Jasper's cock into his mouth, Jasper made a long slow lick up the center of his fragile sac, and Calum trembled. One hard press by Jasper's mouth on the skin between Calum's balls and his hole and Calum's brain melted.

Taking a deep breath, Calum dragged himself back into gear and played on Jasper's crest with his tongue, flicking, licking and laving while his mouth watered and pre-come coated his lips. His mind drifted again as Jasper pulled one and then the other of his balls into his mouth while his fingers wrapped around Calum's cock and squeezed.

Calum moaned against Jasper's cock head. He struggled to remember he was supposed to be making Jasper come too. He struggled to do anything other than feel. Concentration eluded him. It was like trying to lasso a cloud. Not going to happen.

Copy Jasper. The idea was good one. In practice not so easy. White-hot sparks danced along Calum's veins, his entire body preparing to ignite. When Jasper shifted Calum's leg and dropped his mouth onto the stretch of skin behind his balls, Calum's nerves took control of his brain. Somehow he managed to keep sucking Jasper's cock, but as a warm, wet tongue ringed the entrance to his body, Calum felt himself lurch toward lift off. His hips rocked as Jasper licked him, and Jasper's hips bucked too, driving his cock more deeply between Calum's lips.

Please, please, please. Calum wanted to come. Didn't want to come. Jasper pressed into his slit with the tip of his tongue and as he felt Jasper's cock swell in his mouth, Calum's balls detonated. Come flooded up his shaft and spilled into Jasper's mouth, as Jasper emptied himself into Calum's. Calum sucked and swallowed and swallowed as he shook in the grip of an orgasm so exquisitely mind-blowing, he thought it was a good thing he was lying down.

Jesus. He'd never done that before, come at exactly the same time while he had a guy's cock in his mouth. He licked Jasper clean as Jasper did the same to him, and then Calum turned and crawled up to wrap him in his arms.

"You taste good," Jasper whispered.

"So do you."

"You taste better."

Calum laughed. "I needed that."

"The laugh or the blowjob?" Jasper licked Calum's nose.

"Both." He took a deep breath. "I want…" Calum looked into Jasper's dark eyes and sagged. The words had log jammed in his throat.

"What?"

Calum's mouth opened, but he closed it again without saying anything.

"Shall I guess? You want a drink of flat, slightly disgusting champagne? Your father to tell you he's okay with your being gay? A way to cast bronzes? To fuck me?"

"You to fuck me," Calum whispered. "Only…"

Jasper's jaw twitched. "We were fine until the 'only'. Tell me."

"Did you kill your brother?" Calum blurted. *Fucking hell. Am I a complete asshole? Where the hell did that come from?*

Jasper stiffened in his arms.

"I'm sorry, I'm sorry," Calum mumbled.

"No. I didn't kill Ben. In a way, my father did when he hit his horse with his car. I can't imagine how he must have felt when he realized what he'd done. Then my father sort of killed Ben again when he committed suicide five years after Ben came home from the hospital. He sat at the kitchen table and put a shotgun under his chin. I found him and that killed something inside me too."

"Oh fuck. I'm sorry. I didn't mean to push." Tears welled in Calum's eyes.

Jasper put his finger on Calum's lips. "It's okay. It's my past. It's what happened. I can't change it. I have to live with it. Though seeing my father...yeah, well that was hard. I had to keep my mother from going into the kitchen. It was after that, Ben asked me to kill him. And I couldn't." Jasper brushed a tear from Calum's cheek. "He died in the operating theatre having an operation I'd talked him into that might have let him breathe on his own. I knew Ben hoped he wouldn't come round from the anesthetic. He said goodbye to me that morning and I think...we both knew it was the last time." Jasper took a deep breath. "Want to tell me what happened to you?"

Calum closed his eyes and released a shuddering sigh. Jasper had opened his heart, now he had to do the same. *Say it, say it, say it.* "Two guys raped me," he whispered. He'd never told anyone that before. His squeezed his eyes tighter shut. His entire body tensed. Why had he told him? He'd kept quiet all these years. Why now? *I'm so stupid.*

"Oh God, Calum."

He felt Jasper's lips on his eyelids, kissing him. Jasper's arms tightening around him and he couldn't breathe. Nothing would be the same now. The rape would always be there in

Jasper's head. *I should have kept quiet.* Calum jerked away, scrambling for his clothes.

"Don't feel fucking sorry for me," he snapped. "It happened. I got over it." He yanked on his jeans and grabbed his shirt.

"Calum—"

"Shut up. Shut the fuck up."

Jasper caught his arm. "Don't run away."

Fuck, fuck, fuck. He took a deep breath. "I need a minute. Okay. Just let me get my shit together. Sorry." Calum fled.

Jasper stared at the closed door and sighed. *Shit.* He had a feeling Calum had never told anyone he'd been raped, and he could guess what it had cost him to say it. But Jasper had just confided the darkest secrets of his own life and if the bastard cowboy thought he was going to get away with running from this, he had another think coming. Jasper pulled on his clothes. He'd begun to despair of the cab ever arriving and now he didn't want it to.

When the door opened, Jasper expected to see Calum standing there looking sheepish, but two men burst into the room, black hoods over their faces. Stunned bewilderment wrecked Jasper's chances of escape. In the couple of seconds it took him to react, they were on him. Propelled backward onto the bed, the bigger of the two wrapped an arm around Jasper's throat and slapped a hand over his mouth.

Fear galloped through him and Jasper thrashed and kicked out. He tried to bite the hand plastered on his face and received a thump in his side that sent such a sharp pain shooting through him, for a moment he couldn't move. Their hold on him slipped as he went limp and by some miracle Jasper managed to wriggle free. He fell onto the floor, opened his mouth, but before his scream for help was voiced, something hit the side of his head and the room lost focus. Jasper lurched to his feet, stumbled toward the door and this time he was whacked on the back of his head. The next blow targeted his stomach and the air rushed out of his lungs. As Jasper tried to straighten, a fist connected with his chin and he fell back onto the bed wheezing. *What the fuck?* Were they trying to kill him?

"Not his face," one of the men hissed.

That voice…

Jasper saw a piece of wood arcing toward him and tried to roll out of the way, but it hit him and pain radiated through his skull.

Note to self: Don't lose con—

Chapter Fourteen

Jasper came back to awareness slowly. He was moving, more accurately he was being carried, his wrists and ankles tied, a gag over his mouth. His head pounded and his stomach ached. *Oh God, and my jaw.* He lay across someone's back, the guy had an arm looped around Jasper's neck, the other hooked around his knees. Jasper felt more and more nauseous with every jolting step. Except being sick wouldn't be wise when he had something tied around his mouth. The only good news was that he could still get some air through the material.

Oh Christ, what are these guys going to do to me?

He was reluctant to open his eyes fully. Better that whoever held him thought he was still unconscious, but he couldn't stop himself taking a quick peek. Jasper thought they were still on the ranch, but he couldn't be sure. Suffocating fear rose alongside his fury and fear won. Whatever these two wanted, it couldn't be good. That voice—it had sounded like Pete. Was this Calum's father's doing? The guy wanted him gone? But Jasper had been trying to leave all bloody day. Well, most of it.

The guy carrying him was panting. *Good.* Jasper would have made carrying him a damn sight more difficult if he could, but with his ankles bound, and arms tied behind his back, even if he wriggled free, he couldn't run. Where were they taking him? If they wanted him dead, wouldn't they have killed him already? Jasper clung to that faint hope.

In a sudden brainwave, he twisted his hands until he could get his fingers on Angie's bracelet. He tugged hard to break it, gathered as many beads as he could in his fists, then let them fall one by one.

Jasper heard the sound of a door being opened and then closed, and then he was dropped to land on his back in the dirt. The fall knocked the air out of his lungs. The pain in his hands and his back made him arch in agony.

"Oh shit, he's seen my face."

He hadn't, but idiot that he was, Jasper looked up. *Ring. Oh God.* Somehow that wasn't a surprise. The hood over his head must have come off as he'd dropped Jasper. The other guy sighed and pulled the cover off his face. *Pete.* A foot landed in Jasper's side, rolling him onto his face and he groaned behind his gag. *Christ that hurt.* Had he heard a rib snap? It felt like it. It hurt to breathe. Jasper kept his fists clenched and the remaining beads hidden.

"Stop fucking kicking him," Pete whispered.

Jasper lay facedown in the dirt, struggling to drag air through his nose and inhaling dust. *Fuck, fuck, fuck.*

A foot rolled him back again and Jasper blinked in the dim light. They were in a barn he didn't recognize. Pete held a rope with a noose at the end. *Oh shit.* Jasper tugged at his wrists, desperately trying to get free, but he was bound tight. Same with his ankles. When Pete tossed the rope over a beam, Jasper's entire body chilled. His fear escalated and his breathing grew more frantic.

"He's got blood trickling down his face from two places. This isn't going to work," Pete said. "It was supposed to be one tap on the head to knock him out. Fucking fag's got a thick skull."

The rope slithered down to land beside Jasper. He didn't dare feel relief. They'd planned to hang him. And they wanted it to look like suicide. *Oh fuck.* Jasper didn't think that was too much of a jump in logic. He wished it was.

The two men stared down at him, no hint of concern on their faces. *What have I done? I was leaving. For fuck's sake. Please. Please. Please.* Only Jasper knew there was no point pleading, even if he'd been able to. One way or another, they intended him to die. It pissed him off that he didn't know why. Because he was gay? Because of his relationship with Calum?

Or had some megalomaniac partner at his London office arranged to have him killed? *Oh God, oh God.* He'd done nothing to deserve this.

"If we don't have him hang himself, what we gonna do?" Ring asked.

Pete kicked Jasper's ankles. Jasper cried out behind his gag as a steel toe cap made contact.

"Make Calum responsible," Pete said. "They had some sort of fight out here. Calum accidentally kills him and then dumps him. Actually, that'll work better. I should have thought of that earlier."

Jasper was stupidly incensed they hadn't even taken the trouble to work this out.

Pete smiled down at Jasper. "Don't you be thinking a cab company's going to turn up. You called to cancel."

Oh fuck. Jasper sent a mental plea for Calum to come back to his room, find his luggage, come and look for him.

"So we need to rough him up some more?" Ring asked.

Hadn't he been roughed up enough already? Jasper's heart beat so hard, it hurt. But then all of him hurt.

"If there's no marks on Calum, it'll look strange if this one's beat up too bad," Pete said.

"This guy's nowhere near as tough as Calum."

That was painful, even it was true.

"We can tell the police that Calum had a temper," Pete said.

"The police?"

Pete gave an exasperated sigh. "They'll interview everyone. I told you that."

Ring frowned. "Yeah, I know, but this isn't what you said would happen. You keep changing things. First we were going to arrange for him to have an accident at the camp then you said he'd kill himself. Now you—"

"Shut the fuck up and listen."

Keep talking. The longer they talked, the more chance Jasper had of someone coming.

"It's better that nothing happened at the camp," Pete said. "The more distant we are from this, the more innocent we'll look. Everyone thinks we're out there with the other guests. I listened to enough drivel from Melissa. 'Do we have pillows? We've changed our minds, we'd like a tent. Where can I plug my in flat iron?' The woman's a moron."

"You told me to chat her up."

"She doesn't need brains. She has a rich daddy. You should have done more sweet-talking instead of yapping about your bull riding. Christ, anyone would think you'd done it for years."

Jasper stayed still and quiet. Maybe they'd forget he was there. Maybe they'd argue and kill each other.

"She was impressed," Ring said. "I was going to make a move on her tonight until you came up with this plan. Except you keep changing it and now I'm confused. Couldn't we hide him someplace to give us some time?"

Yes, hide me. Just don't kill me. That way there was at least a chance. Jasper wrapped his fingers tighter around the remaining beads.

"Hide him where?" Pete asked.

"Bottom of the grain store?"

Oh fuck. Jasper began to shake.

"That's not a bad idea," Pete said. "He'll be found next week when the grain's delivered." Pete looked down at him. "Or maybe not. The publicity will be bad whatever. British tourist goes missing from the Neilson Ranch. Jasper Randolph found dead. Police launch a murder enquiry. Yeah, Erik will be finished."

So it wasn't about him at all, Jasper thought, but disgruntled employees trying to hurt Erik Neilson. The pair of idiots would surely be caught. All this was for nothing. *You morons.*

"We need to get rid of his luggage," Pete said. "We can hide it somewhere on the ranch. No fingerprints though. We need to be careful how we handle it."

Why did Jasper find that funny? They'd be careful with his luggage but not with him.

"I better carry him up the ladder," Pete said. "I'm stronger than you. You keep a lookout."

"You going to kill him first?"

"The fall will probably do that. He's not going to get out of there. He'll die one way or another. Drag him to the far door. I'm not carrying him any farther than I need to."

Ring grabbed hold of Jasper's shirt and pulled him along the barn floor. Jasper let a couple of beads trickle from his fingers. It was the only thing he could think of to do. He needed Calum to come back to his room, see his bags before they were moved and wonder where he was. Or even better catch these guys taking them. He needed Angie or Calum to see the beads and follow the trail. Fast.

Oh God. Please help me. Calum. Calum.

Ring let Jasper's head drop and then kicked his shoulder. Jasper gasped behind his gag. He desperately tried to suck in air through his nose. If his nose became blocked, he'd suffocate. Jasper's face felt wetter and he guessed he must be bleeding more heavily. Or crying. Both.

His helplessness distressed him. He wanted to fight back and there was nothing he could do. Jasper's mind drifted to his mother, about to lose another son, though depending on her state of mind when the news was broken, she might not even remember she had one. To Calum, who, in time, maybe could have been his. In just these few days, Jasper felt more for him than he'd ever felt for anyone. At least he had that. He'd found someone to love. His friends in London would miss him for a while. His employer and clients would be pissed off at the inconvenience.

Jasper struggled as Pete hoisted him over his shoulder in a fireman's lift. Ring smashed his fist on Jasper's head. The world wavered and the next thing Jasper knew, he was falling, slithering down a slope of grain that avalanched with him.

When he stopped sliding, he lay still in the darkness, heart pounding, barely able to breathe, his face pressed into the gravelly grain. He heard the sound of the cover sliding back into place and then feet descending the ladder on the outside of the storage unit. Surrounded by absolute blackness, Jasper's heart banged against his ribs. *Oh God, is this where I'm going to die?*

He was afraid to move in case he slid down into the grain. He'd be trapped and suffocate. But his breathing had become more ragged. If he didn't get the gag off his mouth, he'd die anyway. Jasper dug into the grain with his heels and whimpered in his throat when almost immediately he touched something solid. The base of the silo. At least he wasn't going to sink. He rolled onto his knees and arched his back to force his bound wrists under his backside. Everywhere hurt, but his chest was so painful, he saw stars in the blackness. One attempt. That's all he had the energy for.

Jasper needed to regulate his breathing, but he was too frightened to slow his frantic inhalations through his nose. When his arms slid under his butt, Jasper groaned behind his gag. He dropped to his side then rolled onto his back and curling up tighter, reached between his legs for his mouth. A desperate scrabble by his fingers was followed by success as Jasper forced the strip of cloth—*ah, my fucking tie*—down over his chin. He sucked in air, tried to fill his lungs, but he was so crunched up, it hardly made any difference. He could call out now, but he didn't want to until he was sure Ring and Pete had gone. Only how could he tell and what was the point? Would anyone be around at this time of night?

He was reluctant to try and maneuver his legs all the way through the loop of his arms. Jasper was flexible but not that flexible, though he might be able to untie his ankles while he was in this position. He tried and couldn't. When his breathing worsened, he gave in and returned his arms to their former position behind his back. The air in the grain silo was thick and heavy. He could taste it, feel it coating his airways, blocking his lungs, slowly killing him. Jasper turned until his feet rested on the metal wall and began to kick. He'd call out every ten kicks because he needed to save his breath, but at the first kick, a flurry of grain slithered over his head and he jerked up, gasping.

Afraid to try again until he'd worked out what was happening, Jasper scooted around, exploring with his hands and his body. He found the wall of grain he'd slid down that probably saved his life, but had no idea how high it was. Maybe the outlet was at the bottom of that, but not a way out for him. In fact if the outlet was opened and he was caught in the grain, he'd be sucked to his death. If nobody came, if for any reason that wall of grain fell to settle on him, if his asthma took hold, Jasper was dead. He retreated as far as he could from the worst danger, lay on his side and kicked and kicked again at the metal.

Calum lay on his bed, with his heart pounding. Why the fuck had he told Jasper about the rape? He'd kept it buried all these years and then just blurted it out. It had happened a long time ago. Why did it even matter? He'd gotten over it. It was done, finished, not forgotten, but— *Oh shit*. Calum rolled and buried his face in his pillow. What was he so scared of? Jasper wouldn't hurt him. The guy had opened his heart and Calum had repaid his trust by running. *I'm such an asshole.*

What should he tell him? Calum shuddered. The truth? All of it? He rolled over and buried his face in the pillow. The first words from his mouth had to be—I'm sorry. He needed to talk to Jasper but he had to get himself under control first. Judging by his racing heart, that wasn't going to be anytime soon.

Calum reached Jasper's room to find he'd already gone. Disappointment sank like a stone in his stomach. Jasper hadn't bothered to straighten the bed. That sort of surprised him because the guy was such a neat freak. The rug was rumpled too. He'd left in a hurry, probably desperate to get away. Calum flung himself facedown on the bed. His hands clenched on the dark cover and he groaned. Wet. Was that his come or Jasper's? But when Calum lifted his hand, it was stained red.

What the fuck? Calum pushed himself up and stared at the cover. There were a couple of dark patches toward the top and he rubbed them. His fingers came away smeared with blood. Maybe Jasper had cut himself shaving. Not that he'd needed a shave. Christ, he could have cut himself on his suitcase, on anything. Then the thought struck him that Jasper might still just be getting into the cab, and Calum ran. He dashed out of the main entrance and sagged. No sign of a cab, though in the distance he thought he saw the shadow of a vehicle traveling without lights.

Too late.

Calum kicked at the dirt. He'd fucked it up. Jasper might have been leaving in a few days, but they could have spent them together. They could have emailed, shared vacations, still *had* something. Calum headed toward the stables and the comfort of Blue, wondering who he was trying to kid. A long distance, under the radar romance? This might be Wyoming but it wasn't Brokeback Mountain. They couldn't live separate lives and steal illicit moments. What if Seth really was his? There was another heap of responsibility there. How many ways could Calum split himself?

Something glowing in the dirt drew his attention. *Raining moonstones?* When Calum bent to see what it was, he sighed. One of Angie's glow-in-the-dark beads. He looked a little farther and saw another. Had she laid a trail? Calum expected it to lead to Misty, but it bypassed the stables and led to the rear barn. He didn't find another for a while. She wasn't exactly making it easy, but Calum knew how thrilled she'd be that he'd followed and now that Jasper was gone, there wasn't much else to do. Plus he needed distracting.

When he found three beads together in the back barn, he saw a patch of something wet in the dust. Calum rubbed it with his fingers. *Oh hell. Blood.* Calum's brain struggled to put two and two together. Blood in Jasper's room, blood here, Angie's beads. Was Angie hurt too? Was she someplace with Jasper?

Calum kept looking and found a couple more beads near the rear door. Another lay at the foot of the silo ladder.

A muffled thud made him jump. *What the fuck?* It sounded like it had come from inside the silo. *Oh Christ, is Angie in there? Playing hide and seek?* Calum banged on the outside of the silo. "Anyone there?" Then he pressed his ear to the metal and listened. He heard something. *A groan?*

Calum sprinted up the ladder, flung open the lid and peered down into the darkness. A figure lay at the bottom. Not Angie. Calum thought his heart was going to stop. "Jasper," he whispered then yelled it, "Jasper!" Calum fumbled at his belt for his phone. Listened to it ring and ring and debated running back to the ranch to wake his father, until finally he answered.

"What the hell—"

"Listen," Calum shouted. "Jasper's trapped in the grain silo. I need rope. I need help and I need it now. Check Angie's in bed and then come."

"How—"

"I don't know. There's no time."

"But Angie—"

Calum wanted to scream at him. "Just check she's okay and then come help me. We have to get him out. He has asthma." Calum exhaled. "I need to go in after him."

"Do nothing until I'm there," his father snapped. "I don't want two of you trapped. I'm coming."

Calum bent over the opening. "Jasper? I can hear you breathing. You keep doing that. In and then out. Don't fuck it up. I'll get you out of here real fast. How the hell did you get in there? Shit. Don't answer that. Just keep breathing. Oh fuck. Hurry up. Not you. My dad."

He thought his heart was going to leap out of his throat. Calum felt around the lid for the safety rope and pulled it up the outside of the silo. He checked the fastening was tight and then tied himself to the end. The moment he saw his father coming, he was going in. *Fuck it, I'm going in anyway.*

"Don't you dare," his father shouted.

Calum sat on the rim of the hole.

"You need to check what the grain's doing or you'll cover him when you go in," Vera called.

They were in robes, running toward him with flashlights.

"Is Angie okay?" Calum asked.

"In bed asleep," Vera shouted. "I've called the emergency services, just in case."

"Gunner's on his way too." His father began to climb the ladder. He was panting when he reached Calum. "What—"

"I don't know," Calum blurted.

Calum took the flashlight and shone it down into the grain store. Jasper lay motionless on one side. On the other side was a slope of grain.

"Lucky we're waiting on a delivery," his father said. "You should be okay, but be careful."

Calum knew his father wanted to tell him to wait and that he didn't say it meant a lot to Calum.

"You can't hold me," Calum said. "I'll drop the rope and climb. When I'm down, pass me the longer rope. Get Gunner to fetch the Jeep to pull us out." Calum shifted and then paused. "He'll need his inhaler," he called to Vera. "Find his luggage and look for it. Hurry."

Calum tucked the flashlight in his jeans and climbed down the rope into the silo, hand over hand, trying to keep clear of the slope of grain. He dropped the last couple of feet, felt the grain cascade over his boots and bent to lift Jasper's head. *Oh God, tied up and looks like he was gagged. This is because of me.* Calum swallowed hard and pulled out the flashlight.

"Hey, Jasper. I have you now. Hang in there."

Jasper's eyes were closed, his pale face mottled with blood, his breathing fast and noisy.

"Dad, I need a knife," Calum shouted. "He's tied up."

"Catch."

"Wait 'til I put down the light."

If the knife hit the grain, he'd never find it. But his father shone a light down and the knife landed smack in Calum's palm. He flicked it open and sawed at the rope tying Jasper's wrists and then at his ankles. Who the fuck had done this?

"Rope coming down," his father called.

Calum tried not to think about Jasper's rapid pulse and shallow breathing, or the blood matting his hair or the graze on his chin because it made him want to kill the fucker who'd done this. He couldn't afford not to focus solely on getting Jasper out of here as fast as possible.

Calum tied the longer rope under Jasper's arms, talking to him all the time, telling him to keep breathing, not to give up. Calum kept coughing. The air was so heavy it was hard even for him to breathe.

"Okay," he shouted to his father. "Pull him up."

"Gunner's in the Jeep. You hang on to the rope too. He'll pull you both up."

"Okay. Ready."

Calum wasn't certain the rope would hold them both, but it would take two of them to get Jasper down the outside of the silo. His father wasn't strong enough to lower him. Calum could hear the roar of the Jeep and then Jasper started to move. Calum kept him straight and grabbed hold of the rope above Jasper's head.

They swung together in the air, hanging face-to-face and Jasper's eyes fluttered open. Calum gasped in relief.

"Flying?" Jasper croaked.

Calum was the one who couldn't speak now.

"Going up? Angel. Good." Jasper gasped the words and then his eyes closed again.

Calum's father shouted instructions to Gunner as they rose in the darkness. When they reached the hole at the top of the silo, his father gripped Calum's wrist and helped him climb out to sit on the rim. Between them, they maneuvered Jasper into Erik's arms and then Calum pulled up the loose rope that Gunner had unfastened from the Jeep. Calum wrapped it around the lid and then around himself before tying Jasper to the other end.

"Can you manage?" his father asked.

"Yes. Climb down the ladder and guide him to the ground."

Calum knew his father was trying to take some of the load of Jasper's weight. How the hell had he been carried up here? As Gunner caught hold of Jasper and the pressure on Calum's arms and shoulders eased, he groaned in relief. Calum untied himself and slid down the ladder, feet and hands on the sides, in the way he had as a kid when his father hadn't been looking.

Jasper lay on his back, Gunner at his side.

"Sit him up," Vera barked as she ran back toward them.

Calum pulled Jasper into a sitting position.

"I can't find his luggage. I don't have his inhaler," Vera gasped. "The paramedics are on their way. We need to keep him calm, try to get him to breathe more slowly. Lift his arms too. They said it helps him breathe."

But when Calum started to lift Jasper's arms his cry of pain stopped him.

"Loosen his clothing," Vera said. "Get that tie from around his neck. What the hell happened? How did you know he was in there?"

"I followed a trail of beads. I thought Angie had left them, but she'd made Jasper a bracelet. He must have snapped it and dropped the beads as he was dragged or carried out here. Who the fuck did this?"

Calum dropped the tie and sat behind Jasper, let him lean back against his chest and reached round to unfasten the buttons of his shirt.

"Christ," Gunner murmured as he shone the light on Jasper. "Looks like he's been kicked."

A ball of fury writhed in Calum's chest. "What the fuck have you done?" he snapped at his father.

"Nothing." His dad stood leaning against the silo, breathing heavily.

"Calum—" Vera began.

"Someone tries to poison him—twice—and now this. He was fucking leaving. What did he do to deserve this? Is it a crime for him to make me happy?"

He felt Jasper's hand settle on his thigh and try to squeeze.

"Shut up, Calum," Vera snapped. "Why would your father have anything to do with this?"

Calum glared at the gray-faced man holding on to the ladder with one hand. He looked shocked and exhausted, his other hand rubbing his chest.

"Ring. Pete," Jasper gasped between a whistling inhale and exhale.

"What about them?" Calum asked.

"Did. This." Jasper forced out the words.

"That's crazy," his father said.

"Call the police," Calum snapped.

"I already have," Vera said.

Jasper's breathing grew worse. Calum could feel him struggling.

"Slow," he whispered in Jasper's ear. "In and out, slow and steady." He dropped his voice even lower. "We'll try fast later."

Jasper fell limp in his arms, unconscious but still breathing.

"Don't die, don't die," Calum whispered.

He looked up when he heard his father groan and then watched in horror as he slithered to the ground at the foot of the ladder.

"Erik," Vera screamed.

"Go help your father," Gunner said and moved to support Jasper.

Calum pulled his father flat. He was utterly lifeless. Not breathing. No pulse. *Oh fuck.* He tilted his head back and breathed into his mouth.

"Wait for his ribs to fall, then do it again," Vera said. "Then chest compressions."

Calum breathed again into his father's mouth. "Does he have medicine?"

"Yes."

"Go get it."

Calum placed the heel of his hand in the center of his father's chest, put his other hand on top and interlocked his fingers. He pressed down then released, and counted. Calum couldn't afford to panic, but he felt as if he were being pulled apart by wild horses. As he worked on his father, maybe the guy who'd ordered Ring and Pete to kill Jasper, his gaze was fixed on the man in Gunner's arms.

After thirty compressions, Calum stopped, tipped back his father's head, pinched his nose and blew into his mouth until his chest rose. Did it again and then went back to the chest compressions. When he heard the groan fall from his father's mouth, Calum sagged. Vera skidded to a halt at his side and pushed a tablet into his father's mouth.

"He's breathing again," Calum said.

"Thank God," Vera panted.

Gunner raised his head. "Jasper's stopped."

Calum flung himself over to Jasper, pulled him out of Gunner's arms and laid him flat.

"Don't you fucking dare die," Calum growled and, tipping Jasper's head back, he breathed into his mouth.

He had no idea if this was right thing to do with someone who'd had an asthma attack, whether he could force air down constricted airways, but he wasn't going to sit back and do nothing.

"Oh Christ, what a mess." Gunner groaned.

"Don't even think about it," Calum snapped. "I'm not kissing you as well."

The sound of an emergency vehicle pierced the quiet of the night and a tear dropped from Calum's eye to land on Jasper's cheek.

Note to Jasper: Don't die. Don't die. Don't die.

Chapter Fifteen

Jasper opened his eyes to see a sweet smile on a face he didn't recognize. A blonde woman stared down at him. *Heaven? Ah, ambulance.* He had a mask over his face and he guessed he was breathing oxygen. *Oh God, I'm alive.*

Shit, I hurt all over.

"Back with us, Jasper? That's great. We're taking you to the hospital so we can check you out." She turned to a man lying on the other side of the vehicle. "How are you feeling, Erik? Pain gone?"

"Yeah," he mumbled through a mask. "Chest feels tight, but I'm okay."

Jasper tried to sit up, and when he couldn't move, fear swamped him. His heart pounded. "Can't...can't..."

The woman turned back to him. "Whoa, boy. Keep that heart rate steady."

"Can't...move," Jasper gasped. *Oh God, what if I'm paralyzed like Ben?*

"That's because we've fastened you down. Don't worry. We'll get the two of you to the hospital fast as we can."

Fear over his own situation subsided under worry about Calum. Would Ring and Pete go after him? Anxiety surged up his throat and emerged as a strangled groan. Jasper couldn't remember if he'd managed to tell them who'd done this. He tried to move again and gasped in pain.

"Slow breaths, Jasper," the woman said. "We think you've broken a couple of ribs. Lie still."

"Water," Jasper croaked.

"You're getting fluids." The woman nodded to a drip.

"His throat'll be dry from the grain dust," Erik said.

"Just enough to wet your lips then."

Jasper sucked at the liquid. Not enough but it helped. The moment he began to relax, another thought popped up and the tension rushed back. What if Calum's father had faked a heart attack so he'd get put in the ambulance to finish what Ring and Pete had started? Jasper clenched his fists on the side of the cot and tried again to push himself up. He moved a little but pain and the woman's hand stopped him from doing more.

"Hey, lie still," she said more firmly. "You can't break those restraints and I want you doing nothing more stressful than breathing in and out. Okay?"

She moved out of sight and Jasper glanced at Erik Neilson. *Ah.* Crazy to think the guy had faked anything. He looked like a ghost under the translucent mask, his skin chalky white, his lips colorless.

"Pete and Ring," Jasper rasped.

"Yeah. You said."

Thank God for that. Hopefully the police had arrested them. Jasper tried to rerun everything in his head, to remember what the two had said to each other.

"Why the hell would they do this?" Erik asked.

"They wanted it to look…as though I'd hung myself."

"Why would you do a damn fool thing like that?"

"Broken heart. I'd been pushed into leaving—poisoned sandwiches, a burr left under a horse's saddle, Calum and I having a fight."

"Christ, I don't need this sort of publicity for the ranch."

Jasper couldn't help wonder what ranked higher in importance—his death or the reputation of the ranch. Why bother wondering? Erik didn't give a shit about him.

"You sure it was Ring and Pete?" Erik asked. "They were camping with the other guests."

"I'm sure."

"Why did they change their minds about hanging you?"

"I was too battered. Ring was heavy handed." It frustrated Jasper he'd not even managed to land a decent punch on either of them. "They'd not planned it well. Pete decided...they'd kill me...get Calum blamed."

"Oh God. Did they think you were dead when they tossed you into the silo?"

"No. They thought the fall might kill me...or the next delivery of grain. They knew I had asthma... They'd gagged me." Jasper trembled. "I thought I'd die." *Christ, I nearly did.*

It was a while before Erik spoke again. Jasper's breathing had eased, his pains now dull aches.

"Why the hell would they want you dead?"

"Apart from the fact that I'm gay, and apparently it's not a good idea to be gay in Wyoming? I think...bad publicity."

Erik stayed quiet.

"Someone want your business to fail?" Jasper asked. "Or you to fall out with Calum." He took a couple of deep breaths. "If Calum thought you'd ordered this done to me, what would he have done? Maybe they have a grudge against Calum or you. Do they?"

"Shit," Erik groaned. "Ring wanted to marry Angie."

Jasper looked across at Erik.

"He spent a few weeks being nice to her, instead of ignoring her. After I said no, he went back to ignoring her. If...if I'd thought he really cared for her, I might have said yes. I want my kids to be happy. But I suspected he angled for a share of the ranch."

You're a liar. You don't care whether or not Calum is happy. But Jasper had had enough. He felt like he'd stirred up a hornet's nest and got caught up in the swarm.

"You know what?" Erik asked in a whisper.

Jasper turned to look at him.

"I wish you'd died."

Jasper's heart shrank, as if it were trying to hide from the cruelty of the words. He could have snapped the same thing back to Erik, but instead he closed his eyes. *I want to go home. I want to remember all the good things and forget the bad.*

After the ambulance had taken Jasper and his father away, Calum slumped. Vera put her arms around him and hugged him.

"Everything will be fine," she whispered. "But you're needed here. I'm going to wake Angie and take her to Jackson. I'll look in on Jasper too and call you."

"Okay."

Not that Calum had any choice. He had to direct the police to the campsite, and sitting in the back of their vehicle left him a sitting target for their questions. He ran through everything that had happened from the moment he saw the glowing beads, but didn't volunteer what had happened before. He wished to hell he knew what Jasper was going to say. What if Jasper denied they were having a relationship to try and avoid problems for Calum?

In the end, Calum was saved from having to say anything by their arrival in the camp. Within moments, the site was in an uproar, Pete and Ring loudly protesting their innocence while alarmed guests huddled in groups outside their tents.

"We've been here since five last night," Pete snapped. "Ask anyone."

"Nothing to stop you sneaking out and sneaking back," Calum snapped.

"You're just looking for someone to blame so suspicion don't fall on you," Pete snarled.

Calum had to fight not to clench his fingers in case the temptation to plant a fist in Pete's face became too much.

"Fucking fag," Pete whispered.

Yep, too much. Calum took two steps before a police officer moved between them.

Despite Pete and Ring's protests, the pair were taken away to answer questions and Calum was left to pacify bewildered guests, soothe bemused employees and argue with one highly agitated guy.

"I have somewhere I need to be," Dean snapped.

"Look," Calum said for what seemed like the tenth time. "There's nothing I can do about this. The police want to interview guests and staff back at the ranch."

"I don't even work for you," Dean said.

Calum took a deep breath. It was hard to be anywhere around Dean without punching him.

"We pay you to do the lasso demonstration and you were happy enough to take Dave's place on this overnight trip."

Dean glared. "Yeah, but that was with the understanding I could leave early. I have a demonstration to do near Laramie."

"Then talk to the detective about it."

Calum left two wranglers to break camp while the others brought the guests back the way they'd arrived, on horseback. Despite the police request he return in their patrol car, he'd insisted he needed to bring back the Jeep, but when they told him they'd need to check it for traces of Jasper's blood, Calum had no choice but to let them drive him back. He called the hospital to ask about Jasper and was told he was sleeping. As was his father. When Calum had demanded more details, the word "comfortably" had been added. It didn't help. Then Vera called and told him the same thing. That didn't help either. He slumped against the window and closed his eyes.

He was resigned to having to refund what the guests had paid for the vacation. Maybe some of them would sue. One was a lawyer. They'd come up with an outrageous claim, persuade some idiotic judge to agree with them and the ranch would go under.

Oh Christ. The ranch was the least of his worries. His dad had a heart attack and Jasper was beaten and almost killed. Calum didn't yet know why Pete and Ring had thrown Jasper in the silo, but they had to have been trying to kill him. The thought of it just about froze his lungs. Calum wanted to kill the fucking bastards himself.

By the time the sun rose, the adrenaline keeping Calum upright and functioning had long gone leaving him heavy-eyed with exhaustion. The formal interview by the police had left him completely drained. He'd told them everything he thought was relevant, including the fact that he and Jasper had a sexual relationship though he didn't include the detail about him being raped. He wondered if Jasper would and panic fluttered in his chest. He didn't think Jasper would say anything, not unless he now hated him. *Fuck.*

Calum helped himself to coffee he didn't want but definitely needed, and sat with a couple of the guests in the ranch lounge. His hand shook as he lifted the cup.

"Sorry about your trip being cut short," he said.

"We'd have been heading back here after breakfast anyway," Janie said. "This is so exciting." She winced. "Sorry."

"The best vacation—ever," Melissa said with no hint on her face of how inappropriate that was.

Calum clenched his teeth so hard, he nipped his tongue and tasted blood. *The stupid bitch.*

"We'll still be able to do the rafting trip this afternoon, right?" Melissa asked.

Calum glanced around to check the expressions of the others. "You don't want to leave?"

"Hell no," said the newly married pair and smiled at each other.

"It's horrible what happened to Jasper—oh and your father—but we're not in any danger, are we?" Melissa asked.

Not as long as you don't think cuddling a bear cub would be neat. Somehow I wish you would. Calum had felt certain they'd make a mass exodus but it seemed he was wrong.

"I presume you have enough staff to continue?" the lawyer asked.

"Yes." Just.

"Why did they do it?" Janie asked. "What had Jasper done to them?"

"Innocent until proved guilty," Matt said.

Calum flashed him a glare but kept his mouth shut.

Matt held up his hands. "Hey, I saw nothing, heard nothing. As far as I know the two of them were in camp all night. The only thing I could tell the police was that I saw Ring deliberately rope him when we were practicing the lasso."

Calum wanted to wrap a rope around Ring's neck and pull it tight so he knew what it felt like not being able to breathe.

"How's your dad?" Gunner asked.

"Doing okay." Last Calum heard. "Vera called to say they planned to schedule him for surgery by tomorrow. A bypass. Vera's on her way back with Angie."

"And Jasper?" Janie asked.

"Fractured skull and a couple of broken ribs, bruises, cuts."

Calum picked up his coffee and sipped the hot liquid. He longed to go to Jasper, and instead he was stuck there, running the damn business.

A hand settled on his shoulder and he looked round to see Suz, Seth by her side clinging to her leg.

"Mornin', buddy," Calum said and mustered a smile from somewhere.

"My name's Seth."

Calum nodded. "Mornin', Seth."

"The guy's here to do the test," Suz said, a smug look on her face.

For Christ's sake. "Not now."

"Yes, now," Suz snapped.

"Daddy!" Seth tugged at Suz's arm.

"What have you been telling him?" Calum said through clenched teeth, but as he rose to his feet and moved away from the guests, Seth pulled away from Suz's hand and went running across the room, straight into the arms of Dean.

Suz pulled at Calum's sleeve, her jaw set. "This is not what it looks like."

Seth buried his face against Dean's shoulder.

"The fuck it isn't," Calum muttered. "Out of the mouths of babes."

Suz set her jaw. "What was I supposed to tell him? Come over here."

He let Suz guide him to the side of the room.

"Seth's yours," she whispered. "Do the test and you'll see."

"So how come he's calling Dean Daddy?"

"Because me and Dean are together."

Since when?

Calum turned and stalked out of the lounge, Suz on his heels. A man sat in the reception area of the lodge, a Styrofoam box on the table at his side. He stood as Calum approached.

"Calum Neilson?" the guy asked.

He was a tall, thin individual with a goatee. The box had Helix Tech stenciled on the side. It looked authentic.

"Yes and you are?"

"I'm a rep for Helix Tech."

"Name?" Calum demanded.

Suz elbowed him. "Stop being such a pain. Just let him swab your mouth and it's done. Two seconds."

"Name?" Calum repeated. "Reason I want to know is I'd like to confirm you are who you say you are."

"My name's John Bishop."

"Wait there." Calum turned.

"I can give you their phone number," the guy said.

Calum shook his head. "No thanks." He stomped over to the phone on the reception, his heart pounding, his mouth dry. He was fairly certain he didn't even need to phone, but he'd play it out. Calum turned to watch the guy as he spoke on the phone.

When they confirmed a John Bishop did work for them, collecting and couriering samples, Calum asked them to describe him. He didn't miss the snap of the guy's gaze toward Suz. The person Calum spoke to had no idea what John Bishop looked like, but Calum made it sound as if she did.

As he put down the phone, Dean came through holding Seth's hand. Calum pointed a finger at the rep as if he were firing a gun. "Game's up."

"I don't know what you're talking about," the man said.

"Your timing's lousy. The police are here and there's a team of crime scene technicians working on the ranch. Still want to tell me you don't know what I'm talking about?"

The guy sagged. "Told you this wouldn't work. You still have to pay me."

"Get out of here, you moron," Suz growled.

Relief swept through Calum. He met Dean's gaze and nodded toward Seth. "He the reason you didn't want to come back to the ranch? In case he saw you and gave the game away?"

Dean exhaled and nodded. "This wasn't my idea. Suz thought if Erik believed he was his grandkid, he'd get left something when he die— Ah shit."

"Shut up, Dean," Suz snapped.

"She seemed more interested in me giving her money now," Calum said.

Dean glared at Suz. "What have you been saying?"

"We need money. More than you get twirling a rope and helping out ranchers who need an extra hand."

"We manage," he barked.

"No we don't," she yelled back.

Calum gave a short laugh. "I saw you."

Dean frowned. "Saw me when?"

"Coming out of our bedroom."

Dean paled. "You never said anything."

"I wanted her gone. I didn't care who she went with. But I wish to hell you'd never come back."

"Sorry," Dean muttered. "And I'm sorry about your father."

Calum sighed. More bad news to break to a sick guy. *The kid you think is mine, well, he's not.*

Calum should have known the police would have more questions. Detectives arrived and he took them to his father's office. He'd been at school with one of these guys, Luke Cannock. Luke had been popular, Calum always on the edge of things but they'd rubbed along okay. The other guy who introduced himself as Harry Kosak, looked the same age as his father.

"Sit down, Calum," Luke said. "How's your dad?"

Calum dropped into the chair. "Doing okay, though they're talking about him needing an operation."

"Why don't you start at the beginning," Kosak said.

Calum mentally sighed at the thought of going through all this again. When the hell was the beginning anyway? When he realized he was gay? When he first set eyes on Jasper?

No hiding anymore.

Calum repeated everything, answered every question truthfully.

"So after you and Jasper...had sexual relations, you left his room in an agitated state?" Kosak asked.

He kept his voice neutral but Calum sensed his disapproval.

"Yes, I walked out."

"Why?"

"It's not relevant," Calum blurted.

Kosak frowned. "Let us decide that."

"I told Jasper something had happened to me that affected the way I felt about certain things. I'd never told anyone before and I didn't wait to hear his reaction. I left. I was angry with myself, not him. It's something personal I'm trying to deal with and it's got nothing to do what what's happened here. By the time I pulled myself together and went back to speak to him, Jasper had already been taken, though I thought he'd left in the cab he'd called to take him to Jackson."

"Pete claims you told them to snatch Jasper, to teach him a lesson," Luke said.

A gasp of disbelief burst from Calum's mouth. "Bullshit."

"Whereas Ring told us they were doing what your father had asked them to do." Kosak twirled a pencil over his fingers. "Father is not very pleased with son." His jaw twitched.

It took a moment for Calum to register he was talking about Ring and Pete and not him and his father.

"Then Ring changed his story and said Jasper tried to force him into sex." Luke stared at Calum.

"No way," Calum said.

"We might have gone some way to believing that one, but Pete didn't go down that road," said Kosak. "And the longer we left Ring, the more he came up with and the more unconvincing he became."

Luke leaned forward in his chair. "The interesting thing is, Jasper's not said much, but one thing he definitely hasn't said is that you are in any way involved with each other."

Calum sighed. "He's trying to protect me." *The stupid, lovable idiot.*

"Why?" Kosak asked.

"Because no one's supposed to know I'm gay."

Luke snorted. "Hell, Calum, we all knew at school. We just ignored it."

Calum managed a small smile. "Guess I didn't do such a good job of hiding it then. My dad is hoping they'll invent a pill to convert me."

"You married, didn't you?" Luke asked.

"Briefly. No one can say I haven't tried to be what my father wanted."

"How do you get on with Marty Shaw?" Luke asked.

Calum frowned. What did Marty have to do with anything? "Like most ranchers get on with their neighbors. Good and bad. Why?"

"When we confronted Ring and Pete over their contradictory stories, they both changed to the same one. They've been working for Marty Shaw to undermine the Neilson ranch. Your father refused to sell this place to Marty but seems he didn't want to take no for an answer."

Calum picked his jaw up off the floor. "Marty said that?"

"Not yet, but I think he will," Kosak said. "He's being questioned."

"Christ," Calum muttered.

"They reckon Marty wanted Erik shut down so he could run the only dude ranch in the area," Kosak said. "It was a win-win situation for Pete. Paid for working as ranch foreman for Erik, he claims he also pocketed money from Marty to make sure guests grew increasingly dissatisfied with their vacation."

Calum's jaw ticked. *The bastard.*

"Pete also wanted your father to grow increasingly dissatisfied with you," Luke added. "It was a two-pronged attack. Marty wanted to persuade your father to sell to him, but he didn't want the ranch left to you if your father died. I suspect Pete had milked his cash cow for too long and either Marty suggested a guest should die or Pete did."

Calum wondered if Marty cared who they'd picked. Had Ring and Pete only gone after Jasper because of him?

Kosak leaned forward. "Before Marty clammed up and asked for his lawyer, it was clear he hated your father's guts. He practically spat when he talked about him."

"Marty and my dad have some sort of grudge that occasionally flares up. I've no idea what it's about."

Kosak sighed. "I do. I was at school with Marty and your dad. Your mom was a mighty pretty woman. She chose Erik, and Marty never got over it."

"But Marty's married. He's been with Lois as long as I can remember. She and Mom were friends." And it had always puzzled Calum that the Shaws had never been invited onto the Neilson ranch.

"When your mother died, Marty got drunk and smashed up a bar in Jackson," Kosak said. "He blamed your father for her death."

Calum felt his world was unraveling. "She died of cancer. How could that be anyone's fault?" The familiar ache hit him in the gut when he thought of his mom and her promise not to die, a promise she'd known she couldn't keep.

"Lois told him your father kept saying it was nothing to worry about and by the time your mother went to the doctor, it was too late." Kosak stared straight at him.

"Oh God. How do you know all this?" *It's my father's fault?*

"Lois is my wife's sister."

Calum spent the rest of the day on autopilot. Vera came back with Angie and the news that his father had been transferred to the University hospital where they'd operate tomorrow. Neither of them had seen Jasper but had been told he was comfortable. *What the hell did that mean?* Kosak had called to say Ring and Pete had been charged with attempted murder. Calum's stomach churned at the thought of Jasper not having been found. If Angie hadn't given Jasper that bracelet, if they hadn't been glow-in-the-dark beads, if…if…if… Calum was desperate to go to the hospital to see him, but he couldn't just walk out.

The ranch was shorthanded. He'd have to double up the guests with the wranglers. Gunner could handle the grain delivery. The kitchen staff could function without Vera's supervision for a day or so. The remaining activities the guests could choose to do were visits to Yellowstone or to the local hot springs. Calum spent an hour in his father's office, going through paperwork, making sure no bills were due to be paid, responding to emails from prospective guests, but his mind constantly strayed to thinking about Jasper.

Calum looked up when he heard the knock at the door.

"You all right?" Vera asked. She looked tired and drawn but keeping it together. Her gaze fell on the desk, strewn with papers. "You don't have to do everything straightaway."

"I know."

"Your father wants to see you."

"Now?" Calum stiffened.

Vera nodded.

He pushed himself to his feet. "The guests okay? Staff okay? You okay?" He wrapped his arms around Vera and gave her a hug. Her fingers gripped him tight for a moment.

"The guests are fine. Staff's overexcited but fine. I'm fine."

Christ, we're all experts at hiding how we feel.

"He should have had bypass surgery a long while ago," Vera said.

Calum pulled away to look at her.

"He kept putting it off, putting it off. Now he has no choice." She gave a grim smile. "You two have so much in common. Avoiding issues, stubborn as mules, letting problems grow into impassable mountains."

"Not impassable," Calum whispered.

"No, that's true. Passable with care. Go and see him, Calum."

He hugged her again and pressed his face into her hair. "Love you, Mom," he whispered.

When he felt Vera shake, regret for what he could have said and done years ago rose into his throat and choked him. She pushed something into his hand and Calum looked down to see another of Angie's bracelets.

Vera smiled and wiped a tear from her cheek. "She wants Jasper to have it in case he gets lost again."

As Calum rode the elevator to his father's room, he glanced at his watch. By the time he made it to the other hospital, he doubted they'd let him see Jasper, but that didn't mean he wasn't going to try. But first he had to speak to the man he didn't really want to see. Had his father delayed his mother seeking medical advice? He was a bull of a guy, never admitting to any of his own aches and pains, but Calum remembered him being gentle with his mother. He didn't want to believe his father would have brushed away her worries over her health.

His father opened his eyes when Calum walked into his room. He looked shrunken somehow, much smaller than the man he knew. The bed was surrounded by machines, and it struck Calum that his father might die and this could be his only chance to make things right.

"How are you feeling?" Calum asked.

"Absolutely fine. Can't understand why they don't let me out of here."

Calum rolled his eyes. "Mom sent these." He didn't miss his father's startled glance.

"Mom?" Erik muttered.

Calum put a bag down on the bedside table. "A book she says you ought to read and your puzzle book. She's ripped out the answers to stop you cheating. She'll be here tomorrow with Angie before your op."

"Mom?" Erik repeated. "What changed?"

"Something Jasper said to me."

Erik scowled.

Calum took a deep breath. "When did Mom find out she had cancer?"

He supposed he deserved the puzzled look Erik shot him.

"Nine months, three weeks and two days before she died." Erik worried the sheet with his fingers. "She found a lump and didn't tell me. By the time she went to see the doc, it had spread. She should have told me. I don't know why she didn't." He sighed. "Maybe I do. I don't like weakness. I didn't allow myself to be ill and I think she thought that applied to her too.

There's not a day goes by that I don't blame myself for her death."

And Calum knew that no matter what Marty's wife had said, his father was telling the truth. Maybe Lois had her own agenda, married to a man who still held a torch for a woman he couldn't have. At least this wasn't something else to blame his father for.

"How's everything at the ranch?" his father asked.

"Fine."

A snort was the response to that. "Two of my wranglers try to kill a guest and everything is fine?"

"Ring and Pete are in custody. The guests think this is the most exciting vacation they've ever had and two of them have booked again for next year."

That brought a smile to his father's face. "Think you're up to handling things until I'm back on my feet?"

Calum bristled and made himself take a deep breath before he responded. "I'll do my best."

"I heard you gave me CPR. Saved my life."

Calum shrugged.

"If you do a good job of running the ranch until I'm back, I'll make you foreman."

And Calum felt his father had thrown a chain around his neck. What he'd once wanted was not what he wanted now.

"Not going to ask why Pete and Ring did it?" Calum asked.

"Guess they feel a little more strongly about gays than I do."

You bastard. "Going to ask how Jasper is?"

"No."

Fucking bastard. And Calum no longer wanted to make things right. The guy would never change and there was somewhere else Calum wanted to be.

"Seth isn't mine," Calum said. "Suz was running a scam. He's Dean's kid. Suz cheated on me. I never cheated on her."

His father's eyes widened. "I thought—"

"I know what you thought, but you never asked." Calum stepped toward the bed and landed a clumsy kiss on his startled father's cheek. "Good luck tomorrow." Then he walked out.

Jasper opened his eyes when the nurse bent over him. The Hispanic guy had a sweet face and smelled of lemons.

"You awake?" he asked Jasper.

I am now.

"You have a visitor. It's after-hours, but I can let him in for a couple of minutes if you feel up to it."

Jasper shook his head. "No, not up to it."

He tried not to wince at the pain. It wasn't just his body that ached but his heart. There was nothing in the world he wanted more than to see Calum, which was exactly why he couldn't, shouldn't, wouldn't. Better for both of them to break like this.

The nurse left and a few minutes later, the door opened again. Jasper held his breath because the idiot part of him wanted Calum to take no notice of what the nurse said and burst in to see him and tell him he lo— *Ah fuck*. The nurse came up to the bed and put something in Jasper's hand. Jasper knew what it was before he looked at it. Another bracelet.

When the police had interviewed him, they'd told him Calum had followed the trail of beads. If it hadn't been for the gift from a sweet child in a woman's body, Jasper suspected he'd be dead.

On the third day, when Calum was told he couldn't see Jasper, he realized it wasn't a medical problem keeping them apart but Jasper's choice. He'd been asked to bring Jasper's bags, discovered hidden behind a stack of timber, and Calum had washed and folded the clothes himself, and then packed them with an immovable lump in his throat. The police had kept the tie that had been used to gag Jasper, but Calum took another from his bag. He wanted it to remind him of how he'd used the tie to pull Jasper in for that kiss. In the heart of the suitcase, he placed a well-wrapped package and hoped it survived the trip back to London.

Calum hadn't wanted to accept that Jasper didn't want to see him anymore but he wasn't going to push. A word with the nurse confirmed there was no point coming the next day because Jasper wouldn't be there. Pete and Ring hadn't made bail yet. Calum hoped they fried the bastards. His father had sailed through the operation and was issuing orders from his hospital bed, most of which Calum had already dealt with. Another load of guests had arrived, half of whom hadn't ridden before. Calum had taken on two more wranglers who seemed to be working out fine.

Note to self: Everything is fine, fine, fucking fine—as long as I stop thinking about Jasper.

Chapter Sixteen

"Two bloody weeks leave? How did you wrangle that, you jammy devil?" Ken Adams asked as Jasper passed him in the corridor.

Ken didn't wait for an answer. Jasper had told his boss not to tell anyone why he was late coming back, including his uncle who was one of the firm's partners, and in any case, Jasper hadn't told his boss the entire truth. Easier to say he'd been attacked, hospitalized, and leave it at that. Even so, Jasper expected the office gossip machine to invent salacious details during the coffee breaks.

After being discharged from the hospital, Jasper had checked into a hotel and spent his time either in or by the pool allowing his body to recover. His heart didn't do so well. His interest in visiting Yellowstone submerged under a myriad of emotions, continuing headaches and pain in his chest, and inertia tightened its hold. He'd kept telling himself everything was fine, but it wasn't then and it wasn't now.

Apart from the fact that he was plagued with nightmares where he suffocated in a grain silo, he couldn't stop thinking about Calum, and when he did, he felt as though a heavy weight pressed against his chest. Feeling it was hard to breathe seemed to be the constant in his life. He'd used his inhaler more over the last couple of weeks than he had in the whole of last year. Jasper suspected he needed to talk to someone, but there was no one he wanted to tell. He could, however, tell his mum tonight, as long as she didn't recognize him.

Once inside his office, he put the box he was carrying down on his desk. He was petrified of dropping it. Jasper hung up his jacket, sat in his chair and swiveled to look out of the window at a gray day, gray concrete and a gray pigeon. His spirits sagged to puddle in a pathetic pool at his feet. He didn't want to work here anymore. He didn't want to do this job anymore. He didn't—

The telephone rang and he sighed. *It all starts again.* Caller display told him it was one of his bigger clients and Jasper turned up his cheerful button before he answered. "Good morning, Simon. Missed me?"

"Been away?"

Fuck you too.

By lunchtime Jasper was exhausted. His head ached and his eyes were sore and gritty. When the phone rang at a minute to one, he did what he'd never done before and ignored it. He picked up the box and walked out.

Fintan's Gallery was a small boutique store selling an eclectic range of artwork. Exquisitely painted wild landscapes that Jasper loved but couldn't afford to buy stood alongside pieces of sculpture he'd have been hard pressed to hold the right way up. He often popped in to look round and he *had* bought one small painting from the owner last year, though he'd refused the invitation to go for a drink. And all subsequent invitations though Fintan was getting more and more inventive.

"How did you know I was gay?" Jasper had asked.

"You're gay?" Fintan raised his manicured eyebrows. "I'll throw in dinner along with the drink."

Fintan was a lovely guy, but flamboyantly gay and twice Jasper's age. He hadn't taken offense at Jasper's refusal and invited him to all the open evenings he held for his fledging artists. Those invitations Jasper *did* accept, though on every occasion, Fintan flirted with Jasper more than anyone else. "I can't resist gorgeous guys. I never give up," Fintan had whispered in his ear.

He was exactly the right guy to show Calum's work.

When Jasper pushed open the door, Fintan threw up his hands in joy—*oh bloody hell*—and rushed toward him. *Please don't hug me.*

"Jasper! I haven't seen you in ages."

Jasper clung onto the box. The contents had crossed the Atlantic. He didn't want it to break now.

"Hi, Fintan. I've something for you to look at. I'd like your advice."

"You only have to ask, dear boy. I'd love to handle something of yours."

Oh God. Jasper put the box on the counter.

"Whatever is that around your wrist? You're wearing jewelry?"

"A present." He pushed Angie's bracelet back under his cuff. He knew he ought to take it off but he just couldn't. *In case I get lost.*

Fintan gently peeled away the layers of tissue paper and took out the clay model Calum had hidden in Jasper's case. It was the figure of two men. One wearing a Stetson leaned back against a rock, knees bent. The other figure had his head resting on the cowboy's chest, legs outstretched and crossed at the ankle. The cowboy's hand was in the other guy's hair. That guy was unmistakably Jasper.

"Oh my," Fintan whispered. He looked up into Jasper's face and gave a tiny smile. "You've just broken my heart."

A shiver trickled down Jasper's spine, as if something had passed from Fintan to him, some knowledge of which Jasper had been unaware.

Not unaware, I'm in denial.

The gallery owner examined the piece from all angles, even took out a magnifying glass, and then stood up and exhaled.

"Is it good?" Jasper asked. He knew it was, but he still wanted Fintan to say it.

"Silly, boy. It's fantastic." He gave a dramatic sigh. "Of course clay is hopeless. It needs to be cast. Who's the lucky cowboy trailing his fingers in your luscious locks? The guy who made this?"

"Yes. His name's Calum Neilson."

"Is this yours?"

Jasper nodded. "I want it cast in bronze. Can you arrange that?"

"Of course. I could sell a bronze version of this for at least £700, maybe £1,000, though it would cost twice that to produce the first one. The most cost-effective way would be to make perhaps ten bronzes, keep one, sell the rest. I'd buy the other nine for £5000. And I'd be keeping one for myself as a memento." He winked at Jasper. "It's stunning. Reminiscent of Remington."

Jasper smiled. Part of him wanted there to be only one bronze just for him. The cost of casting didn't matter, but he imagined how thrilled Calum would be to know people wanted to buy his work.

"Okay. Ten bronzes," Jasper said, "but I get two. And it's still £5000."

"Deal." Fintan stuck out his hand.

Jasper shook on it and didn't miss the extra squeeze.

"He's a lucky guy," Fintan whispered.

For a brief moment, Jasper considered telling Fintan everything, but he knew it wouldn't make him feel better. Probably make him feel like an idiot.

"Fast as possible," Jasper said.

"Spoilsport." Fintan winked. "I love to go slow."

By the time the phones stopping ringing, Wyoming was a fading dream. Back in the noise and bustle of London, those wide-open plains and dazzling Western skies seemed a lifetime away. He'd have to go back for the trial. And see Calum again. How would things be between them? Would Calum have found someone else? Jasper hoped he did and yet even as he completed the thought, pain flared in his heart.

He caught the Tube back to his house and then used his car to drive to his mother's nursing home. It was getting dark when he arrived and lights shone in every window of the converted mansion. All the lights on and nobody home, Jasper thought with a wry smile.

Alcott House had been his mother's residence since Ben had died. She'd slid into a state of shock and never really emerged from it. It had been as though all her energy had been put into looking after her youngest son, and when he'd gone, she had no reason to carry on.

Bronwyn Randolph had seamlessly drifted from a dreamy daze into Alzheimer's, and because Alcott House would take anyone who could pay the exorbitant fees, she'd stayed there. The money from the sale of the family home had been far less than Jasper hoped. His father had remortgaged to buy the best of everything for Ben. His suicide meant no insurance payment because he'd taken out the policy less than two years earlier.

Jasper had managed another year at university before it became clear he couldn't afford to continue. He didn't want to give up his dream, but he had little choice but to leave university and take the job offer with the company run by his father's brother. Four times the salary he'd expect for the first few years as a vet. Huge annual bonus he'd never get as a vet. All to make sure his mother had clean sheets on her bed every day and tea served in the middle of the afternoon with crusts cut off her cucumber sandwiches.

As if she'd fucking know.

Jasper lifted the bouquet of flowers from the passenger seat and climbed out of his car. He hated coming here. He planned his time of departure before he even arrived.

"Mr. Randolph, welcome," said the woman on reception. "Come to see your mother?"

No, I thought I'd come and sit by the bed of some random stranger. He might as well.

"I'll call and tell them you're coming up."

She pressed a button, nodded for him to pass through the security doors, and he headed for the stairs. No smell of old age here. The place was like a five-star hotel. Except the guests never left. Well, only in boxes.

Jasper never knew what he was going find. A mother who knew him. A mother who thought he was Ben. A bewildered stranger. A snarling witch. Ah, that'd be the mother who knew him.

A nurse smiled at Jasper as she came out of his mother's room. "Good evening, Mr. Randolph."

"How is she?" he asked.

"Quite bright today. She'll be pleased you've come."

That'll be the day. When she *was* lucid, she railed at him for putting her in there and accused him of stealing her money when it was more like the opposite. Jasper pushed open the door. His mother sat in a recliner in front of a better TV than Jasper's. She didn't look up when he coughed. He moved so she could see him and she glared.

"You're in the way," she snapped.

"What are you watching?" He glanced at the TV. Football. Jasper almost laughed. As far as he knew, his mother had no interest in any sport.

"It's me," he said and just in case added, "Jasper. I brought you roses."

He put the flowers on her lap and she smiled. "Ben, you spoil me."

Jasper sighed and perched on the edge of the coffee table.

"Have you any news, darling? Will we soon hear the patter of tiny feet?"

"No," he said quietly.

Her face fell. He could have said yes. She wouldn't remember by the time he came again, probably by the time he got out of the building, but tonight he had a perverse desire not to please her. Then her chin wobbled and he regretted not lying.

"Have to find the right person first," he whispered.

"Don't leave it too late," his mother said. "Life's too short."

And yours is too long. Oh fuck.

Jasper dragged his fingers through his short hair. "I've been on holiday, that's why I haven't been in to see you."

"Silly boy. You were here yesterday."

"Ah yes, I forgot," Jasper said.

She either imagined he came every day or accused him of not visiting for months. The specialist's advice was not to contradict, not to argue because it distressed her more. *What about distressing me? Don't I count?*

"I'm Jasper," he said. "Ben's not here."

"Why not?" She turned from the screen to look at him and confusion washed her face. "Who are you?"

Jasper's heart beat faster. "I'm your son, Jasper."

"I don't have a son called Jasper. My son's called Ben. You must be in the wrong room. Go away."

Remember me, Mum.

Jasper looked into her eyes but found no spark of recognition.

"Remember when Ben and I fell in the pond and came out covered with duck weed? You said we looked like sea monsters."

There was no response. She looked as though she'd gone somewhere in her head, a place too far for him to pull her back. It was a waste of time visiting yet how could he not?

"'Bye, Mum," he whispered.

As he reached the door, she called, "Jasper, thank you for the roses."

He had to fight hard not to rush back and tell her everything, how someone had tried to kill him, how he'd found a guy he thought was perfect, how sorry he was that Ben was the one who'd died and not him. But he kept walking.

Jasper slipped back into his normal routine and one week slid into another. Gym before work—taking it easy because of his ribs. Not leaving the office before eight. Eating a meal picked up on the way home. Falling asleep in front of the TV. As the nightmare of suffocating slowly gave up its grip, Jasper switched to dreaming of Calum—the way he talked, the way he felt, the way he tasted. Thoughts of the cowboy became so much part of his life that Jasper found himself talking to him as if he were there. When that habit travelled from home to work and someone caught him addressing an empty chair, Jasper knew he had to do something, though he didn't know what. So he muddled on, growing more and more unhappy.

It took a month before the bronzes came back from the foundry and Fintan sold them all in the first week. When he heard the exuberance in Fintan's voice as he gave him the news, it occurred to Jasper that Calum might not have wanted to sell them, but it was too late now. Jasper shipped one to Calum, paid a fortune to have it express delivered, enclosed a check for $8,200 and wrote, after several attempts—

Dear Calum,

Hope everything is well with you and that your father is improving. I took the liberty of having your fantastic gift cast in bronze. I had ten made and the dealer sold the other eight—I kept one—I hope you don't mind. The check is enclosed. My dealer friend is pestering for more. He's in awe of your talent.

I'm sorry I didn't have the courage to speak to you before I left but I felt it might make matters worse. I wish you all the best with your life. I'll never regret a second of the time we had together. Be happy.

Tell Angie I'm still wearing her bracelet.

Your friend,

Jasper.

The letter sounded more stilted and formal than Jasper would have liked, but for all he knew, Calum's father would open the parcel and read the note. Jasper didn't want to cause trouble. After he'd shipped the bronze, he felt more settled, as though he'd held out his hand and now it was up to Calum whether he shook it or not.

"Calum, Calum, Calum," Angie shouted. "You've got a package."

Angie leapt at him the moment he walked in the door. Calum tried to think if he'd ordered anything. Nothing came to mind.

"It's from England." Angie tugged at his arm to pull him into the family lounge.

From Jasper? Was he sending the model back? Calum had expected him to call or email or write, but he'd heard nothing. He'd been hurt, but then he'd made no effort to contact Jasper. Calum had tried to tell himself it was for the best but he remained to be convinced.

"I need to wash up," Calum said and gently lifted her hand from his shirt.

"No, now," she said and he gave in.

When he saw his father and Vera, he wished he'd resisted a bit harder.

"I got scissors." Angie leapt forward to grab them from the coffee table and then pushed them into his hand.

Vera laughed. "She's been desperate for you to get home. You don't need to open it here."

"It's okay," Calum muttered.

"It's heavy," Angie said. "Feels like a rock. Mom says it cost a zillion dollars to ship it. I don't think it's a rock. Why would someone put a rock in a box? Unless it was from the moon. Is it moon rock?"

Calum lifted the polystyrene box out of the cardboard and peeled off the tape. Angie stood behind him, her chin on his arm. When Calum lifted off the top, he didn't understand for a moment what he was looking at. Then he felt as if he'd been hit with a sledgehammer.

"It's not a rock," Angie said and sounded disappointed.

"Something I made," Calum whispered.

He took out the bronze and set it on the table. Tears welled in his eyes and he blinked hard.

"You didn't make that," Angie said.

"I made it out of clay. It's been turned into bronze."

Vera came to his side. "Oh Calum, it's beautiful. Come and look, Erik."

Calum saw the note tucked in the side and opened it. A check fell out along with a business card for Fintan's Gallery.

"Erik, come and look," Vera said more sharply.

His father dropped his newspaper and huffed as he walked over.

"What's the money for?" Angie asked.

Calum skimmed the note, his heart pounding hard enough to burst through his ribs. "Oh my God. Jasper sold eight bronzes like this. I made over $8000."

He wanted to jump up and down and hoot with joy but the scowl on his father's face wiped the delight from Calum's.

"What are you going to do with the money?" Angie asked.

"Go on vacation." Calum met his father's gaze when he looked up. The tightened mouth told him what his father thought of that.

"Good thing you got that passport before you settled on college," Vera said.

Calum smiled.

"This is very...nice," his father said. "Could we put it where the guests can see it? You might be able to sell it."

"Not this one," Calum said. "Hey, Angie. Jasper says he's still wearing your bracelet."

"That's in case he gets lost again. I'm glad I gave it to him."

"So am I." Calum kissed her head.

Calum landed early on a Friday morning at Heathrow airport. He'd not slept on the transatlantic flight because he was too wired. He could still hardly believe he was there. Calum hadn't told Jasper he was coming because he wanted it to be a surprise, but ever since he'd boarded the first plane at Jackson Hole, he'd worried Jasper might not find it a *good* surprise.

Calum was armed with Jasper's home address from his vacation reservation, and the business card for Fintan's Gallery. He couldn't see the point going to Jasper's house and waiting all day for him so decided to go to the gallery and see if the guy wanted any of the models he'd brought with him.

The Heathrow Express took him into the city, but Calum found the transport system and the number of people and cars overwhelming. Everything was fast and noisy. He'd never been any place bigger than Laramie. London was like an alien planet swarming with life of so many different colors and dotted with amazing buildings that Calum found something to stare at around almost every corner.

He found a bus that took him to London Bridge, which turned out to be a disappointment, just a plain concrete structure. The bus was more interesting, though he worried about going upstairs. Once he got off, he pulled his Stetson harder down on his head, tugged up the collar of his coat and walked, his bag on his shoulder, box in his hands.

Calum stopped for coffee and watched the world pass, people chattering in every language but English. He stopped again at a children's shop to buy a plastic bag of air-drying modeling clay and again at a wine store to buy champagne. He'd been nervous and excited since he got on the plane and now all he could think was—Jasper.

It was almost noon by the time he found the gallery. Calum tipped back his hat and smiled when he saw the bronze in the window. A burst of pride warmed his heart. A sign underneath said—Cowboys Down *by Calum Neilson. Not for sale.* He wondered who'd come up with the title. *Cowboys Down.* He kind of liked it. Calum pushed open the door and went inside.

The only guy in there was dressed in a knee-length blue coat with a stand-up collar. He had his gray hair tied back in a ponytail and was talking on the phone, waving an arm in the air.

"Have to go. A lovely customer just walked in." He put the phone down. "Please tell me I can help you. I'm going to be so disappointed otherwise."

Calum knew his eyes had opened wider, together with his mouth. He snapped his jaw shut.

"Beautiful, blond and dumb? Oh my, I'm in heaven."

"I'm Calum Neilson," he managed to force out.

The guy in front of him squealed. It was an honest-to-God girlie squeal. Calum just about jumped back outside.

"I should have recognized you. You have such a talent. Why didn't Jasper tell me you were coming? The naughty boy."

Were Jasper and this guy more than friends? Calum suddenly felt uneasy.

"Do you have anything to show me in that box? Oh, I'm so sorry. Where are my manners? I'm Fintan Dorian. This is my gallery."

Calum held out his hand. "Howdy."

"I'm going to wet myself," the guy whispered and Calum laughed.

He put the box he'd carefully packed on the counter. Piece by piece he lined up his creations. A wrangler wrestling with a steer. A mountain lion sprawled on a rock. Jasper leaning against a horse. Calum was relieved all the legs had survived intact.

"What do you think?" Calum asked.

"I think you have fantastic hands. You're going to be a very wealthy young man. And I also think you should leave these with me, and go and tell Jasper how much you love him."

Calum swallowed hard. "It's not like that." *How the hell does he know?*

Fintan smiled. "He works at Stonehouse and Taylor. Right around the corner. 117 Fenton Street."

"I'm much obliged." Calum touched the brim of his hat.

Fintan groaned. "Now you've given me an erection."

Calum fled before the guy asked him to do something about it. He'd never seen anyone like that outside of TV. To be honest, he hadn't thought such flamboyant gays really existed. Fintan wouldn't survive five minutes in Wyoming. But could be Calum was wrong. Maybe it was better to be obvious because then people knew where they stood.

No more hiding what he was and what he felt.

Jasper pressed the button to accept the call from the reception desk. "Yes, Jenny?"

"There's someone here to see you."

Jasper frowned and checked his diary. "Do they have an appointment?"

"No, he's not a client, but he says it's important. Something to do with metal futures. Copper in particular."

Jasper's pulse sprinted like an accelerating car. He was being stupid and reading far too much into nothing, but copper was the largest component of bronze.

"Name?" he asked.

"Angus."

Very stupid. His heart slowed again. "Send him up."

Jasper put down the phone. He'd heard nothing from Calum. Jasper didn't even know if he'd received the bronze. He still found himself skimming down his inbox every morning to see if there were any emails from the Neilson Ranch. One day, he'd have to open his heart again, but not yet. He pulled on his jacket and straightened his tie before he opened the door and stood ready to greet his prospective client.

Christ, now I'm hallucinating.

Except…

Jasper's jaw dropped and his cock rose. Stetson in place, Calum walked down the corridor wearing a navy-blue mid-thigh pea coat and faded jeans, a bag on his shoulder. Jasper couldn't have moved to save his life. The only part of him stirring was his cock, inflating behind his zipper. Luckily his suit jacket hid it from view. Everything seemed to be happening in slow motion, as though he were watching a slowed-down film, and for a moment, Jasper's brain slowed too and he wondered if he'd tipped over the brink into madness.

But then Calum came to a halt in front of him, smiled, and the wave of emotion that hit Jasper made him stagger back from the doorway until he hit his desk.

Ken Adams, passing behind Calum, halted. "Are you all right, Jasper?"

"Tripped. New client. Lunch out." *Oh Christ, was that even coherent?*

Calum moved into the room, closed the door, took off his hat and put down his bag.

"Angus?" Jasper blurted.

"Middle name. You have one?"

"Not that I'll ever reveal, no matter how painful the torture. Oh God, God, God." Jasper threw himself at Calum and kissed him. It was a headlong rush straight to frenzied without passing "Go" or collecting two hundred pounds. Calum tasted of coffee and chocolate and that unique essence of him, and Jasper couldn't get enough. Tongues tangled while four hands marauded like Vikings. They pawed at each other, hands squeezing, fingers pulling hair, sliding under clothes as their kiss veered toward biting violence.

Lust roared like a tiger in Jasper's head, but he could feel Calum stroking his back, trying to calm him, and before he obeyed the idiotic voice in his dick and ripped off Calum's clothes, Jasper jerked his mouth away. In an instant, Calum was back, brushing his lips over Jasper's face, whispering words Jasper had no hope of understanding because his brain was about to explode with happiness. As Jasper struggled to control himself, Calum gave him the sort of gentle, lazy kiss that Jasper dreamed of waking to and never had.

Calum lifted his lips from Jasper's and slid his hands to his neck, stroking his nape with his fingers. Jasper's gaze moved over Calum's face in a circle of desire, from his eyes to his lips and back to his eyes.

"Glad to see me then?" Calum whispered.

"My middle name's Aloysius." Jasper said.

"Is that right?" Calum drawled and smothered a laugh.

"See. That's why I don't tell anyone."

"That's not why I laughed. My initials spell CAN and yours spell JAR. Are we a match, or what?"

Oh God. Jasper smiled. "I can't believe you're here."

"I brought over a few more models to that gallery. Fintan's a...character."

"Yep." Jasper kept the smile on his face, but his internal organs sagged. Was that why Calum had come?

"That's not why I came." Calum pulled Jasper closer by the neck and kissed his forehead.

Note to self: Careful what you think. It appears Calum can read minds.

Chapter Seventeen

Jasper looked so smart and handsome in his dark suit, white shirt and striped blue-and-gray tie that Calum was grateful he wore a coat long enough to hide his cock's reaction.

"Hungry?" Jasper asked.

Calum licked his lips, and then chuckled when Jasper growled.

"Leave your bag here. I'll lock the office and we'll—"

"You can lock the door?" Calum's cock twitched.

Jasper's "Yes" came out as a strangled squeak.

"Everyone going out for lunch?" Calum asked.

Jasper nodded. Calum locked the door and took off his coat. When he spotted Jasper's fingers fiddling with the button on his jacket, he shook his head. "Leave it on." he said. "Sit down."

Calum hadn't intended to do this. He'd hoped for a leisurely lunch and then maybe he'd wait while Jasper worked, and then they'd go to his home and fuck each other stupid. Plan B was much better. Jasper sat behind his desk, his eyes slightly glazed, but his attention focused on Calum's face.

"Let me do *everything*," Calum whispered.

He spun Jasper's chair so he sat perpendicular to his desk and then Calum dropped to his knees. Jasper's hands gripped the arms of the chair and Calum leaned to kiss his knuckles.

"Oh fuck," Jasper whispered.

Calum flipped open the solitary button on Jasper's jacket and pulled the two halves apart. He tugged Jasper's shirt out of his pants, and starting from the bottom, unbuttoned it slowly.

Jasper's ragged breathing sounded over-loud in the room.

"You okay?" Calum asked. "Gonna need CPR again?"

"Not by mouth."

Jasper's cock had tented his pants and Calum dragged his fingernail over the raised mound.

"Sh...it," Jasper gulped.

Calum undid Jasper's tie and let it hang loose around his neck. Tight, dark nipples tempted and Calum leaned forward to lick them.

"Calum," Jasper whispered.

Jasper was tight as a wire, vibrating with tension. As Calum rubbed his fingers along Jasper's lower ribs, he laved Jasper's pecs, trailing the tip of his tongue around his nipples before pulling at them with his teeth. Calum let his body brush repeatedly against the bulge in Jasper's groin before sliding down to mouth his cock through the dark material of his pants, exhaling against it until Jasper whimpered.

The phone rang and Jasper flinched. "Fuuuuuuck. Damn. I need to switch to messages."

When he reached out, Calum caught his arm. "Take the call."

Jasper hesitated and then said, "No more biting," before he lifted the receiver. "Jasper Randolph."

Calum opened the button on Jasper's pants and tugged down the zipper.

"Oh, hi there, Lloyd."

Jasper's cock leapt out of the gap in his boxers without Calum having to touch it.

"Yes, I'm fine, thank you." Jasper stared at Calum.

He pulled Jasper's black boxers down until his balls rested on the waistband, and then wrapped his hand around Jasper's dick and blew across the tip.

"G-good."

Calum licked the slit, and then pressed into it with his tongue and Jasper's hips bucked.

"Woohoo…Where I said they'd take five hundred thousand, it looks like they're pushing for another hundred."

Calum smiled at the curse words Jasper mouthed at him while he was listening to the guy on the other end of the phone, but it hadn't escaped his attention that Jasper had not said stop. The taste of him made Calum's mouth water, the salty-sweet pre-come coated his tongue and sent bolts of heat to his groin.

Jasper's cock felt hard and hot and silky in his hand, and Calum thought about what it would feel like inside him. He'd thought about that a lot. Calum wanted it to happen, needed to take that step because until he did, it was as if that one terrible night was controlling his life. Except he didn't know *when* he could make himself take that step.

He licked up the beads of moisture that formed at the tip of Jasper's cock and dipped his tongue deeper into the little hole. Jasper squirmed.

"Fu-funny you should say that." Jasper cleared his throat. "Bluffing was my thought too. So you want to hold on as long as possible and see if they back down?"

Calum rubbed the silky crest across his lips then licked a slow path from there to Jasper's balls. Jasper made a weird sound, a breath bursting out that he'd tried to restrain.

"Sorry, got a tickle in my throat," Jasper said.

Calum kept licking. Both Jasper's cock and Calum's hand were now slick with pre-come and saliva.

"By all means," Jasper said. "Yes, tell me now. That's fine… No. I'm never too busy to listen to you."

Calum rubbed his stubbled chin against the heavy sac hugging the base of Jasper's cock. He licked up and down the engorged stalk, trailing his tongue the length of the dark vein, and Jasper's fingers furrowed into his hair and pulled. Calum looked up, saw the agitation on his face and grinned.

"Bastard," Jasper mouthed.

Incentive enough for Calum to suck harder. While his mouth was busy at the head, his hand pumped at the base.

"Jes…just run that past me again," Jasper said and re-clenched his jaw.

He might be stuttering, but Calum thought his voice sounded impressively calm. His body, on the other hand, grew tenser, his thighs rock hard under Calum's arms. Jasper's fingers no longer tugged his hair but returned to clenching the arm of the chair. Calum swallowed him until the head brushed the back of his throat, and felt the reaction in his own groin as his cock pulsed with delight. Aware of both his and Jasper's escalating need, Calum couldn't afford to let this go on for long. He tightened his mouth and sucked faster and harder.

"Oh God," Jasper blurted. "That…that's wo…worth thinking about."

Calum pulled back to run his tongue around the dip below the swollen crest and then squeezed with his lips as he sucked very fast. His hand around the root felt the change in texture of Jasper's balls and he knew he was moments away. Calum's thrill at making him come like this made his heart hammer. The power, the ability to bring him off while he was talking to a client, the taste and the feel of him, the hardness, the velvet softness, were like strokes to Calum's cock. Calum tightened his mouth and twisted his lips as he sucked.

"No," Jasper snapped.

No doubt that meant him but Calum wasn't stopping.

"Sorry. Sudden pain in my head."

Jasper's cock swelled between Calum's lips, his hips jerked and he came in long bursts, filling Calum's mouth with warm, salty-sweet jets of come. Jasper's eyes were screwed tight shut, his hand pressing the phone to his head was white.

"Sudden headache," Jasper choked out. "I'll be in touch."

He dropped the phone back on the hook and took hold of Calum's hair.

"You complete and utter bastard," Jasper said, but he was smiling. "Good thing I was only talking to the weather guy."

Calum laughed. "I'm not falling for that. He called you." He pushed himself to his feet.

Jasper stood, tidied himself up and refastened his shirt and tie. "My turn."

Calum's hand fell to his pants.

"Not here," Jasper said.

"You expect me to wait?"

"It'll be worth it. Better put your coat on."

Jasper pressed a button on his desk phone. "Hi, Gemma. Is G12 free?"

"For thirty minutes," a woman said.

"I'm taking a client up. I only need it for twenty-nine."

That's optimistic.

"Fine," she said.

Jasper grabbed his briefcase and unlocked the door. He led Calum to the elevator, stepped inside and pressed the button for the top floor. Jasper glanced at the camera mounted in the top left-hand corner and arched his brows. Calum gave a sight nod, and Jasper relaxed his shoulders.

The door opened on the twelfth floor and Calum followed Jasper out into the corridor. Jasper took a key ring from his briefcase and unlocked a room. Calum walked in and gasped. The wall facing the door was ceiling-to-floor glass with a spectacular view over the city.

"It's the boardroom," Jasper said. "There's something special about it."

Calum looked at the highly polished table.

"Not that." Jasper laughed and locked the door. "Scratch that and I'm dead."

"The view?" Calum wandered over to the window. The river looked like a black ribbon winding through the city. London stretched as far as the eye could see, swathes of green swirling around the buildings.

Jasper lifted the coat from Calum's shoulders and tossed it onto a chair. "The view is excellent, but that's not what's special."

Calum turned and took another look at the room. "Apart from you?"

"Apart from me," Jasper said with a smile.

"I give in. My cock gives in. My balls have already given in."

"The glass."

Calum frowned. "The glass is special?"

"We can see out but no one can see in."

Calum gulped. "No cameras in here?"

"Nope. What would you like me to do?"

"Twenty-nine minutes?"

"Twenty-four now."

"Take your clothes off."

It took Jasper longer than Calum to strip, but by the time Calum retrieved a condom from his wallet and a little sachet of lube, Jasper was buck naked as well, his cock lengthening as Calum watched. *Wow, the guy recovers fast. Oh God, he's still wearing Angie's bracelet.*

"Face the glass, spread your legs." Calum slipped on the condom, squirted lube onto his palm and rubbed it over his cock, wincing at the need that flared inside him.

Calum stood behind Jasper and pushed his legs even wider with his knee. He spread Jasper's butt cheeks, positioned his cock at the entrance to his body and rocked his hips gently so the crest of his cock nudged Jasper's anus.

"Oh Christ, do you know how many times since you left I've imagined doing this?" Calum whispered.

"About as many as I have."

"Not in front of a window, though just about everywhere else." He laughed.

Calum slid his hands to Jasper's hipbones and held him firm as he pushed harder against the puckered entrance to his body, bending his knees as he pulled Jasper down onto his cock.

"You going to let me in?" he asked.

"Knock three times and say the password." Jasper groaned as Calum's tip breeched the barrier.

When he heard Jasper exhale, Calum slid into him, a long, deep push that shoved Jasper against the window.

"Oh Christ," Jasper gasped.

"Sorry, sorry. It's just that you feel so good." Calum licked his neck. "I swear I could come without moving."

"I missed you," Jasper said in a quiet voice.

"I missed you too." *Oh God, how I missed you.*

"Seventeen minutes. You're going to have to count. I'm losing track already."

Calum picked up his pace, feeling Jasper clench around him as he lunged back and forth. Jasper gave a loud groan and the sound wrapped around Calum's heart. He looked out of the window onto the city below and wished just for a moment that they *could* be seen, that everyone could witness how much this guy meant to him.

"Shit, shit." Jasper had dropped one hand from the glass to pump his cock.

Calum circled his hips as he thrust into Jasper, and judging by the sounds of pleasure bursting from him, Calum was hitting his prostate.

"If only I could stop time," Jasper gasped. "I should have asked for that when I was ten instead of Monopoly."

Calum chuckled. He was pounding now as tension began to overwhelm him, tightening his muscles, quickening his breath, tormenting his balls. Jasper took every inch of him into his body, and Calum shuddered with pleasure as his balls hit Jasper's backside. He slid his hands from Jasper's hips to settle on his shoulders.

"Oh Christ," Calum panted.

It felt like sparks from a campfire flickered up Calum's shaft. His balls had knotted tight, drawn up at the base of his cock as if they were trying to climb it.

"Yes, yes, yesssss." Calum cried out as he came, the sound muffled as he bit down on Jasper's back. His hips jerked as his cock pulsed and filled the condom. His knees shook as he rode firecracker aftershocks, and then Jasper's ass clamped tight around him as Jasper spurted ribbons of come onto the glass.

"Where did all that come from?" Calum asked panting.

"Fuuuuuck," Jasper groaned.

Calum withdrew his softening cock and removed the condom. "Much as I'd like to linger, I don't want to get you sacked." He reached for his boxers. "How are we going to clean that up?"

Jasper sighed and left his boxers off. When they were dressed, he wiped the glass with them, tucked the condom into the boxers, wadded them up and handed them to Calum. "It'll spoil the line of my suit."

Calum dropped the boxers in a wastebin once they'd left the building.

"I could have washed them," Jasper said.

"I'd rather you went without."

"It's drafty."

Calum laughed. "So where are we going?"

"A pub. I have to be back at the office by two-thirty but we finish early on Friday. After we've had some lunch, you could go for a wander and meet me back here at four thirty or you can sit in my office and drive me mad with longing."

"I'll stay with you," Calum said. He hadn't come all this way to go sightseeing when the best view was right next to him.

"Talking of staying." Jasper glanced at him. "How long do I have you?"

"A week." Calum had argued for longer, but he hadn't even known if Jasper would want to see him. He bought a round-trip ticket and reckoned he could cope with a week on his own if necessary.

"Have you called and told them you've arrived?"

Calum shook his head. "I didn't set up my phone to work over here."

Jasper handed him his. "You need to dial 00144 before the number. This is the pub. Stay outside, it'll be too noisy in. Want a beer? Sandwich?"

Calum nodded. He tapped in the numbers and waited, hoping his father didn't answer.

"Neilson Ranch," said Vera.

Calum relaxed. "Hi, it's me."

"Calum! Are you in London?"

"Yep. I've met up with Jasper. He's fine." *More than fine.* "We're about to have lunch in a pub. Is everything okay?"

"Fine. Did the gallery want your sculptures?"

"Yes. He was kind of excited."

"That's great, Calum. I'm so proud of you."

Calum swallowed the lump in his throat. "This is Jasper's phone. I better not chat. Give my love to Angie. And Dad."

"I will. Enjoy yourself."

Jasper was against the bar, standing out in the crowd. Not many men wore suits. None were as handsome as Jasper. He turned as if he sensed Calum there, smiled and nodded toward a table. Calum sat down and snagged another stool before he took off his coat. Jasper brought over beers in tall glasses, went back for two plates of sandwiches and sat down.

"I can't believe you're here," Jasper said. "I'm so happy I could explode."

Calum knew what he meant. He felt like he had a firefly inside him, darting around, lighting up his entire body.

Jasper lifted his pint and knocked it against Calum's. "To us."

"To us," Calum echoed.

But as Calum sat in Jasper's office, half-dozing in an armchair, he listened to a guy he thought he knew and realized he didn't at all. Jasper sounded different—self-assured, efficient, controlled. As he sat there brokering deals worth millions, persuading and cajoling those on the other end of the line to accept his recommendations, Calum suspected there couldn't be an "us". Jasper was smart, polished and perfect. He spoke French and what sounded like Japanese, but then even some of the English words and phrases he used sounded foreign. Amortization, illiquidity, fill or kill. It made Calum feel stupid.

As one phone call ended, another began. Jasper had three computer screens in front of him and seemed able to do a million things at the same time—talking, typing and flicking through paperwork as well as rolling his eyes at Calum and mouthing *wanker*.

Calum remembered the clay he'd bought and took it from his bag. He warmed it up, molding it in his fingers until it was soft enough to work and made an erect cock and balls. Jasper snorted into the phone when he saw it.

One blow with his hand and Calum flattened the clay again and this time turned the gray lump into Bessie, sitting looking up at him with that sweet expression on her face he knew so well. Calum always felt she expected him to know what she was thinking. Course, if it was dinnertime, he did.

He used his fingernails to make her fur look real and borrowed a pencil from Jasper's desk to add more detail. Calum became so absorbed in what he was doing that he hadn't noticed Jasper come up behind him.

"That's just like her," Jasper said. "She has that look on her face of complete and utter devotion."

"Want it?" Calum asked and set it on a plastic sleeve on Jasper's desk. "It's kid's clay. It hardens in air."

"I'd love it. Thank you."

"Thanks for getting that bronze made. I could hardly believe it when I opened the box. Angie had guessed it was a piece of rock from the moon."

Jasper smiled. "I bet she was disappointed."

"She liked it. Hell, even my dad seemed to think it was something to have on display, though he wanted to sell it. Not going to happen."

"What did Fintan say when he saw what you'd brought him?"

Calum squirmed. "He doesn't hold back, does he?"

Jasper laughed. "No. I'd guess you've replaced me as the object of his desire."

Calum frowned. "Have—"

"Don't you dare complete that thought," Jasper snapped. "He's a great guy but not my guy."

Since he stared directly into Calum's eyes when he said that, it left Calum in no doubt who was his guy. The moment hung in the air, like a huge wave, before it broke to swamp him with breath-stealing emotion.

"Ready to go?" Jasper asked.

There was a knock on the door and an older guy walked in. He glanced at Calum and said, "Sorry, am I interrupting?"

"What do you want, Kurt?" Jasper asked.

The guy dropped a large orange file on Jasper's desk. "I need you to check this. They're expecting the email tonight. You should have it done in a couple of hours."

He turned to leave and Jasper said, "No."

The guy turned back. "What do you mean—no?"

"I don't have time. You'll have to get someone else."

The guy snatched up the file and stormed out. Calum swallowed. Was he distracting Jasper from his work?

"Do—" Calum began.

"No. I've not spent the afternoon tying up loose ends to get involved in Kurt's problems. His couple of hours is more likely to be five or six. I've better things to do. We're off, though we need to hurry before Kurt calls my uncle to moan about me."

"Your uncle?"

Jasper packed up his briefcase. "He's one of the partners in the company."

Calum put on his coat and shouldered his bag. "So shouldn't you—"

"Yes, but I'm not. I already told you, I have better things to do." He brushed his thumb over Calum's lips and smiled.

As Jasper led Calum down the tree-lined street to his house, he felt nervous. He knew it was clean and tidy. It always was. But would Calum feel comfortable there?

"This one's mine," Jasper said.

"Why don't you drive your car to work?"

"Too expensive, too time-consuming, nowhere to park." Jasper stared at his blue Vauxhall, wishing it would turn into a Porsche or even better a Ferrari.

He climbed the three steps to the front door, opened it and bent to lift the mail from the mat. When he heard Calum growl behind him, Jasper laughed. Calum closed the door and put down his bag.

"Come here," Calum whispered.

Jasper dropped the mail and walked into his arms. His cock had been semi-hard all the way home, now it completed the journey north. Calum's tongue slid between Jasper's teeth and then pulled back to trace the line of his lips.

"You still taste of beer," Calum whispered. "Christ, why do I love kissing you so much?"

He pressed his lips against Jasper's and slid his hands over his back and up to his neck to hold him exactly where he wanted him. Jasper's hands gripped Calum's butt under his coat, his fingers grinding the seam of his jeans into the crease. Then they were shedding clothes, pulling at each other's buttons while they kept their faces together in a frantic lips-nose-tongue kiss that grew wilder by the moment.

They left a trail of clothes along the hall, up the stairs and the length of the landing as they stumbled and laughed and snogged their way to the bedroom. Calum broke away, panting, his gaze fixed on Jasper. Calum was naked while Jasper still wore black socks—and that bracelet.

"Think I've got socks-appeal?" Jasper asked.

"Loads of it, but I want you naked as me."

Calum pushed Jasper to lie back on the bed and then pulled the socks off with his teeth. When Jasper felt Calum's lips around his toes, he shuddered, closed his eyes and wrapped his fist around his cock. One nip of his big toe and all but a couple of Jasper's organs turned to soup.

"Like that?" Calum asked.

"Speak. Can't. Sense. What. Fuck."

Calum laughed. Jasper opened his eyes and pointed to the bedside cabinet. "Lube, condoms, nipple clamps, handcuffs, raclette."

"What?" Calum gaped at him.

"It was a joke."

Calum narrowed his eyes. "Which of them don't you have?"

"The raclette's downstairs."

Calum yanked open the drawer and threw lube and a string of condoms onto the bed. "I don't know what the hell a raclette is, but we'll leave that for another time."

He pushed up Jasper's legs and leaned through the V to lick his nipples. When he drew his teeth in tight and tugged, Jasper sucked in a breath at the bite of pain.

"Aaah shiiiit," he hissed.

Calum licked him all better and then bit him again. Jasper held Calum's head, fingers threading his hair, pulling him off, pushing him down. The rough stubble of Calum's cheek, together with his hot, wet tongue had Jasper writhing. Calum lowered himself onto Jasper, pushing their cocks together, and they rutted, lips joined, panting into each other's mouth. Jasper slid his fingers into the seam of Calum's backside and massaged his butt cheeks with his palms.

Calum licked his way to Jasper's neck and whispered, "I want to fuck you so bad. Can I?"

What could Jasper say but yes? It wasn't that he didn't want to be fucked by Calum, but he had to push back the disappointment that once again he was on the bottom.

Note to self: I have to talk to him about this.

Tomorrow.

Mmm.

Maybe the day after.

Chapter Eighteen

Jasper melted under Calum's caress. He still couldn't quite believe the cowboy was here. *In my bed.* Jasper lay on his side, Calum behind him, panting into his ear as he held up Jasper's leg and slid into him. *So good, but I wish I was doing this to you.* It took only moments before Calum grunted and cried out, his hips jerking as he spurted into Jasper. Jasper's hand pumped at his cock but his heart wasn't in it. They needed to talk. Now. Not tomorrow or the day after.

Barely a heartbeat passed before Calum withdrew. He pulled Jasper onto his back and buried his face in his shoulder. Jasper's hand fell from his softening cock. He slid the condom from Calum's dick, put it aside and then wrapped him tight in his arms. Another heartbeat and Calum was asleep.

A smile curved Jasper's lips at how fast Calum had zonked out, though the smile didn't last. He hadn't had the chance to talk to Calum about the rape. Back in Wyoming, Calum had blurted it out, rushed off, and Ring and Pete had burst in. Jasper guessed the rape was at the root of Calum's reluctance to bottom, but how the hell could he bring it up? Maybe Calum didn't want to talk about it—ever. What if he thought merely telling Jasper was enough? If they only had this week together, then maybe it should be left to rest, but that meant always being the subservient partner. *That's not me.* And the longer it went on, the harder it would be to do anything about it.

Jasper had no idea how to handle this. Or if he should even try to. *Fuck it.* Maybe he was already handling it by lying here and holding Calum and saying nothing. Jasper brushed his cheek against Calum's tousled hair. He was the first guy he'd ever had in this bed. Not that he'd wanted it that way, but Jasper was cautious. He never rushed into anything.

Usually.

"I'm sorry," Calum whispered.

Jasper stiffened. *Had he even been asleep?* "What for?"

"For not coming back to your room soon enough," Calum mumbled into Jasper's shoulder. "For what Ring and Pete did. For not letting you fuck me."

Jasper tightened his hold. "First of all, you're not responsible for Ring and Pete's actions."

"Yeah, I am. If I'd taken it more seriously about the burr under the saddle, the sandwich making you sick, the stuff about the mountain lion, maybe I'd have been able to stop what followed. If I hadn't shown any interest in you, they'd never have picked on you like that."

Jasper shuffled down so that he lay face-to-face with Calum. "But I showed interest in you as well. And you *did* come back to my room, which was the important thing. If you hadn't spotted those beads, the outcome would be very different. You saved my life. I don't think I ever said thank you." Jasper kissed him. "Thank you."

"You're welcome."

Jasper smiled. "What lovely manners."

Calum thumped him in the kidney. Not hard.

"What did your father think about you coming over here?"

Calum winced and then stroked Jasper's neck. "Pointed out a whole load of reasons why it was a bad idea. I had to come. I have to… I want to…" He shuddered and pulled away to sit on the edge of the bed with his back to Jasper.

Jasper swung his legs on either side of Calum's hips and sat behind him to massage his shoulders, pressing his thumbs into tight muscles, willing Calum to talk.

After a couple of minutes' silence, Jasper gave in.

"I've never found it easy to talk about personal things," Jasper said. "I think that's true for most men, but even as a boy, if I had a problem, I kept quiet. I was bullied at school for a long time and it was only Ben blabbing to our father that eventually stopped it. I was geeky, wore glasses, always did my homework, always came top of every test and it was my hand that rose in response to questions no one else could answer. The phrase 'Teacher's pet' could have been coined for me. I appeared on the surface to be the perfect child—biddable, smart, polite, always well groomed."

"Christ, I'd have bullied you."

"No, you wouldn't." Jasper pressed his thumbs harder into the knotted muscle, and Calum rolled his shoulders with a moan. "The thing is, below the surface I was different. Sex mad, constantly jacking off in the school toilets after I'd showered surrounded by cocks, not understanding why boys' butts turned me on, why I was entranced by the size and shape of those dicks, fascinated in the way balls hung and knowing that if anyone caught me even taking a glance, I was dead. My Latin teacher was an accident waiting to happen." Jasper took a deep breath. "Not quite an accident. It was me who seduced him."

Calum sighed. "You were fourteen. He should have said no."

Jasper kneaded down the sides of Calum's spine. "I was very persuasive and I feel the guilt of that even now."

"He should have said no." Calum turned to look at him.

"He did. I ignored him. Christ, I don't know what had got into me that day. Desperation maybe. I unzipped him, took his cock in my mouth and made him mine."

Calum's Adam's apple rose and fell. "He could have stopped you."

Jasper nodded. "You're right, but it must have been like a dream come true for him. A fantasy he might have jacked off to but never imagined acting on. Sex with one of his pupils. So did I create a monster? Would he have ever thought of touching Ben if I hadn't encouraged him to touch me in the first place? See why I feel guilty? The consequences are that I never, ever make the first move on a guy."

"I don't remember throwing myself at you." Calum leaned back so his head rested on Jasper's shoulder.

"I said you were perfect for me. We collided head-on." Jasper snuggled tighter to Calum's back and swept his arms round to hug him. His fingers brushing the scars from the lion attack. It was a reminder of how close Calum had been to death.

He could feel Calum's heart pounding under his palm, the rapid rise and fall of his chest, the tension in his body. Jasper kissed Calum's neck and waited.

"I got a fucking erection and I came." Calum rushed out the words.

Jasper held him close because he understood what Calum had just confessed. The tension evaporated and Calum shrank in his arms.

"I must have wanted it, right?" Calum whispered.

"Of course not. It means nothing that you came."

"Don't talk crap."

Jasper hugged him tighter as Calum tried to move away.

"They got me on my back. One guy sat behind me, his thighs pinning down my arms, holding my legs up while the other guy fucked me and I not only got an erection, I fucking came all over my chest."

All the tension flooded back and it was like holding a piece of stone. Jasper swallowed hard. "You think that means you must have enjoyed it?"

"I fucking didn't enjoy it, but other people would think that, wouldn't they? That's what they'd have said if I'd reported it."

"Listen," Jasper whispered in his ear. "Ejaculation is not the same as orgasm. It's an involuntary physiological reaction. They wanted you to come because they knew you'd be ashamed and at the same time it lessened their guilt. It doesn't mean you wanted to be raped or that you enjoyed it. Just because you were aroused does not mean you consented."

Jasper felt the tension sliding from Calum, but he didn't loosen his grip.

"I couldn't tell anyone," Calum muttered.

"I know."

"We're supposed be able to protect ourselves."

He sounded like a little kid, not a grown man, and Jasper's heart ached for what had happened to him. "Not against two guys, and it seems to me there's no right or wrong in keeping quiet. I get why you said nothing, why a lot of rape victims keep quiet. Talking about it somehow makes you the victim you tried not to be. You can't know how family and friends will react, or the police, or what the bloody bastard rapists would claim. But one thing's certain, you have to stop thinking that in some way you wanted it, or you'll never get over what happened."

Calum dragged Jasper's arm up to his mouth. "I didn't even freak out," he mumbled into his wrist.

"Because most guys wouldn't. I bet you were calm and composed afterward, maybe a bit subdued. It's the way men cope, but you've buried the issue in shifting sands. You're still struggling."

"How come you know so much?"

"I read the back of cereal packets."

Calum sighed. "I want you to top me, I'm just worried I'll freak out or..."

"Or what?"

"Not get hard," Calum blurted.

Jasper kissed his neck. "You don't think I wouldn't understand?"

"It's not you I'm worried about. I did try once to let someone top me. My head filled with flashes of what happened before, what they did and said, and my cock stayed limp. I swore I'd never let myself feel that helpless again and now I'm frightened how I'll react with you because I don't want—"

"It's okay," Jasper whispered. He pulled Calum back so he lay flat on the bed and then settled next to him. "I can wait."

"But—"

Jasper put his finger over Calum's lips. "When it's right. I would never push this. I will never hurt you."

"Hold me," Calum whispered.

"Always."

That was the sound of my heart breaking.

Calum woke with a jolt, for a moment disorientated. When he realized he was alone in the bed, his heart thumped. *Is it over already? Fuck, I shouldn't have told him.* He turned and his cheek landed on a piece of paper.

You looked so peaceful, I thought I'd let you sleep. Breakfast downstairs when you're ready.

Calum exhaled. He levered himself out of bed, stretched and took in what he'd been too distracted to notice last night. Jasper's bedroom was…stark. Light wood furniture, light brown carpet, cream drapes. But the bronze of the pair of them sat on the top of a chest of drawers on an eye line with the bed. Calum's bag lay in the corner, the clothes he'd discarded last night, neatly piled on top. Calum thought of the clutter in his bedroom and gulped.

The bathroom was tiled floor to ceiling, the showerhead above a place where the floor dipped, a circular drain in the center. The towels hung in a regimented line on a sail-shaped set of chrome rails. It was hard to believe anyone had ever used the room.

A hot shower revived Calum's spirits and he pulled on boxers and jeans before he went barefoot down the stairs. More pale paint on the walls, the same carpet everywhere. He heard Jasper hiss "Shit" and pushed open a door at the end of the hall to find him crouched down in the kitchen. Calum smiled. Here was the mess, pans and packets all over the counters, egg all over the floor.

"Morning," Calum said.

Jasper stood and growled. "You look good enough to eat. And that's just as well because I'm not sure breakfast will be edible." He pulled Calum into his arms and kissed him. "Yep, definitely good enough to eat."

Calum laughed and pulled away. "What are you trying to do here?"

Jasper sighed. "I nipped out to buy the sort of things you served on the ranch. I thought I'd better have a practice first. The results are in the bin."

"What were you trying to cook?"

"Toast."

Calum laughed.

"Eggs, bacon, pancakes. Who knew it was so hard to crack an egg without breaking the yoke?"

"Want me to do it?" Calum asked.

"You can cook?"

"I can do breakfast."

Jasper stepped aside. "Be my guest. I'll clean up the mess."

Calum kind of liked that Jasper wasn't perfect, though it did occur to him that this might have been deliberate. When he caught sight of the burned eggs in the trash can, he changed his mind.

"Is there anything you're desperate to do today?" Jasper asked.

"Nothing I'm desperate to do." *Except fuck you.*

"Good." Jasper came up behind him.

Calum shivered when Jasper's hands slid over his chest. The feel of Jasper's breath hitting his neck made his cock stir.

"Oh God, I can't believe you're here," Jasper whispered. "I think that had to be the best surprise of my life."

Calum chuckled. "Set two places and get me a couple of plates."

"Yes, chef."

Jasper chattered away as Calum cooked and he sensed Jasper's anxiety, as if he was afraid to leave a gap in the conversation. *Christ, is this going to sit between us like a sheet of toughened glass?* Maybe he'd be better to drag Jasper upstairs and tell him to go ahead and fuck him.

Calum put the food on the table and Jasper groaned as he stared at the plate. "Oh God, it looks delicious. I can't tell you how excited I am. Well, I probably don't need to. I haven't shut up, have I? I want to take you everywhere and show you everything. London is a fantastic city—well, if you ignore the traffic and crowds. But not just London, the UK's stunning too. Admittedly not the open plains—oh shut up, Jasper."

Maybe it wasn't anxiety, just excitement, and it was infectious.

By the time they were dressed and ready to leave the house, Calum was buzzing too. Jasper had told him to put on the oldest things he'd brought, which wasn't a problem, but Calum couldn't help laughing at Jasper's version of old.

"You look as though you're going to dine with the Queen," Calum said.

"Hey, I've left off my tie."

Calum sniggered.

"Bring your coat. We'll be doing this outside."

Jasper carried a bag out to the car and put it in the trunk.

"Where are we going?" Calum asked.

"Surprise."

Two hours later, after they'd passed through a village called Camber, they paid to park in a small lot, and Jasper led Calum up a sandy track. As they reached the top, Calum's jaw dropped. Ahead stretched a line of undulating dunes, followed by an expanse of flat sand and then water. *The sea.*

"Christ," Calum whispered.

He took a deep breath. The air smelled different—fresh, untainted, salty. A cloud hid the sun and the color of the sea changed from dark blue to dull gray. Calum looked up. Not the wide blue skies of Wyoming, but there was a lot of blue up there.

Jasper slung his arm over Calum's shoulder. He didn't say anything and Calum was glad. He wanted to drink this in—the water, the sand, the wind. It calmed him somehow. How could he worry about things when there was a vastness like this to drown his concerns?

"Thank you," Calum whispered.

"Have you seen the sea before?"

"Not for real. Are we going to swim?"

"You can. I've got more sense. It'll be freezing." Jasper glanced at his watch. "We should have time to get to the surf. Come on."

He ran down the sand dunes and Calum whooped and followed. Once the sand turned hard underfoot, the going was easier and he ran alongside Jasper until they reached the water. Jasper was breathing heavily.

"You okay?" Calum asked. "Don't tell me you forgot your inhaler."

"In my pocket. I'm fine."

Calum jumped back as a wave rushed toward his feet. He turned to Jasper. "I really want to go in."

"Christ, in October? It's freezing. It's freezing in July as well, for that matter."

Calum moved back to where the sea couldn't reach and took off his coat.

"Oh fuck." Jasper groaned.

Calum shivered as he pulled off his shirt. The wind bit just as hard as in Wyoming. He wrapped all his clothes and his shoes in his coat and beamed as Jasper grumbled at his side and did the same. They stood there shivering in their boxers, Jasper's teeth chattering.

"We going to go in naked?" Calum asked.

"We'd get arrested. Not that there'd be anything to see. My cock has shrunk to the size of a peapod and my balls have retreated to the back of my kidneys."

"Come on, then."

"After you. I only need to delay two seconds and you'll be running back out screaming."

Calum held out his hand.

"Bugger," Jasper said and took it.

Jasper had been wrong about the two seconds, Calum thought. One just about did it. *Fuck, it's cold.* But once he'd started, he wasn't going to give up. He dragged Jasper through the waves, both of them yelping as the water got deeper until they stood up to their waists.

"Oh God, I've lost the feeling in my toes," Jasper moaned.

"My cock's whimpering."

"Let's get out."

"Not until we've swum."

"Oh Christ." Jasper threw himself forward into the waves and emerged swearing. "Jesus fucking Christ, it's freezing." He swam a little way and then turned to look at Calum who hadn't moved. The marks the mountain lion had made on his upper chest looked white in the cold. "Get in here."

"It's too cold. I'm getting out," Calum said.

Jasper stood up and Calum gulped. Water glistened on Jasper's chest, his nipples tight peaks. He looked frozen.

"Get in here," Jasper called.

"Don't think so."

Jasper growled when Calum waded as fast as he could toward the beach and he raced after him, roaring. He caught Calum by his knees and brought him down in the surf. Calum came up spitting water.

"Now fucking swim, you little shit," Jasper barked.

Ten strokes before Calum gave in. More than Jasper thought he'd manage. They bounded out of the water, laughing, and shook themselves like dogs.

Several people were heading onto the beach with a trailer, so Jasper put on Calum's coat to slip out of his wet boxers and pull on his jeans. By the time they were dressed, Calum's lips were blue. Jasper wanted to kiss him and warm him up, but with others around, he wasn't sure how Calum would feel about that.

"What are they up to?" Calum nodded to the guys dragging equipment off the trailer.

"That's the second surprise," Jasper said. "They're kite buggying. We're doing it too. I booked it this morning while you were sleeping."

Calum's eyes lit up and Jasper's heart skipped. He wanted so much to make Calum happy.

They went over to the group and introduced themselves. Jasper and Calum were the only two learning to kite buggy. The others were kitted out in wetsuits ready to kite surf. Jasper had thought about booking that, but now they'd been in the water, was glad he hadn't.

Their instructor was called Brian. It didn't take long to master flying the kites. The only reason Jasper's crashed twice was because he was looking at Calum, watching the smile on his face and the way he bit his lip when he concentrated. They were kitted up in helmets and protective gear before they were allowed in the three-wheeled carts. Those who could already do it were whizzing around at the far end of the beach. Brian explained how to use their legs for steering, arms to control and fly the kite and the way to safely stop.

"Not many on the beach today but you still need to keep your eyes peeled," the instructor said. "Remember to start off with the buggy pointing downwind and the kite overhead. If the kite crashes, you need to get back into that position before you try again. Drop the kite into the wind in the direction you want to go and you'll speed up. Work the kite back and forth to go faster."

Jasper got the kite in the air and the buggy shot off. *Shit.*

"Bring the kite behind the line of travel and then back overhead to slow down," Brian shouted.

But Jasper didn't want to slow down. He picked a point to head for and let the kite catch the wind.

"Practice stopping," Brian yelled.

Maybe I should. Jasper used his feet to turn through the wind, and then steered upwind and the buggy slowed.

"Well done," Brian called. "Now have fun."

Calum was yelling and whooping somewhere on his left. Jasper didn't yet feel comfortable enough to turn and look for him. Then he didn't need to turn, Calum was ahead and getting faster. This was something Jasper would never have done on his own and he felt a pang of regret he'd probably never do it again. He mentally slapped himself. No way did he want to ruin this week thinking of Calum going back to Wyoming.

Jasper harbored a tiny hope that Calum wouldn't want to go home. He could stay here on a visa for six months, except what happened then? Jasper could only stay in the States for three months because of visa restrictions. How could they work? What would they do for the other three months? *Shit.* Too much thinking and not enough concentrating. Jasper was heading straight for the sea. He turned fast into the wind and the buggy spun in a one-hundred-eighty-degree circle. His heart pounded, but that had been fun. He set off again, following Calum.

When they were done, they sat in the shelter of the dunes and ate the sandwiches Jasper had bought at the petrol station.

"That was great," Calum said. "I don't know why you haven't done it before. I suppose we could offer it at the ranch, but it would have to be on the pasture. Not as good a surface as sand. We certainly get enough wind. Maybe too much. Thanks for bringing me."

Jasper wanted to feel joy at the sight of Calum's happy smile but he couldn't. *He isn't thinking about staying.* Jasper knew he was being idiotic but he longed to make Calum want to stay, even if he didn't.

"What do you have lined up for tomorrow?" Calum asked.

"Base jumping. Course I can't do it because I'm recovering from a fractured skull, but I'll watch."

Calum gulped and Jasper laughed.

"Bastard," Calum hissed.

"Today isn't over yet. You might be too tired to do anything tomorrow."

Calum lay back on the sand with his arms behind his head. "As long as I'm with you, I don't care what I do. Except I'm not throwing myself off a building. Or going back in the sea." He sighed. "God, I like the sea."

So did Jasper. When he felt anxious, this was where he came. When his head buzzed with problems, the sea drowned them out. Something in the rhythmic ebb and flow of the waves soothed him.

"It's a little like looking at the stars," Calum said. "So vast it makes me feel insignificant and yet it's comforting to know I'm still part of the universe no matter how small I am. I'm made from the earth, one day I'll return to it and become part of something else."

"That's a bit morbid." Jasper leaned over to plant a kiss on Calum's lips.

"We're all going to die one day." Calum slid his fingers into Jasper's hair. "Which is why it's important not to let something die inside you while you're still alive."

Oh God. I...I...

Calum gave Jasper the sweetest, softest kiss followed by a smile.

Note to self: I love him.

Chapter Nineteen

Calum woke as Jasper pulled up outside his house. He stretched and chuckled as he looked through the car window. "We're back? How long have I been asleep?"

"About an hour."

"I feel sticky." He unclipped his seat belt.

"It's the salt. We need to shower."

Calum stared straight at him and smiled. "Is that right?"

"Yep." Jasper's grin hardened Calum's cock. "I do love the way you say that."

"Is that right?"

Jasper laughed. Calum followed him into the house and slung his coat over the bottom of the stairs. When he saw Jasper take off his shoes, Calum removed his.

"Want a coffee first?" Jasper asked.

"No thanks."

"Something to eat?"

"Yeah." Calum took Jasper's hand and tugged him up the stairs.

When they reached the bedroom, Jasper started to pull his sweater over his head, but Calum pushed his hands aside. "Let me undress you."

Calum unwrapped him as if he was a precious gift, slowly removing layer by layer until Jasper stood naked. Calum took in every dip and curve, every beautiful inch of him, his gaze sweeping from eyes to toes and back again.

"You're embarrassing me," Jasper muttered. "My ears are hot."

"Not just your ears. You're hot all over."

Jasper snickered. "I'll go start the shower."

The moment Jasper walked away, Calum stripped in a rush, and then stepped to the bathroom door. Not that Calum's cock needed more stimulation, but the sight of Jasper standing with his butt toward him, hands resting on the tiled wall, water hitting his shoulders and pouring over his back just blew Calum's mind. Perfect shoulders, perfect legs, perfect ass. The dude was pure sex.

Calum filled his palm with shampoo and slid behind Jasper to wash his hair. The moment his fingers began to rub, Jasper groaned. As Calum massaged Jasper's scalp, the guy arched back into him, reaching round to plant his palms on Calum's butt cheeks.

"Oh God, there's a strange man in my shower," Jasper said.

"Hey, who are you calling strange?"

Calum danced his hands down Jasper's chest, sliding his thumbs over his pecs, around the taut nipples and then dropping farther, trailing them back and forth across solid abs. Jasper sighed and rubbed his butt into Calum's cock. Jasper's hands tightened on Calum's butt, fingers creeping into the crease, sending sparks skittering up Calum's spine.

"Much as it pains me to say it, if you let me go, I'll wash all of you," Calum said at his ear. "Put your hands on the wall."

Jasper obeyed and Calum dropped to his knees behind him. A bottle of shower gel sat within reach and Calum lathered his hands. He rubbed Jasper's ankles and pressed his face into the back of his thighs, licking and sucking at the taut skin.

Calum's heart rate had doubled, not just because of what he was doing but because of what he was thinking of doing. Had the moment come where he'd let Jasper fuck him? Calum kneaded, stroked and rubbed his way up Jasper's legs and onto his butt.

When Calum caught sight of Jasper's fingers creeping onto his cock, he snapped, "Hands off."

A long sigh and Jasper pressed both palms against the wall. Calum shouldered Jasper's legs apart, clamped his hands on Jasper's butt and ran his tongue down the seam of his backside. Jasper's knees sagged and then straightened.

"Your tongue's a dangerous weapon," Jasper said with a groan.

Calum spread his ass cheeks to expose the puckered star of his hole and licked it.

"Oh God, God, God," Jasper grunted and one hand slid off the wall.

"Touch your cock and I'll stop," Calum said.

He pressed his face into the line of Jasper's butt and let his tongue play around the opening to his body. Water streamed over Jasper's backside and splashed off Calum's face as first he rimmed him then pressed two fingers slowly inside him.

"I give in," Jasper gasped. "Yes, it was me who broke my mother's best china plate and not Ben. I sat on my violin deliberately. I did inhale."

Calum laughed as he turned him round. But when he looked up past Jasper's swollen cock to the intense, desperate expression on his face, Calum's breath lodged in his throat. He'd never forget this man—ever. Calum's fingers drifted to the back of Jasper's thighs and held tight.

Jasper brushed a thumb over Calum's nose. "I don't think I've ever been this close to coming from just a look," he whispered.

"You didn't notice my fingers in your ass?"

Jasper quirked his lip. "Oh yeah, but it's the look on your face that makes my balls tighten and my heart leap and my gut clench. Your beautiful face... Oh God...I..." He stroked Calum's wet hair, twisting the short strands in his fingers.

Calum felt as if Jasper had reached into his chest to caress his heart. "Jack off. I want to watch."

Jasper released a strangled laugh. "Don't blink or you'll miss it."

"Want me to stop you coming?"

Jasper raised his eyebrows. "I'm not sure even a knife at my balls would stop me." He frowned. "Well, yeah, it might actually."

Calum slid his hand between Jasper's thighs and pushed his finger into his ass.

"That's not going to work," Jasper choked out.

Calum pressed hard with the thumb of the same hand onto a spot midway between Jasper's balls and his hole. When he looked up, Jasper's eyes had closed and his head was tipped back, water spraying over his face, his fists clenching and unclenching at his sides. Calum licked his cock, bottom to top, top to bottom, mouthed his balls and then nibbled a lazy path back to the crest where he laved the tip in slow circles.

"God, that feels good," Jasper mumbled.

"You'll have to help," Calum said. "When you start to feel yourself coming, tell me."

"Now," Jasper spat out.

Calum laughed.

"I'm serious." Jasper opened his eyes and blinked down at him, the water on his lashes shining like tiny gemstones.

Another squirt of shower gel and Calum wrapped his hand around Jasper's cock, ignoring the pleas of his own. He dragged his fingers down, tightening them at the base and loosening his grip when he brought them back to the crest. Calum's balls throbbed.

"Oh God, now. I mean it."

Two identical passes and Jasper hissed, "Fucking definitely now."

Calum pushed harder on the pressure point near Jasper's balls and Jasper shuddered, sighed and uncurled his fingers.

"Okay?" Calum asked.

"Are my balls blue? They're about to drop off."

Pre-come seeped from both cocks. In driving Jasper to distraction, Calum travelled along the same path. He let Jasper calm down before he took the head of his cock between his lips and sucked, and at the same time massaged the shaft below his mouth with his hand. Calum's finger was still in Jasper's ass and now he circled within to rub his prostate.

"Jesus bloody Mary fuuuuck," Jasper gasped.

Which Calum took as a need to press harder on that midway point to halt orgasm.

"Can't, can't, can't," Jasper muttered.

Calum let him rest, did nothing more than press on that magic point and keep his finger motionless in his ass before he started again. But every time he did, he brought Jasper more and more quickly to the point of no return before he pulled back. Jasper was panting now, excitement, frustration, anticipation all over his face.

"No more," Jasper whispered.

His cock was rock hard, dark with blood, the snaky blue veins like 3-D tattoos. His balls were drawn up tight at the base, and Calum tried not to touch them, knowing how sensitive they'd be.

"Calum, you have to let me come."

"Not yet."

He dragged his fingers up Jasper's cock to twist around the head and Jasper's legs buckled. More pressure pulled him back from the brink. Calum knew how Jasper felt because he'd done this to himself, a teasing stop-start jacking off that made his balls ache, his head throb and his skin prickle, but when he came, oh Christ—when he came, it was fan-fucking-tastic. On the other hand, he'd never done this to someone else and timing was everything.

One suck at the head and Jasper barked, "I'm coming."

Oh no you're not. Not yet. Calum dug his thumb in hard on the midway point, and judging by Jasper's strangled cry, he'd stopped his orgasm in its tracks. One spurt escaped from the head of Jasper's cock and Calum pressed harder.

"Let. Me. Come," Jasper begged.

Calum licked down the length of the steel-hard shaft, scooping up the pre-come before the water washed it away and then took his hands off Jasper. Calum wrapped his fingers around his own cock, pumped fast and looked up into Jasper's face as he licked once across the swollen tip of Jasper's dick. Jasper cried out as he came in long, shuddering contractions, ribbons of come landing on Calum's face.

The ache in Calum's balls intensified. Pressure built, synapses firing, electric impulses passing the message faster and faster until the dam burst, his entire body tingled and his balls exploded. White sparks flashed behind his eyes and he gasped as come sprayed over his chest and Jasper's legs. Jasper slid down the wall until he sat on the floor, his chest heaving.

"Worth waiting for?" Calum asked, bringing come from his cheek to his lips.

Jasper smiled through his gasps and reached out to rub his thumb over Calum's jaw. Calum tipped his head to the water and closed his eyes, letting the spray wash his face and his chest. While he knew Jasper had liked what he'd done, a worm of guilt nibbled at his heart. Would Jasper think it was a delaying tactic?

Was it?

Calum opened his eyes and blinked water from his lashes. He wanted and didn't want Jasper to fuck him. The conflicting needs coursed around his brain, one chasing the other, until he could barely think straight. When he looked at Jasper's face, Calum knew he understood and wouldn't push.

Jasper reached up to turn off the shower then tugged Calum round until he sat with his back to Jasper's chest. Jasper draped his arms over his shoulders, resting his chin on Calum's head.

"How energetic are you feeling?" Jasper asked.

"Why?"

"Want to go dancing?"

Calum turned to look at him. "Where?"

"Somewhere we won't get laughed at." Jasper kissed the water from his cheeks.

"Okay."

Calum thought it was ironic he'd agree to pretty much anything Jasper wanted to do and yet found it so hard to say yes to being fucked. Much as the idea of base jumping scared the shit out of him, if Jasper had thrown himself off a cliff, Calum suspected he'd have followed. He wanted to make Jasper happy, he wanted to do things together, and while he was okay about going out, Calum would have been just as happy to stay in and watch a movie. Anything, as long as he was with Jasper.

Jasper would have liked to stay in, order pizza and watch a movie, but with Calum only there for a week, he was desperate to show him what he and London had to offer in the hope that Calum would stay longer, want to come back, maybe not want to leave.

"Wear your tie," Calum said. "That thin gray one. Leave it loose at the neck over a white cotton shirt, top button unfastened."

Jasper laughed. "Anything else?"

"Blue chinos."

Calum pulled on jeans and a T-shirt that said *Dirty Cowboy* across the front. Jasper rolled his eyes.

"I bought it at the airport," Calum said. "Oh, and Angie sent you yet another bracelet in case you get lost again." He handed it to Jasper. "I keep thinking, what if—"

"Don't," Jasper said and tied the bracelet around Calum's wrist. "Let's not tempt fate."

He looked at Calum then, thinking how near death he'd been, and saw the same thought cross Calum's mind. Their hands joined for a moment, and Jasper squeezed Calum's fingers.

They went into London by double-decker bus and sat on the top in the front seats. Calum was like a small boy and his childish excitement was infectious. Jasper pointed out landmarks and kept up a barrage of trivia.

"London has three-thousand five-hundred pubs, over two hundred museums, more than one hundred theaters and over two hundred gay and lesbian bars and clubs."

"How come you know so much?" Calum asked.

"My father told me, well, not about the gay bars."

"Did he know you were gay?"

Jasper rubbed his jaw. "We never talked about it. I think the fact that I never mentioned girls, never went out with girls must have registered, but after Ben had his accident, my dad stopped noticing a lot of things."

"And have you been to all two hundred bars and clubs?"

Jasper shook his head. "I've been to a few but…"

"But what?"

"When you're on your own, they're like a meat market and I seemed to attract the wrong…well, it will be different with two of us because we're not looking for anyone."

"Speak for yourself," Calum said.

Jasper grabbed him in a headlock and rubbed his knuckles into his scalp. Calum laughed as he pushed him off and levered himself upright again.

What was it about this guy that made him feel like a kid again? It was as though Jasper was relearning how to have fun.

They ate in a Thai restaurant where diners reclined on the floor around low tables. The waiting staff was so taken with Calum's outspoken delight they kept bringing small dishes of food for him to try. Jasper smiled as he watched Calum eat.

"More than five thousand restaurants in London," Jasper said.

"You're beginning to sound like a Texan."

"Ah, showing off, sorry. I just… I want…"

Calum's hand settled on his. "I know."

I'm trying too hard to make him happy. Even so, Jasper had already decided not to go to work next week. He still had days left and though taking leave again so soon would be frowned on, if they said no, he thought he might just walk out and never go back.

Except I won't.
Only what if I did?

His heart hammered in his chest. Calum had taken a chance and come halfway around the world without telling him, why shouldn't Jasper take back control of his life? But then, if Calum wasn't part of his future, what did it matter?

Jasper had to fight hard not to let his anxiety show. If he wasn't careful, he'd ruin the time they had by worrying about the time they wouldn't have.

They walked from the restaurant to a club near Charing Cross Station.

Calum nodded at a flashing vertical white sign. "Zero. That where we're headed?"

"Yep."

"Been here before?"

"A couple of times. It's tamer than some of the other clubs."

Calum grinned. "You mean we get to keep our socks on?"

Jasper laughed. Calum slipped his arm around him as they stepped inside and a rush of pleasure in the show of affection made Jasper flush with heat. They checked their coats and headed toward the music.

Calum gasped as they walked into the main room. "Geez."

The room was packed with guys, the heavy beat of the music shaking the floor in Saturday night fever. Most of those dancing were young and slim and in various forms of undress. Older guys stood on the edge, watching bodies they longed to have in more ways than one gyrate to the music. Somehow they were always the ones Jasper attracted. Calum's hand dropped to grip Jasper's and tightened.

"Don't let me go," he said in Jasper's ear. "I don't want to get lost."

Never.

Jasper bought beers, managing not to wince at the cost, and they leaned back against the circular glass bar and looked out onto the dance floor. Sweaty guys rocked and rolled and writhed against each other, bare chests glistening under the lights. Hips kissed, circled and bumped, bulges evident at groins. Hands fondled, groped and stroked, inside and outside pants.

"This is tamer?" Calum asked in an incredulous voice.

"It's been awhile since I came."

Jasper hadn't remembered it being quite so raunchy. His gaze wandered to a couple in the corner and he gulped. If they weren't having sex, they were making a good job of looking as if they were. Maybe this hadn't been a good idea. He and Calum would have a dance and leave.

A tall, slim, good-looking black guy in his forties sidled up. "You two together?"

"Yes," Calum spoke before Jasper could.

"Looking for a third?" the guy asked.

"No, sorry." Jasper moved closer to Calum, a spike of jealousy searing a hole in his gut.

"Shame." The guy smiled and moved on.

Only to be followed by another, a short older man in black leather pants.

"Looking?" he asked.

"No," Calum and Jasper spoke together.

"Pity." The guy wandered off again.

"Christ," Calum whispered. "It must be your aftershave."

"It was you he wanted, idiot."

Calum elbowed him. "You're the idiot."

As they stood drinking, Jasper caught the gaze of several men and moved closer to Calum before they got the wrong idea. Calum was not available.

"I want to dance," Calum said. "Think if we pick a quiet corner no one will notice us making fools of ourselves?"

Since Calum shone like a bloody beacon, Jasper doubted it. Calum grabbed his tie and pulled him into the middle of the dance floor.

"This isn't a quiet corner," Jasper said.

"Changed my mind. I'm done hiding."

Calum began to dance and Jasper's jaw dropped. The cowboy had an innate sense of rhythm, his movements exactly in tune with the music, his hips swaying like a snake, his face wreathed in a broad smile.

"Dance," Calum urged.

"Can't."

"This was your idea."

"Concrete shoes," Jasper mumbled.

Calum wrapped his arms around him and kicked his feet. As Jasper began to sway in sync, Calum licked his throat.

"Oh God, I can't dance and do anything else at the same time," Jasper said with a moan.

But he could and he did. With Calum's encouragement Jasper slowly unwound until he forgot where he was. The music and Calum filled his head. The only man he could see was the cowboy. Calum had stolen his heart and Jasper knew he'd never get it back.

Jasper tripped as they stepped out into the night, only Calum's grip kept him upright. Jasper hadn't drunk that much. Just being in Calum's company made him lightheaded.

"I was thinking of punching the next guy who came on to you," Calum said. "Either that or get them to line up and charge them."

"Me? It was you they couldn't take their eyes off."

They argued good-naturedly about which of them had been the target of all the cruising. Guy after guy had strolled past, flirting with their eyes, flashing follow-me smiles, some of them made blatant advances.

"Christ, of course they wanted you," Calum said. "Just look at you." He caught Jasper's tie and pulled him round for a kiss.

Jasper chuckled. "That's why you wanted me to wear it? Want me to get a collar and lead?"

"Would you?" Calum opened his eyes wide.

Jasper knew he was joking but he growled deep in his throat. "Better run, little boy, before this wolf eats you."

Calum scampered down the road, high on life, and Jasper bolted after him. Another breathless kiss in an alley, another on a street corner before they carried on heading toward the river, pushing and shoving, cuddling and teasing. Calum was effervescent with happiness, and it made Jasper almost burst with pleasure. Everything they saw, Calum loved. Everything they did, he marveled at.

"London's fantastic," Calum said.

"The buildings are beautiful.

"Tower Bridge is gorgeous.

"The people are amazing."

Calum wanted to go on the London Eye, and see the city from above, but it was closed. He wanted to go on the Thames, but the boats had stopped running. Tomorrow, tomorrow, Jasper promised and wondered how he could deny this guy anything.

Jasper eventually hailed a cab. He had a feeling Calum would have wandered around all night, and then as they sat in the back of the taxi, he wondered if that's exactly what Calum had hoped for because he didn't want to let Jasper to fuck him. *Ah crap.*

They held hands, but Calum had his face pressed to the window. Was he seeing the other side of the capital now? The grubby pubs at street corners with their faded plastic flowers decorating hanging baskets, the bands of hooded youths lurking in shop precincts, their oversize jeans clinging to their hips by sheer willpower, the seedy underside of the city with drug dealers, drug takers, pimps and prostitutes, male and female and somewhere in between.

"What a fucking amazing city," Calum whispered. "But I don't know how you can stand to live here. It's exciting and manic, and beautiful and ugly all at the same time."

Jasper's heart shriveled.

Calum turned to look at him. "Makes me realize how much I take Wyoming skies and the quietness for granted. I'd go crazy here."

Jasper thought if he opened his mouth now, a sob might escape.

The cab dropped them back at the house, and Jasper stumbled as he walked to his front door. Calum laughed and propped him up.

"You shouldn't have had that last drink," Calum said.

Jasper wished he was drunk. He'd tried hard to get drunk but had stayed distressingly sober. Calum took the keys from Jasper's pocket and opened the door.

"Need to lie down," Jasper mumbled and headed for the stairs.

Calum followed. By the time Calum emerged from the bathroom, Jasper was putting on the performance of his life as a man sound asleep. He lay naked on his stomach under the duvet, face planted in the pillow, and under it his fist was clenched tight. The bed dipped as Calum climbed in the other side.

"What's wrong?" he whispered.

To speak or not to speak? By the time Jasper accepted he ought to say something, he'd felt Calum turn away and the bedside light went off. How hard was it to tell Calum how he felt? He just had to open his mouth and let those three words out.

Only Jasper had never said them to anyone since he'd last said them to Ben.

Nothing was wrong.

Everything was wrong.

Jasper wanted Calum to stay. He didn't want to let him go, and every moment they spent together made the thought of their parting more painful. And yet he knew how idiotic that was. Wasn't Ben's accident enough of a lesson? Seize hold of every second of time you're given. The thought of not having Calum in his life made Jasper physically hurt.

Jasper rolled over at the precise moment Calum rolled to face him.

"I love you," Jasper blurted.

Then he saw Calum's eyes were closed and he was sleeping.

Calum didn't move a muscle. *Oh Christ.* It would be the easiest thing in the world to open his eyes and say those words back, so why couldn't he?

Because Jasper had only said them because he thought Calum was asleep. Or maybe Jasper was talking in his sleep.

Fuck it. Open your eyes. Say it back. But when Calum's eyes opened, Jasper's were closed, the regular puffs of air from his mouth evidence that he was sleeping. Calum closed his eyes and whispered, "I love you too."

Jasper didn't stir. His breathing stayed the same.

Calum had never slept with a guy before. He'd dozed after sex, but never spent the entire night in a guy's bed. He hadn't wanted to. Now, he couldn't think of anywhere he'd rather be. Except instinct told him he'd upset Jasper in some way. Something he'd said? Done? Not done?

Calum lay awake, rerunning everything and came up with nothing. So it had to be because he hadn't let Jasper fuck him. Maybe Jasper didn't want to be fucked. Maybe he thought he was doing Calum a favor by not pushing. *Fuck, fuck, fuck.*

After he'd lain awake for an hour, wishing the word "maybe" didn't fucking exist, Calum slid out of bed, pulled on his boxers and padded out of the bedroom. He wasn't tired, but wired. In the kitchen, he poured himself a glass of milk and went in search of something to read. The room opposite the lounge was a study, shelves lined with paperbacks, DVDs and CDs, and facing the window was a desk with a laptop and printer. Calum put the milk on the desk, and as he ran his gaze over the books, he frowned. Advances in Equine Nutrition. Textbook of Veterinarian Anatomy. Fundamentals of Biochemistry. Neurophysiology.

"I studied veterinary science at university," Jasper said.

Calum spun round in shock. Jasper stood in the doorway wearing boxers, his dark hair mussed.

"You're a vet?" Calum asked. "Is that how you knew about the laminitis and the tumor?"

"I'm not a vet. I didn't finish my degree."

"Why not?"

"I needed to earn more than I would as a vet."

Calum frowned. "Why?"

"There was the mortgage to pay on the house where my mum and Ben lived. Wages for additional care assistants. Money for all sorts of crap—extra heating, another opinion from yet another consultant, state-of-the-art equipment for Ben. I tried to keep studying. I really wanted to be a vet, but after a full day at the university, I had to work in a bar every night just to keep us afloat, only we were sinking faster and faster. When my uncle offered me a job, I took it. Ben told me not to do it, but my mother pleaded with me to work for my uncle. I thought I could maybe go back to studying at some point in the future, but then Ben died, my mother needed care too and I was trapped."

Jasper turned to look at the books. "Don't know why I kept them really. I'm thirty-one. The dream's over."

"Why does your mother need care?"

"She has Alzheimer's. She doesn't remember who I am. And sometimes I think I've forgotten too." His jaw twitched.

Calum stepped forward and pulled Jasper into his arms. He pressed his face to the side of Jasper's head.

"I've had to be what everyone else wanted for so long," Jasper whispered into his hair. "I was lost and you found me."

Note to self: Jasper isn't talking about the beads.

Chapter Twenty

Calum got out of the car outside the nursing home and closed the door. He shivered and wished he'd brought his coat.

"Sure you want to do this?" Jasper asked.

Calum stared at him over the roof of the car. "Don't you want me to come in with you?" He wasn't sure whether Jasper wanted him with him or not.

"She might not recognize me anyway," Jasper said in a glum voice.

Calum walked with him to the door. Jasper clutched a bouquet of flowers and had a box of chocolates tucked under his arm. It was his mother's birthday.

Time had seemed to speed up over the week. Jasper had spent a couple of hours in the office on Monday and taken the rest of the week off. They'd explored London together, wandering around museums and parks and eating leisurely lunches over a bottle of wine. They'd gone bowling and Calum had chuckled at how competitive Jasper was. They'd gone bike riding, and Jasper had even taken him sailing. It seemed to Calum that the guy was trying to fill every minute of every day.

In the evenings, they lay entangled on Jasper's couch and watched movies, their legs and fingers entwined. They ate in, they ate out, they laughed and kissed and fucked, though Jasper shied away from topping him. Calum wasn't sure why. Because Jasper sensed he wasn't ready? Because he really *wasn't* ready?

Jasper gave their names at the reception desk and they were buzzed through. Calum caught hold of Jasper's clenched fist and rubbed his knuckles with his thumb. Jasper shot him a smile.

"Shouldn't take long," Jasper said. "Unless she thinks you're Ben."

"Won't the accent tell her different?"

"She sees and hears what she wants to."

Since Calum had arrived almost a week ago, he'd sensed a quiet desperation building in Jasper, and he understood it because he felt it too. Jasper was intent on them having as much fun as possible, and Calum was determined to have as much fun as possible. He had and yet there was always that knowledge that they were trapped—by circumstance, by a sense of duty, by inertia, but maybe most of all by fear of trying to make this work. It made Calum's heart ache when he laughed hard enough to bring tears to his eyes, made his stomach clench when Jasper looked at him as though he was the most special person in the world. They loved each other. They'd admitted it and yet neither of them seemed able to say it again when the other's eyes were open. Calum had tried a couple of times and the words had dried in his mouth. They needed to talk about the future and yet neither of them seemed capable of bringing it up.

Jasper halted outside a half-open door. He knocked, took a deep breath and went inside. Calum followed.

"Happy birthday, Mum," Jasper said.

She sat in a recliner in front of a flat screen TV though it wasn't switched on. Calum thought she looked too young to have dementia. Her nails had been painted with bright pink polish, her dark hair was neatly coiffed and she wore a pretty dress and jacket. Jasper bent to kiss her cheek and she glared.

"I don't like those," she said, nodding at the chocolates that Jasper had told him were her favorites.

Jasper stiffened. "Okay, I'll take them away."

"You might as well leave them now," she snapped. "The staff can eat them."

Jasper rolled his eyes.

"I brought a friend." Jasper beckoned him. "This is Calum."

Calum walked forward with his hand out. "Pleased to meet you."

"Ben! How lovely. Sit down and tell me what you've been up to."

She beamed at him, and Calum flashed Jasper a look of desperation.

"Mum, this is Calum. He's my friend from America."

"Go away, Jasper," she said. "I want to talk to Ben alone."

Jasper winced and his shoulders slumped. "Mum—"

"I said go away," she barked.

"It's okay, Jasper," Calum said. "We can chat for a while." Calum wished he could talk some sense into her, but knew he couldn't. He'd had plenty of practice at talking to people who didn't want to hear what he had to say.

Jasper mouthed "Sorry" and left the room. Calum could imagine how much it hurt to have a mother who didn't even recognize you. It made him feel even guiltier for not calling Vera his mom sooner. Jasper's mother grabbed Calum's hand and pulled him onto the chair beside her.

"Jasper's trying to kill me," she whispered.

Calum gaped at her.

"Are you a policeman?"

"No, I—"

"A doctor?"

"No."

"Jasper killed his father and his brother and now he's trying to kill me."

"No, that's not right," Calum said.

"Are you an angel?"

Oh Christ.

"You look like an angel." She smiled at him and he saw Jasper in her smile. "You were always such a good boy. You did as you were told. It was all Jasper's fault." She began to wring her hands and rock in her seat. "I don't understand why it happened. We had everything and then we had nothing."

Calum patted her fingers and wished Jasper would come back. "It's okay," he whispered.

"Michael swerved so he didn't hit Jasper and instead he hit you. He was so sorry." A tear trickled down her cheek. "He broke my heart that day along with his. Better if he'd hit Jasper. Jasper always bounced back. But you didn't, sweetheart. You were broken and no one could mend you." She clutched his fingers.

"You've wearing a lovely dress," Calum said in desperation.

"Jasper was in the way. That's why Michael had to swerve. Jasper should have died."

She looked toward the door and Calum turned to see Jasper standing there, his lips pressed tight together, a muscle twitching in his cheek.

"I don't feel well. I don't want any visitors." She let Calum go and closed her eyes.

Calum tried not to run as he left the room. Jasper nodded toward the stairs and Calum followed. He reached for Jasper's shoulder, but he pulled away. Calum stayed on his heels all the way back to the car. When Jasper wrenched open the driver's door, Calum pushed it shut before he could get in and slipped to stand in front of him.

"Don't," he whispered. "Don't push me out. I don't know how the hell you cope with her. She doesn't know what she's saying. She thought I was Ben, an angel, a doctor, a policeman. She didn't mean what she said."

Jasper's head sagged. "Yeah, she did. When Ben lay there, tubes in his mouth, and in his backside and in his cock, alive and yet not alive, she turned and said it would have been better if I'd died rather than have this happen to my brother. I wanted to believe she didn't mean it. The accident wasn't my fault. Ben had been messing around, not paying attention, but that isn't what she wants to have happened. Easier to have someone to blame."

Calum's heart ached in sympathy. "After all you've done, all you gave up… It's not fair."

Jasper pressed his mouth to Calum's ear. "News flash. Life isn't fair." Then he straightened and gave a tight smile. "But I'm not going to let her spoil our last night. That really wouldn't be fair. Come on, get in."

All the way back, Jasper worked hard to dispel the pall of his mother's outburst. Calum recognized that Jasper didn't want to talk about her but he was doing a skilful job of not talking about anything that mattered.

"Is she like that every time you visit?" Calum asked.

"I never know what I'm going to find. Do you want to stop and pick up a couple of pizzas?"

"I'm not hungry. Does no one else visit her?"

Jasper sighed. "A few relatives."

"I don't know how you deal with it."

"I've learned to clear my mind the moment I leave. Would you rather get a Chinese takeaway?"

"I'm really not hungry."

"Want to go to the pub?"

"I want to go home. We need to talk."

After that, Jasper didn't say a word, but his grip tightened around the steering wheel. Calum wanted to pull him into his arms and tell him everything would be all right, that they'd find a solution, though it flittered through his mind that in some ways, it might be kinder to concoct an argument and make the break unpleasant. If Jasper thought there was no hope, maybe he'd find someone else to… *Christ.* It wouldn't be difficult. They already had an unresolved issue. Jasper hadn't topped him. All Calum had to do was tell Jasper he didn't want him to, that he didn't trust him. The lump in Calum's throat threatened to choke him. *God, I can't tell him that.*

Jasper spun the car into the drive and switched off the engine. They hadn't stopped for food. They'd eaten before they went to see his mother, so Calum had guessed the hollow feeling in Jasper's stomach was anxiety, and maybe he didn't want to come home.

Calum followed Jasper inside and closed the front door. Jasper leaned against the wall and sighed. Calum thought how hard it must be to have a mother who didn't recognize you, who said cruel things even if she didn't know what she was doing. It reminded Calum yet again how lucky he was to have Vera and knew there was no way he could deliberately hurt Jasper. He was ashamed he'd even thought about it. Calum pulled him into his arms. Jasper's Adam's apple shifted up and down and Calum leaned in to kiss it. He slid his hands to Jasper's neck and stroked the line of his chin with his thumbs.

"The moment I saw you, I wanted you," Calum whispered. "I didn't even know if you were into guys and I still wanted you. And every day since, I've wanted you more and more. I thought maybe after a week here, I'd be full, but I'm just as hungry."

"Then stay," Jasper choked out.

Calum exhaled. "I can't. This isn't my world."

"You can sculpt here, you can *make* it your world." Jasper's eyes were bright with unshed tears. "You're allowed to stay in the UK for six months."

"And then what? My father's sick. My mom needs me. Angie needs me. Even if I could stay longer, it only makes parting harder."

Jasper trembled. "I could come to Wyoming. I'm allowed to visit for three months."

Calum let his gaze wander over Jasper's face, taking in every detail. "And what happens after that? You'd lose your job. What about your mother?"

"I want to make you happy," Jasper whispered. "I want to wake up with you by my side. I feel…responsible for your happiness. It's like something burning inside me, a feeling that making you happy is what I'm here for, my reason for being."

Oh God. Calum sighed. "I love you."

Jasper closed his eyes for a moment and then looked straight at him. "I love you too."

Calum dropped his hands to Jasper's and clutched them. "Take me to bed and make love to me."

Jasper swallowed hard. "No."

Calum took a deep breath. "Jasper, we have one night. This is what I want."

"No." Jasper tightened his jaw.

Calum let his hands slide from Jasper's. "Why not?" he snapped. Calum stamped away and then stormed back, his cheek twitching. "Why the fuck not?" Maybe he didn't need to concoct an argument. Maybe this was it.

"Because it's…a big thing for you and I think it should be something that should wait until you meet the guy—"

"I *have* met the fucking guy." Calum tried not to shout and failed. "I want to do this with the guy I love." He lowered his voice. "That guy is you."

"But—"

Calum caught hold of Jasper's hair and held him so they looked each other in the eyes. "Don't keep giving me an out. You don't think I'm nervous about you shoving that monster cock in my ass?"

Jasper released a strangled sound—half-groan, half-laugh.

"Anyone would think you didn't want to fuck me." Calum rapped his knuckles on Jasper's head.

"I *do* want to," Jasper whispered. "If you ask me to stop, you know I will."

"I trust you."

Calum did trust him, but as Jasper took his hand and led him upstairs, his throat clogged with fear.

What if I can't get hard?

Because that was a distinct possibility. Now he'd set off on the path to this happening, his cock had shriveled. Considering what he'd confessed to Jasper about the rape, the irony didn't escape him.

What if I freak out?

He might yell, scream, or worse—burst into tears. *Fuck it, not that.*

The moment Jasper got into his room, he stripped off and leapt onto the bed. Calum's skin crawled with awareness as Jasper watched him undress, but Jasper's gaze never shifted from Calum's face. Jasper dragged his hand up and down his shaft as he stared and the sheer puppy-like eagerness of his expression began to melt Calum's fear and turn his cock hard. *This is Jasper. I love him.*

Calum crawled onto the bed from the bottom and lay on his side, his face next to Jasper's.

"Got everything we need?" Calum asked. "Condoms, five bottles of lube?"

Jasper laughed and pulled Calum in for a kiss. His fingers encircled the back of Calum's head and then their tongues brushed and played together. Jasper groaned against Calum's mouth, licking at his tongue as if he were starving. Calum stopped worrying about his cock, it was as rigid as Jasper's, and as their hips melded, their dicks rocked and kissed in their own special way. Jasper's tongue plunged in and out of Calum's mouth in a promise of what was to come and Calum's fear crumbled like a drying sand castle.

"I want to fuck you so much," Jasper muttered into Calum's neck. "I am scared shitless I'll muck it up and come before I even get inside you."

And Calum realized Jasper had his own issues here.

Then Jasper's mouth was back on his, their lips frantically mating as they writhed against each other. The need to come sank its claws so deep into Calum he had a feeling he might have the same problem as Jasper. This could be over before it started. Still, they had all night.

Jasper reached out to grab the lube and condom off the bedside table and Calum ran the flat of his hand down Jasper's outstretched body, letting his fingers slide over the satiny skin, teasing soft hair and skimming chiseled abs until Calum reached Jasper's cock.

Oh shit, he is fucking huge.

"How come I didn't notice how big you were before?" Calum muttered.

"And you're not?" Jasper laughed.

He relaxed into Calum's touch like a large cat, stretching arms and legs, almost purring as Calum rubbed the dark curls at the base of his cock.

Jasper stroked his head. "Are you sure?"

Calum tried to say yes but the word log jammed in his throat.

"You don't have to." Jasper feathered his lips over Calum's.

"Will you still respect me in the morning?" Calum asked with a smile.

Jasper growled. "Put me under pressure, why don't you?"

He pushed Calum onto his back and kissed a slow, wet path from his lips, over his chin, down his throat and onto his chest. Calum closed his eyes and flexed into Jasper's touch, threading the fingers of both hands into Jasper's hair as the guy fluttered his mouth over his nipples. Calum's breathing lurched in fits and starts as Jasper moved from one side of his chest to the other, teasing his nipples until they were so tight and sensitive, each touch made Calum shiver.

When Jasper's mouth reached his cock, Calum groaned. His hips constantly shifting, he bucked into Jasper's face, his hands still on Jasper's head holding him tight. It was hard to think when every cell in his body was bent on pleasure. Jasper's hot, wet tongue licked around his crest and then blazed a trail down to his balls. Calum opened his eyes and looked at Jasper's dark head between his splayed thighs and willed his body not to let him down.

Jasper licked and petted and stroked him into an impossible mix of high tension and deep relaxation. Afloat on a sea of sensation, Calum had only enough sense to wrap his hand around the base of his cock and squeeze. That might earn him a couple more minutes. Jasper's tongue was working magic on his asshole, sending spirals of pleasure coursing down

Calum's veins, but at the wash of cool lube, Calum sucked in a breath and flinched.

"It's okay," Jasper whispered. "I squeezed too hard and emptied half the tube on your butt. It's very shiny. You'll probably slip through my fingers and end up on the floor."

Calum laughed, which was what he guessed Jasper had intended. But when he felt Jasper's finger press on his anus, Calum stiffened and closed his eyes.

Jasper moved from between his legs and slid to Calum's side. He rested up on his elbow and shifted his finger back to play around Calum's hole.

"I love you," Jasper whispered. "Whether we do this or not, I still love you."

Jasper's voice calmed his frazzled nerves. Calum tried to relax as Jasper's finger circled and pressed. When the insistent digit breached the muscle barrier, Calum released a noisy breath.

"Okay?" Jasper asked.

Calum nodded and rubbed his face against Jasper's hair, filling his lungs with the citrus scent of his shampoo. One finger in his ass became two, and Calum gave an involuntary hiss at the slight burn. Jasper kissed him as he slid his fingers in and out, kissed him harder when he twisted them and pleasure began to seep through Calum's body, overwhelming trepidation, swamping memories. He tightened his grip on his cock and began to squeeze in time with Jasper's thrusts, letting the river carry him toward the waterfall.

When the fingers withdrew, Calum groaned, wanting them back. He'd been close to coming. He opened his eyes to see Jasper rolling on the condom and smothering himself with lube. *Oh God.* Calum's heart was already beating fast, but now it beat faster. Jasper shifted to the bottom of the bed and knelt between Calum's spread thighs. He ran his wet fingers over Calum's where he gripped his cock and smiled.

"Trying to strangle your dick into submission?" Jasper asked.

"I'm a little tense."

"You're a big tense."

Calum rolled his eyes. "Yeah, bad joke. That helps."

Jasper edged closer and trailed his hands down the inside of Calum's thighs to part his butt cheeks.

"Know how to tell the difference between erotic and kinky?" Jasper asked.

"No."

"When you want to go for erotic you use a feather. Kinky, use the whole chicken."

Calum laughed. He was still smiling when Jasper lined his cock up with the entrance to his body.

"You can still say no," Jasper panted.

"Fuck me," Calum whispered.

The rounded head of Jasper's cock nudged harder and Calum took a deep breath and pushed back against the pressure. He wasn't freaking out, he wanted this, he wanted Jasper buried balls deep inside him. He stared into Jasper's face as Jasper stared into his and then Calum's ring of muscles relaxed to let the wide flare of the cock slip just inside his hole.

"Oh God," Calum gasped, one hand clutching harder at his cock, the other trying to pull a tightly fitted sheet into his fist.

In a mix of pleasure and slight pain, his muscles burned at the intrusion.

"Fuck, fuck, fuck," Jasper whispered.

He leaned over to rest on his arms on either side of Calum's head, then smiled and kissed him.

"Want all of you," Calum gasped into Jasper's mouth.

"You've got it."

Calum choked out a laugh. "Liar."

"You can—" Jasper began.

"Fuck me. Do it."

"I've changed my mind," Jasper said, but he was laughing.

Calum needed all of him. Now. "You bastard. Want me to beg?"

"That would be nice."

Calum narrowed his eyes. "Please."

Jasper pushed hard and deep. He sighed as slid into Calum's body, his face suffused with pleasure. Calum lifted his legs and wrapped them around Jasper's hips to pull him as close as he could. The feeling was so good, the sensation of being filled, that Calum could scarcely believe it. Jasper began to move, rocking his hips to drive his cock through the nerve-rich tissue of Calum's ass.

"Christ, you're tight," Jasper panted.

Calum squeezed down on him with his rectal muscles and Jasper sucked in a breath. Then there were no more words, just a shared gaze as Jasper picked up the pace and powered into him. Calum pumped his cock, the head hitting Jasper's belly. They were both moaning and grunting as they climbed together. Calum rocked his hips up into Jasper's downward thrust, their rhythm perfectly matched. Then Jasper twisted his pelvis and his cock hit Calum's prostate. White-hot sparks shot up Calum's spine and his entire body caught fire.

Jasper rode him faster and faster, pulling back and thrusting forward harder, and Calum loved it, every inch of it. He was glad now that he hadn't been able to do this before because it had been as if he'd been saving this for Jasper. Calum took his hand off the sheet and slipped it between their bodies, down behind his balls, feeling the place where they were joined. Jasper's thrusts grew more frantic. Fire burned at the base of Calum's cock, his balls drew up and as he flew over the falls and into the plunge pool, he clamped down hard on Jasper's cock. Calum's back arched and as come spurted onto his chest in long, hot ribbons, Jasper stiffened and cried out. Calum felt Jasper's cock swell inside him and then he was coming, gasping his release.

They collapsed together, wrapped in each other's arms, aftershocks carrying them on the final part of the journey. Calum's throat was so dry each rasping breath seemed to make his lungs rub against his ribs. Jasper panted into his ear, his hand clutching one of Calum's. Slowly, their breathing calmed and they kissed and kissed and kissed.

Note to self: Find a way to keep him.

Chapter Twenty-One

Jasper stood at passport control with his arms wrapped around Calum and bit the inside of his lip to stop himself crying. Didn't work. His tears fell into Calum's tousled blond hair.

"Shit, don't cry or I'll start," Calum muttered.

Jasper pulled himself together, straightened and tried to put a smile on his face. He'd see Calum again when he went back to Wyoming for the trial, and for the time being they could email and talk on the phone, but in the grand scheme of things, Jasper suspected that would just make everything more painful. His stomach twisted into a tight ball.

"Oh God, look at you in your suit," Calum said with a groan. "My poor cock. This is not the time and place for a hard-on."

Jasper snorted. Calum flipped his tie and then slid his fingers to the back of Jasper's neck. "Thank you," he whispered. "But I feel like the luckiest and unluckiest guy in the world."

Jasper couldn't speak. His throat was clogged.

"I left you a gift. Not sure you'll want it cast. Maybe you'll think of me when you look at it."

"A well-hung stallion?" Jasper blurted.

Calum laughed and glanced toward the doors. "I have to go through."

Jasper nodded and Calum's hand fell away. He stared at Jasper, gave him one last brilliant smile and walked away.

"Wait for me." Jasper whispered the words too faint for Calum to hear, but the cowboy hesitated for a moment before he continued on his path. Jasper stood watching until Calum moved out of sight. He couldn't move. It seemed impossible that he was still breathing, that his heart kept beating. His love for Calum couldn't be turned off. It ran through Jasper like a tumbling mountain stream.

He made his way back to the train with heavy steps, fingers fumbling with the bracelet around his wrist. Neither he nor Calum had slept last night. They'd talked and made love and held each other until it was time to go to the airport. Now Jasper had a boss to placate. He might have been due the days of leave he'd taken, but to go in for a couple of hours and then give so little notice of taking the week off was hardly professional. Jasper didn't care. He was a different person now. A better person, but a sadder one.

At the end of a hectic morning, after a lecture from his boss about reliability and responsibility, Jasper left the office to get some air. When he found himself outside Fintan's Gallery, he stopped and stared at the bronze in the window. *Cowboys Down.* He remembered lying in the aspen grove with Calum and gulped at the sharp pain in his chest. A tap on the other side of the glass and Jasper looked up. Fintan beckoned.

Jasper pushed open the door. At least the guy would be a distraction.

"Where's your lovely cowboy?" Fintan asked.

Oh fuck. "Gone home."

The gallery owner clapped a hand over his heart. "You let him go?"

"He has a ranch to run, family to look after."

"You let him go?" Fintan repeated.

"He has responsibilities, he—"

"You let him go?"

"Fuck it, I had no choice," Jasper snapped. "I can't live over there. He can't live over here."

"You—"

"If you say that one more time, I'll—" He glared at Fintan and then his shoulders dropped and he stared at his shoes. They could do with a polish, but Jasper didn't care.

"You don't like your job," Fintan said and Jasper glanced up. "I've seen you walking around with a face like a wet lettuce. I also know that you trained as a vet."

Jasper gaped.

Fintan reached out with one finger and lifted Jasper's jaw. His teeth clacked together.

"How the hell did you know that?"

"When I have a little...crush, I like to learn everything I can about the object of my desire. It wasn't hard to find out your academic details. And about your family. I'm sorry. Life has been difficult for you."

Jasper swallowed hard.

"I know I'm not your type." Fintan puffed out a breath and fluttered his hand over his face. "Doesn't stop me wanting though." He gave a sad smile. "Follow your dreams. That was what my mother said to me. So I set up in the art business and I looked for love. At least I'm successful in one of those. Why don't you finish your studies, qualify as a vet and go rope your cowboy?"

Jasper gave a short laugh. "I'd probably have to start studying from the beginning all over again. Five years? Then the chances of getting a job in the States would be remote."

"Mr. Negative." Fintan glared. "Why do you have to study here? Why not in America? You can afford it, can't you?"

"My mother—"

"For Christ's sakes, Jasper. Find a way."

"She's got senile dementia."

"Then she won't even know if you've gone. You can come back and see her. You're not planning a trip to Mars. *I'll* go and check on her."

Jasper felt as though a bee had flown into his ear and was buzzing around in his head. He'd given up on the dream of being a vet, but now black-and-white images turned to color.

Ideas flashed one after the other—plans, thoughts, dreams coalescing, converging to become a future reality. Maybe his former university tutor would write him a reference. He'd kept up-to-date with a lot of the advances in veterinary science. He could afford to study in the States if he liquidated everything here. His mother—well, what would change?

Oh Christ, can I do this? He'd need a visa, acceptance on a US study course, to sell his home, to— *I* can *do this if I want it enough.*

He smiled and Fintan let a long sigh.

"Thank you," Jasper said.

"Want to thank me by coming to my party?" Fintan fluttered his eyelashes. "I promise not to misbehave."

"All right. When is it?"

Fintan flung his hands in the air. "Now I'll have to plan one. Oh God, what theme? Go away, I need to think. I'll call you."

Jasper's smile widened. He headed for the door and turned. "Don't say anything if Calum should contact you, just in case it doesn't work out."

"Lips sealed." Fintan pulled an imaginary zipper across his mouth.

When Jasper returned home from work to be greeted by an empty house, he wanted to weep. He hadn't realized how lonely he'd been, how he'd done little more than exist for the last few years, how much time he'd wasted. But then, if he hadn't, maybe he'd never have met Calum. That afternoon, Jasper had made some calls, expecting to hear the word no and instead heard maybe. Now he had to turn maybe into yes.

Calum's gift sat on the coffee table in the lounge. A clay model of the two of them making love. Jasper on top. *Oh fuck.* Where had Calum found time to do that? A piece of paper had been pushed under one corner and Jasper pulled it out.

Hey Dude, don't be sad. It's your smile that lights my world even if I can't see it.
I love you.
Calum.
It was some time before Jasper could smile again.

By the time Calum got back to the ranch, he was exhausted. Gunner picked him up at the airport and filled him in on what had been happening. Nothing much by the sound of it. As Calum stepped into the family living room, Angie turned, yelled and flew at him. His mom came up to give him a hug and his father nodded from his chair. *Nope, nothing much has changed.*

"Did you meet the Queen?" Angie asked.

Calum smiled. "No, but I saw where she lived. Big house."

"Did Jasper like my present?"

"Yep he did, but he gave it me so I wouldn't get lost coming back. He sent something for you. I brought you something too."

Angie's gaze switched to his bag.

"How was Jasper?" his mom asked.

"He's fine. He took the week off to show me round London."

Angie tugged his sleeve. "Do you need help unpacking?"

Calum bit back his smile. "Nope, I'm good." He turned to his father. "Gunner said things have been quiet."

"Had a damn fool guest who got too close to an elk but luckily the elk took one look at him and fled."

"Calum," Angie whined.

"Horses okay?" Calum asked.

"Calum." Angie's voice had grown louder.

"Stop teasing your sister," his father snapped but he had a smile on his face.

Calum opened his bag. "I bought you this." He handed his mom a book called *British Baking*.

"Oh that's lovely, thank you." She turned the pages and oohed at the pictures.

Calum took out another gift and gave it to his father. It was a book about British horses from Shetland ponies to carthorses. His father looked stunned to be given anything.

"Thank you. I'm going to have to learn how to read now."

Fuck it. A joke? "Don't worry, I picked one with lots of pictures," Calum said.

His father grinned and Calum's spirits lifted.

"A book." Angie sounded so miserable Calum had to withhold his snigger.

"This is from me. This is from Jasper." Calum put two wrapped gifts on the coffee table.

She opened Calum's first. He'd bought her a necklace, a silver star on a chain.

Angie sucked in a breath and then exhaled. "That's so pretty. Thank you." She kissed him quickly on the cheek and then bent to Jasper's gift and ripped off the paper. "Wow. It's a dress." She held it up in front of her. It was pretty blue dress with wide shoulder straps and a crossover front. Calum hadn't been sure it was the right thing to buy, but looking at Angie's face, he saw he'd been wrong.

She rushed off to try it on and Calum caught his father's glare. The welcome home hadn't lasted long.

"A dress?" his father barked.

"Erik," his mother snapped. "It was kind of Jasper to send it to her. This recipe book is lovely, Calum. I shall have to try out some of these cakes."

Calum knew she was trying to deflect his father and was grateful. "Jasper said you might have to look up something to convert the measurements from grams to cups."

"I can do that. My mouth's watering already. Scones with cream and jam. They sound delicious."

"Ta-da," Angie shouted and posed in the doorway.

Oh God. What had Jasper done? The dress fitted her perfectly, clinging to her curves, showing the swell of her breasts. She looked...*Oh God*...she looked like a normal young woman dressed up to go out.

"You look lovely," he told her.

Angie turned to her mom.

"Stunning, sweetheart. That color really suits you." Vera swallowed hard.

"Who are you?" asked his father.

Angie stomped over to him. "Me, silly."

"So it is. You look gorgeous, sweetheart." His father smiled at her but Calum noticed it didn't reach his eyes.

Vera put her hand on Angie's shoulder. "Go and take it off so you don't get it dirty."

Angie's shoulders slumped. "I'm never going to get a chance to wear it anyway." She looked at her father. "I could if you'd let me go to Casper."

His father bristled. "Now we discussed this."

"No we didn't," Angie said. "You just said stuff and told me to listen." She turned to Calum. "There's a vacancy that has come up in a special house in Casper. I could live there Monday to Friday and come back at the weekend. There's people who can help me find a job."

"I don't think you're ready," his father said.

"Yes I am," Angie said. She went to sit on her father's knee and wrapped her arm round his neck. "I know you don't think I can cope, but how do you know until you've let me try? You have to let people be who they are. Everyone deserves a chance."

Calum felt as though she'd reached into his chest and stroked his heart.

"Not sure your mom can cope without you," his father muttered.

Angie glanced at her mother. "I'd have to cope without her, so she could try."

"Not sure I could cope without you," said her dad.

"But Mom said you'd have to cope if Calum didn't come back and he does a lot more around here than me."

Calum's heart skipped. They'd talked about him not coming back?

"You think I should go?" Angie asked Calum.

He stared straight at his father. "I think you're right, Angie. Everyone deserves a chance."

It had been three long months since Calum had kissed Jasper goodbye. Thank fuck Ring and Pete's trial started in two weeks. Calum hoped to pick Jasper up at the airport and stand by his side through the entire ordeal. He shook the snow off his duster and kicked the powder from his boots before he opened the door of the ranch. Calum shut it quickly behind him, took off his Stetson and slapped it against his legs, letting the snow fall on the mat.

He sighed at the warmth that hit his face and bent to stroke Bessie who'd come up, wagging her tail. Felt strange not to have Angie around, but she was spending a couple of days a week in the house in Casper with others of her age who had learning difficulties. She had a job working in a craft store part time and if she got on okay, that might turn out to be full time.

"Coffee?" his mom asked, walking toward him with a steaming mug.

"Thanks. Guests in the hot tub?"

"Yep."

The Neilson Ranch wasn't ideally placed for ski vacations, but the journey to Jackson was doable with the right transport. He'd convinced his father to invest in a better vehicle and they'd marketed themselves as a place to cross-country ski, snowmobile, hunt and snowshoe. Calum had just come back from hauling guests to Yellowstone. The group of married couples had talked on the way back about sitting in the hot tub drinking champagne while the snow fell around them, and Calum wished— He shook the thought off.

"I had to call the vet. About Blue."

Calum straightened. "What's the matter with him?"

"Gunner said he was listless, not wanting to feed, generally out of sorts."

Like I've been.

His mom sighed. "I didn't want to worry you over nothing, but the vet's still here."

Calum handed his coffee back and put on his hat.

"Bring him in for a bite to eat," she said as he hurried out.

The wind whipped the snow across his face and Calum tucked his head down into his coat as he trudged over to the stables. He slid the door open just enough to slip inside and then closed it.

"Frank?" Calum called.

"Here."

The muffled voice came from the direction of Blue's stall. Calum headed down there. *Oh God, if there's anything wrong with Blue...*

"Hello."

A guy in a long gray coat stepped out of Blue's stall and Calum's heart stopped.

"Jasper?" he gasped. "Oh fuck, am I seeing things?"

Calum's knees shook and as he staggered, Jasper caught him.

"What...how...fuck," Calum mumbled. He looked over at his horse. "This was just a trick to get me out here? Mom said the vet... Oh God, I can't believe you're here. I've missed you so much."

Jasper ran his thumb over Calum's lips. "Frank's given me a part-time job. I'm registered at Laramie. I have some credit for what I've already studied but I plan to continue my vet training here in the States."

"Laramie's three hundred miles away."

"That's not better than five thousand?"

"Fuck it." Calum wrapped his arms around Jasper and kissed him, inhaled the scent of him, drank in the taste of him, felt the hardness of him even through their coats.

When he pulled back, he still couldn't believe it. "Did Mom know?" he asked.

"Not until today."

"Why didn't you tell me?"

Jasper smiled. "I wanted it to be the biggest surprise of your life."

Calum laughed. "Congratulations." He swallowed hard. "What about your mom?"

"A plane ride away. She's getting worse. Fintan said he'd keep an eye on her. I don't mean to sound selfish, but we only get one chance at life, and I don't think the mother I once had would want me to give up mine."

"God. So Blue's okay?"

Jasper laughed. "Blue's fine."

"Fuck." Calum took a deep breath. "You're supposed to come into the house for a bite to eat. You're staying here, right?"

"If you'll have me. I start after Christmas at Laramie. I need to rent a house. I thought you could help me look. Maybe I could live there in the week and come here at the weekend?"

"Oh fuck."

"Is that all you can say?" Jasper asked.

"You've had months to get used to this. I feel like I've slid down a rainbow."

"Ah yes, talking of that, I've brought a check with me from Fintan for a hundred thousand dollars. He upped the prices on those pieces you took to London and sold them all."

"Oh my God." Calum gulped. "A hundred thousand?"

"He's pissed off he didn't ask more."

Calum almost choked.

"The market's huge. He's talking of going to Europe with more pieces for an exhibition. Wants to know what else you've got and if you'll go. He still has that bronze in the window, but when I showed him the sculpture you'd left, he almost hyperventilated. That's his new favorite. Mine too. He called it *Cowboys Getting Down.*"

"Christ."

Jasper took a deep breath. "Something else I need to tell you. I spoke to your father this afternoon."

Calum grabbed his hand and held it. "That you're still here says something. Tell me he didn't yell or say something sexist."

"We had a long chat," Jasper said. "I told him about Ben and my father, and how I felt about you. I know I'm not what he would have chosen for you, but I pointed out it wasn't his choice to make. I think he'll tolerate me, maybe one day he'll smile at me. He seemed impressed Frank had given me a job and that I was going to study in Wyoming."

Jasper shivered and Calum tugged him to the door. "You need proper gear to wear, not a London coat, though it's turning me on big time." He turned to look at Jasper. "You did bring your ties?"

"Yep." Jasper laughed.

They left the barn and headed for the ranch, snow still falling heavily.

"Course, when I decided where I'd like to study, I didn't know it was so damn cold," Jasper said. "Maybe I should have gone to California. Probably not too late to change."

Calum growled and leapt at him, knocking him to the ground. They rolled around in the snow, laughing. Calum's Stetson blew away and Jasper stuffed a handful of snow down his neck and in return received a handful down his.

Eventually, Calum pinned him down and landed a wet kiss on his lips. "I know what you've given up for me. Thank you."

"California sun. But it wouldn't have been the same without you there."

"You've made me so happy."

Jasper smiled and licked a melting snowflake from his lips.

"I'm cold and I'm wet," Jasper said.

"Is that right? Sounds like you need a shower, cowboy."

Jasper's smile widened. "Want to wash my back?"

Calum tugged him to his feet. "And your front."

He slung his arm over Jasper's shoulder as they headed for the ranch.

Note to self: Now that I have him, don't ever let him go.

Jasper's heart was so full, he wondered if it could burst. All those weeks waiting for paperwork to be sorted, for the right people to say yes—it had all been worth it to see that look on Calum's face.

Note to self: Now that I have him, don't ever let him go.

About the Author

Barbara Elsborg lives in West Yorkshire in the north of England. She always wanted to be a spy, but having confessed to everyone without them even resorting to torture, she decided it was not for her. Vulcanology scorched her feet. A morbid fear of sharks put paid to marine biology. So instead, she spent several years successfully selling cyanide.

After dragging up two rotten, ungrateful children and frustrating her sexy, devoted, wonderful husband (who can now stop twisting her arm) she finally has time to conduct an affair with an electrifying plugged-in male, her laptop.

Her books feature quirky heroines and bad boys, and she hopes they are as much fun to read as they are to write.

Visit Barbara online at www.barbaraelsborg.com or barbaraelsborg.blogspot.com.

It's all about the story...

Romance

HORROR

Retro ROMANCE

www.samhainpublishing.com

CPSIA information can be obtained at www.ICGtesting.com
Printed in the USA
BVOW030849191212

308680BV00001B/1/P